Jane Fairfax

Joan Aiken was born in Sussex, and is the author of many classic books for children, as well as a number of historical romances and contemporary thrillers. She is married to the American painter Julius Goldstein. They divide their time between Sussex and New York.

Jane Fairfax is one of Joan Aiken's four Jane Austen sequels. *Eliza's Daughter* and *Emma Watson* are published by Gollancz and *Mansfield Revisited* is now available in Indigo.

JOAN AIKEN

Jane Fairfax

A novel to complement EMMA by Jane Austen

INDIGO

First published in Great Britain 1990
by Victor Gollancz Ltd

This Indigo edition published 1996
Indigo is an imprint of the Cassell Group
Wellington House, 125 Strand, London WC2R 0BB

© Joan Aiken Enterprises Ltd 1990

The right of Joan Aiken to be identified as author of
this work has been asserted by her in accordance with
the Copyright, Designs and Patents Act, 1988.

A catalogue record for this book is
available from the British Library.

ISBN 0 575 40042 0

Printed and bound in Great Britain by
Guernsey Press Co. Ltd,
Guernsey, Channel Isles

96 97 98 99   10 9 8 7 6 5 4 3 2 1

For
Liz Francke
in New Zealand

BOOK ONE

Chapter 1

The marriage of Miss Jane Bates to Lieutenant Fairfax was accompanied by the usual good omens: church bells rang, the sun shone, and many handkerchiefs were waved. But these omens were to prove delusive, for the Lieutenant, an excellent officer and a most deserving young man, had the misfortune, not more than three weeks after the wedding, to be posted overseas with his regiment, and killed in action before he had another chance to revisit his native land. His young widow, soon sinking under the combined assaults of consumption and sorrow, bequeathed the care of the fatherless child to her elderly parents, for Lieutenant Fairfax possessed no family of his own.

The Reverend George Bates, vicar of Highbury, a man already in frail health and advanced years at the time of this occurrence, proved unequal to the unwonted exertions and fatigues laid on him by the addition to his modest household of a lively four-year-old girl: an attack of the bronchial affection to which he was at all times subject soon carried him off. His widow and remaining unmarried daughter (considerably older than her sister Jane) were thereupon obliged to remove themselves from the vicarage and since he, a man of keen intelligence but little judgment and much given to impulsive, unthinking generosity, had left them remarkably ill-provided for, their new quarters must necessarily be very humble: the drawing-room floor of a house in the middle of Highbury village. The ground premises were occupied by people in business (a barber shop); the establishment owned no garden. The village itself, however, enjoyed a pleasant, airy situation in the lovely county of Surry, and early anxieties that the little girl might inherit such a weakness of the lungs as had despatched her unfortunate mother and grandfather were in due course allayed. All that the fond care of a doting grandmother and deeply attached aunt might accomplish was done; and nobody had any expectation but that little Jane would remain in Highbury, taught only what very limited means could command, growing up with no advantages of connection or improvement to be engrafted on what nature had given her in good understanding and a pleasing person.

That the child's disposition and capacities were both above average was a fact not lost upon either her affectionate relatives or on more impartial and discerning neighbours; and such services as might, without offence, be offered were soon at her disposal. Mrs Pryor, wife of the incoming vicar, who had seen her own four children carried off untimely by the cholera, was very ready to teach little Jane her letters and multiplication tables, finding the child an eager and biddable pupil. Equally advantageous, but on a more mundane level, was an attention from the chief family of the village: wearing-apparel, very little spoiled and of excellent quality, was contributed by Mr and Mrs Woodhouse, who had two daughters, both of larger size than the orphan. Isabella, the firstborn, was seven years older, while Emma Woodhouse, though born in the same year as Jane, was so remarkably healthy, well-grown, and forward for her age that she had the appearance of being at least two years older. — This system of outgrown clothes being handed on was begun so early, while the children concerned were not of an age to comprehend the difference between worn or new garments, that it soon became a matter of accustomed usage by most of the parties to it. Indeed the scheme was so sensible, and so well-intentioned, that none of the adults involved ever paused a moment to conjecture as to the possible effect on a proud and sensitive nature of being perpetually obliged to appear in the village street clad in bonnets, boots, and pelisses, however superior in quality, which were already familiar to neighbours as having been worn several years previously by the young Misses Woodhouse, and having been chosen, in the first place, to fit the tastes and measurements of another.

"That cerise muslin becomes you far better than it ever did Emma Woodhouse, especially now that it has faded," some old lady would be sure to exclaim, encountering small Jane on her way to daily lessons at the vicarage; or, "Bless me, child! you must take to growing a little quicker, indeed you must! Why, I can remember that Isabella wore that pelisse when she was but four years old, and here you are turned six and it still fits you well enough!"

Little Jane remained, indeed, over a number of years, diminutive for her age, possibly due to the somewhat cramped and airless circumstances of her nurture; at this time she was a thin, dark, soft-spoken child; pale to a fault, her single manifestation of possible future beauty a pair of large expressive dark eyes inherited from her father; her Aunt Hetty continually lamented the lank straightness of her hair, while the similarly lanky proportions of hands, feet, and limbs appeared to indicate that in years to come her present deficiency of stature might be rectified. — She never made any outward complaint when the parcels of used clothing were delivered at the shop below-stairs, but silently attended as her aunt and grandmother clucked and contrived, patching and re-lining articles where necessary, fitting the sleeves of one garment to the bodice of another; she stood in patient compliance while petticoats were tried on her and deep tucks pinned into them, sleeves shortened and hems adjusted; only, sometimes, she would let out an involuntary, almost inaudible sigh; and once, upon her grandmother's thoughtfully remarking, "I wonder that poor dear Mrs Woodhouse will so often put little Emma into that particularly brilliant shade of puce, I do not think it a very becoming colour," little Jane was heard to murmur a heartfelt "Yes!" of agreement. Her Aunt Hetty, a woman of boundlessly kind nature but not distinguished either for intellect or observation, made no conjectures as to why Jane would sometimes linger wistfully outside the windows of Ford's the draper's shop, studying the goods therein displayed, but was simply thankful that their darling should be so well and warmly clothed at so little cost to themselves; and Jane, who was noticing and intelligent well in advance of her years, rapidly began to understand how straitened were the means that provided her home, how every halfpenny must be stretched to its limit and beyond. — She had never owned a new garment in her life.

Besides wearing-apparel, the Woodhouse family supplied another benefit which was reckoned at an infinitely greater value by its recipient.

Mrs Pryor, while teaching her apt pupil various nursery songs and ballads, had soon discovered in the child a sweet true voice and a remarkably accurate musical ear. Accordingly she ventured to suggest to the well-disposed Mrs Woodhouse the possibility of little Jane's being permitted to share the services of Signor Negretti who came twice weekly from London to give Isabella and Emma instruction on the pianoforte. A request so reasonable and so practical was instantly acceded to, and it therefore became a matter of habit that Patty the maid should, every Tuesday and Thursday, escort Jane round to the shrubbery side-door of Hartfield, the large comfortable house on the outskirts of Highbury where dwelt Mr Woodhouse and his family.

Soon, for Jane, those two days would become the most precious of the week, haloed around with joy.

The peculiar disposition of Mr Woodhouse, a nervous man, whose flow of spirits, never high, could easily be irritated by unwelcome sounds (such as the jangle and repetition of juvenile finger-exercises on the pianoforte) had rendered essential the introduction into his establishment of a secondary instrument, used solely for the children's lessons and inevitable hours of practice, situated at a sufficient distance from the rooms normally occupied by the master of the house to afford him no source of distress. A disused store-room adjacent to the housekeeper's parlour was allotted for the purpose, and to this haven Jane was soon permitted to repair whenever she chose, her right to make use of it seldom, if ever, challenged by the Woodhouse young ladies, and her ingress by the side door precluding, in general, the necessity of encountering either servants or members of the family. How many hours of solitude and happiness were passed by Jane in this chamber it would be impossible to compute, but the portion of her childhood thus occupied became paramount in shaping her whole character and therefore her subsequent career.

After a year of lessons, to the great wonder of all the village, Signor Negretti put forward a request to Mrs Woodhouse that he might be permitted to give Jane tuition on her own, since she had wholly outstripped both her fellow-pupils, even the thirteen-year-old Isabella.

"And I should be most happy to teach the young lady gratis, for nothing," asseverated the enthusiastic teacher, who of course was well aware of his pupil's circumstances, "for she has a talent quite formidable — prodigious!"

But this offer the generous Woodhouses would not, for a moment, consider: "They were only too happy to pay for the dear child, were rejoiced at her talent, the more especially since this might afford the means of her being able to earn for herself a respectable living in years to come."

Young Miss Isabella Woodhouse had no ear at all for music, and no taste for it. The day when, after numerous entreaties, her parents permitted her to discontinue the lessons with Signor Negretti was the happiest of her childhood. But little Emma, her junior, though sadly idle and disinclined for practice, possessed a good ear and considerable taste and could, if only she would apply herself, play charmingly; it was a thousand pities, and the teacher's continual despair, that her application was so infrequent and so unequal. "Ah, Miss Emma!" he lamented, week after week, "if only you would give yourself to practise as does little Miss Jane."

These declarations Jane, of course, did not hear; she only observed that the teacher, invariably weary and discouraged-looking when she first entered the music-room and Emma skipped out of the door, would appear refreshed, and gradually return to better spirits as her own lesson proceeded.

Emma Woodhouse was at this time a cheerful, handsome, easy-tempered child, on to whose fundamentally amiable and carefree disposition beautiful manners were being engrafted by her gentle sensitive mother. In the fullness of time Emma would grow completely aware of what was due from her to persons less fortunate than herself. But her character was not, and had no capacity to be, a highly perceptive one; alertness to the feelings of other individuals would never form a prime factor. And to find herself adversely compared, week after week, to a child in all other ways so seemingly inferior, so less well endowed in every visible particular: birth, looks, residence, manner, family — and one who, furthermore, was invariably dressed in her own outworn garments — was something she found perplexing, equally hard to bear and hard to understand, the hardest thing, in fact, yet encountered in her otherwise indulged and comfortable existence.

The connection between the two children remained, simply, that they shared the same music teacher twice a week; no spontaneous friendship had ever sprung up.

"Should we not invite little Jane Fairfax round to play with you some time, Emma dear?" was a proposal sometimes tentatively put forward by Mrs Woodhouse, whose own relations with the Bates ladies had been established when the former vicar was still alive, and were both benevolent and cordial, taking into consideration their very different styles of living.

But Emma would always answer her mother's suggestion with: "Oh, Mamma — need we? Jane is so stiff and dull, she never has anything to say, except about books."

"Well, but, my darling, that is because poor Jane leads such a narrow, confined life, shut up in those three small rooms with her aunt and grandmother; kind, well-meaning ladies to be sure, but both of them past their first youth; whereas you have dear Bella to teach you I do not know how many games, and Papa and myself to take you for drives with James, and our big garden to roll and run and jump about in; only think how lucky you are compared with poor Jane."

Such arguments carry remarkably little weight with the young, however; and liking cannot be forced; apart from their parity of age the natures of the two children were really so dissimilar that, lacking some cataclysm, there seemed remarkably little chance of a bond between them ever forming.

Mrs Woodhouse possessed too much good nature, and also too much sound common sense, to exert the weight of authority in such a matter over her extremely strong-willed younger child, where the issue would be of only doubtful benefit to either of the parties concerned. For would it, in the end, be a true kindness to little Jane Fairfax to be instilling in her a taste for such a wider and more agreeable existence as she might never again experience, destined, as she seemed to be, for a life passed in the service of others? And would it advantage little Emma, already rather too fond of her own way, to expose to her almost certain domination a silent, gentle, more self-effacing child upon whom, because of her humble circumstances, Emma was accustomed to look as inferior?

Solicitous to protect Jane, Emma's mother did not reflect that the boot might conceivably be on the other foot; that Jane, because of her mental attainments, might be in a position to give Emma some salutary set-down.

The value of friendship between two rather lonely children began, in any case, to seem of minor importance to Mrs Woodhouse, beset, as she was, with greater cares, the chief of which were well-founded anxieties about her own health and about the ability of her husband, a kindly and devoted but not strong-natured man, to shoulder the responsibilities of the household, should she be obliged to take to her bed for any protracted period. — She was in expectation of a confinement which, judging from her two previous experiences, might be difficult, even dangerous. Her frame was not robust. Many matters must be set in order before the approaching event. And a fervent wish to avoid any discord or household upset, such as might ensue if little Emma were constrained to some course that did not please her, became the overriding factor. Mrs Woodhouse did not attempt to enforce her private, intuitive feeling that a friendship between the two children might be of value to both. Only the unspoken wish was picked up and, as such things do, may have influenced her daughter in a contrary direction.

Mr Woodhouse, a valetudinarian himself, in continual agitation about his own health, was acutely afflicted by the sight of indisposition in others, even the thought of it; therefore, on the increasingly frequent occasions when she found herself unfit for the kind of lively, cheerful conversation he preferred, it became his wife's habit to plead household duties and betake herself to the housekeeper's parlour where Mrs Hill, a kindly woman with understanding far in advance of her education, would leave her mistress in peace to enjoy the solace of music. For, from here, if the door were left ajar, the sound of Jane's piano practising could be heard, and the pleasure this afforded to Mrs Woodhouse it would be impossible to over-estimate. She would sit for a half-hour or so, listening to whatever Jane chanced to be playing, whether Haydn, Scarlatti, or Cramer, then return, refreshed and with strength and optimism renewed, to the demands of her husband's company.

In the month of October, after a disastrously mismanaged birth, Mrs Woodhouse was interred, with due ceremony, in Highbury churchyard, along with her third and stillborn child. Her husband, utterly stricken by this event, found himself obliged to take to his bed, from which, three weeks later, he arose, aged, apparently, by ten years, piteous and woe-begone, with white hair and faltering gait.

At the commencement of this period of mourning, thirteen-year-old Isabella had been carried off by kindly cousins to stay at their house in Kent. But six-year-old Emma refused to be removed from her home into what she envisaged as a place of exile. She kicked, she screamed, she wept, she stormed, and in general behaved herself so abominably that the invitation on her behalf by the cousins was hastily withdrawn, since they had no confidence that they would be able to manage the child.

"I have never known her behave so," said Mrs Hill the house-keeper, into whose charge Emma was, perforce, relinquished.

Some days of total solitude were therefore passed by the unhappy orphan, and it was left to the compassion and initiative of a friend and neighbour, young Mr Knightley, a sensible and well-disposed man still in his twenties, to undertake the search for a governess who might be able to come at short notice and undertake her charge. — He achieved this through the Pryors, who, by great good luck, were acquainted with the very person for the task, a young lady, a connection of theirs, recently obliged to quit her first post at Weybridge, not through any fault of her own, but because the family were departing abroad. She was free to commence her new duties at the end of a week, did so, and rapidly grew to be so much a part of the Woodhouse family circle that Emma, for once, apparently almost forgetting her own mother, turned to dear Miss Taylor for all the affection, the kindness, the support, and continuous, happy, unimpeded intercourse that would normally be expected from a parent. All these Miss Taylor was able to provide without stint, and the only evil of Emma's new life must be, as before, that of being allowed rather too much of her own way.

Soon she had forgotten, or at least pushed out of memory, the terrible days before Miss Taylor's arrival.

On the first of these, little Jane Fairfax had arrived, unheralded, at the house. News of the death of Mrs Woodhouse had, of course, been passed in hushed tones about the village and discussed with due solemnity. But, such is the natural self-absorption of early childhood, Jane had not related this event in any way to her own doings. It never occurred to her, for example, that the fatality might affect the twice-weekly visits of Signor Negretti. For almost a year, now, she had been accustomed to take her way unescorted to Hartfield whenever she chose; Patty, her grandmother's sole servant, had a thousand daily tasks to perform, and it was such a short way through the village that no one felt the least anxiety about the child. Nor did her aunt think to warn her that at present the usual music classes must very probably have been suspended; so, as was her custom, she ran eagerly along the narrow path among the Hartfield laurel-bushes—only to stop short when she reached the lawn, startled at the wholly unwonted sight of Emma, huddled miserably on the low, broad bench that encircled the cedar tree.

Not only was Emma never to be found alone in the garden at such a time of day, but this was an Emma never seen, never even imagined by Jane before: an utterly wretched, crumpled, tear-drenched Emma, her cheeks pale and smeared, her shoe-laces undone, hair uncurled, hardly so much as combed, and, most astonishing of all, instead of her usual carefully chosen attire, she wore a plain, unbecoming black serge dress at least two sizes too large for her. (It had been one of Isabella's, made at the time of their grandfather's death four years previously, which nobody had, as yet, found time to alter.)

"Oh — Emma — " exclaimed Jane, pausing irresolutely, "I am sorry, I did not know — that is, I was told you had gone away into Kent — "

She was very ready to turn tail and run homeward, for at various former encounters Emma's manner to her had been decidedly rebuffing. But this time, perhaps, might be different?

Emma looked up. Her hazel eyes were reddened, hardly to be glimpsed between swollen lids. She cried out wildly, "Jane, Jane, my mother is dead! Mamma is *dead*! How shall I ever go on without her?"

Jane was much struck. That Emma, always so surrounded by friends, comfort, affection, should appear thus solitary was strange indeed.

"But — have you not your papa still — Mr Woodhouse?"

"Yes; but he is in bed, where he lies and cries, and if I go near him he only tells me to run away to Mrs Hill."

"Well, but you do have Mrs Hill — and Serle, and James, and your maid Rebecca — "

"They are only servants!"

"And your sister — Miss Isabella — "

"She is not the same as Mamma! Besides, she is in Kent."

This was unarguable.

"Oh, Jane!" cried Emma. "What shall I ever *do*?"

An appeal so simple, so heartfelt, was not to be resisted; certainly not by Jane, who, though she could not recall her own mother with any clarity, was all too familiar with the anguish of a loss only a few years past; she remembered, also, what a kind, gentle, solicitous lady Mrs Woodhouse had always been, not infrequently stepping into the music-room for a moment to say a kind approving word.

Without a moment's hesitation she ran to the bench, flung her arms round the other child, and embraced Emma tightly, crying out, "Oh, poor, *poor* Emma! I am so truly sorry for you! Indeed it is dreadful — I do not know how you can bear it."

Such sympathy, so spontaneous, direct, utterly sincere, was the only thing, just then, that could have done Emma any good, and she laid her head on Jane's shoulder and wept abundantly for many minutes.

"What shall I ever do?" she repeated, over and over. "Who is there to take care of me? Mr Knightley sent a message to Papa that he is finding a governess. A governess! I am sure she will be hateful. How can she ever, ever take the place of Mamma?"

"Well; if she is hateful," said Jane stoutly, "I will stand by you."

The thought that she might actually be of use to Emma was sweet indeed.

"Oh, yes!" cried the other. "Do! We shall be friends for ever, shall we not? And tell each other all our secrets!"

"Everything," said Jane, who had no secrets to impart. "And love each other best, always. And never be cross or unkind."

This promise ratified, over and over, many times, they huddled together, clasping each other like two fledgling birds blown from a nest, until Serle's voice calling, "Miss Emma! Miss Emma! Where ever have you got to? Come in, now, like a good girl, to your dinner!" brought Emma to her feet and, for the time being, separated them.

Jane, finding the hour so late, turned homewards to her own dinner, deep in thought. But her step was unusually elastic, and her head held high; pity, aghast pity for Emma's stricken state being, within her breast, almost equally combined with a species of wondering joy at this undreamed-of friendship that had, like a gift from the gods, been so suddenly and unexpectedly bestowed. A friend! Emma Woodhouse has offered to be my friend! thought Jane. Now we shall be able to do so many delightful things together. We can take walks — perhaps Mr Knightley will come with us — he is very fond of Emma, I know — and she will come back to my house, sometimes, and look at all the drawings I have made for Mrs Pryor, and my paper dolls, and Aunt Hetty will bake one of her sweet cakes for us, I am sure. We can have pretend tea-parties, using acorn tea-cups; and play house under the table with the red cloth cover.

In preparation for which events, she collected a great many acorn-cups and persuaded Aunt Hetty to cut her out a new set of spillikins.

Before any such plans could be put into execution, however, Emma's mourning dresses must be made; she could not endure to be seen outside the grounds of Hartfield looking, as she said, such a fright, in clothes that fitted her so ill. With which feelings, Jane could only sympathize.

For six days, therefore, with the cordial permission of her aunt and grandmother, Jane went daily to Hartfield, where the two children, usually in the garden, for the season was fine, mild, and open, amused themselves with I-spy, Bilbocatch, conundrums, and other quiet pastimes considered permissible during the period of mourning: cards, counters, dolls, and other such playthings were naturally put by for the time.

Jane's first suggestion had been for hide-and-seek. Ever since the commencement of her visits to the house, she had been longing to explore the Hartfield gardens. Now that, for the first time, she was at liberty to roam about the shrubberies, walks, and wildernesses of the extensive grounds, she had discovered in herself considerable skill for locating crafty, unexpected places in which to hide, crouched among the ivy against a wall, perched in the mossy niche over a lion's head fountain, or just above eye-level in the fork of an old willow; but hide-and-seek proved unsatisfactory as an activity, involving, as it did, long spells of solitary waiting, or of solitary search for the other player, during which periods Emma rapidly became bored and restless. If she were the seeker, her attempts to find Jane would grow more and more languid and desultory; if the hider, she would begin, from her place of concealment, to call impatiently, "I'm here! I'm here! Come and find me. Jane, Jane, I am here!"

And, when Jane had reached her, "I'm tired of this game. Let's do something else. Let's play weddings." Since Emma was the hostess, she must of course command the choice of game; Jane, too, had been taught good manners. Yet to her this "wedding" game, which consisted of planning imaginary nuptials for all the inhabitants of Highbury, seemed intolerably slow and dull.

They would sit for hours together in the revolving summer-house and discuss the imaginary ceremonies down to the most minute detail; Jane, who had never attended a wedding in her whole existence, sometimes wondered at Emma's grasp of the procedure.

"And what about Mr Knightley? Whom shall he marry?" she asked, stifling a yawn, when the Misses Cox and the Gilberts and the Otways had all been run through, with their hymns, gloves, bouquets, lace trimmings, white satin, the love scenes, the wording, the proposals, and the presents.

"*Mr Knightley?* He is *by far* too old to marry. — His brother, now, Mr John, I have sometimes wondered — but Mr Knightley is much too old. And so is Mr Weston. In any case, Mr Weston is a widower, he was married before . . . "

Emma's voice faltered. Mr Weston's marriage had been brought to an end by the death of his young wife, and that was a subject too closely allied to her own trouble. Jane, with ready comprehension, said quickly, "Well, then, how about Miss Bickerton, the young lady who has become a parlour boarder at Mrs Goddard's school? What gentleman would do for her?"

"Miss Bickerton? She is scarcely older than my sister — *far* too young to marry. In any case, I daresay she will have to become a teacher; or an old maid; Mrs Goddard told Papa that she has no family, but is paid for by charitable subscription."

This careless comment cast Jane into silence. Young though she was, she had already begun to speculate, with a great many doubts, on the subject of her own future.

"Who else could be married?" demanded Emma, yawning in her turn. "Come on, Jane! Think of somebody else, do! You are so quiet; you never have ideas."

"Am I quiet?" said Jane in surprise.

"Yes; too quiet."

"Well:" said Jane after some thought, "I suppose it is because Aunt Hetty talks so much."

On the following morning at breakfast Aunt Hetty's usual flow of incessant conversation was, for a wonder, stilled; the cause of this, to Jane's observant eye, seemed to be a long white envelope with a red lawyer's seal which Patty had brought from the post office. For once, Aunt Hetty did not try to persuade Jane to eat a second slice of bread-and-butter; her request to leave the table and make herself ready for the daily visit to Hartfield was absently granted, and as she put on her pelisse (for the mornings were growing chill) she heard a low-voiced conversation between her elders.

"Should the child be informed? What is your opinion, ma'am? So *very* kind! So very unexpected! I hardly know what to think — "

From the old lady, her grandmother: "Had we not better wait and invite the opinion of some gentleman with greater knowledge

— it may, you know, be our legal duty to tell her — but Mr Knightley, perhaps — or Mr Pryor — "

"Run along, Jane dear," said Aunt Hetty. "That is right. I daresay Emma will be waiting for you so impatiently — "

But on that morning Jane, with the acute sensitivity of the natural solitary, detected a change, a coolness in Emma's welcome.

"Oh, are you there, Jane?" she said listlessly. "It is very cold today. What shall we play to keep warm?"

"Shall we stay indoors? Go to the music room and play duets?" Jane suggested.

This plan had, for some days, been lurking at the back of her mind, since there were a few pieces for four hands on the piano which she had long been eager to try; they had been procured by Mrs Woodhouse for her daughters before the day of Isabella's rebellion against music, and from that time had lain in their place unopened.

But — "*Duets?*" cried Emma with a look of disgust. "I thank you, no! What a disagreeable idea! Duets are wretched things! You only say that — " she checked herself, looked, for a moment, very downcast, then burst out irrepressibly, "You need not think yourself the best pianist in Surry, just because Mamma left you one hundred pounds! It is no great matter, after all!"

This remark was so incomprehensible to Jane that she stood perfectly still, wondering if she had heard amiss.

"What can you possibly mean, Emma? Your Mamma left me one hundred pounds? What *can* you be talking about? She did not leave me anything."

"Yes — she did," muttered Emma resentfully. "Her Will was read yesterday. Mr Cox the lawyer came and read it to Papa. Mamma had money of her own, and she left one hundred pounds 'to my young neighbour Jane Fairfax, to be used for her education, because of the very great pleasure her music has given to me.' "

"One hundred pounds! But I do not understand." Jane was totally puzzled. "Mrs Woodhouse never came into the music-room while I was practising — except, perhaps, for a moment sometimes, just at the end . . . " her voice faltered as she remembered the thin, pale, elegant lady who would now never come again. At this moment she began to comprehend the full permanence of death. "I do not think Mrs Woodhouse ever heard me playing, above once or twice," she said doubtfully.

"Well: she did." Emma's tone held all the outrage of the child who has been unjustly excluded from some privilege enjoyed by his siblings. "She used to go and sit in Mrs Hill's room and listen; Serle told me so. And now she has left you one hundred pounds. She has not left *me* any money — nor Isabella; not until we are twenty-one when we shall have thirty thousand; but what use is that? I think it is very unfair."

"But, Emma," began Jane, "you have everything now — " She looked about her at the gardens. A thick frost today whitened the lawns.

"I don't have Mamma!" cried out Emma passionately.

"It is far too cold, sitting here like this," said Jane in haste, to forestall an imminent outburst of tears. "Let us run races. Quick, Emma! I will beat you to the chestnut tree."

Jane, though so small for her age, was nimbler than the more heavily-built but somewhat clumsy Emma; she won two races out of three.

Soon tiring of this diversion — "Let us go and talk to James and the horses," Emma proposed. "If we ask, I daresay Serle will give us some bread for them."

Jane, in secret, was a little afraid of the huge glossy carriage horses, but of course offered no objection to this plan; however, when they reached the cobbled stable-yard they found the stalls empty; neither James nor the horses were there. Tom, the stable-lad, told them James had taken the carriage to Kingston to meet the new governess and, he added, ought to be returning very shortly with his passenger. Accordingly, after loitering about the yard and jumping off the horse-block a few times, they dawdled round to the front carriage-sweep with its great iron gates, and so were at hand to witness the arrival and descent from the conveyance of Miss Taylor, who proved to be, not at all the severe elderly lady of Emma's imaginings, but young, pretty, and kind-faced.

"Which of you is my pupil?" she asked immediately, and, on being told, "What game were you playing? May I not play it too? Or should I first go and introduce myself to your Papa?"

"Oh, no. Papa does not at present come from his chamber until two or three in the afternoon," explained Emma, while Jane excitedly cried, "Do, please, ma'am, play hide-and-seek with us!" — longing to put to use a few of the ingenious hiding-places that she had discovered.

"Very well!" answered the new governess, laughing. "Do you, then, go and hide — what is your name? Jane? — while Emma and I begin to make one another's acquaintance. We shall give you no more than three minutes by my timepiece, then come in search. Away with you!"

Overjoyed, without observing Emma's discontented expression, Jane sped off. Emma has found a grown-up friend, she thought comfortably; that lady will be kind to her, I am sure. Buried under this pleasant impression remained the strange radiance of that one hundred pounds. What a thing, what a thing to have happened! That must have been what Grandma and Aunt Hetty were talking about at breakfast.

Jane knew just where she planned to conceal herself, in a kind of double laurel-hedge that formed a boundary between the shrubbery and the lawn; one of the trees in it was already of large stature and had a fork, several feet above the ground, where she could perch hidden in a nest of greenery. Thither she flew, and, as soon as she was in position, called out loudly, "*I am ready!*" and settled herself to wait in patience.

Great patience was required of her, for the seekers proceeded at what seemed to her a most dawdling pace. Several times she saw them in the distance, talking to one another, but walking in the wrong direction, and she was tempted to call again, but restrained herself.

And then, unexpectedly, she heard their voices close by; apparently they were strolling down the wide dry walk that lay along the border of the shrubbery.

"And is Jane Fairfax your great friend?" Miss Taylor was asking kindly. "Does she share lessons with you and your sister?"

"Oh dear — *no!*" came Emma's reply, in a tone of pitying astonishment. "Jane's family are quite poor. She has no father or mother, and lives with her grandmother over a barber's shop. Mamma used to call on them, but it was out of kindness. And Jane will never be able to marry, for they have no money, none at all. Except — " Emma hesitated, then went on. "When she is grown, Jane will be obliged to earn her living, she will be — "

There she halted, possibly because she had been on the point of saying, "be a governess." Belated caution had overtaken her.

"Well," commented the new governess in a neutral tone, "that is very sad for Jane, to be sure, but it would not, surely, hinder your being friends?"

"No; but, the thing is, Jane is so dull!" declared Emma roundly. "She does not talk about things that interest me. And the only games she knows are so babyish — like this one. *Hide-and-seek!* Or running races — such games are only fit for boys, I think."

"But would you not like to learn your lessons with her?" suggested Miss Taylor. "Lessons, I believe, are better not learned alone, but in company. Perhaps if you did so, you would have more things to talk about. You would come to know her better, and like her better."

"Oh no, I am very sure I should not! I should not like that plan at all! Once we were used to take music lessons together but Signor Negretti said — "

The voices died away along the laurel walk.

Jane sat petrified in the tree for a few minutes, then scrambled down, stiff-legged, and ran trembling away in the opposite direction. She felt quite sick and breathless; bewildered, too, with pain, as if some organ, her heart perhaps, had been dragged bodily from its proper site. She would, unthinking, have made her way directly homewards, but, by chance, encountered the other two, face to face, while crossing the carriage-sweep.

"Why, *there* she is, after all! In what clever place were you hiding, Jane? We quite thought we had searched everywhere!"

"She must have been in the hay-loft," asserted Emma. "But we had agreed that was to be out of bounds."

Jane said neither yes or no to this, but murmured in a low tone that she must go home; she had seen the stable-clock, it was late, Aunt Hetty would be growing anxious.

"Are you ill, child? You seem so pale?" said Miss Taylor, troubled, a little, by something in her manner.

"Oh — Jane is always pale!" cried Emma. "It is nothing out of the common."

Jane declared, stiffly and gruffly, that she was not ill, not the least bit; she dared say no more. Without another look or word she turned and trudged off down the driveway, between the gates.

"What a queer, abrupt little creature," said Miss Taylor, puzzled, looking after her. "But — I suppose — no one has had time to teach her deportment — "

"She is very dull," repeated Emma. "And selfish; she only wants to play the games that she is good at, not what other people enjoy. — But, Miss Taylor, never mind about Jane! May I come and see you unpack your boxes?"

"Of course, my dear, you may."

Jane, when she arrived home, gave no account to her aunt and grandmother of the conversation she had overheard, merely explained that Miss Taylor, the new governness, had arrived, that she appeared a kind, pleasant lady, that Emma seemed ready to like and trust her.

"I am very glad to hear that," observed old Mrs Bates. "Poor little Emma! She is said to be somewhat hard to please. It is very fortunate for her that she has had you to keep her company during her lonely days."

Jane made no answer to this, but endeavoured to eat her dinner. It was soon remarked, however, that she had no appetite, and, soon afterwards, upon her falling into a severe fit of shivering, which rapidly increased to tears and nervous fever, she was put to bed by her anxious relatives, and Mr Perry the apothecary summoned. — This was to be the first of a series of acute headaches accompanied by violent sickness which would at intervals, from that time on, afflict Jane for many years of her life. None of the usual remedies, eagerly applied by Mr Perry or her aunt, were of the least efficacy to the sufferer, who lay prostrate for three days, tossing and turning wretchedly upon her narrow cot in the small stuffy chamber where, since it was shared with her aunt, she could at no time be certain of any privacy. — She could not even weep in peace.

Listeners hear no good of themselves, she thought. Well, Aunt Hetty has often told me that; and now I can see that it is true. I hope that I never, ever, have the misfortune to overhear anything, ever again. *Very dull! Very dull!* Emma Woodhouse thinks that I am very dull. But, if she thought so, why then did she offer to be friends with me in the first place? She did not have to. I am sure I would never have asked it.

Poor Jane's sore, sensitive mind was not, at that juncture, capable of comprehending the fact that Emma, in distress and bewilderment after the first true calamity in her secure and cherished life, was crippled by misery and temporarily incapable of justice or kindness: such a conclusion would, in any case, be far above a child's understanding. The only thing clear to Jane was a sense of utter betrayal, of having the ground cut from under her feet.

"And I will never, never," she said to herself, turning wretchedly away from her aunt's hopeful proffer of custard-pudding, "I will never, ever again, make such a promise to anybody; nor trust any other person, no, not in the whole of my life."

"Do try just a mouthful of the pudding, dear; you have taken nothing for so long!"

"No, thank you, Aunt Hetty."

The pudding was sorrowfully withdrawn, and Jane lay staring at the blank wall, deaf to the pleas of her aunt, while in her ears, over and over again, she heard the receding echo of that other voice and its illusory promise: "We'll be friends for ever, shall we not? And tell each other all our secrets. And love each other always!"

The Knightley brothers, George and John, who inherited the Donwell Abbey estate, about a mile outside Highbury, were old and valued friends of the Woodhouse family. John, the younger brother, was just now away at university, reading law, but George, his father's death occurring shortly before he attained his majority, had succeeded to the not inconsiderable property and its responsibilities; he, therefore, lived at home in the Abbey, looking after his lands. Having been acquainted with the Woodhouse girls from birth, he was regarded by them in the light of an elder brother, and so regarded himself; he was prepared to counsel, reprimand, or rejoice, as occasion offered; and entered with the fullest sympathy into their distress at the loss of their mother, having himself so recently suffered a similar bereavement; and he lost no time in establishing a friendly alliance with their new governess in order to promote the welfare of the girls in any way that might occur to him.

"Emma," said he to Miss Taylor, "has a great need of more company and more competition; she is far too apt to consider herself the pinnacle of perfection, since Isabella, being sweet-natured and so much the elder (and far from Emma's intellectual equal), has always given way to her; Emma can wind Isabella round her little finger. Do you not agree, Miss Taylor, that Emma ought to have other children to play with, and to learn with?"

"It might be better, undoubtedly," replied the new governess with some hesitation. "But there is so little choice, in this neighbourhood."

"There are the Cox girls."

A doubtful, troubled expression passed over Miss Taylor's countenance.

"Emma dislikes them exceedingly. And I must confess I should be sorry to see the dear child acquire any of their pert mincing ways."

"Well then, the Martin sisters."

"Farmers' daughters? I do not think Mr Woodhouse would agree — "

"They are decent, wholesome children," said he impatiently. "Emma could come to no possible harm amongst them."

"Oh, I am sure not! But she herself is so very reluctant also — "

"Well, then, how about little Jane Fairfax? Her family are unexceptionable, and she is a quiet, thoughtful, well-behaved small person; very forward at her lessons, I understand from Mrs Pryor; she would give Emma some healthy rivalry — "

"Oh, I agree." Miss Taylor looked even more troubled. "But, for some reason, Jane and dear Emma do not seem to get on well together. Where the fault may lie, I cannot pretend to say. You know how unaccountable children can be, Mr Knightley. And Emma — a sweet and most engaging child but she can at times be a little wilful — seems to have set her face absolutely against having Jane here, either to play or to share instruction — except for the piano lessons, of course, but those in any case Jane receives by herself. And when she comes for them, or to practise, she slips in and out as silently as a little ghost. You know that it can be difficult trying to persuade Emma into a course that she has set her mind against — "

"Say rather, impossible! In fact she has you, too, under her thumb! Well," he said, "I shall see what I can do myself to remedy the situation."

Mr John Knightley had, some four years previously, with the cordial sanction of Mrs Woodhouse, taught Isabella to ride upon the old grey pony which had been the childhood pet and companion of the Donwell Abbey boys. This faithful friend had long since been laid to rest, but Mr Knightley took pains to search out and buy a pair of gentle, well-behaved ponies from one of his tenant farmers, and now proposed to Emma that he should teach her, in her turn, to ride.

"For I have often heard you grumble about the tedium and familiarity of all the walks around Highbury: down Vicarage Lane and back; along Donwell Lane and back; over the Common Field; whereas, in the saddle, you could venture a great deal farther afield and see much more."

Emma was quite enraptured at the plan.

"Oh yes, yes! Dear Mr Knightley, when can I start? — Does Papa agree?" she added as an afterthought.

Mr Woodhouse, in his present melancholy and enfeebled condition, had, in fact, been exceedingly difficult to convince as to the advantages of the proposed scheme. "Poor dear little Emma tired so very soon; and, just supposing the horse took fright and she was thrown? that did not bear thinking of; horses were such unaccountable, restless, nervous, fidgety beasts; he was sure he should be cast into a wretched state of anxiety and distress of spirits all the while that the lesson was taking place."

But Mr Knightley was able to assure his elderly friend that the pony in question was one of the most aged, peaceful creatures imaginable, with a pace that seldom accelerated beyond a slow walk; also that, since it was of diminutive stature, no possible risk from falling off it was to be apprehended. "It would merely be like falling off a chair, my dear sir." And he engaged to fetch in Miss Bates and Mrs Goddard to sit with Mr Woodhouse and allay his anxieties with their cheerful conversation each time that a riding lesson was in progress.

So far, very good; and Emma was, in truth, so eager to commence learning without delay that she even agreed to make use of her sister Isabella's old riding habit, while waiting for a new one of her own to be made; the broadcloth skirts were accordingly pressed out, and Miss Taylor escorted her pupil to the paddock where the lessons were to take place, Emma chattering gaily all the way.

"When I have learned to ride, Miss Taylor — can *you* ride, by the by?"

"Yes, my love; I was brought up in Wales, you see, where almost everybody has to be able to ride, because the villages are so very far apart — "

"Then Mr Knightley can lend us his mare and we can go exploring to Burgh Heath and Box Hill and a great many pleasant places. Highbury is so dull! James can come with us on one of the carriage horses — "

"Hardly as far as those places, I think, my dear; however, we shall see!"

These grandiose projects, unfortunately, were destined for speedy extinction when Emma discovered, to her deep dismay, that Jane Fairfax was to be her companion in riding instruction.

"For two can learn as fast as one," said Mr Knightley briskly. "A great deal faster, in fact; since one will learn from the other's mistakes. William Larkins is going to lift you up on to Dapple, Emma, while I lead Jane up and down on Ginger. Hold yourself a little more upright, Jane; you lean forward too far. There, that is capital. No: do not hold on to your pony's mane; it was not put there by Nature as a handle. Very good, Emma; the left knee just a trifle farther back, shoulders well dropped, chin high."

As the first lesson proceeded, it began to appear that Jane, thin, but naturally wiry and active, and most eagerly bent on pleasing her teacher, would prove a better pupil than Emma, who, at this stage of her development, tended somewhat to plumpness and sloth; she was, furthermore, decidedly out of humour at finding that she was not to be the only and favoured pupil. Towards the end of the lesson, taking advantage of a moment when Mr Knightley and William Larkins were changing places, she contrived to give her mount a kick which set it into a lumbering trot; then, sliding from the saddle, she tumbled herself on to the grass and lay there looking piteous, until Miss Taylor ran to her assistance, followed at a slower pace by Mr Knightley.

"Don't concern yourself, ma'am, there is nothing amiss, I saw exactly what happened. You will take many a worse toss than that, Emma, before you are done! Come, jump up and let me mount you again; you should always get back into the saddle directly after coming off."

Emma, however, declared that she was badly shaken and bruised, and had had quite enough; somewhat tearfully she demanded to be taken home. And on the way back to Hartfield she remained unwontedly silent. But the account that she rendered to her father of the incident was enough to evoke his complete ban on all further essays into equitation. "He could not endure," he said, "to picture the continual danger that his darling might be undergoing; his nerves could not support the anguish of apprehension; and, after all, what possible need could there be for dear Emma to ride on horseback? There were quite sufficient dry walks around Highbury to serve anybody's need for exercise; he himself saw no occasion ever to venture beyond the shrubbery of his own garden, except once in a way to take tea with Mrs Goddard; Emma was far better off within the precincts of Hartfield, which were neither muddy in winter nor dusty in summer; people should remain upon their own estates; all this gadding about the countryside for pleasure was a thing quite unknown in his childhood and highly undesirable, a product of the new century, a most ill-conceived restlessness. Emma could always use the carriage, after all, if she had a real need to go farther afield. It had been obliging of Mr Knightley to offer the lessons, but he had known from the start that the scheme would not answer; it certainly would not answer; and his doubts had been abundantly justified."

Mr Knightley, deeply chagrined, sold one pony and continued to give little Jane lessons on the other. Proving an apt pupil, she soon developed into a capable horsewoman.

"And it has done wonders for Jane's colds," her grateful aunt told Mr Knightley. "For Jane was used to be such a delicate child, you know, my dear sir, we were in continual dread about her; as soon as she stepped out of doors she would begin sneezing, and her sore throats were our despair; but since taking all this exercise with you, Mr Knightley, no such thing! she has become another creature, why, when she comes back from a ride, her cheeks are positively pink, and she chatters on in a manner you would scarcely credit; we were used to hope, you know, that Jane and little Emma Woodhouse would be great friends, but," (with a sigh) "the difference in their situations, I suppose . . . Well, as I was saying, in the general way Jane, you may not be aware, is rather silent, not a talkative child, not like myself, I am rather a talker, you know, my tongue runs on, but after one of her rides with you, Jane chatters on in a manner you would — which is so very — ; and her having learned to ride may, I dare say, stand her in excellent stead, for she is bound, poor thing, to earn her living as a governess, circumstanced as she is, we see no help for it; and if she can ride horseback, why then, should she be fortunate enough to obtain a good position with a superior household, she would be able to accompany her charges on horseback, if that should be required of her."

Accepting defeat after the episode of the riding lessons, Mr Knightley gave up his attempts to inculcate a friendship between Jane Fairfax and Emma Woodhouse.

From that time on, it was rare for the two girls to exchange half a dozen words in the course of a year; Emma took care to keep herself removed from Jane's path on music-lesson days, Jane came and went as softly as a ghost; and if, by chance, the two encountered one another in the village, each one would keep to her own side of the street, and pretend that the other was not there.

Chapter 2

When Jane Fairfax attained the age of eight, it became her proud
duty to run along, every morning, to the post office, past the Crown
Inn, and the butcher's shop, and Ford's the draper's, and the baker,
and the blacksmith, to fetch the mail. Very seldom was there much
to bring back, for the Bates ladies were growing old, and had few
correspondents, beyond some second cousins in Shropshire who
rarely found occasion to put pen to paper. But the morning air and
exercise was thought salutary for Jane, who had recently begun to
grow apace, continually requiring to have the tucks taken out of
Isabella Woodhouse's cast-off pelisses, but who, if left to her own
volition, would probably have spent the major part of her time
indoors, practising the piano up at Hartfield.

One breakfast-time she returned in triumph waving a large white
envelope.

"Who in the world can it be from?" puzzled old Mrs Bates,
peering over the rims of her spectacles. "It is, to be sure, a hand
that I do recollect to have seen before, but I cannot at this time
recall precisely when or where. Open the seal with great care,
Hetty, so that you do not tear any of the writing inside."

The letter, fortunately, was not a long one, for it was read and
exclaimed over so many times during the next few days, by the
Bates ladies and their friends and neighbours, that there was hardly
time for any other occupation.

"Mrs and Miss Bates have had a very kind, friendly offer," said
Mr Knightley, reporting on the matter to Mr Woodhouse. "They
discussed it with Mr Pryor; and he advised them that they should
have no hesitation at all in accepting, after he had talked it over
with me. And I have said the same thing to Miss Bates. It would
be decidedly for the child's material advantage. I knew that you
would be most cordially interested, my dear sir, since you have
given such notable help in the matter of music lessons."

"Ay, so I have; poor Mary wished it, and I have always continued to carry out her wishes. The music lessons will be of sovereign value to the poor girl in time to come. But what precisely was the offer, Mr Knightley?"

"Yes, what was it?" demanded Isabella eagerly, while Emma cried out with sparkling eyes, "Has somebody left Jane Fairfax a fortune, Mr Knightley?"

"No, not a fortune," he said, smiling at her. "I know you always wish for the fairy-tale ending, Emma, but I fear it is not that. Yet, who knows, it may turn out even better. A friend and former commanding officer of Jane Fairfax's father, a Colonel Campbell, has returned to this country after many years of active service overseas. He is now about to retire, due to wounds, and proposes to take up residence in London with his wife and daughter, who is about Jane's age. He says in the letter they showed me — which is a very open, straightforward, gentlemanly worded missive — that he had entertained the greatest possible regard for Lieutenant Fairfax, who was an active, promising young man; and he had, further, been indebted to Lieutenant Fairfax for such attention, during a severe bout of camp fever, as, he fully believed, had saved his life. He was aware that the child, bereft of both parents and supported by relatives, themselves in straitened circumstances, had very uncertain prospects. These were claims, these were adversities which the Colonel does not intend to overlook, although to take action on them, hitherto, had been beyond his power, engaged as he has been on active service abroad during the five years since the death of poor Fairfax. But it is now his intention, with the permission of her friends, to seek out the orphan and take notice of her, inviting her to stay for a period with his own family in London, and, if matters turn out as he hopes, extending the visit indefinitely; he offers, in fact, to undertake the whole charge of Jane's education."

"And *then* he will leave her a fortune!" exclaimed Emma.

Mr Knightley indulgently shook his head.

"No; Colonel Campbell makes it plain that such a financial settlement does not lie within his power. He is not a wealthy man. The plan is, simply, that Jane shall be brought up for educating others. The colonel's fortune is no more than moderate, and must be for his own daughter."

"Educating others!" said Emma with a look of disgust. "So what is the good of her going to stay in London if *that* is to be the end of it all?"

"Why, my dear," said Mr Woodhouse in his slow, pondering way, "who knows what may occur during the course of the time that Jane remains with the good Campbells, if she grows up an obliging, pretty-behaved young lady, as I daresay she will? All manner of good fortune may yet befall her. On the whole I am not in favour of residence in London; it is a great pity, to be sure, that Jane must be taken out of Highbury, where she was born, and which is such a surpassingly healthy locality; people should certainly remain where they are if it is within their power; yet, in this case, I do not know but what it may be all for the best."

"Lucky Jane! she will see all the sights of London!" cried Isabella.

"But what is the use of that, if she must, at the end of it all, become a governess?" objected Emma.

"Hush, my love, such opinions are not very kind to our dear, good Miss Taylor — who, I am sure, is just as much a part of the family as if she had been born among us. Where is that lady, by the by?"

Miss Taylor at that moment entering the room revealed that she had been to pay a call on the Bates ladies to offer her services in hemming linen, in contriving and preparing Jane's wardrobe for her first visit to the Campbell household, which would take place in the very near future; Colonel Campbell had announced his intention of visiting Highbury to convey Jane back to London (with her friends' permission) during the following week, so soon as he had his own family settled in Manchester Square.

"Manchester Square?" murmured Mr Woodhouse. "Dear me; now what was somebody telling me, not very long ago, relative to Manchester Square? — But no, that was Manchester Street; ay, that was it to be sure; only I cannot just at this moment recollect who it was mentioned Manchester Street; nor precisely what it was that he said — "

"Oh, Miss Taylor," cried Emma, "could not Jane have my figured cherry cambric gown and jacket that I have never liked? That, I think, would serve her quite well for a best gown in London?"

"That must be for your papa to say, my love — "

"And she could have my lavender sarsnet that has a tear in the back breadth; if it were taken in to Jane's size the tear would not signify," suggested Isabella practically.

"My loves, you are very kind, thus to remember the needs of your little friend," said Mr Woodhouse fondly. "But then you are both of you, always, good, generous girls."

A somewhat ironic smile hovering on Mr Knightley's countenance, as Emma ran off to fetch the garments in question, indicated his lack of credence in the word *friend*; he said to Miss Taylor, "Jane Fairfax has now, for Emma, been translated into a fairy-tale princess, the heroine of a story; as such she will command considerably more indulgence than in her former role of an unfortunate neighbour."

"I fear you are right," replied Miss Taylor, smiling and sighing at the same time. "Emma's inveterate passion for making up stories about her acquaintances must be the concern of all her mentors; besides being a shocking waste of time that could be more usefully spent, it tends to lead her into false views and imprudent actions. I do, I must own, endeavour to discourage it as far as I can."

"Which means, not at all! If I am any judge of Emma's power to go her own way — But still, I must acknowledge, she never fails to surprise one," he broke off to add, as Emma came back, her arms draped over with garments and carrying, also, in her hands, a little rosewood desk.

"Papa, may I give this to Jane? It is the one, do you recall, that my cousin Eliza in Kent sent me for my seventh birthday, and, as you know, I have Mamma's, which I like much better, besides very seldom needing to write letters to anybody; and this one is very nicely fitted up, you see, with the ink well and the wafers and sand-box and little drawer for seals and pens and the lock and key; if Jane is not to live in Highbury any more, she will often be wanting to write letters to her aunt and grandmamma — "

"Softly, softly, my dear, you talk so quick I scarcely understand you; and nobody, you know, has yet said anything about poor little Jane quitting Highbury *entirely*; this time, at least, it is only for a visit — "

Emma's face fell. She said, "But I thought — Mr Knightley said — there was talk of 'extending the visit indefinitely'?"

"Well, that may be so if all the parties take a liking to one another," explained Mr Knightley. "As, indeed, there is no reason why they should not. I have always found Jane an intelligent, responsive, good-hearted girl," he added, looking directly at Emma and, because he saw a cloud come over her brow, he went on, "But it was a truly kind thought, Emma, to wish to give her your desk, and I think it is an offering that, coming from you, she would particularly appreciate, since the two of you have never — have never found yourselves able to make friends. — And, after all, if Jane returns to Highbury at the conclusion of this visit, she will be leaving behind her a new set of connections in London, with whom she will certainly wish to maintain a correspondence. Your present will serve her well, whether she is there or here. If you concur, my dear sir — " to Mr Woodhouse, "I think the gift should be made."

"Ay, that will be best," agreed Mr Woodhouse. "Poor little Jane. I daresay she will get a great deal of use from that desk — it was well thought of. And Emma has her mother's, after all; my poor dear Mary," sighing deeply. "But still it is very sad that the child should be obliged to go from the place of her birth . . . "

Three other persons who found it sad that Jane must go from her native place were Jane herself and her aunt and grandmother. During the process of setting Jane's wardrobe to rights for this bold venture into the world of London, and adapting such gifts from neighbours as proved suitable, their tears fell copiously and almost continuously.

"Aunt Hetty, Grandmamma, do I truly have to go?" was a question put by Jane over and over again. And, "Yes, my dear, you must," was the answer invariably returned by the two ladies as they sat at their stitchery. "It will be a most dreadful loss for us, indeed," said her Aunt Hetty, wiping away the tears that would fall on the muslin kerchiefs she hemmed, "and there is no denying that we can hardly bear to part from you, our own dear, dear, good child; but you must remember, my love, that Grandmamma and I are not growing any younger; the day might come when she may be laid up, and all my care will be needed to nurse her — "

"But I would *help* you, Aunt Hetty — "

"My love, I know you would, and with the greatest goodwill in the world; but then, you should be learning at your books, not having to tend grown folk; and then too, you see, I am not so young any more myself — for your poor dear mother was so much younger than I — and if I should fall sick, there would be nobody but Patty to look after you — "

"But if you were ill, Aunt Hetty, then who would take care of *you*?" cried Jane, horrified.

"Why, my dear, I do not at all suppose that such a thing is likely to occur, for I am, I am thankful to say, remarkably stout and healthy as a rule, as indeed is dear Grandmamma; but it will be such a relief to us to know that you are comfortably established with kind Colonel Campbell and his good lady in their house, and that we need not be worrying our heads any more about your future, for that will all be taken care of by the Colonel; such a kind, excellent letter as he writ: 'to provide for her entirely is out of my power,' says he, 'but she shall be trained up for educating others; and I am glad to undertake this in token of the very great esteem in which I held Lieutenant Fairfax (your dear father, you know, my love) who, I am persuaded, was the cause of saving my life when laid low with a severe attack of camp fever.' Just think of that, my dear! No good action ever goes unrewarded! To think of your excellent father's kindness bearing fruit so very long after the event."

When neighbours came in, Mrs Goddard, Mrs Pryor, or Miss Taylor, the tears were quickly wiped away and smiling faces shown. The kind gifts that the visitors brought, sets of handkerchiefs, watch-cases, thimbles, needle-books were admired and displayed and thanked for most earnestly; the Bateses and their child could hardly have done praising a beautiful little work-basket offered by Mrs Pryor, who told them with sincerity how much she would grieve to lose her best pupil.

"But where you are going, my dear, you will have the best masters, I don't doubt, and will very soon have gone far beyond what I could teach you."

Jane acknowledged all these kindnesses very prettily, for her manners were excellent, but when the good ladies were departed she was obliged, sometimes, to lie down upon her bed for many minutes in stricken silence.

When Emma's charming little rosewood desk was sent down from Hartfield by a gardener, and unwrapped from its felt and sacking, Jane asked, "Need I accept this, Aunt Hetty?"

"Oh, my dearest child, what a question! How can you possibly think of not accepting such a kind, kind thoughtful present — precisely what you will be needing in London, you know, for Grandmamma and I shall be so eager to hear from you as often as it is possible for you to write — every day would not be too often for us, would it, ma'am? — if it were not for the cost of postage — and that is, I do believe, little Emma's very own desk, the one that

Mrs Goddard told us about that was sent to her last year from those great-cousins of Mr Woodhouse in Kent; but, however (and who could blame her?) Emma has always preferred to use her own dear Mamma's desk, Mrs Goddard said. But it really is the most useful convenient piece of furniture that I have ever seen, fitted with all that you might possibly require, and we must be fully sensible of Emma's great kindness in remembering you, especially as the two of you have never quite seemed to . . . Therefore the best thing you can do, indeed, my dear, is just to sit down this very minute and write dear Emma a nice note of thanks for it."

Accordingly Jane sat down as instructed and wrote, "Dear Emma: thank you very much for the beautiful desk. It is just what I need." Then she sucked the end of her pen and, after a few minutes, added, "It will remind me of Hartfield."

"That is right, my dear," said Aunt Hetty, satisfied. "That is doing as you ought. Now give the note to Patty, when you have it folded, and she can take it up when she goes with the bread to Mrs Wallis to be baked — "

"May I not take it myself, Aunt Hetty?" said Jane. "I shall be glad to, for, you know, I have sat indoors most of the day sewing — and I want to say goodbye to all our kind neighbours — "

"True, child, that is well thought of and shows a proper attention; yes, you should go to the vicarage — and Mrs Goddard — and the Perrys — only wrap up warmly for these autumn afternoons grow chill."

With this franchise Jane ran out into the cobbled street where she had lived all her life: the street of humble, unpretentious little houses, some brick, some stone, some tiled, some thatched, each of which, with its occupants, she knew nearly as well as her own. Here lived Mrs Ford, here old John Crow, here the Otways, here the Perrys. Here John Saunders, the blacksmith, blew a bright fan of sparks with his bellows, and Jane stood and watched for a moment, beside the patient cart-horse, as she always did. Sometimes Mr Knightley could be found here, having a horse shod, exchanging news with a farmer; he was not here today. Over the way was Mrs Wallis, the baker, with a few gingerbread men and glossy halfpenny buns still in her bow window.

After Jane had paid her duty calls she walked to where the houses ended, where the fields began, on the road to Donwell, and looked wistfully in that direction. Every hedge, every gate, every puddle, every pollard had some part in her own history. The apples in the vicarage orchard hung red and heavy, ready for picking; I shall not see them picked, thought Jane. I am obliged to leave, I have to go from here, and why? It is no fault of my own. I love this place, it will break my heart to go from it. In London all the faces will be strange to me.

Still she lingered, but at last turned back along the dewy, silent road. Plumes of blue smoke rose from the chimneys. The villagers were at home. Evening meals were in preparation.

Jane let herself in through the faded blue door in the high brick wall which protected the extensive grounds of Hartfield from the public view. She walked, as she had done so many times, quietly up the winding path among the laurel-bushes. As usual, the side door stood unlocked, and she could make her way to the music room without much risk of encountering any member of the household.

Seated at the old piano she laid her head for a moment on the keyboard lid, with its faded brown velvet cover, then raised it, revealing yellowed keys, and began softly to play. This evening she embarked on no classic airs, no concert pieces, but an old friendly tune, taught her when out riding by Mr Knightley:

> *Dulce, dulce, dulce domum*
> *Dulce domum resonemus*
> *Home, sweet home . . .*

She had not been playing more than a few moments when the door gently opened and Mrs Hill the housekeeper tiptoed in.

"Oh, Miss Jane dear — ! And is it really true that you are off to London tomorrow?"

"Yes, Mrs Hill. I just came to — to say goodbye to the old piano. And to give you this note for Emma. And to thank you," said Jane with a tight throat, "for all the pieces of cake you have brought me in this room."

"Oh! Miss Jane! Such a pleasure as it has been to all of us — to hear you play. And when I think of how poor Missis used to enjoy listening to you — " The housekeeper dabbed her eyes with her apron. "Serle and James ask me to say goodbye to you, Miss, and to wish you the very best of good fortune in London. Which I am sure you *will* have, miss; if only because of your beautiful music; why, His Majesty himself would think it a treat to listen — "

"Oh, Mrs Hill, I am afraid that is not true. Though it is kind of you to say so. But I am very sorry — very sorry indeed — to leave Highbury — and my aunt — and Granny — "

"Never fear, miss, we'll see they go on as they should; Master's a good soul, he will not forget them, you may be sure. And nor will I. I'll see that James steps down there, every two-three days — "

"Oh thank you, Mrs Hill. Here is the note for Emma — "

"Serle shall give it to her." The housekeeper took the paper, folding her lips inward. "*There's* one as walks with her nose uplifted. Has a high notion of herself. You'd ha' thought — but there! Dreadful pity it was that her ma died when she did. Such a sweet, good mistress, Mrs Woodhouse. No puffed-up conceit about *her*. And yet she was a true lady, never forgot what was anybody's due. Which one could not say the same — never mind! My lips are sealed."

Since, despite this declaration, Mrs Hill's lips plainly were *not* sealed, Jane made haste to take her leave, and ran out quickly into the dusk.

To her surprise — and considerable dismay — on approaching the shrubbery she encountered Emma who, she had reckoned, would be safely indoors at this time preparing for dinner, which the Bateses ate at a much earlier hour than their rich neighbours. Emma had been sitting on the bench under the cedar tree and now stood up as Jane was obliged to pass her.

"Oh — there you are — Emma — " stammered Jane, much confused. "I came — that is — I brought a note — a note thanking you for the desk — it was very good of you — "

Emma seemed almost equally at a loss. She stood silent for a moment, then said stiffly, "The desk was nothing. I use Mamma's, you know, which I like far better. And Isabella was given a handsome one, all her own, made of walnut, by Mr John Knightley. So nobody needed this one. — Well, and so you are going to London." Her tone lightened, as if she were relieved by the prospect, Jane thought. "Are you glad?" she asked.

"Glad?" said Jane in surprise. "No, why should I be glad? I am sorry — very, very sorry — to be leaving Highbury — and my house — and Aunt Hetty, and Grandmother — "

"But you live in those tiny dark rooms — where there is so much furniture that you can hardly walk about — and your grandmother is so very old — and your aunt talks all the time — you said so yourself — how can you bear it?"

"Excuse me," said Jane, gulping. "I have to go home now. They will be waiting for me. Mrs Cole was to come in to drink tea and say goodbye — "

"Oh — Mrs Cole! But wait a moment, pray wait," said Emma. "There is something I wished to say — "

Jane waited obediently, but as nothing seemed to be forthcoming, repeated, "Aunt Hetty will be wondering what has become of me. I *must* go, Emma."

Emma still hesitated, then said rapidly, "That stuff looks better on you than ever it did on me — it was improved by taking off the bugle trimming. But I do not think you should wear a stuff dress in London — cashmere would be better — "

"I do not know — I suppose the family, the Campbells, will tell me how to go on — goodbye — " stammered Jane, hardly aware of what she was saying, and ran away down the path among the bushes, leaving Emma again solitary by the cedar tree.

As she let herself out through the door in the wall Jane thought over the few words that had been exchanged, and then about what Mrs Hill had said. I would not agree that Emma is puffed-up, exactly, she decided. No. She is not that, whatever Mrs Hill may say. She does not have a high notion of herself. But she is very hard to please, when it comes to other people. That is because she is so easily bored.

Emma's words returned to Jane. "So you are going to London. Are you glad?"

Almost, Jane thought, as if she envied me. Almost as if she herself would be glad to go. Yet she has a father who dotes on her, a loving sister, a kind governess, friends like Mr Knightley, fine clothes, playthings, books, a grand house, a beautiful garden — why is she not satisfied?

Running homeward along the village street, Jane wondered suddenly: will the Campbells have a piano?

Returning home, she was stricken to learn that Mr Knightley had called, had been sitting with her aunt and grandmother twenty minutes, hoping to say goodbye to her, but was finally obliged to go off to a churchwardens' meeting.

Chapter 3

Colonel Campbell was a tall, active-looking man, aged about fifty, his complexion much bronzed and weathered by long service abroad under blistering suns. His grey-brown hair had mostly receded, leaving him half bald, and his keen, intelligent countenance was further marred by a scar, the legacy of a bullet-wound, on the left side of his temple. He walked decidedly lame, and was deaf in one ear, another effect of the head wound.

"You will have to speak loud and clear when you address me, my child," was one of the first things he told Jane, in the harsh, carrying tone of the partially deaf. "For otherwise, you see, I shall be continually urging you to *speak up, speak louder*, and that, you know, will be a very tiresome waste of our valuable time."

"Can you hear me if I speak like this, sir?"

"Ay, that will do very well; you have a fine, clear, pretty voice, my dear. I do not doubt but that we shall do very well together."

Miss Bates and her mother naturally wished to entertain the Colonel lavishly with currant-wine and sweet-cake from the buffet; they wanted to call in the neighbours and make their visitor known to half the village; but he swept aside all these proposals with military briskness. Endowed, under his abrupt manner, with a kind heart and a discerning eye, he perceived that both the elderly ladies, and also Jane herself, were suffering acute strain at the thought of the imminent parting; the ladies had sat up after midnight, crying and completing last-minute tasks, and all three had slept very ill, if at all, during the remainder of the night; the greatest kindness he could do for them was to remove Jane with all possible speed.

"Come, my dear, if you are ready, let us be off; the horses have had all the bait they need; it is only sixteen miles to London, after all! Nothing of a journey. Once you are finally and permanently fixed with us, I daresay we shall be trotting it up and down three or four times a quarter."

"Oh — but *this* time I am coming only for a visit, am I not, sir?" urgently and anxiously protested Jane, as he lifted her into the carriage, after many and tearful embraces of her grandmother and aunt.

"That's of course!" He pinched her cheek, but turned to say privily to the two trembling ladies in their shawls, "We had best make it a tolerably long one, this time, hey? to allow the child space to settle and put down a few roots, you know; for I can see that she is one of the sort who forms strong attachments, I can see how much she loves her home here (and indeed it's to her credit); and such bonds take time to form — There, now, have we all on board that we should have, every basket, bundle, posy, and carpet-bag? Excellent — capital — that was most expeditiously done. Now, my dear ladies," he added with a certain impatience, "pray do you step indoors, for this wind will give you a shocking chill otherwise. I guarantee that we shall not start off until I see your faces at the window upstairs — Look out through the glass, now, Jane, and wave your kerchief to your friends — that's the dandy — there they are, snugly established up in the bow. Now then, let go, driver! and let us see how fast you can get us back to Manchester Square."

Jane did not require any instructions to look out and wave; her face was pressed against the carriage glass; but it was doubtful how much of the external world she was able to see, for the tears streamed continuously from her eyes. Still, so long as any of the landscape remained familiar, she continued to crane her neck and gaze out at all the beloved scenes so as to fix them in her memory; and when, as very shortly happened, they had travelled beyond any familiar landmarks, Colonel Campbell kindly and sensibly pulled out a newspaper and absorbed himself in it, allowing her to have her cry out in peace; after which, being really exhausted by her disturbed night, she fell sound asleep.

When she next awoke, over an hour had passed, and they were already threading the new-built streets of suburbs. A small rain fell, and Jane was dismayed by the view through the glass: rows and rows of small shabby houses, interspersed with fields of cabbages and straggly orchards.

"Is this London, sir?" she asked.

The Colonel laughed at her tone of horror.

"No, this is only the outskirts; set your mind at rest, my child! You will find that the neighbourhood where I and my family have chosen to settle is pleasant enough; only ten minutes' walk from a fine, handsome park, not to mention streets of elegant shops. And my daughter Rachel will be so eagerly looking out for you; you can have no notion of how many questions she has asked about you, and will have to ask. She is overjoyed at the thought of having a companion. She and her mother, you see, have scrambled over half the world after me — France, in which country Rachel was born — and Corsica — and the West Indies — and the Low Countries — and Ireland — they are regular camp followers and have hardly ever been lucky enough to have a settled place in which to live. So poor Rachel has completely missed attending dame school, and music lessons, and dancing classes, and birthday parties, and all the other things that well-brought up little girls, such as yourself, take for granted. She is hoping — and, indeed, so are her mother and I — that you will be able to help and advise her in ever so many ways."

The Colonel said all this with great friendliness, and Jane was encouraged, as he had intended that she should be. She said, "Oh, but, indeed, sir, I don't, either, know very much about birthday parties and dancing classes. I — I have always lived very quietly, you see, in Highbury, with Grandmamma and dear Aunt Hetty; there were so few other children."

"But you have learned your lessons with good Mrs Pryor — I am told that you are an exceedingly well-informed young person. And you know a great deal about music, so in that department you will be able to help Rachel, who loves to sing, and has picked up, in the course of our ramblings, various peasant ditties; she will be able to tell you a great many tales about mules and mountain passes, but has only been taught by her mamma, and has hardly ever had the good fortune to get near a pianoforte."

"I love to sing too," said Jane shyly. "Perhaps we can sing together."

Her curiosity began to stir about this unknown Rachel. How very delightful it would be, she thought, if there were ways in which she, Jane, could be of use to the other, could help or inform; how fortunate if Rachel were actually to be grateful for her presence, if the benefits were not to be all on one side. What an unexpected notion that was! She had grown to accept her rejection by Emma as being an example of what life was bound to offer, and to believe, humbly, that because she was so dull, and not interested in making up stories about weddings, nobody could wish for her company. But here, it seemed, was somebody whose early childhood had been even more deprived of amenities than her own.

"How old is Rachel, sir?" she asked.

"Just your age, my child; she will be nine in February. We had hoped, for a long time, that she might be blessed with younger brothers — or sisters; but, alas, that was not to be; so *your* companionship will be all the more welcome. And, I hope, hers to you. I know you have had the company of your good aunt and grandmother but you must, often, have wished for friends of your own age."

Jane could not feel, truthfully, that this was so. She had become used to her solitude, had often consciously enjoyed it, had never been aware of loneliness; she could pass hours in perfect content playing her music, or sitting on the bank of a brook watching the minnows, or at her needlework, absorbed in the memory of some book that she and Mrs Pryor had been reading together.

"Indeed I have never had a friend," she said thoughtfully.

"Well, now you are furnished with one — friend, sister, companion — ready made, on offer! Which is enough, I daresay," remarked Colonel Campbell drily, "to make you both detest one another on sight! But let us not tempt Providence by supposing any such thing, for now we are arrived, and yonder I perceive Rachel and her mother on the step, ready to greet you."

In fact the carriage had, while they were talking, rolled into a spacious new-built square, with a circular garden in the centre, protected by railings; and, close at hand, outside of a handsome modern red-brick mansion, a lady and child were waiting with eager expressions of curiosity on their faces.

"Well, my dears," called the Colonel jovially as the horses came to a halt, "here she is, I have brought her to you, and now you can pet her and play with her to your hearts' content."

He spoke so cheerfully, opening the door of the carriage, that Jane was startled to see the child on the step throw him what seemed a nervous, apprehensive look, as if she were not prepared to believe in his good humour.

Next moment the lady, presumably Mrs Campbell, a thin and frail, but brown-visaged and intelligent-looking person, dressed in a very plain, almost Quakerish fashion, was helping Jane to alight, and embracing her in the warmest possible manner, while exclaiming, "Welcome, a thousand welcomes, my dear child! We are so happy to meet you. I was well acquainted with your father, you know, before his sad, untimely death — the kindest, most delightful young man. Oh, you have quite a look of him — his eyes exactly — has she not, James? For his sake, and for your own too, we are most happy to have you here. Are we not, Rachel?"

The child beside her drew a half-strangled breath. With a sudden flash of astonished comprehension, Jane realised that she really was terrified of something — almost too terrified to speak. Stepping forward, with a most unwonted initiative, Jane caught hold of her hand — a piteously thin, cold hand it was, like a little bird's claw — and said quickly, "I do so hope that we shall be friends! Your papa has told me a great deal about you!"

Two skinny arms came round her neck. "I am s-s-s-certain we s-shall!" said a hesitant little voice in her ear. "I want to l-love you like a s-s-sister!" Over her shoulder Jane felt Rachel cast a scared glance at her father.

"That's right, that's right — but come along, Rachel, don't be dawdling there, do not keep poor Jane shivering on the step!" he said impatiently. "Bring her indoors where she can see the house, and get warm, and grow accustomed to us all."

Flinching, Rachel would have retreated, but Jane held fast to her hand, thus allowing herself to be drawn into the hall, where the Colonel was loudly exclaiming, "Come, where's my dinner? Where's my leg of mutton? I am downright famished, and so, I dare swear, is poor Jane — hey, Jane, are not you?"

Rachel winced again, at her father's brusque demand, but Mrs Campbell answered tranquilly, "Dinner will be quite ready in ten minutes, my dear. Before that I daresay Jane will like to see where she sleeps — come with me, Jane, my child — and to wash her face and tidy her hair a little."

During which process — which revealed to Jane that, for the first time in her life, she was to have a capacious bedchamber all to herself — Mrs Campbell, who accompanied and assisted her with the greatest kindness, also addressed her the following words of earnest advice:

"My dear Jane, we are *truly* glad to have you with us, for your dear father's sake, and shall do our utmost to make your stay here as happy as possible. We are not rich people, you know. My husband, due to his wounds and — and other reasons — was obliged to sell out of the army sooner than he would otherwise have wished; though, for myself and Rachel, I am very pleased to be back where there are houses and pavements and libraries! But our style of living will be very plain; there will be no grand entertainments, or anything of that kind. But all that we have you shall share."

"Thank you, ma'am," quietly answered Jane (but thinking, as she looked round her spacious chamber, observing the bed with a quilt, the well-polished chest-of-drawers, the closet full of shelves, the slipper-chair and dressing-stand, that the Campbells' style of living, however plain, was greatly superior to that of the Bates ladies in their three rooms in Highbury).

"There is, however, one thing that I should like to say to you directly," continued Mrs Campbell, glancing towards the door to make sure that nobody was within earshot, "and that is about Colonel Campbell. As you will have discovered, he is somewhat hard of hearing, and this makes him — on occasion — a trifle impatient, if he cannot catch what other people — especially children and servants — are saying. He is not *at all* an ill-tempered man — I would not wish you to think that — but he *can* be hasty. All will be very well so long as you speak up clearly and address him without fear. Indeed I am rejoiced to see that you and he are already on such pleasant terms. Just speak so that he can easily hear you, and I am sure he will love you like a father."

"Yes, ma'am. I quite understand. My grandmother is a little hard of hearing too. And I am very much obliged to you for having me to stay," answered Jane.

This was not, at the moment, strictly true; she was in a misery of homesickness, wondering how in the world Aunt Hetty and Grandmamma were managing without her — they would have finished their early dinner long ago and now, most likely, she thought, would be sitting shedding tears with no Jane to wind wool and read aloud to them. — But, most likely, kind Mrs Goddard or Mrs Pryor would have stepped in, knowing how they must be feeling this first evening without their precious child. Encouraged by this notion, Jane looked up at Mrs Campbell, whose thin, brown, clever face was bent down to hers in earnest goodwill.

"Colonel Campbell was so *very* fond of your excellent father, my dear — who, indeed, saved his life on at least two occasions. And he is ready to be equally fond of you. He — " Mrs Campbell glanced again towards the door, as if she would have said more, but at this moment Rachel came shyly round it.

"Ah — Rachel my love. That is right. Now you can take Jane downstairs, and show her the way to the dining-room."

Jane, seeing them again side by side, was struck very much by the resemblance between mother and daughter. They both had the same very thin, long faces, long noses, and small delicate mouths; but where Mrs Campbell's eyes were bright brown and sparkling, Rachel's were pale grey, similar in colour to her father's, and rather close-set. Her nose, too, had a tendency to pinkness. Lank brown hair hung straight round her face; she was, in fact, poor child, decidedly plain. Yet, thought Jane, there was a quality instantly attractive about her thoughtful, interested, inquiring expression and the light in her grey eyes, suggesting that she would eagerly welcome all new impressions, all new encounters, and put them to excellent use.

As before, she caught Jane's hand, saying in a half whisper, but very warmly, "After d-dinner I have s-s-so many things to s-s-show you — "

"Make haste!" came the Colonel's clarion shout from below, and they hurriedly scampered down the stairway.

Before she fell asleep that night, Jane had many tears to shed. The noises in the street outside were disturbing: strange, loud, and unfamiliar, hoofbeats on stone, shouts of link-boys, wheels rattling on a paved roadway; and she thought of poor Aunt Hetty, lonely in her tiny chamber where the other bed stood empty for the first time. Jane longed for the silence of her own village, where the loudest sound at night would be the hoot of an owl or bark of a kennelled dog. — But, beyond sorrow and homesickness, what a multitude of new things she had to occupy her mind! And, foremost, making all other details of this new existence sink into the background, was the visibly unhappy relation between Colonel Campbell and his daughter. Each time he addressed her, she shrank and trembled — and small wonder, thought Jane, for his manner to her was so harsh, irritable, lacking any kindness or patience. How *can* he be so unreasonable to her? wondered Jane, when he is so understanding and kind to other people? Poor Rachel did not help her own cause, it could certainly be seen, for when she did address her father in reply to his questions (never spontaneously of her own accord) her voice was frequently so low and timid that he furiously ordered her to repeat almost every sentence. And her stammer, less observable when she conversed with other people, became, when she spoke to her father, so severe, so crippling, that the shortest phrase, or even a single word, often took her several minutes, while the Colonel waited, irritably tapping fingers on the table, or the arm of his chair. It was painful, it was distressing, to watch and listen to them. — Whereas Rachel, on her own, was a different being. With what eager pleasure did she display to Jane all her collections of pressed flowers from the West Indies, her tiny Corsican doll — "We had so little room in the s-saddle bags, you s-see, that she was the only toy I was permitted — " her drawings of foreign castles, and the few books she had already acquired since their arrival in England. "Now you are with us I hope we s-shall get m-many m-more! Do you find my English accent v-very odd, Jane? G-Grandmother Fitzroy says that I roll my r's dreadfully; I had a Corsican nurse, you see, I spoke Italian before I learned English (or not even Italian, exactly, but the language they s-speak in C-Corsica, Aunt Sophia s-says it is dreadful g-gibberish;) poor Giannina, she cried when we left, and s-so did I; then there was S-Seraphina in Santa Lucia, and G-Grizek in K-Krabbendam, and M-Maire in Ireland — I have had so many nurses, and each one s-spoke a different language! And now we are to have a g-governess, P-Papa says he hopes she will teach me to s-speak correctly. We have only, you know, been in England three weeks; I like it well enough, but not s-so well as the West Indies. But now you are with us I am s-sure I shall like it m-much better!" hugging Jane. She had innumerable questions to ask about England, which Jane answered to the best of her ability.

"And were there f-friends that you were s-sorry to part from when you came to us?"

"Dear Aunt Hetty and Grannie I was *very* sorry to leave — but you will be meeting them by and by, I hope."

"F-friends of my own age, I really m-meant?"

"No; not precisely," Jane answered after a moment's hesitation. "The only one of that sort was Emma; but she was not a friend."

"Who is Emma?"

Jane endeavoured to give an account of her relation with Emma; the made-over clothes, "I am still wearing them now"; the music lessons, the imaginary wedding game, the horse-riding fiasco.

"Emma, you see, is the one who has to lead, she feels obliged to be first in any company. If she may not lead, then she does not choose to be part of it at all."

"How very s-strange!" cried Rachel. Then, after some thought, "How d-does she occupy herself all day? If they are s-so rich?"

"I hardly know," answered Jane, who had often asked herself the same question. "She learns her lessons with Miss Taylor, of course; and talks to her sister. But Miss Isabella is a great deal older; indeed it is said that Mr John Knightley has begun paying her attentions, and will marry her. If Isabella were to marry him, and go to live in London, Emma would be very lonely, I think."

"It is delightful that you can ride so well," Rachel said, harking back to the days on Ginger with Mr Knightley, "for we can go riding in the park. P-Papa has promised that. And we are to have m-music lessons, of course."

This part of the programme, which had been a source of some inquietude to Jane, was ratified next day. Not only were the music lessons to be continued: her dear Signor Negretti was to continue giving them. He had written in dismay to Mr Woodhouse when he heard of the plan for Jane's removal from Highbury; Mr Woodhouse had shown the letter to Mr Knightley, who spoke of it to the Bateses, who had mentioned it to Colonel Campbell, and the upshot was that Signor Negretti, who lived in Wimbledon, would travel to London once a week, so as to remain in touch with his favourite pupil.

"Oh, I am so glad!" Jane cried out joyfully when this news was communicated to her. "I am so *very* much obliged to you, Colonel Campbell."

"Well, well, we shall expect a plentiful reward of fine music to delight our ears — so soon as Broadwoods have seen fit to send up the new instrument — hey, miss?" He looked down at Jane, smiling and indulgent. Oh, why cannot he ever look at Rachel like that? she wondered. Rachel's face lights up so when she smiles, but her papa never sees her smile; whenever his eye is upon her, she looks more as if she might at any moment burst out crying.

Mrs Campbell had taken advantage of a time when Rachel was paying an essential visit to a dentist, under the escort of a maid, to open her heart rather more to Jane on the subject of the Colonel's relations with his daughter.

"I am treating you, my dear Jane, almost as a grown-up person, for I can see that, no doubt because of having lived always in the company of grown-ups, you are sage and sensible far beyond your years. And I rely on you to help us as much as you are able; indeed I have high hopes that your being all day long in company with Rachel will greatly help to remedy matters which have come to such a sorry pass. My husband, you see, was greatly displeased at Rachel's birth; firstly, he thought I should have returned to England before the event (but transport was very difficult and uncertain just at that time; also I did not, *at all*, wish to leave him); and secondly he was, I fear, greatly disappointed that Rachel was of the female sex. He would so much have preferred a son. Especially as, in the sorrowful event, she was not to be followed by sisters or brothers. And then, it was most unfortunate that she learned to speak from so many foreign nurses; first some Italian dialect — and then a kind of peasant Spanish; and, when her father reprimanded her, and obliged her always to speak English, it was found that she had this stammer — "

"Did she not, then, ma'am, speak with the stammer in the other languages?"

"Not near so bad; a friend of ours — your own father, in fact, my dear — wondered if it was the being compelled to change languages when she was only three that brought on the impediment. Your dear papa was used to be endlessly kind and patient with Rachel, my dear — he was such a *good* young man — of course she cannot remember him now, she was only a baby then — "

Jane felt a queer pang of envy that this other child should, even if so fleetingly, have known her own father whom she herself had never met.

"So you see, what I am hoping you can do, my dear Jane, is to encourage Rachel, by your own excellent example, not to be so timid with the Colonel, for he, though in general quite a reasonable man — and *truly* benevolent and kind-hearted — cannot be brought to understand that Rachel is unable, simply by making an effort, to surmount her speech impediment. And, of course, the more impatient *he* grows, the more apprehensive *she* becomes."

"Yes, I can see that, ma'am."

Jane thought that she was being set a most difficult, an almost impossible task. For the Colonel, when in a state of exasperation, could be an alarming spectacle: his eyes flashed, his voice rose to parade-ground pitch, he was not a man to suffer opposition or frustration easily. If he were to turn the battery of his anger on herself, she did not think she would be able to behave any more courageously than Rachel.

However she of course promised to do her best.

"That's my good child. Never be afraid of the Colonel, my dear," urged Mrs Campbell. "If your cause is good — stand up for yourself! He will like you all the better for it!"

Jane was presented with an opportunity to do this more quickly than she would have wished when, two days later, the longed-for piano was delivered.

Colonel Campbell called for her to come downstairs from the schoolroom, where she was sitting with Rachel and the new governess, in order to try out the instrument.

"For, if you don't approve it, miss, back it goes! *You* are the musical expert in this house."

A little abashed at such a responsibility being laid on her — yet reasonably confident — Jane played a few exercises and small pieces, and soon pronounced the piano to be of superior quality, as, indeed, it was. Signor Negretti would, she was sure, approve.

"Very good," said the master of the house. "Then it shall stay! Place it over there, by the fireplace, if you please," he told the carriers who had brought it.

The family were at that time assembled in the main drawing-room of the house: a large, front-facing apartment.

"Oh, sir!" cried Jane in dismay, "you will surely not have it in *here?*"

"I certainly shall, miss! How, otherwise, can you delight us and our company every evening after tea?"

"Oh, but sir, pray consider! Rachel and I will be needing to learn our lessons on this piano; and to practise, each of us, for several hours daily; Rachel has never learned before, she will need to practise a great deal. So, indeed, do I; the more one learns, the more hours of exercise are required; Signor Negretti, when he comes, will tell you the same. You and Mrs Campbell will not, for sure, wish to have all those scales and exercises rattling in your ears, hour after hour, while Mrs Campbell is at her work and you are reading the newspaper!"

"What? What?" he said, half smiling, half annoyed. "Why, where the plague *is* it to go, then? In there?" — gesturing to the rear half of the apartment, which was cut off by a pair of folding doors.

"No sir; for the sound would travel through those doors much more than you would think — step in there a moment, and I will play, and you shall see for yourself."

She obliged him to do so.

"Well then, what do you suggest?" said he, returning. "Here we have a musical prodigy in the house — and a new instrument of tip-top quality — how are we to delight our friends, of an evening, if the piano is to be hidden away in some attic — hey? Or do you expect me to acquire two instruments — one for the schoolroom, one for the parlour? Well, I can assure you, I am not indulging in any such expense!"

Jane had been devoting rapid, intensive thought to the matter.

"Sir, why should it not go into the conservatory? I have heard Mrs Campbell say that is the one room in the house she has no use for — as she does not care for hot-house blooms — and the conservatory is not so far distant from here but that, if all the doors are opened, the sound could be heard — it is only down a few steps, after all — and then, I believe, if a large screen — such as that one, there — were to be placed between the piano and the conservatory door — the sound of our lessons and practising would be greatly diminished — perhaps hardly heard at all. While, at other times, when you wished to enjoy the music, the screen could be taken away and the piano, perhaps, advanced a little closer to the doorway — "

Colonel Campbell, who at the outset of this speech had begun by scowling in a highly unreceptive manner, glanced at his wife and burst out laughing at her nod of approval.

"She has it all planned, has she — hey? The quiet little mouse is not so quiet as we thought — has a head on her shoulders, indeed! Major General Moore should have had you on his campaign staff, madam minx! So Mrs Campbell has to forego her orchids and lilies — "

"Indeed, Colonel Campbell, Jane is quite right," quickly put in his wife. "I was saying, only this morning, that, with all my charitable committees, I have better things to occupy my time than watering a quantity of sickly flowers which nobody ever looks at."

"Oh, very well, very well! Take the instrument down those steps," he told the delivery men. "Though the black gentleman himself only knows how you will persuade it to go round that corner. — Well, my dear Jane, I shall expect some particularly heartbreaking music this evening as a reward for depriving our drawing-room of its new asset." It was a lucky circumstance that the Colonel's partial deafness did not impair his enjoyment of music, to which he was very partial; a melody was for him easier to catch than the variable tones of the human voice. "I had particularly intended that corner for the piano," he added. "Now it is going to look decidedly bare."

"You could place a tub of orchids and lilies there," ventured Jane. The Colonel made a mock-threatening gesture, and pinched her cheek; then he ran down the stairs to the front door, calling back to his wife that he was off to his club and would not be back until dinner-time.

Rachel, who had been listening, huge-eyed, to this dialogue from a distant corner, said to Jane afterwards, "How you *dared* speak to Papa in s-such a way — !"

"Oh, but it was necessary," said Jane seriously. "He would have been much more inconvenienced — and — and put out — if he had been obliged to hear us playing our scales all day long. That would really have overset him and put him in a bad skin."

The governess, Miss Winstable, pursed her lips and shook her head.

"Pray, Jane, my dear child, do not let me hear such expressions on your lips! They are not at all the thing when you are referring to your kind guardian and benefactor — or, indeed, at any time."

Miss Winstable had been Mrs Campbell's own governess and mentor in time gone by, and had then, for many years, looked after the education and morals of Mrs Campbell's sister, Lady Selsea's, children, until that family removed to Lisbon, when, by pure good luck, Miss Winstable was free to offer her services to the Campbells.

Or by pure bad luck, Rachel said.

Miss Winstable was like a wisp of cobweb. She seemed to slow down, hamper, and hinder Rachel and Jane at every turn, without herself being precisely visible or tangible.

"Dear old thing," said Mrs Campbell vaguely, "*how* Sophy and I used to laugh at her when we were young. The only product of all her teaching that I can remember was a landscape picture, worked in silk, which took me seven years to complete . . . I have a notion that it is still in Grandmamma's house in Bath somewhere — " And

Mrs Campbell took herself off to preside over one of the various committees framed to promote public feeling and action on penal reform, prevention of the slave trade, abolition of flogging in the armed forces, and extension of the franchise, which, with other charitable and benevolent activities were, now that she was returned to England, her principal interest and concern. Having supplied her child with a governess and an intelligent companion, she felt that she had sufficiently disposed of her parental responsibilities for the time.

Jane, in desperation after a few days, nerved herself to face Colonel Campbell in his library, which at the moment was furnished sparsely enough with two armchairs, a table, and a pile of bound issues of *The Rambler*.

"Sir — may I trouble you?"

His tone of reply was brisk. "Well — what is it?" — lowering the newspaper an inch to look at her over the top.

"Sir — we are learning nothing from Miss Winstable — except carpet-work. I am sure she means to be very kind — but — but if I am to be trained as a governess — and, and Rachel wishes to know all manner of things — "

"Did not Mrs Campbell engage masters for you, then?" Jane shook her head. "Cecelia is so engrossed in her own concerns, now we are back where she can get at them," he said indulgently. "Well, well, this must be seen to. You were very right to come to me. What then — astronomy? history? languages? geography? literature?"

"Oh, yes, sir, if you please, all those," Jane said, greatly relieved to have her request so reasonably received. "And drawing. And mathematics too, I should think; Rachel has a great wish to learn mathematics."

"Has she indeed?" He seemed startled. "Very well, your educational programme shall be attended to without delay. When does your music teacher resume his duties?"

"Today, sir."

"Excellent." And he crackled his newspaper as a sign of dismissal.

Signor Negretti was enchanted to find his star pupil established so prosperously in London (where he gave many lessons) with benevolent patrons and a brand-new piano. And he was, of course, not averse to a new pupil, even one who, at the advanced age of nine, had received as yet no keyboard instruction. He soon discovered in Rachel a fair ability, along with a high degree of quickness and intelligence which made her eager to make up for lost time as fast as she could.

"Mees Rachel will not too soon equal *you*, Mees Jane," he said privily to Jane, "for you are indeed the best pupil I ever have, but she has a nice small talent and we shall make the best use of it. Also she shall have a pretty contralto voice. Together you shall sing some charming duets."

"What about the stammer?" Jane asked anxiously.

He made a gesture of extreme impatience.

"Idiocy! this can all have been avoided, if it were not for stupid parents."

Jane sighed. Many parents, she thought, might be a great deal worse than Colonel and Mrs Campbell who, after all, did not seem so very stupid.

"But singing lessons will help her, will they not, Signor Negretti? I recall you told me once that somebody who could hardly speak at all learned to sing very well — "

"Yes, yes, yes, singing shall much help her; and also you, Mees Jane, shall perform with her each day some throat and face exercises which I show you."

Miss Winstable came fluttering back into the room, very agitated at having left her second charge alone with the music master for so long lacking the presence of a chaperon. Jane had in fact seized the opportunity of poor Rachel's being afflicted with a nosebleed — a not infrequent misfortune with her, sometimes the result of excitement, or, more frequently, a consequence of having been spoken to harshly by her father. She had been hurried away to lie down on her bed with cold compresses and hartshorn.

"Poor little dear! — Such a tiresome, unladylike affliction! How I hope she soon grows out of it!"

"Signor Negretti," said Jane, at the conclusion of the first lesson, "you still go to give Emma Woodhouse her lessons at Highbury twice a week?"

"To be sure I do, Mees Jane, and what a sad change! To veesit that house where I have passed such profitable hours of joy, and have only naughty Mees Emma to teach, who never practises as she ought! Do you wish me to take some message to her? I shall be very happy to do so."

"Oh, no, thank you," quickly answered Jane, thinking how very relieved Emma must be to have Jane wholly removed from her proximity. A reminder in the shape of a message would probably be the last thing she would want. "No, but, I was thinking, as you ride, on your way there, right past my grandmother's house — might I entrust you sometimes with a letter for her and my aunt?"

"Of course, of course!" beamed the Signor. "As often as you please! And I shall have the happiness of telling them that you grow well, and learn well, and become every week more beautiful! And I can bring back letters to you, also."

"Oh, gracious me, my dear, I do not know if that is a very wise or proper thing to do — sending letters by a *music teacher* — " worried Miss Winstable, whose first impulse, on hearing about any course of action proposed by her charges, was to forbid it, on grounds of impropriety, or rashness, or unladylikeness, or any slightest tincture of those dread possibilities. — Or, simply, on the principle that the young should be continually thwarted and chastened.

But Jane had instant recourse to Colonel Campbell, who stopped reading about the Treaty of Amiens only long enough to snap: "Of course, of course! Send as many letters by the fellow as you please; perfectly in order. Never trouble me with such trifling matters again!"

Such an arrangement was an immense comfort to Jane, saving, as it did, so much postage for the poor ladies in Highbury, and for Colonel Campbell too. Jane had, of course, written home immediately on arrival to assure her friends of her safe establishment in Manchester Square, to describe the kindness of her hosts and friendly reception by Rachel, and had added a pitiful postscript: "Please give my very best remembrances to Mr Knightley. I was sorry not to be able to bid him Goodbye." Colonel Campbell had franked the first letter for her. But, prudently, she did not wish to trespass on his kindness too often.

A few weeks after the establishment of a regular teaching routine, when, one afternoon, the girls were returning from a botanical ramble in Kensington Gardens with Miss Winstable, Jane thought she recognised, ahead of them in Wigmore Street, the backs of two very familiar figures. She hesitated a while, for, accustomed as she was to know every face she met along the street of Highbury, she still found it hard to accept the largeness of London and the fact that every person in the street must necessarily be a stranger. But as they overtook the group ahead — for the two gentlemen (who were accompanied by a boy, Jane now saw) had come to a halt, apparently to bid one another a long and conversational farewell — they were to be recognised, indubitably, as well-loved, familiar neighbours.

"Mr Knightley! Mr Weston!" burst out from Jane, irrepressible with joy.

Miss Winstable turned on her a scandalized countenance.

"Jane! *My dear child!* Ladies do not *ever* call out to persons in the street — most particularly not to unknown gentlemen. I can hardly believe it of you!"

"But they are not unknown gentlemen, Miss Winstable—they are friends!"

Despite this endorsement, Miss Winstable was for instantly hurrying her charges away from such potentially dangerous and undesirable contact, when the two gentlemen, approaching and removing their hats in the most civil manner, contrived to block her escape.

"Jane, my dear child! What a fortunate chance! I was just on my way to deliver a note and a packet to you from your aunt — I believe it consists of a pair of mitts, or a pair of socks, or some such article. I told her I was coming to London to visit brother John in Brunswick Square and asked if there were any article she might like conveyed to you." He bowed to Miss Winstable, and Jane made haste to introduce him as "a very old friend of my grandmother's. And this," she added quickly, "is Mr Weston, another neighbour, who lives part of the time in Highbury, and part of it in London." The governess fluttered, unsure of what course to follow, but both gentlemen were so polite, and seemed so truly genteel and unexceptionable that finally, with reluctance, she permitted them to accompany her charges a short way along the street; indeed she could see no means of preventing it.

"And you must also allow me to introduce my son," added Mr Weston beaming. "My son Frank, you know. Frank and I were just returning from the park when we encountered Knightley here, so we turned to walk along with him, as he said he was intending to call at Colonel Campbell's; Frank informs me that his guardians, Mr and Mrs Churchill, are acquainted with the Colonel and Mrs Campbell."

The boy Frank was meanwhile regarding the two girls with ingenuous interest, and they studied him with a similar unaffected friendly scrutiny. He was older than they by some three or four years — a slender, fair-haired, open-faced boy with a fresh colour and ready smile.

"Do you go to school in London?" Jane asked him.

"No, in Yorkshire," he told her. "But my guardian has come to London to see a doctor, so I was granted a holiday to come with her — only I am obliged to visit a dentist, so it is not all pleasure." He laughed, puffing out his cheek and making a gesture as of an enormously swelled jaw, and the girls laughed too.

"I have just b-been to a d-dentist also," said Rachel shyly. "It is a d-dreadful experience!"

"Don't forget, my boy, that your dental trouble gives us this happy chance to see one another," put in his father. "And that is a great joy, for me at any rate."

They were parting from the Westons, on the corner of Manchester Square, when, by chance, here came Colonel Campbell back from his club, so the introductions must be made over again, and Miss Winstable, inexpressibly agitated at being discovered by her employer in the company of three strange males, was at least relieved to have the situation ratified and regularized by the Colonel's total lack of displeasure and outrage. He even expressed happiness at making their acquaintance, said he had heard a great deal about Mr Knightley from the Bateses, and about Mr Weston, from the Churchills. Indeed he pressed them to come in and take a glass of wine, but both gentlemen pleaded other engagements. Mr Weston must escort his son to the dentist. Mr Knightley said, "Another time, I shall be happy," smiling kindly at Jane. "Your aunt and grandmother will indeed be glad when I tell them I have seen you looking so well — " and he strode off along the street while Jane gazed wistfully after him.

The girls were obliged to hear a great many more strictures from Miss Winstable, after re-entering the schoolroom, as to the appalling impropriety of addressing any male person in the street. "Not at *all* the kind of thing that any of dear Lady Selsea's girls would do!" If it had been Rachel, accustomed only to the wilderness of Flanders or Corsica, it might have been a little more excusable, but for Jane, brought up in a region of such unimpeachable respectability as Surry, she could only feel vicarious shame. "I blush for you, my child, I do indeed!"

Her thin cheeks were indeed reddened, and the look she gave Jane was one of disapproval, unmixed with any liking.

"I am sorry, Miss Winstable," Jane repeated politely for the third time, adding, "But you see, Mr Knightley is such a very, very kind neighbour. He sends my aunt and grandmother two great loads of firewood every winter, besides I do not know how many bushels of apples. And he taught me to ride — I would not for anything in the world be behindhand in paying him proper attention." Her voice faltered, remembering the happy freedom of those rides, and Rachel cast her a glance full of sympathy.

That evening Colonel Campbell demanded more information about Jane's acquaintances, and she was pleased to tell him what she knew: Mr Knightley, Mr John Knightley, the beauties of Donwell Abbey and its estates were carefully described.

"And Mr Weston? What is his story?"

A sad one, Jane told the Colonel. Mr Weston's young wife, who came from a proud Yorkshire family, the Churchills, had died, leaving him with a baby son. Since so young a man, still with his way to make in the world, seemed no very adequate guardian for a baby, the wealthy Churchills had offered to adopt the boy, Frank, and had done so when he was but an infant. During the subsequent nine or ten years Mr Weston, now engaged in business with his two brothers in London, had prospered very well, and had been able recently to exchange the small house in Highbury where his leisure was spent for a small but handsome estate adjoining the village. He still divided his time between London and Surry, but was looked up to, respected, and greatly liked by all his village neighbours. And he had never lost touch with his son, for the Churchills, coming south to London every spring, raised no objection to Mr Weston calling at their house in Manchester Street and taking Frank on educational excursions to see the Elgin Marbles, or less educational ones to Astley's Amphitheatre.

"He seemed like a pleasant, good-humoured lad," remarked the Colonel. "Surprising, that — hey? For his aunt, Mrs Churchill, has the reputation of being the most froward, ill-tempered woman, and her husband the most downtrodden and hen-pecked; is not that so, Cecelia?"

"Yes, perfectly true," said his wife. "I have sat with Mrs Churchill on several committees, and a more difficult, assertive person I have seldom encountered; one quite despairs of getting any motion passed if it is opposed by her, for she simply repeats her own opinion over and over, without listening to a word uttered by anybody else. But I am glad to hear that the boy is so sweet-natured; no doubt he takes after his father. I hope he will make a pleasant playmate for our girls."

Miss Winstable looked as if she would have liked to oppose any scheme involving the entry of youthful males into her schoolroom sphere; but Jane explained that most of Frank Churchill's time was spent at school in Yorkshire.

"Perhaps then we may see him at Easter. And now, how about a little music — hey?"

Jane had earnestly impressed upon Signor Negretti the value and importance there would be in Rachel's being able, within the least possible time, to demonstrate her rapid attainment of musical proficiency.

"For if he sees she can do one thing well, that will encourage him to believe that she may do others. And that will greatly encourage *her*."

To this end, a piece of music for four hands by Dussek had been selected by the Signor which, while demanding a bravura performance from the player of the first part, left the second player little to supply but a few chords and single notes. As it was a lively, cheerful écossaise, the girls had practised it with great diligence and no little amusement, making as much noise as they could, until Miss Winstable, at her carpet-work in the drawing-room, urged them to hush! or they would disturb dear Mrs Campbell, so busy reading parliamentary reports.

So, when the Colonel called for music, Jane suggested, "Shall we play him our duet, Rachel?"

Mutely, Rachel nodded, the screen was removed, and the two young ladies took their places. The well-rehearsed piece was played with tremendous panache, indeed both the girls were in fits of laughter as they brought it to its rattling conclusion.

"You stole my note, Rachel, you wretch!"

"N-no, I d-didn't — you stole *mine!*"

Even Mrs Campbell raised her head from her minutes long enough to call out "Bravo!"

To Jane's dismay the Colonel left his seat and came into the conservatory to stand by them.

"Well, that was a very spirited performance, indeed!" he said, appearing to note with surprise his daughter's pink cheeks and laughing look. At his approach, however, all laughter left her; she became pale, gulped, and looked down at her hands.

"Now let me hear you play something on your own, Rachel," said the Colonel.

"Oh, n-no, p-pray, P-Papa, I c-couldn't!" she faltered.

"Hey-day? What sort of foolishness is this? If you can play with Jane so nimbly, you can surely play by yourself. And your mother and I naturally wish to hear you. We wish to know how your capacities are progressing. No nonsense, now, if you please! Play something — anything — no matter how simple."

"Oh, p-pray, *pray* P-Papa — d-do not make me — "

"Are you a girl or a worm?" thundered the Colonel furiously, thumping on the lid of the piano so that it boomed, and all the sheets of music flew about. "Enough of this ridiculous missishness. I demand to hear you play!"

"Oh, come, James — if the child can't, just now, perform by herself, then she cannot — " called Mrs Campbell, too late, from the other room, for Rachel, in a burst of tears, with blood pouring from her nose, fled from the conservatory, leaving Jane staring stormily at the Colonel.

Twice she opened her mouth to speak, twice she closed it again.

"Ridiculous affectation! Can't play, indeed? *Won't*, is more like it. What — are we to expend good money on music lessons for a little squeaking milksop who is too delicate ever to be heard in execution? A fine thing for my daughter, upon my word!"

Fuming, he turned on his heel, strode through the double drawing-room, and down the stairs. A moment later they heard the front door slam behind him.

Jane could only be thankful that Miss Winstable, pleading indigestion (to which indisposition she was a martyr) had retired early to bed. Very devoutly Jane hoped that she would never come to hear of this scene, for in any dissension between the Colonel and his daughter, the governess could be relied on to come down heavily on the parental side, and descant at immense length on the importance, the absolute necessity, of sparing no pains, stretching every faculty to its utmost, in order to please parents, those givers of life and arbiters of destiny. "Not to play when your Papa wished it! Fie, for shame, miss! Lady Selsea's daughters would have played for days together — for *weeks* together indeed. It is too bad — disgraceful — the outside of enough!"

Chapter 4

The process of encouraging Rachel not to be afraid of her father, of persuading Colonel Campbell not to terrify his daughter advanced, it seemed to Jane, by infinitesimally slow degrees. True, with Jane's co-operation and assistance Rachel, who had a very pretty alto voice, had learned the second part of a duet which Signor Negretti had himself arranged from a French ballad, a chanson Béarnaise and, this accomplished, they went on to an Italian song, "Arietta Veneziano". Singing in French or Italian, Rachel was able to forget her speech difficulty and warble away with fair confidence. It had been Jane's hopeful scheme that, on his birthday, which fell late in March, the two girls should entertain the Colonel to a little concert.

But, alas for such schemes! Just before the birthday, by unhappy mischance, Miss Winstable came across, and angrily drew to the Colonel's notice, an exercise book belonging to Rachel which, instead of having its pages dutifully covered with French irregular verbs, was filled with drawings of people: "Not even portraits so much as *caricatures!*" gasped the outraged governess. Unfortunately most of them were all too recognizable: Miss Winstable herself, swathed in veils and gauzy shawls, hovering irresolutely outside a closed door as if uncertain whether to enter or to listen at the keyhole; one of Mrs Campbell, so deeply buried among pamphlets and piles of minutes that only a wisp of brown hair and the tip of a long nose, perfectly familiar, were to be seen; one of the Colonel's valet, Tonkin, tiptoeing up the stairs with an armful of starched white cravats and a comically apprehensive expression on his face; one of the redoubtable Mrs Churchill, laying about her with an umbrella; and, worst of all, one of the Colonel, his brow as black as Rachel's pencil could portray it, his lower lip out-thrust, and his daughter before him on her knees, quivering with such terror that she was reduced to the shape of a dish of lemon jelly which stood beside her.

The Colonel summoned his daughter, raged at her, roared at her, and at last dismissed her in such a state that she had to be put to bed for three days.

Then Jane was sent for in her turn, and the tongue-lashing she received was hardly less in degree than poor Rachel's: ranged over the various heads of Subversion — Disrespect — Encouragement of Rachel in these faults — and, in general, of inciting Rachel to disobey her governess and make fun of authority.

"That book was meant for French verbs, not for impertinent drawings!" he thundered.

Jane, unlike Rachel, stood up for herself, though terrified.

"Sir! You are unjust! Firstly, Rachel *knows* all the French irregular verbs — she speaks French perfectly well — quite as well as a French person, I believe, and a great deal better than Miss Winstable."

Jane herself spoke French with tolerable fluency, for it was Signor Negretti's second language and they had conversed in it for the past two years; she was therefore well aware of the governess's shortcomings in this area.

"Nonetheless the book was allotted for a specific educational purpose, not for vulgar scribbles. Young people must learn to be systematic and obedient, whether they understand the reasons for their activities or not."

Jane took a deep breath and said, "*Still* I think you are unjust, sir. When — when you brought me here, both you and Mrs Campbell told me that one of the reasons for my coming was because you wished me to — to help Rachel become more — more confident and less timid. How can she ever learn these things if — if she is to be scolded and put down when she does a thing that she can do well — such as her drawing? And how can she ever learn to be sure of herself — if, if she is reminded all the time only of her faults, of her difficulties?"

Throughout this long speech her heart beat very fast in her breast, but she stood her ground, trembling and gazing resolutely at the Colonel, trying not to think what her relatives would say if she were to be sent back to Highbury in disgrace.

There was a moment's silence. Then — "I am not angry with you, Jane," said the Colonel presently, in a more moderate tone (though she thought that he was, still, judging by the spark in his eye and the curl of his lip). "But I wish you, child as you are, to stop a moment and consider the difference between Rachel's position and your own. There is a difference, though we try to make as little of it as may be. Rachel, when she is grown, will have twelve thousand pounds of her own. Which is well for her, poor girl, for she will never have even passable looks with which to entice a suitor. And even her twelve thousand won't see her far in the matrimonial stakes, unless, as well, she learns the feminine art of attracting by her ways, her manners, her amiability, and her accomplishments. For you, my child, it is different; being, most regrettably, un-dowered, you must, perforce, take up a profession, and your friends have chosen for you the useful, and not too disagreeable or arduous one of teaching — for which, being naturally clever, you are well-suited. You may — I don't doubt you will — go far, supposing that a suitably well-connected position may be found for you. (Rachel's grandmother was at school with the Duchess of Rich-mond; and Mrs Churchill is a friend of Lady Castlereagh, so we may have good hopes; these things must be thought of and planned for, well in advance.) Your future, though hard-working, is therefore assured; you will be independent and self-supporting. But, for Rachel, if she is to take any sort of place in the world, it is otherwise; she must marry; she must learn to please a man; and she will certainly not do that by stammering, fumbling, and going red when she is spoken to, or by making silly and vulgar drawings in her French copy book."

"Sir," said Jane stoutly, "Rachel draws very *well!* Professor Kramer said so. He awarded her a gold star at our last lesson. He had never given a gold star to any of his pupils before. He said so."

"I rejoice to hear it," the Colonel replied drily. "Then let Rachel apply herself to landscapes and water-colours and — and subjects appropriate to females. There — that will do, Jane; run along. And pray let me not hear Miss Winstable complain of you again."

"And certainly not impertinent caricatures," she heard him mutter to himself as she left the room.

Shortly after this interview Jane was told that she would be permitted to return to Highbury for a visit.

She had, for some time, been making gentle but persistent demands: "Pray, sir, pray, Mrs Campbell, pray allow me to go home now; Grandmamma and Aunt Hetty must need me, I am very sure they do; they have not said so in their letters, but I cannot imagine how they can go on for so long without me to perform a hundred little tasks that need doing for them — " But on each occasion some reason against her visiting Highbury had always been found by the Colonel or Mrs Campbell. "The winter was a bad time to travel; Jane would be better in London, in a large, warm, well-aired house than in the damp, foggy country, sadly subject as she was to colds and rheumy affections of the chest and throat," "Maria Dickons was to take the part of the Countess in *The Marriage of Figaro;* it would be a shocking pity to miss such an important performance and Rachel would be sorry to hear it without her friend," "there was a concert at the Pantheon of songs by Purcell which Signor Negretti had particularly recommended," "Colonel Campbell's friends the Dixons, from Ireland, would be in London after Easter, and Rachel was always so much more at ease in company if she had Jane to support her."

All these excuses had sufficed to keep Jane in town through January, February, and March; but now April was come, and Jane became even more urgent to return to her native place. She thought of the daffodils, the green haze of honeysuckle buds over the hedges, the brooks running high with rainwater; although she had developed a true attachment to Rachel, felt towards her, indeed, as she might to a dear sister, yet she longed for home. No 12, Manchester Square certainly was not yet considered as home, though, as the Colonel had foretold, she was beginning to put down roots.

In point of fact the long-deferred permission to revisit Highbury was intended, when it came, she strongly suspected, not in the least as a piece of indulgence but more as a lesson, a remedial exercise to remind her, by a taste of the adversities and inconveniences she had left behind, that she had a great deal to lose by failure to please her benefactors; that her presence in Manchester Square was still on sufferance, dependent on conformity and submission, revokable at any time.

"But they cannot possibly guess," she thought, "how very much I long to be back in Surry, or they would never suppose sending me there to be a form of discipline." Indeed she was so overjoyed at the permission when it came, thanking the Colonel and Mrs Campbell over and over again with unfeigned delight, that she received confirmation of her suspicions by overhearing the Colonel (who was often unaware of the loudness of his own voice) remark to his wife, "I wonder if we do right in arranging this visit? Jane plainly regards it as a treat." "And why should she not?" calmly returned Mrs Campbell. "I am convinced that she is a sensible, deserving child. She loves her relations as she ought. And she has certainly worked hard at her lessons. Rachel is devoted to her and will miss her sadly; I believe Jane will miss Rachel also." "Humph. That may be no bad thing," muttered the Colonel. "I daresay, at all events, that she will soon have had enough of being cooped up at Highbury."

Indignant at this, and wishing to advertise her presence in the conservatory (where she was sorting music) Jane thumped down the piano lid, which caused a startled silence in the next chamber, followed by the sound of hasty retreating footsteps.

On this occasion, perhaps because she was slightly in disgrace, Jane was not escorted into Surry by the Colonel, but merely sent in charge of a servant, one of the maids, who chanced to have parents at Bookham and was not at all averse at being given the opportunity to visit them.

Jane and Rachel had exchanged many farewell promises.

"I shall write to you every single d-day," vowed Rachel, wiping away tears, "And d-do you do the s-same! Then I shall give S-Signor Negretti s-seven letters to carry to you. C-Come back soon; p-pray pray, d-do not stay t-too long."

Jane had asked if it would not be possible for Rachel to come and pay a visit to Highbury. "I would so love to show her all my favourite places, and for her to meet Grandmamma and Aunt Hetty."

Mrs Campbell seemed inclined to listen favourably to these suggestions. The fresh country air would certainly be good for Rachel; she had always been well and happy when they were scampering about on foreign mountainsides. But the Colonel pointed out to her, privately, that this indulgence would undermine all his disciplinary intentions. "Let the pair of them be parted for a while. Then they will learn the results of disrespect and selfwill."

It was, therefore, arranged that Jane should remain with her Highbury friends for a month. Then, perhaps, depending on a number of contingencies unnamed but understood pretty well by all parties, Rachel might be permitted to accompany her father when he came to fetch Jane.

"Oh, I do hope so much that you may! For then you can meet all the people that I love; and perhaps there might be time to go to Donwell Abbey and see Mr Knightley . . . "

The promised interchange of letters commenced at once; Jane kept a copious daily memoir of her simple life at Highbury; and Signor Negretti, on his visits to Hartfield, was able to hand over a fat bundle of correspondence from Rachel, who wrote a remarkably adult hand, with very few crossings-out or spelling errors, embellishing her epistles with tiny skilful sketches; and was able to tell her best, her dearest, most cherished Jane that the Dixons had arrived from Ireland (where Colonel Campbell had originally met them while on military duty in that country); that the parents, Major and Mrs Dixon, were lively, friendly, and well-bred, whereas the two boys, Matt and Sam, were a shocking pair of hobble-de-hoys, from having been permitted to run wild and consort with ragged Irish peasant boys, their language at times was almost incomprehensible; but still they were very friendly and good natured and could at times, she must admit, be extremely entertaining. Colonel Campbell was wholly scandalized at their uncouth manners, and the advantage of this was that Rachel's own defects, for once, paled into insignificance and were often overlooked. "But just the same I miss you every hour, every minute! Come back very soon, my dear, dearest Jennie. And, meanwhile, give me all the intelligence of Highbury: Sig. Negretti informs me that you have returned to lessons and practise at Hartfield. How is the horrid Emma? Is she still as horrid as ever? I almost hope so, for if you were to become great friends, I should be so jealous! And how is kind, handsome Mr Knightley? Is he still as kind and heroic as ever ? Does he take you riding? — The Churchills are back in town and Mrs Churchill brought Frank a-calling. She and my Papa fell out about the slave-trade and she gave him a great set-down. Frank C is grown handsome and by his air and manner makes the Dixon boys seem like wild savages. Here are drawings of them all three: Matt is the one with the wild shaggy black hair. Papa tells Matt and Sam that they should take Frank C for an example, which makes them die of laughing for they think he is a coxcomb. — Your deeply attached, loving faithful friend Rachel Campbell."

Jane wrote back, via the Signor: "Darling Rachel, your letters are a joy. I laugh and cry over them and can see Manchester Square, your house, and all the people in it as I read every line. I miss you so very much! But I am glad that you have so much company to amuse you, and that the terrible Dixon boys divert your Papa's severities from you. — About your Papa, my grandmother, who is the wisest person I know, said a curious thing. I had been telling her about your troubles (I know you will not mind my having done so, for I love you both so very dearly) and she said, 'Rachel ought to ask the Holy Ghost to help her.' I said, 'Why the Holy Ghost, Grandmamma?' She said, 'Frederick (that was my grandpa, you know, who used to be vicar of Highbury) Frederick always used to say that when a person was in trouble or embarrassment, or sudden danger, the Holy Ghost was the most convenient Authority to apply to for help.' 'Why so, Grannie?' 'Well, you see, my child, God the Father and Jesus are so very much occupied with all the great, terrible troubles of the world. They may be too busy to come at once. But the Holy Ghost is like a Curate, always ready to attend to the needs of small people.' She assured me that the Holy Ghost had very often helped her. 'Tell your friend Rachel this, and she will soon find that I am right.' So here I am telling you, and hope from the bottom of my heart that her advice will be useful.

"Yes, I have seen the horrid Emma! She is not near so plump as she used to be, and has grown quite handsome. But I felt equal to her just the same because, for the first time in our lives, I was able to face her wearing nice new clothes of my own (for which I am abundantly, eternally grateful to dear Mrs Campbell) instead of being rigged out in used clothes of Emma's. 'Well, and so, how are you, Jane?' says she, looking me up and down. 'Do you enjoy life in town?' 'Oh yes, pretty well,' said I, and told her such tales of going to Concerts, Astley's, seeing the King and Queen driving in the park, and Lord Elgin's carvings, that she was quite silenced for a moment. Then she said that she had rather have seen the Rosetta Stone and the royal princesses, and was it true that fashionable persons now always wore a green eye-shade? I felt — believe it or not — almost sorry for her; there she is, confined to Hartfield and its grounds (for even with Miss Taylor she seldom ventures outside) while I am now acquainted with so many more people than she is, and have witnessed so many more agreeable and varied scenes. Imagine it! she has never even been as far as Kingston, for Mr Woodhouse is now such a sad Invalid.

"Yes, I have seen dear, dear Mr Knightley! He took me for a ride (not on Ginger who, to my grief, has been sold, but on his little mare Doucette, who is a treasure). We rode over Highbury Common and had a glorious gallop — it has been the greatest joy of my visit so far, apart from the continual happiness of being with Grannie and Aunt Hetty.

"Mr Knightley told me that his brother John has at last proposed for the hand of Isabella Woodhouse — which everybody knew that he would do, sooner or later. This has thrown poor old Mr Woodhouse into a sad turmoil; he cannot bear the idea of Isabella leaving Hartfield and going to reside in London, where Mr John now practises Law. It will take years, Mr George Knightley believes, before Mr Woodhouse can be brought to consent. — Emma had not mentioned this to me, but Aunt Hetty spoke of it also. I daresay it makes Emma, too, very unhappy, for Isa has always been a kind elder sister to her.

"Do the Dixons still remain with you? I am very curious to see them, I must confess! And does Frank Churchill stay in town with his aunt and uncle? His father's new house is being built and goes on slowly; Mr Weston has called here several times and kindly offers to bring me back to London; but that must depend upon your Parents' consent. We have walked out once or twice on fine days to see the house, which is to be called Randalls, for it is built on land belonging to Farmer Randall; Mr Weston is busy laying out pleasure-grounds and planting fir, mountain ash, acacia, and Lombardy poplars to screen the offices. But it will never be the equal of Donwell Abbey, where Mr Knightley lives. — This comes with my strong and enduring affection, dearest Rachel . . . "

When Jane stated that the ride with Mr Knightley had been her happiest time at Highbury so far, she spoke no more than the truth. Mr Knightley had always appeared to her the best, handsomest, most intelligent, kindly and upright adult of her acquaintance (apart of course from dear Grannie and Aunt Hetty) and now, in comparison with the irascible, erratic Colonel Campbell, he appeared even more an example of kindness, good judgment, and probity. To be sure, Colonel Campbell meant very well, had excellent intentions, but he often proved so fallible, whereas Mr Knightley had never been known to deviate from the path of sovereign intelligence and benignity. Happy would be she whom he invited to preside over his establishment at Donwell Abbey. — That is, supposing he ever took such a step; Aunt Hetty held the opinion that he would never marry, for who in the world was good enough for him?

One aspect of her present sojourn at Highbury troubled Jane deeply. This was that, contrary to expectation, and distressingly fulfilling Colonel Campbell's prediction, she did not, in fact, find herself so unfailingly happy as she had expected to be. The village was just as delightful, familiar, and welcoming, as anticipated; every tree, leaf, window, chimneypot, thatched roof, every smiling neighbour, every clump of daffodils had the expected charm. And Grannie and Aunt Hetty were overflowing with love and expressive joy at the return of their nurseling. Also, thank heaven, they seemed well; the winter without Jane had not adversely affected their health; neighbours had been unremittingly kind; they had never lacked for company or help when they had required it. But, Jane was obliged to admit to herself after a few days, she now found existence in Highbury more than a little monotonous, more than a little confining; she could go out from the house and walk about the village, of course, but that meant unkindly deserting the two who set such store by her company; and then, the three rooms were so very dark and tiny, airless and crammed with furniture; it was queer that she had never noticed this before. And there were no books. And Aunt Hetty did talk such a great deal! Detesting herself, tortured by unhappy feelings of guilt, Jane could not help a decided hankering for the large sparsely furnished rooms (for Mrs Campbell, as soon as there was a barely adequate supply of chairs, tables, and beds, had quite lost interest in improving her establishment, and immersed herself in philanthropy) at Manchester Square. Jane longed for the large, airy schoolroom, for Rachel's clever, sympathetic company, for all their books and occupations, for Mrs Campbell's occasional shrewd, pithy observations, even for Colonel Campbell who, when in affable mood, could be both entertaining and instructive about such issues as the Peace of Amiens, what Buonaparte might do next, and the relations between the King and the Prince of Wales. — Whereas conversation at home seldom related to anything farther afield than the story that some pigs had escaped from the Abbey Farm and done great damage to Mr Perry's cabbage beds, or the rumour that Mr Pryor, finding the work of the parish grow too much for him, was to provide himself with a curate.

Jane could not help, from time to time, recalling Emma's words: "You live in those three dark rooms where there is hardly space to walk about — and your grandmother is so very old — and your aunt talks all the time — how can you bear it?"

She loved Highbury deeply, and always would, but she knew now, with anguish, that it could not supply with her with all she needed. — Ungratefully, she sometimes wished that the Campbells had never taken her away to teach her this lesson.

Nor could she avoid sometimes recalling the conversation with Colonel Campbell in which he had outlined the different futures lying ahead for her and Rachel.

"Your friends have chosen for you the useful and not disagreeable profession of teaching . . . But, for Rachel, it is otherwise; she must learn to please a man."

Why, thought Jane, because we have the ill-luck to be born girls, why are these the only two choices open to us? Boys can elect for the army, the navy, the church, the law, or medicine, or politics; they can write histories, or become painters or musicians; but girls, it seems, can only be mothers of families, or teach; those are the only futures allowed to them. Or they remain spinsters, like Aunt Hetty; and what in the world will become of Aunt Hetty when Grandmamma dies? Her future does not bear thinking about. I only hope that by that time I shall have become governess to some grand family, so that I can let her have a portion of my earnings. Jane shivered a little at the prospect. She thought of Miss Taylor with the Woodhouse family, Miss Winstable with the Campbells. Miss Taylor was used well, treated in every way as one of the family; but there was no blinking the fact that the Campbells regarded Miss Winstable as being of small account, hardly rated on a level with the family or their friends. "And that is only fair," thought Jane, "for she is a stupid woman; her only skills are embroidery and the ability to make filigree baskets; and besides that she is malicious and a tale-bearer. But then, what chance has she ever been given to learn anything more? She has spent her entire existence in charge of other people's children, probably spoiled, peevish, indulged children. Is she what *I* shall have become in thirty years' time?"

The thought was enough to cast her into deep depression.

"But then, on the other hand, will Rachel's lot be any better? She must learn to please a man. But what sort of man? A clever, well-informed kind person like Mr Knightley? Or a touchy, un-reasonable, uneven-tempered man like Colonel Campbell? And how can poor Rachel ever hope to please any man when she begins to stammer, or breaks into a nosebleed, at the very thought of talking to one of them?"

Chapter 5

"There has, here, been a most unexpected Occurrence, my dearest Jenny," wrote Rachel after Jane had been at Highbury for a couple of weeks. "My Grandmamma Fitzroy has come to live with us. Neither Papa nor Mamma were aware that she had any such intention; so far as we all knew she was comfortably established in Bath. But it seems that she has had reverses in her investments (or something that I do not fully comprehend). At all events she arrived three days ago with all her trunks and bandboxes and some furniture and a shrieking parrot in a cage and her French maid Fleury, and the two of them have already contrived to throw the whole household into disorder. The Dixons were obliged to cut short their visit, for which I am sorry, as I had come to deal very comfortably with Matt and Sam; their queer English, which made me laugh, had begun to improve, and we were practising a number of Irish ballads, for both have good voices and are very fond of music. But, even if there had been sufficient room in the house, they would not have wished to remain here with Grandma Fitzroy. They have removed to friends in Chester and will then return to Ireland, much to my disappointment. I so much wanted you to meet them.

"Also I am afraid that you will find this house not near so comfortable when you return. You will soon see why! But I am ever and always your devoted Friend. I hope you will come back soon. I embrace you . . . "

And indeed, not long after, the Campbells accepted a friendly offer from Mr Weston, who had driven his carriage down to Highbury with a load of furnishings for the new house, and was now about to return to London with plenty of empty space.

"I can just as well take you as not," he told Jane comfortably. "Colonel Campbell perfectly approves, and we can have a fine chat all the way up to town."

Which they did, Mr Weston being a cheerful, garrulous man,

very ready to discuss the engagement of Isabella Woodhouse to John Knightley — "Mr Woodhouse has said they must wait at least four years before the wedding takes place. But Miss Taylor, a charming woman of great sagacity and discernment, thinks they may whittle it down to three; after all, poor John Knightley is nearly twenty-seven; he will be one-and-thirty before he is married. A man should marry young, in my opinion." They talked about the new young lady pupil at Mrs Goddard's school: "She is a very pretty little thing; nobody knows who her family may be; the Cox girls think it the most romantic business, and that she must be a princess incognita." And, of course, they talked about his son Frank, a subject upon which Mr Weston was at all times happy to descant at boundless length: "Such a fine, handsome, cheerful boy, and not in the least spoiled, though the treatment he receives from that Churchill woman would, you would think, be enough to turn the head of any boy. Sometimes they are so amazingly liberal, allow him the least thing he asks for; and then, at other times, Mrs Churchill is downright tyrannical, and will not permit him even to see his friend Thomas Braithwaite or leave the house for so much as half an hour. Her temper is shockingly unreliable."

"So I have heard Mrs Campbell say," agreed Jane. "It must be very difficult living with such an unreasonable person."

"Ay, but it is true that Mrs Churchill suffers from wretched health and is often in quite severe pain; some of her variations of temper must be put down to that."

And the same, Jane supposed, might be said of Colonel Campbell, who experienced frequent pain from his head-wound, and his lame leg, besides the exasperation of his deafness; she wondered how he was managing to put up with his mother-in-law.

Mrs Fitzroy had been a Despenser, as she lost no time in informing any new acquaintance considered worthy of the honour; one of her ancestors had been the last Justiciary of England and another had been Earl of Winchester, executed in 1322 by Queen Isabella. "No doubt she had her reasons," Colonel Campbell was in the habit of darkly muttering to himself when he chanced to overhear one of his mother-in-law's not infrequent repetitions of this piece of history. Marriage to General Fitzroy had been a decided come-down in the social scale for Amelia Despenser, but sweetened by his five thousand a year, for the Despensers had by that time ceased to count wealth among their assets. Some fairly severe mismanagement of his funds while the General still lived had, however, reduced their income, and, after his death, which had occurred five years previously, his widow had, by her foolishly improvident and extravagant habits, so seriously diminished the remainder of her capital as to be obliged to throw herself on the good-nature of her son-in-law. Colonel Campbell, a man of rectitude and high principles, did not attempt to evade his duty by his wife's mother; "but," as he said to Cecelia, "I doubt if we shall have a single comfortable day in the house ever again. Our chance of a peaceful family life is quite cut up." "Oh, I daresay we shall all rub along tolerably once Mamma has settled down," Mrs Campbell replied calmly. "You will simply have to spend longer periods at your club." Mrs Campbell herself, who made no hypocritical pretence of the least attachment to her mother, contrived to pass even more of her own time in charitable meetings with her various committees. Consequently the brunt of Mrs Fitzroy's presence in the household as a fellow-inmate was felt by the children.

Miss Winstable, of course, was an old ally of the lady, having been hired in the first place, long ago, as governess to Mrs Fitzroy's own two daughters. She, naturally, was overjoyed at the arrival of her old employer in Manchester Square, and continually held her up to the girls as a pattern of all that was elegant and ladylike.

"Such a manner! Such an air! Such dignity! Blood will tell! Why, the queen herself, girls, could not come near it."

Mrs Fitzroy was, in fact, remarkably elegant — "So she ought to be, considering the cost of her wardrobe," sourly observed Colonel Campbell. Indeed, before Paris had been cut off by the Terror, Mrs Fitzroy had always paid regular annual trips to the capital of fashion, and never bought so much as a chemise anywhere else; after the regrettable events culminating in the death of the French king and queen she was obliged to intermit her visits, but still contrived to maintain a correspondence with persons in the front line of the mode, and so to receive drawings, patterns, snippets, and samples, long in advance of the general British public. She knew about shades such as *terre d'Egypte, nègre,* and *gris-antique* long before any of her acquaintance, and had participated in the shocking fashion of wearing a red velvet ribbon round the neck, symbolical of la Guillotine, to the outraged disgust of her daughter Cecelia who, fortunately, was out of England at the time, only informed of her mother's conduct by the letters of scandalized friends.

In appearance, Mrs Fitzroy resembled her daughter and grand-daughter: she was thin to emaciation with a long nose, thin-lipped mouth, pale stone-coloured eyes set close together, and an exquisite pink-and-white complexion, most carefully tended with Gowland's Lotion and a whole pharmacopoeia of other preparations. Her pale straw-coloured hair, tending to white, was much frizzed, and piled up in classic Grecian mode. Her clothes were the admiration of all the females in the household, excepting her own daughter.

"It is singular that Mamma should be so v-very different in her t-tastes from Grandmamma," observed Rachel to Jane. "If they were not so s-similar in feature, you would never b-believe they were related to one another."

Jane did not think it singular; she could quite comprehend how any daughter of Mrs Fitzroy might wish to be as different from her as possible — particularly a person of such intelligence and good sense as Mrs Campbell.

Mrs Fitzroy, for her part, never let slip an opportunity for gentle denigration of poor Cecelia's taste. "I am afraid — my daughter's clothes — *well!* I believe she must have picked up her notion of fashion from some Corsican fisher-woman. Perhaps it is not too late to hope that I can instil *some* notion of propriety and good taste into my unfortunate granddaughter. But, how all circumstances combine against me ... Her father — so uncouth, so abrupt! And this house — the furniture; indeed the building can hardly be said to be furnished at all. One might as well reside in a barn ... "

Mrs Fitzroy had, fortunately, brought a quantity of her own possessions with her, to improve the comfort of her apartments, making them, the Colonel said, more like some cursed Eastern bazaar than a habitation for humans. But unless obliged to do so, he hardly ever set foot within those doors.

Mrs Fitzroy's bedroom was a source of considerable grievance.

She had, naturally, stipulated for a chamber with an adjoining room for her maid Fleury. The only practical solution to this request, in the view of Colonel Campbell, was to transfer the two children, who had adjacent rooms, to the rear of the house, and instal Mrs Fitzroy in the room previously occupied by Rachel; that of Jane, smaller, next door, was allocated to Fleury the maid.

But Mrs Fitzroy found this accommodation shockingly inferior and did not hesitate to say so.

"In front of the house, where I must hear all the noise of the street! No sun! Dark and cold! And why, pray, should I have a room smaller than the one assigned to that upstart Fairfax child? Why should not I be at the back?"

"My dear madam, you yourself insisted on having your maid next door. You also have a sizeable powdering-closet. Why should your maid sleep in one of the biggest and best chambers in the house?"

The dispute was never resolved, and never would be. It sputtered on for weeks, months, finally years, exploding into open hostilities when relations were especially strained, conducted at other periods as a form of guerilla warfare, in sudden ambuscades, unexpected volleys of fire, or subterranean tunnellings. And it was the original cause, though there were, of course, many others, for Mrs Fitzroy's fixed dislike of Jane.

"So very *odd* to bring in a child from outside — such an atrocious mistake! — unknown origins, probably no better than they should be — Fairfax all very well, but Bates — what sort of a name was *Bates?* — child just what might be expected from such a mongrel background — encouraging Rachel to insubordination and all manner of foolish nonsense — music? of what importance, pray, was music? So long as a gal could accompany herself in a ballad or two — all that study far from desirable — Rachel's arms deplorably thin, no benefit to be derived from displaying them in performance — the last thing she needed was to acquire a reputation as a bookish bluestocking — a totally different case from that other wretched girl who must of course earn her living — "

Mrs Fitzroy saw no necessity for Jane's continued residence with the Campbell family after her own arrival, and lost no opportunity for making this opinion audible. On the whole, this militated in Jane's favour: Colonel Campbell so disliked his mother-in-law that her invincible, unceasing hostility towards Jane must necessarily restore and raise the latter in his favour. Former faults and imperfections, errors of encouraging Rachel's insubordinate activities were overlooked or forgotten; the household drew together against the common foe. In fact, the Colonel was obliged to admit to his wife, "it was a lucky thing Rachel had her dear crony there so they could console one another when the old Termagant had been more than commonly devilish."

Here he maligned Mrs Fitzroy who could never, at any time,

have been described as a termagant. Acid sweetness was her forte, trickled on to a victim drop by venomous drop.

"My *dear* child! Turn around. Your petticoat! Your tucker! *Whence* had you that handkerchief? It is a disgrace. And your hair is out of curl. Do, I beg, stand up straighter — feet together when I am addressing you. Now let me hear you recite a hymn. Grace and manner are of the very first importance — pray make an attempt to look a trifle more like a young lady of breeding, and less like some dreadful little orphanage creature."

All these sentences delivered in a high, incisive carrying tone; unfortunately for Colonel Campbell, his deafness availed him not at all in this particular context, for Mrs Fitzroy's voice was of the shrill, resonant kind that, as he complained "went through your head like a perditioned tuning-fork." He could easily hear her, *and* her cursed fowl, three rooms away.

The parrot, more properly a macaw, an evil-dispositioned bird, loved by none but its mistress, was kept, during the daytime, in the conservatory, an arrangement which soon led to more hostilities.

To begin with, Mrs Fitzroy thought it very remiss, not to say odd, of her daughter, to use the conservatory merely as a music room.

"The place is as bleak as a tennis-court! The one room in the house that might, with very little pains, have been made to support the aspect of a gentleman's residence. Why, pray, *have* a conservatory if you do not propose to furnish it with blooms?"

"It c-came with the house; it was th-there," pointed out Rachel, her mother having, as usual, quitted the field with a vague and inattentive murmur relating to business elsewhere.

Another and bitter grievance arose from the treatment of the macaw, who, suffering from surplus energy, since he was obliged to remain covered up in his mistress's room all night, tended to shriek all day, most especially when the girls were practising on the piano. His volleys of clamorous squawks obliged them to drape a shawl over his cage to silence him while piano lessons or practice were in progress.

Mrs Fitzroy was outraged when she discovered this.

"My poor Mistic! Treated like a coal miner!"

Nor did she see the necessity for locating the piano in the conservatory. It would be far better situated in one of the saloons.

Mrs Fitzroy's greatest, and most bitter grievance against Jane was one which must necessarily remain unvoiced. This was the superiority of Jane's looks over those of her own granddaughter. Rachel, because of her long nose, patchy complexion, and close-set pale eyes, could never boast any pretension to beauty or even prettiness, despite the most careful attention to hair-dressing, countenance, and dress, although her eager, intelligent expression must always attract friendship and interest from those well-disposed or acute enough to remark it. — Whereas Jane was beginning to grow apace, doubtless because of the more healthful and spacious environment and more liberal regime and diet afforded her by the Campbells; her height seemed to increase weekly, her hair lost its lankness and became glossy, thick, and dark; her eyes were large, grey, and lustrous; her complexion, though it would always remain pale, was clear and fine; she was, above all, endowed with that quality of innate elegance which Mrs Fitzroy laboured so unremittingly to instil into her own grandchild. And, from observation of Mrs Fitzroy (who, with all her faults, must be acknowledged a model of good taste) Jane could not but help acquire greater grace, greater elegance.

"Your grandmamma has such a way of wearing her clothes," Jane observed to Rachel. "Disagreeable though she is, one cannot help admiring her. Even a simple twist of gauze is given a clever, fashionable air by the way she adjusts it."

"B-but all to what p-purpose?" objected Rachel, who was imbued already with many of her mother's republican and utilitarian sentiments.

"It is simply an art in itself — like your drawing."

Rachel drew as naturally as a bird sings; and, from long practice, had acquired a startling ability to catch a likeness.

"Yes; but my art is *for* something; I should like to become a political cartoonist — like Gillray or Rowlandson."

"For mercy's sake, never let your grandmother hear that! She would forbid you ever to take a pencil in your hand again."

Rachel sighed, leafing nostalgically through the pages of a portfolio filled with portraits.

"Which is Sam, and which is Matt?"

"That one is Matt — with the longer hair. Here is Sam, playing the flute; that is Matt again . . . I am so s-sorry you d-did not meet them. They were mighty curious to m-meet you, after all that I had t-told them about you. I wish they might ever come back! But how can they, now Granny Fitzroy is here? — There is Frank Churchill — the one holding the book."

Frank Churchill, also, had left London to return to his school in Yorkshire, and was not expected to reappear until midsummer, at which time the Churchills sometimes hired a house in Richmond or Twickenham.

"B-but by then, I think," said Rachel, "we s-shall not be here. P-Papa said s-something about going to the s-seaside."

"The seaside!" Jane had never been to the sea.

Rachel chuckled. "I th-think he hopes to leave G-Grandmamma behind."

Before the family removal to the seaside, however, occurred what Jane would ever after think of as the bracelet affair.

It began when Mrs Fitzroy, animadverting disparagingly on Rachel's untended apparel and appearance, advised that her grand-daughter should have a maid of her own to look after her.

"Soon she will be ten, Cecelia! It is high time she took more care of her toilet."

"Do you really think so, Mamma? I should hardly have considered it necessary. However, if you insist . . . "

Mrs Fitzroy did insist. Where money was to be spent by some other individual, her ideas were still on a lavish scale. And, to the amusement of Jane and Rachel, a tiny personal maid was forthwith engaged, by name Sukey, aged thirteen, whose duties consisted solely of ministering to the two young ladies, tending their hair, stockings, and nails, making certain that they did not walk abroad with petticoat frills unhemmed, cutting their curl-papers, mending their laces, cleaning their gloves, collecting lemon peel to soften their fingertips, and preparing clove-oranges to sweeten their linen-drawers. Sukey and her two young mistresses were soon on the very best of terms, she told them about her large impoverished family in Spitalfields, and they enlisted her as an ally in many of their activities.

Unfortunately, however, not many months after Sukey's instal-lation in the household, many small articles began to disappear: fans, beads, feather ornaments, pins, scissors, girdles, silk stockings, and, last and most valuable, a pearl and opal bracelet belonging to Mrs Fitzroy.

Mrs Fitzroy set great store by her jewellery. From her diamonds, lodged in the bank, down to the humblest pin, they were continually enumerated, thought about, cleaned, re-set and exulted over; when this loss was discovered, she raised a great outcry.

"General Fitzroy had given it to her upon their betrothal; it had the very deepest sentimental value to her — besides its intrinsic one, which was not inconsiderable; she did not wish to cast suspicion — but what was one to think?"

Fleury, Mrs Fitzroy's maid, went about with a very lowering aspect. This was not hard for her, since she was at all times a lean, dour, sallow, black-avised creature with not a good word to say to any member of the household except her mistress and the macaw, which she tended solicitously. After the bracelet's loss had been discovered and broadcast, Fleury spent whole days in a restless pacing of the house, peering in the most unlikely spots, under dish-covers, behind clocks, in coal-scuttles, with her lips pressed savagely together as if she accused the whole family of having conspired to steal her mistress's treasure.

Then it became known that she had made some discovery which seemed to afford her a kind of angry satisfaction; she was closeted first with Mrs Fitzroy, who forthwith summoned Colonel Campbell. He, unluckily for himself, had just returned from his club.

"Look, sir, what Fleury has discovered in that child's box!" Mrs Fitzroy announced, waving a pink ostrich plume in his face. "Mine! which had been missing since last Thursday sennight!"

"What child's box? I do not perfectly comprehend you, ma'am," replied the Colonel, impatiently, but with an anxious frown.

"Why, that Susan — the maid, my granddaughter's maid. Hired, sir, by you! This was found in her box! And if she has this, who knows what else she may have purloined? I demand that constables be fetched immediately, and a search of her belongings be made!"

"Seems that it has been, already, ma'am," rejoined the Colonel, not at all happy at this disruption in his household, though relieved that the plume had been located in the maid's box and not (as for one hideous moment he had apprehended) among the possessions of his daughter or her friend.

The constables were duly summoned, and poor Sukey was interrogated. Sobbing and trembling, she denied all knowledge of how the pink plume came to be in her box: "She had never seen nor touched it, no, *that* she hadn't, nor would never dream of doing such a thing. She loved her young ladies, was very happy with them, had everything her heart could wish, why would she want to make off with something she could never use?"

But her box was diligently searched by the officers, and other vanished articles were found there — scissors, a pair of stockings, a packet of pins.

"I never put them there!" wept Sukey. "Some wicked person done it out of spite, to lay blame on me! I never prigged nothing from no one."

The evidence, however, was too strong against her, and the officers prepared to take her away, assuring Colonel Campbell that further questioning of the culprit, at the constabulary office, would most likely discover the whereabouts of the bracelet.

Jane and Rachel had not, at the outset, been informed of these happenings, but the presence of constables in the house, their loud footsteps and voices, could not be concealed, and the girls were in the front hall, aghast and pitying, as tiny Sukey was brought down quaking between two burly officials.

"I am sure, I am perfectly sure she did not do it!" whispered Jane in horror, and Rachel stammered, "Oh, S-Sukey, p-poor Sukey! I d-do not, no I c-*cannot* believe she would do such a thing — "

When Sukey saw the girls in the hallway she pulled herself out of the officers' grasp, exclaiming in a choked voice, "I *must* bid goodbye to my young ladies — " ran to them and hurriedly kissed their hands, repeating over and over "I *never* done it! *You'll* believe me, won't you, Miss Jane, Miss Rachel — ?" then without waiting for the constables to regain their grasp of her, she fled like a mouse through the open door, down the steps, and out into the square.

With angry shouts the two men pursued her, but, light and fleet of foot, she eluded them and raced away down Duke Street.

"I hope — oh, I do hope she gets away from them — " gasped Rachel.

"But, *poor* Sukey, what will become of her? She has lost her place and her good name!" Jane was horribly troubled. "With us, Sukey was always so very honest. On any little commission we gave her, she always rendered such strict account, down to the last farthing. No, I cannot believe she took those things."

"Wretched child, I fear she has dished herself by this flight," muttered the Colonel. "It does seem an admission of guilt. If she had been prepared to stand her trial, she might have been proved innocent — "

"Ridiculous!" cried Mrs Fitzroy. "It is perfectly evident the girl was guilty! I could have told you so — I knew it from the very start!"

Rachel and Jane, terribly distressed by this occurrence, could think of nothing else. They sat in the schoolroom, shivering and crying, quite regardless of Miss Winstable, whose view of the matter ran precisely counter to their own.

"Of course the girl had taken the bracelet. And it is to be hoped the constables rapidly apprehend her. No doubt they will then discover the whereabouts of your grandmother's valuable bracelet, at some thieves' kitchen."

This was not to be, however. Later that evening Colonel Campbell came to the room with a grave face to tell the girls that Sukey, being pursued by the constables through the traffic of Oxford Street, had dashed recklessly in front of a coach-and-six, gone under the hoofs of the horses, and had been picked up lifeless.

"Oh, *n-no!*" whispered Rachel. "Oh, P-Papa!"

Jane, without a word, stood up and left the schoolroom to make her way to her own chamber.

Unthinking, blind with tears and numb with misery, she, without considering, opened the door, not of her own room, but of the one now occupied by Fleury.

Made aware of her mistake immediately by the different arrangement of the furniture, she was retreating when a gleam on the white coverlet of the bed caught her eye, and with a cold shock of horror she recognised Mrs Fitzroy's opal-and-pearl bracelet.

"So Fleury took it!" breathed Jane. — She was about to dart forward and pick up the trinket when it struck her that if she were to carry it to the Colonel, there would be only her unsupported word to assert that that was where she had found it. Let the Colonel see for himself — !

She flew down the stairs and whispered to him urgently: "Colonel Campbell! Please to come with me for a moment! It is of the greatest importance and urgency or I would not ask you! Do, please, come quickly!"

"What is it, child?" Puzzled, he allowed her to lead him to the door of the maid's room.

"Now go in, sir, and look before you. Look on the bed!"

He went in, but there was a shriek of wrath from within. Fleury had returned, and was demanding by what right her privacy was violated. "Not so much even as a knock! Most disgraceful!"

"Look on the bed, sir!" said Jane.

But of course there was nothing on the bed.

"I *saw* it — Mrs Fitzroy's bracelet. It was here but now!" Jane kept reiterating.

"Lies! The child is telling monstrous, scandalous lies!" screamed Fleury. "Just because her wicked little *fille de chambre* was found guilty — now she must accuse me — who nevaire took nossing!"

"I am afraid I must ask for this room to be searched, nonetheless," said the Colonel calmly. "An accusation has been made — we cannot have the whole house in an uproar until this business has been thoroughly investigated."

The constables were fetched back; but they found nothing. Jane repeated, over and over, her absolute conviction that she had seen the bracelet on the bed.

"You were wholly mistaken! Of *course* you were mistaken!" angrily declared Mrs Fitzroy.

But the Colonel, to Mrs Fitzroy's outrage, declared his entire belief in Jane's story. "She is a careful, observant child. I have never known her anything but utterly truthful; and why should she lie? I am sorry, ma'am, but, in the circumstances, I cannot tolerate the maid's continued presence in this house. She is under considerable suspicion, which I, for one, believe to be justified. And I also believe that, by planting false evidence, she caused that unfortunate girl's death. — She must go, and without delay."

Mrs Fitzroy at first furiously declared that, where her maid was not welcome, she herself could not possibly remain. At this hearts throughout the whole house beat high in hope. But unfortunately Mrs Fitzroy presently recollected that nowhere else would she be able to live board and rent-free, within reach of her friends, and in a tolerably fashionable quarter of London. Her other daughter, Lady Selsea, was married to a man with whom Mrs Fitzroy was not on speaking terms; no hospitality could be hoped for in that quarter. With an exceedingly ill grace she decided to accept the situation. Fleury left the house, in a cloud of wrath and contumely. Another maid was hired, and two lasting results of the affair were a deep and continuing sense of grief and injustice in the hearts of Jane and Rachel, and a greatly strengthened dislike of Jane Fairfax in the heart of Mrs Fitzroy, who, from that time on, lost no opportunity of injuring Jane if she could do so inconspicuously.

Shortly after this, thinking it best for all the parties to separate, Colonel Campbell took his wife and children off to Weymouth, leaving Mrs Fitzroy in undisputed possession of the house.

Rachel was in high hopes of finding the Dixon family at Weymouth. "They often do go there, and Matt wrote saying they planned to do so this year. I am longing for you to meet them, Jenny — " But, alas, this was not to be. Matt wrote again, with news that his brother Sam had been laid low by a rheumatic fever. It was not thought advisable to travel.

In the autumn, when the Campbell family returned from Weymouth to London, there was an unexpected postscript to the bracelet affair.

A great-aunt of Colonel Campbell's had died in August, leaving her nephew a certain amount of property including some old-fashioned jewellery which Mrs Campbell, who never wore personal adornments herself, decided to dispose of.

"The money may as well add to Rachel's dowry; in any case, the things are hideous. You would not want them, would you, Rachel?"

"Not in the very least, Mamma," said Rachel, to whom the whole topic of jewellery just then was distasteful. In any case she would far rather have had drawing lessons.

"In any case," continued Mrs Campbell absently, "I understand that Mamma plans to leave you her jewels."

Rachel did not trouble to say how much she disliked this prospect, but dutifully accompanied her mother to Gray's, in Sackville Street, on an errand which both regarded as somewhat trivial and time-wasting.

While Mrs Campbell was displaying the jewels and discussing their value with one of the shopmen, Rachel wandered in boredom to the other end of the counter, and came back in a moment, very excited, to say breathlessly, "M-Mamma, d-do l-look here! D-do but look! There — I am sure — is G-Grandmamma's bracelet!"

There, indeed, it was: neither of them could mistake the bracelet, which they had seen a hundred times before. — Asked who had brought it in for sale, the shopman could not in the least recall. There were so many assistants in the place, it might have been received by any of them. — But, in fact, when all were questioned, one elderly man did chance to recall that the article had been brought in and sold to him by a female who looked and spoke very quick and sharp-like, as if she had been a furriner; a Frenchy, mayhap.

"Would she have looked like this?" inquired Rachel, and drew a rapid sketch on the little ivory tablets that she carried always with her in her reticule.

"Ay, that's her — that's the very moral of her, missie!" nodded the man. "It be wonderful the way you caught her likeness!"

A police warrant was issued for the arrest of Fleury, but she was never apprehended. Colonel Campbell, with much dislike for the transaction, bought back the bracelet and restored it to Mrs Fitzroy, who received it with no very effusive expressions of thanks. "I shall always think of it as having been the occasion of my losing the best, most faithful maid I ever had," she declared.

Colonel Campbell, whose dislike of his mother-in-law had grown apace since she had become a member of his household, kept in his own breast the suspicion that Mrs Fitzroy herself had employed the maid to sell her trinket and then cast the blame on the unfortunate Sukey.

The repercussions of this affair were a very long time in dying away.

Chapter 6

Jane's visits to Highbury necessarily became shorter and less frequent after the arrival of Mrs Fitzroy in Manchester Square. Buttressed by the company of her friend, Rachel was less vulnerable to her grandmother's interference, and she continually begged Jane not to desert her. It had always been the Colonel's plan that the major part of Jane's time should be spent in his household, "for," as he declared, "though they meant as well as might be, the poor dear Bates ladies had nothing at all to contribute towards the child's welfare or education; moreover the situation at Highbury was far from beneficial, mewed up without air in those confined quarters."

He had begun to observe, furthermore, that Jane's returns from Highbury to London were accompanied, very often, by an unsettled mental state, a mixture of homesickness with the sad realization that Highbury was no longer her true home. — The Colonel's insight here, as he grew steadily fonder of Jane with the passing of time, came far closer to the truth than any of his perceptions of his own daughter. Having Jane's welfare truly at heart, he contrived that her visits to her birthplace should be reduced to a minimum. A few days passed with them at Christmas and at Easter gave Jane the only chance to see her aunt and grandmother; often during these brief interludes she got no glimpse at all of other Highbury acquaintance; though she always made the strongest endeavour to see and talk with Mr Knightley, and felt bitterly deprived on the occasions when this was not achieved.

The wedding of Isabella Woodhouse to Mr John Knightley afforded one such meeting and also a rare encounter with Emma, the sole bridesmaid, now a self-possessed young lady of fifteen in snowy book-muslin over a white silk underdress, and her dead mother's pearls twined in her light-brown hair. Emma greeted Jane very graciously: "Jane Fairfax, *of course* she remembered her; very well indeed!" And Emma turned, smiling, to Mr Knightley, who chanced to be nearby: "Such playmates as we used to be! What a long time it seems now since those games of hopscotch and I-spy, when we told each other all our secrets, and you were obliged to wear my old outworn dresses. How you must have disliked it!" — inspecting the other girl at the same time with unaffected, unembarrassed curiosity. Not true, thought Jane. We *never* played hopscotch — while replying, meanwhile, in similarly courteous and friendly terms.

Emma's air, Jane was bound to admit, Emma's manner to every guest at the wedding was beyond praise, just as cordial and graceful as it could be; she had the same smiling, friendly, unstudied address, whether to the Bates ladies, in their mended shawls, to Mrs Perry the apothecary's wife, or to old John Abdy, bobbing, cap in hand, at the churchyard gate. Emma's public manner was irreproachable, could not be faulted; but just the same, thought Jane, it is like a clever piece of acting; why should that be so? It is a lesson that she has learned just as well as she can, like playing a sonata by Piccini on the piano; somehow I am aware that her heart is not behind it; under those smiling polite phrases I am certain she criticizes us all the time, and feels superior. Oh, how I wish — and here Jane astonished herself with the vehemence of her own feelings — how I wish that once, just once in my life, I could see Emma Woodhouse receive a real set-down!

The two girls conversed again at the wedding breakfast. Emma inquired with easy interest about life in London, and Jane, this time sensitively mindful that Emma still had never set foot outside Highbury, confined her replies to a few guarded descriptions of Mudie's library, public breakfasts, scientific lectures, and boating parties to Kew. — Emma did not seem impressed. She has, Jane thought, the gift of making the things she herself does appear interesting and somehow superior, even if they be faults: "Oh, I never do that — I never read that sort of book — I have a strong dislike for such adornments — " at once reducing the objects in question to the kind of tawdry pleasures only favoured by persons of vulgar taste and low mental attainment. In a situation where any other person would have apologised or felt the need to defend her lack of knowledge or deficiency, Emma, by complete confidence, made hers into a virtue. Reluctantly, unwillingly, Jane found herself impressed; and, though she did not like Emma any the better, came away from this encounter marvelling at such an impervious self-satisfaction. "Where can it come from? Isabella has it not, nor Mr Woodhouse." Idly, Jane wondered how Emma and Mrs Fitzroy would deal together, and concluded that they would probably like one another very well, much better than Mrs Fitzroy liked her grandchild, or her grandchild's friend.

The property bequeathed to the Colonel by his great-aunt had included, besides a sum of money and the pieces of old-fashioned jewellery, a modest estate in the West Indies which was, unfortunately, the subject of legal dispute; other parties, possible legatees, contested the bequest, and the plantation was, furthermore, encumbered with debt. After several years, and copious correspondence on the matter, the Colonel's lawyers advised that by far the best way for him to submit his claim and reach a practical decision would, without question, be for him to visit the spot himself and settle matters in person. Following much careful deliberation he decided, not only to go, but to take his family with him.

"You and the girls may as well come along, Cecelia. You know that you will be glad to acquire more evidence relative to the slave trade, and your London committees can, I daresay, manage without you for a year or so. Rachel, doubtless, will be pleased to revisit old haunts, and the trip may help to dispel some of the poor girl's continuing awkwardnesses; travel will open Jane's eyes to the world — " thus the Colonel glossed over the fact that he was really fond of Jane and looked forward to showing her foreign scenes — "the warm climate, moreover, will be advantageous for her bronchial troubles."

And, best of all, the Colonel thought but did not say, we shall leave your mother in England. For relations between Mrs Fitzroy and the family were still far from happy; and Mrs Fitzroy had not the slightest intention of quitting London on a visit to uncivilized foreign shores — Paris being one thing, but the Windward Isles, infested with snakes, scorpions, and Yellow Jack, quite another. She had announced her intention of remaining in Manchester Square. Her continued residence in the house would preclude a profitable rental of the property, which must be a disadvantage; even so, the Colonel considered the loss of income greatly outweighed by the happiness of losing his mother-in-law's company. Indeed, he nourished an unspoken hope that by the time of their return the old lady might have been gathered to her fathers.

The lawsuit proved, as legal matters invariably do, far more difficult and slower to settle than had been apprehended; nearly five years passed before the family were able to return to London, the Colonel having, finally, sold the estate for less than he had hoped, for a sum, indeed, which did little more than cover the expenses of the double journey. To add to his chagrin, the Colonel, just before his return, contracted a severe case of Yellow Fever and was taken on board in a lamentable condition, his eyes suffused with blood and, after a frightful bout of Black Vomit, his faculties almost suspended. Only his invincible obstinacy made him succeed in forcing his womenfolk to have him carried on to the ship and embark as planned. In fact the sea voyage was probably instrumental in saving his life: an excellent surgeon on board and treatment with Eau Vulneraire, a medicine made by infusing a quantity of herbs in alcohol, in the end pulled him through. Jane and Rachel nursed him devotedly, but if he felt gratitude for this he did not show it; his temper was greatly impaired by the disease, and the good relations which had begun to obtain between him and his daughter had worsened again. With all the impatience of a convalescent he grumbled about Rachel's tanned skin, her freckles, her sun-bleached hair — "Why in the world could she not wear a straw hat like sensible Jane, there, who kept her pretty pale skin unblemished through the tropical heat?" It was greatly to the credit of both girls that none of this made the least difference to their affectionate relationship, each being perfectly aware that the only reason Jane wore her hat all day had nothing to do with her complexion but was to avoid the severe headaches which still, at times, came to plague her, occurring for no ascertainable cause, and obliging her to take to her bed for two, or even three days when they came, for no remedy was of the least use.

They arrived back in England to news of the old King's collapse into complete insanity, and expectations of his death. The Prince of Wales had been appointed Regent, and the war still continued in Europe.

A dispute on a smaller scale, but waged with equal vigour, now arose in Manchester Square, where Mrs Fitzroy was still ensconced, much to the Colonel's unspoken disappointment.

She had taken one look at her granddaughter and let out a wail of horror.

"That girl's hair! Her teeth! Her complexion! How in the world is she ever to be brought out?" the old lady demanded of her daughter.

"Brought out?" vaguely inquired Cecelia, abstracting her attention momentarily from a memorandum on the slave trade by Wilberforce, which she had been eagerly perusing.

"Brought out in society, Cecelia! Presented! How will she ever acquire a husband if she does not make her debut?"

"Oh, my dear mother! Surely you do not believe that my poor Rachel should be put through that antiquated charade? It is like entering a beribboned cart-horse in the May Day parade! I am sure that Rachel would detest it, would you not, Rachel?"

"D-detest what, M-mamma?" inquired Rachel, who entered the room at that moment.

"Why, being presented at court, going to Almack's, court breakfasts, balls, all that flummery."

"You are n-not g-going to m-make us d-do that?" gasped Rachel, huge-eyed. "I sh-should hate it of all th-things! And I am sure Jane f-feels the s-same."

"There would be no question of *Miss Fairfax* being presented," interposed Mrs Fitzroy coldly. "She is a nobody, and has no future. But you, my granddaughter, must certainly take your place in proper society, and to that end I have saved up a thousand pounds, to cover your wardrobe and expenses."

So, to Mrs Fitzroy's credit, she had, but only, the Colonel grumbled, out of the very comfortable annual allowance she received from him.

"But I will not d-dream of d-doing anything that Jane can't d-do!" said Rachel, "and in any case I d-do not at all wish to be p-presented, thank you, Grandmamma."

Outraged, Mrs Fitzroy carried her grievance to the Colonel. "Something must be done about that girl, James! She needs — she needs intensive grooming," she declared, using the words with distaste, but aware that they might have an impact on her son-in-law. "Otherwise she will remain an old maid."

For once, although it went against the pluck with him, the Colonel was inclined to take Mrs Fitzroy's part. Impatiently, for he would have preferred peace and congenial company at his club, he entered the lists on his mother-in-law's side. It was true, he said to Cecelia, that Rachel needed polishing up. She was now nineteen, nearly twenty, time she looked about her for a husband, and how could she attract the notice of any sensible male when she had such freckles, such a gap in her teeth, such a stammer, above all, such complete lack of confidence when in polite society?

"She must begin going to parties; at least a few small, select parties."

Rachel, whose only wish was to attend art classes at the Royal Academy, was appalled.

"What about J-Jane? Will she come too?"

"Certainly not!" snapped Mrs Fitzroy. (Rachel's mother, soon tiring of the subject, had gone off to prosecute a copious correspondence with Samuel Whitbread.) "Jane has no need to learn the ways of society; in fact it would be quite improper. Jane must now find a position as a governess. Whereas you, my love, when you are twenty-one, will have twelve thousand of your own."

"I sh-shall sh-share my f-fortune with Jane!" declared Rachel.

Mrs Fitzroy left the room in a fury.

Deeply perturbed, Rachel took counsel with Jane.

Of course they had known, both of them, vaguely, always, that in time to come their ways of life must diverge, must part; but now, suddenly, the future was here, was on top of them, long before they were prepared to accept it.

Jane, secretly, had been to a registry office in Wigmore Street to discover the terms and conditions under which governesses were hired, and had come away deeply depressed, not only by the scantiness of the salaries, but by the downtrodden, dejected air of the applicants for positions, and the contemptuous, disregardful manner in which they were used by the people who ran the office. Because of her elegant clothes and manner she had been taken for a prospective employer, and she had not enlightened anybody; after watching and listening for a while she had walked away, castigating herself for a coward, while she made excuses: "Colonel Campbell said I need not commence my career until I am twenty-one; or until Rachel is married. Which will happen first?"

"If — if only we had s-some friend to take our p-part!" said Rachel.

Jane thought longingly of Mr Knightley; but he did not, and never would, stand towards her in that kind of relation; he was only the subject of her wistful, childish dreams.

Jane had, of course, visited Highbury immediately upon the return from the West Indies; had been happy and relieved to find

Aunt Hetty and her grandmother enjoying their habitual good health and spirits, embarked securely on that long, tranquil span, between age fifty and seventy, during which persons of untroubled moral and physical conformation exhibit hardly any change from one decade to the next. — With Jane, of course, it was wholly different and her elders could not have done exclaiming over her growth, her beauty, her widely increased range of knowledge and accomplishments, her musical brilliancy. The entire village must meet their returned darling. Unfortunately the entire village on this occasion did not include Mr Knightley, who had gone to a sheep-shearing festival at Holkham to study modern theories on leguminous crops and feeding oil-cake to cattle: "Doddy new-fangled ways," grumbled his man William Larkins, meeting Jane in the street, "no good will come of any of 'em you mark my words," and Jane could only shake her head in melancholy agree-ment, bitterly regretting the absence of the one person, outside of her family, whom she had really wanted to see.

At last, after many anxious and fruitless hours and days of family argument about Rachel's come-out, it was Rachel herself who hit upon the solution that satisfied all parties.

"I have had a very good idea," she announced one morning to Jane.

"What is it?" the latter inquired with considerable caution. Some of Rachel's plans in the past had included such schemes as Jane's becoming an author and writing novels, which would be illustrated by Rachel; Jane, strictly a realist, knew they might as well expect to make a living from piracy.

"I had a letter from Matt Dixon — " Rachel, to the extreme disapproval of her grandmother had never lost touch with the two Dixon brothers, maintaining a sporadic, intermittent, but lively and friendly correspondence with them. "Matt tells me that Sam has been ill again, but now they propose visiting Weymouth in hopes that the air will do him good. Let us suggest to Papa that we go to Weymouth also!"

Jane did not precisely see how a visit to Weymouth was to solve their problems. Did Rachel expect the Dixons to rescue her?

"Well, no — not precisely — b-but — they m-may have some helpful ideas. And — and Weymouth is s-such a f-friendly, easy place. Remember what a good time we had there — even without

M-Matt and Sam. I sh-shall feel more c-comfortable there, if we m-must go to p-parties. Even G-Grandmamma might agree that it would b-be b-better to b-begin at Weymouth."

Surprisingly, Mrs Fitzroy did agree. The London season was, in any case, almost over, people of the ton were leaving town for their country estates. Her grandchild might as well acquire a little polish in the more relaxed, less formal atmosphere of the watering place; while at the same time an intensive campaign was waged on her complexion with Gowland's Lotion, on her hair with eggs and rosemary-water, on her hands with salts of lemon, and on her lips with resin and spermaceti.

Miss Winstable had accompanied the family to the West Indies ("and had been a dead bore," said the Colonel, "always screaming at the sight of a centipede, terrified of the natives, invariably falling sick when she might have been of some use"); on the return to England it had been decided, to everybody's joy but her own, that her time of usefulness was past, so she was handsomely pensioned off by the Colonel, and the girls drew a breath of relief. Prematurely: for a new female chaperon, Mrs Consett, was hired, whose duty was to instil in them those ladylike qualities which, for one reason or another, Mrs Campbell had never inculcated.

"I had rather have kept Miss Winstable," said Rachel ungratefully, after a few days.

The journey from London to Dorset took them three days, for Mrs Fitzroy would not be hurried. She always travelled with her own sheets, and insisted upon inn bedrooms being aired for half a day before she would set foot in them.

Jane had hoped, humbly, that the route to Weymouth might lie close enough by Highbury to afford the chance of a visit there, but this suggestion was instantly vetoed by Mrs Fitzroy. "Absurd, to waste several hours of valuable travelling time! And for what? To visit a set of unimportant persons with whom no one but Jane was acquainted. Quite unnecessary."

Jane had longed for Rachel to meet dear Grandmamma and Aunt Hetty; also, just possibly, to catch a glimpse of dear Mr Knightley; but when the refusal was made she began at once to feel that she had been unreasonable in entertaining such a hope.

"Never mind," said Rachel, squeezing her hand, "perhaps we may contrive to stop there on the way back. All kinds of things may have happened by then!" She gave Jane a conspiratorial grin;

it had already been agreed between them how very convenient it would be if only Mrs Fitzroy were to fall overboard from some sailing vessel.

Weymouth, when they reached it, was still thin of company, but there were enough respectable names entered in the book of the Assembly Rooms to make Mrs Fitzroy feel quite comfortable.

"Hmn, Ponsonby, yes — Abercrombie — Ross, Acton, Drummond — hmn, hmn — ah, Lady Pytchley, she has two girls of Rachel's age, very good — Wheeler — *that*'s no name — Dalrymple, ah, Felix, that will be the Viscount's younger son, he has not a feather to fly with — Baring, Windham; yes, yes, we are assured of very tolerable society. Windham inherits his great-aunt's estate."

If the name Dixon were there, she did not announce it.

As had been the family's habit on former visits, they stayed a few days at the Royal Hotel in the north part of the town (once known as Melcombe Regis, but now more frequently referred to as New Weymouth). Meanwhile they looked about for a comfortable house to hire, and found one in York Buildings, facing the sea, and the great curving swoop of bay, which had given Weymouth its nickname "the Naples of Dorset".

"Ah, you couldn't have got a house like this so easily ten years ago," declared the landlord sadly. "When His Majesty was used to come here, you'd be lucky to hire so much as an attic, this time of year. They say his poor Majesty's altogether confined now — shut up by his London doctors. 'Tis a sad shame, *I* say. He was the pleasantest, affablest old gentleman you could wish to meet; used to take his dip every morning in the sea, right over there. And there's his bathing machine still, to prove if I lie."

There it was; in fact there were two, kept carefully painted, as they later discovered; an octagonal one on wheels, and a large floating structure, like a houseboat, moored in the river below the Nothe headland. The machines were coloured red, white and blue, and had gilt crowns on them. After His Majesty's daily dip, the landlord told them, the crowds on the sea-front had been used to halloo and huzza, and the band of the Royal Dragoons played "God Save the King".

It was sad that those stirring times were over; and yet, Jane thought, Weymouth seemed still a very cheerful, lively town. There might be no more royal receptions in the Assembly Rooms, these days, but weekly balls were still held there, a variety of plays and entertainments were to be seen at the Theatre Royal on the Esplanade, there were the New Rooms, and the Old Rooms, there was Harvey's Library and Card Assembly, not to mention other minor libraries, where newspapers might be read and books borrowed. The old town, with its picturesque narrow little streets, had fascinating shops, where fishermen's nets and glass balls, or fossils from Lyme might be bought by the tourists; and there was Ryall's Toyshop, next to the theatre, where Queen Charlotte and her daughters had purchased sponge cakes and sugar-sticks. Besides those delights, the Radipole barracks beyond the Narrows were seething with troops and officers, and the harbour was bristling with naval craft, still heedfully keeping watch for a possible French invasion.

Mrs Fitzroy might turn up her nose and say that Weymouth was a paltry little place compared to Bath, but Matt Dixon, who had been to school there, said that Bath was the dismallest black hole on earth, situated in a dank dell, where it never stopped raining. Weymouth, Matt said, was infinitely preferable, for besides the advantage of the sea it had all kinds of agreeable excursions: to Sandsfoot Castle, and the island of Portland, Radipole Lake, the wishing-well at Upwey, Lulworth Cove, the Durdle Door Rock, and Corfe Castle.

"We can be exploring for ever," he told Rachel. "Oh, what fun it is that you are here at last! What larks we shall have! And what a lucky thing that you young ladies are such excellent horsewomen!"

"It is only too bad that poor Sam cannot accompany us," sighed Rachel.

The Dixons, already installed at Weymouth, had a pleasant bow-fronted house in Trinity Road, on the older side of town, overlooking the harbour. They or their friends in York Place could cross the harbour by ferry when they wished to visit one another, go for a dip in the sea, or walk on the Esplanade.

Mrs Fitzroy made no secret of the fact that she did not think at all highly of the Dixons. She had met them just once before, at the time of her first descent on Manchester Square, and could concede, only, that the boys were not quite so uncouth as they had been at that time.

"But, *Dixon!* I ask you! What kind of a name is *that?*"

Colonel Campbell, ignoring his mother-in-law's animadversions, continued to like the Dixons very well. The Major had been an old friend, carried off, most regrettably, by a ball at the battle of Vimeiro. But both the Colonel and Mrs Campbell were sincerely attached to Mrs Dixon, a kind, untidy, cheerful lady, who hoped by much sea-bathing to become a little less plump. "For I am too round, my dears, indeed I am!" But as, after every dip from her bathing-machine, she insisted on keeping out the cold by munching several little queen-cakes, bought at Ryall's, before a luncheon of lobster patty and pickled pears, it seemed unlikely that her ambition would be realised.

Jane, from the start, was most favourably impressed by the Dixon brothers, and could readily understand why Rachel had always remembered, always corresponded with them. They were not precisely handsome; no, one could not say that of them, especially, for instance, when compared with the memory of Mr Knightley. But their looks, particularly those of Matt, were striking and poetic to a degree. And that was as it should be, for Matt, he confessed, had taken to writing poetry; he had completed several odes already, kept a daily notebook, which he termed his "skeleton diary" and hoped to follow the profession of letters.

They were Anglo-Irish — "Ancestors went over with Cromwell, you see, vulgarly recent; the Normans and the true Irish think nothing of us, we are merely the scaff and raff of the country," Sam explained to Jane with a grin. But, she guessed, there had been considerable intermarriage with the true Irish since Cromwell's day; both boys had black Celtic hair, Matt's indeed was a positive mane, rough, shaggy and curling, reaching to his shoulders; they had high cheekbones and large dark grey Celtic eyes. They were fluent and brilliant talkers; they could, said Rachel "chat a dormouse out of its winter sleep," using a wealth of lively gesture and dramatic declamation, besides effervescent jokes and wit. Their manners, once so uncouth, were now as polished as anybody — except Mrs Fitzroy — could wish. Even Mrs Consett, the chaperon, found them delightful.

"Excellent address!" she sighed. "And so romantic in appearance. And there will be a title for Mr Dixon, in due course, when his uncle Lord Kilfinane dies. But what a pity poor Mr Sam is so sickly."

"An *Irish* title!" sniffed Mrs Fitzroy. "What use is that? And only a little scrap of an estate — all bog, no doubt."

Nothing could recommend the Dixons to Mrs Fitzroy. She found them encroaching — affected — puffed up with affectation and nonsense — and then, Dixon! What a name. "It smacks of the grocer's counter — that is all you can say."

Meanwhile Rachel and Jane got along with the boys very comfortably. Somehow the term "boys" came naturally to mind when referring to them, though Matt was twenty and Sam nineteen. Matt was at Cambridge; Sam, because of his various illnesses, had not yet applied to enter a university but hoped to do so perhaps next year. Matt, in course, would inherit his uncle's estate and title; "That's if I don't do anything to annoy the old crotchet; the title I am bound to come in for, but he can cut me out of his will if he so chooses, and would do so, I'd take my affidavit, at the drop of a pin, if he took the fancy, for he has all sorts of quirks in his head, and don't like me above half." Sam was destined for the church, as soon as he could throw off his inconvenient weakness of the lungs. His mother, that cheerful, carefree lady, seldom allowed herself to be troubled for too long by anxieties and perplexities, but even she found cause for concern in his state at present; the family had come by sea from Cork to Weymouth and had, unfortunately, encountered quite severe gales off Land's End; poor Sam had been wretchedly ill and had coughed himself into a haemorrhage; but the good air and sea bathing of Weymouth would be bound to restore him very soon. Mrs Dixon was of an unconquerably optimistic turn of mind. It was too bad that, after his morning dip in the sea, the poor boy was so fatigued he had to lie down upon a sopha until noon, but he would soon feel more the thing. In the meantime Sam did not allow a little physical debility to quench his spirits — he was as gay as could be, and throve on company; almost every day he contrived to persuade the group of young people to repair to the house in Trinity Road, where Mrs Dixon, a devoted mother, had hired a very fine piano. Both her sons adored music, Matt loved to sing and had a beautiful tenor voice. Sam played the fiddle and loved to sing also, but it made him cough. Rachel and Jane participating, they could manage an immense variety of glees, duets, trios, and quartets; Sam was overjoyed to find in Jane such a superior performer, and the house, as Mrs Dixon often said, "sounded like a nest of humming-birds all day long." In the afternoons Matt and the two girls hired horses and rode out into the surrounding countryside; sometimes Frank Churchill accompanied them; he too, with his uncle and redoubtable aunt, had now arrived to take the waters at Weymouth. But Frank, compared with the eloquent, imaginative, brilliant Dixon brothers, appeared like a kind, friendly, but rather dull young man; he was not often invited to the house in Trinity Road.

Mrs Fitzroy could and did complain that her granddaughter spent far too much time with those Irish hobble-de-hoys, but Colonel Campbell had no objection, so long as Mrs Dixon or Mrs Consett sat with the young people.

"But they are not making the acquaintance of *any* of the right society of Weymouth!" was Mrs Fitzroy's daily complaint. "There are Lady Pytchley's girls — and the Dalrymples — and Miss Acton — all from a really elevated level of society — from whom Rachel could pick up a little manner, a little address — instead of which, all she does is sing Irish airs and go flying about the countryside acquiring more freckles!"

"Possibly so, ma'am, but she is decidedly less nervous than she was, and seems at last to be conquering her stammer just a trifle."

This was true. What all Signor Negretti's exercises had failed to achieve was brought about by laughter, enjoyment, and time spent in congenial company. After two or three hours' singing with the boys, Rachel could talk with less constraint, almost without the painful locking, or having to struggle with her breath. Sometimes the group played charades, or verse games, declaiming and reciting; it was remarkable how well Rachel managed those too. All the cheerful conversation and friendly companionship did wonders for her self-confidence. And her looks, Jane thought, were improving visibly, day by day: her nose was not so pink, the regular applications of bandoline had certainly helped her hair; and just the fact that she spent so much of her time laughing added immeasurably to the animation of her countenance!

Frank Churchill's aunt, a professed invalid, was seldom to be seen about the town; she had hired a handsome house in Augusta Place and mostly remained indoors, receiving doctors and masseurs. She never ventured her person into the sea, but took, instead, expensive daily hot and cold baths in the establishment set up for that purpose upon the quay. Her husband, on the other hand, rented one of the one-and-sixpenny umbrella bathing vehicles (with guide) and was to be seen every morning at seven scurrying from his sedan chair up the steps of the umbrella machine and into its sandy recesses; the machine was then drawn into the water until a sufficient depth had been reached; the horse would be unhitched and led away so that the bather could descend from the seaward end of the apparatus and take his dip, under the umbrella, with or without the help of the attendant. Finally the horse would be re-harnessed to the shoreward end, so that the bather could be restored to dry land.

Colonel Campbell, after trying a bathing machine once, voted the whole process "far too fiddling, jolting, and devilish bone-shaking"; he much preferred to swim in the sea without all that nonsense. Accordingly he and Matt Dixon and Frank Churchill would betake themselves to a northerly part of the bay, near the barracks and half a mile out of town, where they could splash and swim away from the eyes of females without the need to worry about anybody's modesty.

Jane and Rachel greatly wished that it were possible for females to do likewise; they agreed that the bathing machine routine was very joggling and uncomfortable; moreover the attendant always returned long before one was ready to come out (there were only about forty bathing machines for the whole beach, so these were always in brisk demand). Still, they enjoyed the bathing; "and c-certainly the s-sea was d-doing wonders for Papa's lame leg," Rachel said.

Mrs Fitzroy, now in her mid-seventies, had become acutely rheumatic while the Campbells were in the West Indies, and now walked very lame with a stick. She often accompanied Mrs Churchill into the hot bath, and, as well, swallowed numerous potions and mineral waters. The remainder of her days were passed in elegant company, playing whist and cassino and commerce for small points, and acquiring information. Mrs Churchill, whose temper was quite as difficult as report had ever made out, possessed no friends and few intimates; but still, she considered Mrs Fitzroy to be a tolerable sort of creature, and did not disdain, now and then, to discuss the affairs of the young people with her, while the ladies were taking the bath together.

It was agreed between the pair of them that a match between Mrs Fitzroy's granddaughter and Frank Churchill would be an excellent arrangement. Frank (supposing his aunt so chose) would be very comfortably situated, and Rachel would have her twelve thousand. That, said the ladies to one another, would make for a decent, well-settled establishment. And if Frank, it must be admitted, was just a touch volatile, just a trifle too light and unreliable, Rachel's seriousness and good bottom would soon sober him down.

"For she is, I won't conceal from you, ma'am, a thoughtful, clever gal; takes after her mother in that respect; and also, like Cecelia, I don't doubt she'll make a sensible, affectionate wife. Unlike my other granddaughter Charlotte who is a sad flirt! I only wish that Rachel could be detached from that Fairfax creature, tiresome chit; the sooner *she* is sent packing, the more comfortable we shall all be."

"Does your son-in-law dower Miss Fairfax also, if she should marry?" inquired Mrs Churchill, who took an almost professional interest in all such arrangements.

The two ladies were at that moment partaking of tea and wafer cakes in John Harvey's Library after (with considerable disfavour) watching the Dixon and Campbell families depart, in three curricles, to make the circuit of Radipole Lake.

Mrs Fitzroy was on the point of answering in the negative when a military band, outside, struck up such a deafening rendition of "Rule Britannia" that all conversation was temporarily suspended: and while the noise lasted she was given time to consider.

The result of her cogitation was that when Mrs Churchill, again with the most single-minded wish for information, repeated her question: "Is it your son-in-law's intention to give that girl a portion, should she be so lucky as to receive an offer of marriage?" Mrs Fitzroy had a reply prepared and could say, "As to that, ma'am, I cannot, of course, answer for his intentions. He does not open his mind to me. But he *is* excessively attached to the girl, that I do know. Such a thing is not at all out of the question . . . "

For something she had heard, earlier in the day, about the Dixon brothers, had suddenly put into her head a notion for queering the Fairfax girl's pitch — not, of course, that Mrs Fitzroy would ever employ such an ungenteel expression.

"I had understood the young lady was destined for a teaching career."

"That, indeed, was the original purpose, ma'am. But my son-in-law grows so fond of the young person that her quest for a post has been continually postponed."

Here, Mrs Fitzroy did not exaggerate. Jane had several times, since reaching the age of eighteen, represented to the Campbells that it was high time she became independent, that she should not be a burden on them any longer, that it was almost robbing Rachel that she should continue to be a charge on the household; but both the Colonel and his wife had replied that they could not possibly consider parting with her yet. If — *when* — Rachel was settled in the world, had left the nest, then, of course, such a step must be taken; but, in the meantime, poor Rachel would be utterly wretched at the thought of parting from her crony. "She is so much more animated and at ease when in your company, my dear Jane," insisted Mrs Campbell. And in this matter Jane had, though with considerable private reservations and doubts, acquiesced; it was undoubtedly true that Rachel was more at ease on social occasions when her friend was by, and might therefore be thought more likely to receive an eligible offer (which, of course, was everybody's secret wish for her); but, after all, thought Jane, sooner or later she must learn to do without me, and meanwhile I am living in a kind of fool's paradise, growing to depend on pleasures and treats that I am not entitled to, and that will most likely never come my way again. The Campbells do not consider my side of the matter. — When Colonel Campbell had finished with his daily newspaper Jane regularly scanned its advertisement columns with a cold, terrified distaste; only that morning, doing so, she had read: "Wanted, Young Person of excellent education & unimpeachable references to take charge of a Fine Family of six children & instruct them in Languages, Drawing, Mathematics, Use of the Globes, Music, & Deportment. Salary £10 per Half Year." She recalled the grim and dismal scene in the Wigmore Street office. That, she thought, is what I shall have come to in a year or so; and for a moment she was filled with a frantic urge to cut herself immediately adrift from the Campbells, to plunge away and commit herself at once to the bleak life of drudgery that awaited her. She had few illusions as to the lot of a governess in however elevated a family: socially distanced from her employers, disliked, more often than not, by the spoiled children of the family, regarded as a kind of upper servant, the instructress lived a solitary, bat-like existence with no assigned place in the household, and with duties that might and often did range from teaching Euclid and Latin to bathing the baby and formidable quantities of household needlework. The life of Miss Winstable or Miss Taylor had been luxury indeed compared with other females employed by families on visiting terms with the Campbells. — Jane had once asked Mrs Campbell if there were no other form of employment in which a well-educated girl might hope to earn her living — Mrs Campbell, mixing so much in public affairs, must surely know of *something*? But the lady had shaken her head.

"Nothing that *pays*, my dear Jane; all the ladies with whom I associate perform on a strictly voluntary basis; that is why only the rich can afford to be social reformers."

(Privately, both of Rachel's parents thought that Jane, even lacking a dowry, could not fail of attracting some eligible young man, with her handsome looks, musical endowments, and her striking poise and elegance. This was the prime reason why her request to establish herself in a post was continually deferred.)

All these considerations rose and subsided, like troubled tides, in Jane's mind. Today, forming one of a party of pleasure to make the tour of Radipole Lake, she decided that since she was positively instructed to enjoy herself, she might as well do so, for however short a time. Let somebody else be found to take charge of the fine family of six children! And she gazed around her with unaffected interest at the lake and the enormous number of swans apparently resident upon it.

The excursionists had been accommodated in three open one-horse chaises, hired from the Royal Hotel, of which Frank Churchill drove the first, with Rachel and Mrs Consett as his passengers; Colonel Campbell was in charge of the second, with Sam and his mother; and Matt Dixon drove the third, with Mrs Campbell and Jane. Mrs Campbell could very rarely be persuaded to take part in such excursions, and, indeed, on the present occasion, had brought along the annals of some learned body set up to report on the prevalence of lung-disease in the china clay industry, which she read intently, ignoring the scenery and paying only desultory attention to the talk of her companions.

Matt was telling Jane about his home, Baly-Craig.

"I wish you could see it, Miss Fairfax! So beautiful it is! The mountains sweep right down to the lough, and at evening, or sunrise, they turn all manner of colours, from lavender to indigo to brilliant gold; words cannot describe those hues! And the little homesteads are white as pearls, down by the water's edge; indeed it breaks my heart to go away to Dublin, every time, it does."

"And have you spent much time in Dublin?" Jane wanted to know. "Is Dublin a handsome city?"

"The grandest in the world, sure it is! With all the bridges, and its fine streets, and beautiful river; some talk of Venice, but, for my part, I think Dublin far superior."

He ran on at length, extolling the beauties of Dublin; and then they talked of books, for they had discovered many tastes in common, and of music, and reminded one another of favourite airs, and tried to remember others which lay forgotten, just beyond memory. "Sam knows the one I mean," Matt said, referring to a theme by Corelli, "he will be able to sing it for you in a moment." That led on to Sam's state of health. "Poor fellow! It is a thousand pities he is so pulled-down by the journey, for my mother hoped that the summer here would set him up for next winter. I worry about him: this morning he declared that he will never marry, for his constitution is such that he feels no woman should be called upon to look after him; but it is a terrible pity, upon my word it is, for he is the best-natured creature in the world, and worth fifty of me! When he goes into the church, as he plans, he will become a saint, entirely."

"You and Sam are very fond of your home," said Jane thoughtfully. "You are both deeply attached to Ireland. And yet you come away. When you are here, do you not miss your own place?"

"Faith, Miss Fairfax, we do! Some days the thought of Baly-Craig is like a continual sorrow at the back of my mind. A hurt that can't be healed, or ignored. The greenness of the place, and the shape of the hills, and the sound of cattle lowing, and the call of the plover on the hillside; I can tell you truly there's no minute of the day when some part of me isn't missing it."

"And yet you come away from it all? You come here to England. I wonder why?"

"Ah, now you put your finger on it, Miss Jane." He turned his dark, lively, intelligent face to look at her. "I come away. Why? Because there is not enough in Baly-Craig to content a man like me."

Jane sat quietly. Her look encouraged him to continue.

"I love the place, ma'am, as dearly as my right hand, but what can I do there? Fish the river, go out sailing down the coast in my little boat with one or two of the lads, spend the day on the hills after snipe, or out on the bog — what kind of a life is that, for a man of education? I am to be a writer, I need others of my kind to brush minds with. Sometimes I think my father should never have sent me to Cambridge, he has ruined me entirely! I need talk, clever talk, the life of the mind, I need to see the wheels of the world go round."

"And perhaps a little female society as well, hmnn?" inquired Mrs Campbell, emerging suddenly out of her learned report.

"That too, ma'am, faith!"

"Perhaps if you had a clever, conversible wife, she would reconcile you to the solitude of Baly-Craig."

"And perhaps if I had a clever wife *she'd* go melancholy mad alongside of me in the deep silence of the place!"

"Wives have a trick of supplying a man with a whole tribe of children — and then there's an end to your solitude and silence!" said Mrs Campbell.

"As to that, ma'am, perhaps I'd sooner be left in my desolation!" But he laughed.

Mrs Campbell returned to her pamphlet.

"It is queer that you should feel like that about your home," Jane remarked thoughtfully. "For I understand the feeling so very well. I was born and brought up in a little village — oh, nothing like so remote as Baly-Craig — and yet it lies distant enough so that you may not see a stranger ride along the street from one week's end to the next — especially in winter. I am truly attached to my home and all the country that lies around it — as I think any person of sensibility must be, to the place of their birth — and yet, now, when I return home, I find that it does not entirely satisfy me. I miss the things I have come to depend on in London — books, music, conversation, even the sight of faces other than the familiar neighbours of every day."

"Ah, you do indeed understand!" cried Matt Dixon. "You have the marrow of it."

"But what can we do? Is it wrong to feel so? It seems like a betrayal — "

"It cannot be that. The love is still there — "

"But why should we feel this? Our forefathers were content to remain in one spot, they built their houses and tilled their ground — "

"Not all of them," again put in Mrs Campbell, lifting her eyes from the report. "Or Christopher Columbus would never have discovered America. Some stay at home, others sally out. And there is no history book that says Columbus was not homesick — But I perceive that the others, ahead of us, are stopping. They appear to have encountered some acquaintances."

As the chaise rolled on — Matt, absorbed in conversation, had allowed his horse to lapse to a dawdle — Mrs Campbell exclaimed, "Why, bless my soul, it is Robert and Charlotte! I did not know that my sister Selsea proposed coming to Weymouth! How very singular of her not to inform us that she had such a scheme in mind."

The other two carriages had halted at the head of the lake, where a wide, sandy space permitted foot passengers, if they so wished, to walk down to the shallow brink of the water. The carriages were drawn up under spreading oak trees beside another one, and there, to be sure, were Rachel's cousins.

"Aunt Cecelia! Uncle James! Cousin Rachel! We inquired at the hotel and heard you had gone this way, so hoped, if we made a little speed, coming the other way, to meet you hereabouts! Is not this an agreeable surprise? Was not this a charming plan? We were staying, you know, with Lord Fortuneswell at Abbotsbale, and so we persuaded Mamma to come on here, just for a frolic. For it was very slow at Abbotsbale, was it not, Rob?"

"Lord, yes! Slower than a stopped clock! Old Fortune proses and dozes, and the bath water is only luke warm, and all the billiard cues are warped. And we knew that you were here, for Ma had had a letter from Grandmother."

"So are you not delighted to see us?" chirped Charlotte.

"That's of course!" replied Colonel Campbell in rather a dry tone. And Rachel, coming up to Jane, whispered in her ear, "*What* a misfortune! Now all our c-comfort will be quite c-cut up!"

Mrs Campbell's sister Lady Selsea bore a very close resemblance to her mother in looks and dress; her habits of fashion and society were the antithesis of her sister's. Of her children Charlotte, the elder, some four years older than Rachel, was a remarkably silly girl with small blue eyes, a profusion of light curly hair, and an artless effusiveness of manner that would always, in some circles, be called charm; it concealed, quite often, more than a touch of malice. She never troubled to make friends among her own sex, reserving all her attention for gentlemen. Her brother Robert, two years younger, was already in a way to becoming a finished coxcomb; he thought of little but dress, food, and play, and his complexion bore witness to his excesses.

"Let us hope that they find Weymouth dull and don't stay long!" Jane whispered back softly. She could see that the Dixon brothers and Frank Churchill did not look with any particular kindness on Robert Selsea, though they greeted him civilly; his sister, full of laughter, smiles, and chat, was welcomed with more amiability. She knew Frank Churchill by sight, but she had never met the Dixons before, and Jane could see that she was greatly struck by both of them, especially with Matt; she began at once to engage him in fluent conversation, asking many questions about the neighbourhood: pleasant walks? pleasant rides? which were the most picturesque viewpoints? which inns provided meals at midday?

Now a young gentleman who had hitherto stood at a distance sauntered up and was introduced as Robert Selsea's most particular friend, Tom Gillender; he, Jane thought, looked even more of a dandy than his companion, for he wore primrose-coloured pantaloons and a most elaborate stock, inspected the world through a glass, which he continually raised to his eye with an air of ineffable fatigue, and made a habit of always taking snuff before committing himself to any opinion. He had already been staying at Weymouth for several days, he informed them, and indeed Jane recollected seeing him at leisure upon the Esplanade, casting a disparaging eye over the females in their seaside muslins.

" 'Pon my soul, Mrs Campbell, ma'am, I see you share my opinion of Weymouth and all its tedious surroundings — slow, hideously, abominably slow! I wish I, like you, had thought to bring a gazette or a journal to beguile away the time, 'pon my soul I do!" — as Mrs Campbell, reluctantly abandoning her pile of reading-matter, joined the group of young people.

"Do you attend the Assembly tonight, Cousin Rachel?" inquired Charlotte, turning momentarily from her conversation with Matt; and, upon Rachel's glancing doubtfully at Jane, cried out in affected horror, "Come! Come! Do not tell me that you had no plan to go? Why, the Assemblies at Weymouth are the only occasion for visiting the place. La! I declare, my dear cousin, you are turning into a regular bluestocking, and it is high time Robert and I came by to give you a reminder that there are other things in this world besides ink and paper. Amn't I right, dear Aunt Cecey?"

Mrs Campbell, who had once been heard to say that her niece reminded her of a buzzing gnat, had already turned away and was talking to Sam and Mrs Dixon — but the Colonel, whose manners in company were always kindly and correct, said to Charlotte,

"And so *you* will be attending the Assembly, I collect, miss, in all your finery?" adopting the slightly bantering air that he customarily used when engaging foolish young ladies.

"That's of course, Uncle James! And Robert and Mr Gillender will be escorting me; so I hope we shall have the pleasure of seeing you there, Rachel — " her eye passed entirely over Jane — "and — of *course* — you other gentlemen as well?" with a sparkling look at the Dixons. "An assembly cannot have too many gentlemen, can it, Rachel?" And she smiled very winningly at Frank Churchill, adding, "I have not yet had the pleasure of being introduced to *this* gentleman — though I have seen you, I believe, at the Harrogate Assemblies? — but I am sure he agrees with me, do not you, sir?"

"Why, my dear, this is young Frank Churchill, an old friend and neighbour of ours in London," explained the Colonel, at the same time as Frank most readily replied,

"Why, yes, indeed, ma'am, I am entirely of your way of thinking. Dancing, for me, is one of the first pleasures, and if somebody else will provide the music, I will engage to continue dancing until daylight, and that without the slightest fatigue! I could just as well dance for a week as for half an hour. The inventor of the cotillion, the polonaise, the gigue, the strathspey, deserves, in my opinion, to be ranked far above such minds as those who have merely hit upon gunpowder, or the arch, or the wheel."

"Frank, Frank, you are a frivolous fellow," cried the Colonel, shaking his head at Frank, but kindly enough, while Charlotte clapped her hands, exclaiming, "Famous! Famous! I can see that you will certainly attend tonight's Assembly, Mr Churchill, and I hereby guarantee to equal your prowess in dancing every single dance."

Politeness, of course, now constrained Mr Churchill to engage Miss Selsea for any two dances that she chose to designate, and Mr Gillender, languidly approaching Jane, solicited the honour of her hand for the first two dances.

"For, 'pon my soul, I won't, like our friend here, guarantee to remain in the place for more than an hour or two. But one owes it to the society of the town, don't you agree, ma'am, to show oneself at the commencement? Public duty and so forth."

"I am sure the citizenry of Weymouth must feel very much obliged to you," drily commented Mrs Campbell.

"I thank you sir," answered Jane, who was not at all favourably impressed by Mr Gillender, "but I think it quite improbable that we shall be attending the Assembly," for she had received a signal from Rachel, a very decided shake of the head.

But Colonel Campbell exclaimed, "Come, Rachel, do not disappoint your cousins. Let us have a little less of this conventual attitude. Your grandmother will most certainly wish you to go. And I daresay Jane will not object — will you, Jane, hey?"

"That is entirely as Rachel chooses," replied Jane. "For myself I have no strong feelings one way or the other." Which was not entirely true, since her great feeling for music extended into a lively enjoyment of dancing. But she certainly had no wish to enforce upon Rachel what might, for the latter, prove to be an evening of penitential suffering and boredom.

"Ah, have a heart, let you, the two of you!" exclaimed Matt Dixon. "Surely you would not wish to deprive me of the pleasure of dancing with each of ye in turn? For as long as the evening lasts? and Miss Selsea, too, of course!" With a warm smile at that lady. "And, though Sam cannot dance, poor fellow, I know he will take prime pleasure in watching you."

To which Rachel, with a slight stammer, replied, "V-Very well, if P-Papa wishes it, we will go! Th-thank you, Matt! I shall be very happy to dance with you."

Mrs Campbell was now heard declaring that they must return home, or the girls would never have sufficient time to rest themselves before the evening's gaieties, and the party reassembled itself into carriages. Robert and Charlotte drove off smartly (she lavishing smiles on Matt Dixon to the last) accompanied by Mr Gillender on horseback; this time Frank Churchill drove Jane and Mrs Campbell, while Matt had charge of Mrs Consett and Rachel.

Jane had not, hitherto, engaged in much conversation with Frank Churchill. She frequently felt a little sorry for him, though she would have been hard put to it to give any reason for this. He was a very good-looking young man — height, air, address, all were unexceptionable. His countenance was full of spirit and liveliness, yet the lively manner adorned what appeared to be a basis of excellent sense. There was a well-bred ease in his manner, and a friendly readiness to converse upon any subject. All this stood high in his favour. So why, Jane asked herself now yet again, why did she continually have this feeling that, with all these advantages, he was somehow to be pitied?

As they drove along the shores of the lake, and he chatted with great fluency and animation about swans — castles — sea-bathing — music — books — poetry — folk-tales and superstition — whatever came to his mind or his ready tongue — Jane tried once more to analyse her feeling about him.

Was it because somehow he seemed always to be standing on the outskirts of their group, a little wistfully hoping to be invited to join the central core of it, but aware that he had, as yet, no place there? He is like, Jane thought, a smiling, friendly, handsome dog, with wagging tail; always ingratiating, always on best behaviour. — I suppose he has learned to be like that, poor fellow, because his tartar of an aunt is so exigent and unpredictable.

For Jane was well acquainted, of course, with Frank's history: how his mother, from a wealthy and ancient clan, the Churchills, had married to disoblige them, had married impecunious young Captain Weston from Highbury; and upon the poor young mother's early death after a three-years' marriage — a death hastened, some said, by the hostility of her own family — the Churchills had proposed to Captain Weston that they should adopt the child, whose name was accordingly changed to Churchill.

His story is not unlike my own, thought Jane; except that his will have a happier conclusion, for he is truly the Churchill heir, by blood as well as by adoption, and will in time inherit a fortune, besides having a fond, indulgent father always ready to receive him at Highbury, should the Churchills consent to such a visit (so far, she gathered, they had not); but, on the other hand, I am far luckier than Frank Churchill, for I love and am loved by the Campbells, whereas with the best will in the world I cannot discern any signs of attachment between Frank and the Churchills. They have bestowed wealth and comfort on him, but no true affection; I believe he has, all his life, been starved of honest feeling; that is it! And I am sure that is why he stands waiting so wistfully, so eagerly on the outskirts of our group. It is because he longs for what he can see we all feel for one another. And he has learned always to be on his best behaviour in order not to fall foul of the bad-tempered aunt. Poor fellow! Yes, he is really to be pitied; my instinct was right, and in future I will endeavour to show more friendship, more genuine, sincere friendship towards him.

"There is a famous wishing-well at Upwey — we must certainly make an exploration to that spot," Frank was saying. "Do you believe in wishing-wells, Miss Fairfax?"

"I have never been so fortunate as to come across one, Mr Churchill," she told him. "But I am not, I believe, superstitious in general. I have not so far in my life had sufficient good fortune to place much credence in the magical granting of wishes."

Mrs Campbell, immersed in her documents, was here heard to give an assenting grunt.

But is that really true? Jane asked herself, while Frank, turning to her a most animated countenance, exclaimed, "*You*, Miss Fairfax? Not had good fortune? But you seem to me the heiress to the best fortune in the world!"

"I, Mr Churchill? An orphan, destined to make my living by teaching?"

"Oh, never mind that!" he cried. "I mean, yes, of course I know that you are an orphan, with no father or mother, which, to be sure, is exceedingly sad, but you have the happiness to reside with a family who love you dearly — any simpleton can see — and then, you know, a myriad chances may affect your future; for who in the world can ever venture to prophesy what may befall them? Look at you and look at myself, Miss Fairfax; our fortunes are alike in this, that we were both suddenly displaced from the course allotted to us and set elsewhere; we are a kind of companions in unexpected circumstances, are we not?"

How singular, thought Jane, that his thought should thus echo mine of a few minutes back.

And she began to view Frank Churchill with a little more interest; he was not, she admitted to herself, unintelligent; though she would never regard him with the same admiration as, for instance, Mr Knightley. Or Matt Dixon.

There was something brilliantly spontaneous and expansive about Matt: a native intelligence and warmth which owed nothing to artifice or education. Whereas poor Frank Churchill had learned to think twice before he spoke; he had learned the art of pleasing, and, though it came easily to him, as to his father Mr Weston, one cannot, thought Jane, have so much respect and esteem for such a person as for one, like Matt, who speaks his mind straight, with no thought for the effect on the auditor.

"If you were to be granted a wish, Miss Fairfax," Frank Churchill was continuing eagerly, "as, of course, you will when we visit Upwey and drink the waters of the well — if you had a wish, what would it be?"

On the instant, Frank's laughing, cajoling face vanished from Jane's view and she was whirled backwards into the most consuming, the most frequent, the most wholly unrequited longing of her later childhood: that Mr Knightley should appear, mounted on his black horse Brutus, leading the mare Doucette, and say, "Come, Jane, come with me," and that then, riding at his side over Highbury Common, she should hear him utter the words, already heard a hundred, a thousand times in reverie, in fantasy: "Jane, will you be my wife?"

Vain dream!

Very seriously she turned to Frank Churchill and said, "But, Mr Churchill, you *must* know better than to ask such a question! All the fairy-tales tell us that if we utter our wish aloud, the bad Fates will intervene to prevent its being granted."

"I had not given you credit for so much waywardness, dear Miss Fairfax! Just now you would have me understand that you were the most rational of young ladies!"

She looked thoughtfully at her gloved hands.

"Even the most rational among us entertain *one* private superstition, I believe. Why, Colonel Campbell himself, the most level-headed of men, has a strong distaste for driving an equipage drawn by a black horse with one white sock. You may smile, but so it is!"

"I would not dream of smiling," he replied (though his features belied his words), "I, too, have the great aversion to such an animal and would never allow one in my stable. But now, Miss Fairfax, as we are at the end of our journey — " for the carriages were pulling up outside the Royal Hotel — "may I solicit the honour of your hand for two dances this evening — perhaps the first two country dances?"

Resolved on the immediate implementation of her plan for behaving more friendly to Mr Churchill, Jane at once accepted his offer, and they said a temporary farewell.

Chapter 7

To the annoyance and dismay of Rachel, who had many things she wished to discuss with Jane, and to the politely concealed boredom of Rachel's mother, Charlotte and Lady Selsea came round to call at York Buildings that very afternoon, and the ladies all sat together for upwards of an hour.

Lady Selsea had much to tell her sister about the company at Lord Fortuneswell's, the conversation, the excursions, the music, the cards, the violent detestation between Fortuneswell's wife and his sister, the old-fashioned notions of his mother, the reprehensible habits of his son " — the merest puppy, sister, I can assure you that dear Charlotte very quickly saw through the falsity of *his* pretensions and flirtatious looks!" — and the tiresome affectations and fine airs of his two daughters. "Just because their grandfather was a duke they seemed to think they had a right to behave towards my poor Charlotte as if she were a stupid nobody!"

"Indeed?" said Mrs Campbell, raising her brows. "I wonder you care to visit a house where, it seems, you can have so little cause for enjoyment."

"Well, but, sister, it is the most elegant establishment in the south country, and half the ton was there; one would be thought quite singular to stay away from such a party."

Meanwhile Charlotte, her small blue eyes fastening sharply on every detail of her cousin's unimpressive toilette, was in a perfect spate of communication with Rachel, who sat listening with a look of mingled distaste and incomprehension on her face.

Both visiting ladies, of course, wholly ignored Jane, who remained silent in a corner, wishing heartily that she might remove herself to another room and practise "Robin Adair" (Matt's favourite song) on the rented pianoforte which the Colonel's kindness had procured for the girls.

When the visit was concluding — "And shall we look forward

to seeing you again this evening at the Assembly, sister?" said Lady Selsea.

"My dear Lady Selsea, not on any account," responded her sister gladly. "I assure you, I have better things to do with my time. But I believe that James will be there, for he thinks it his duty to escort the girls, and our mother, of course, and Mrs Consett."

"Ah yes — Mamma — how does she go on?" inquired Lady Selsea, who had up to this moment shown no particular solicitude as to the health or whereabouts of her parent.

"She has struck up a friendship with Mrs Churchill, and they are at present trying out the new hot-sea-water douche. No doubt she will tell you all about it tonight."

With effusive farewells for sister and cousin, and the slightest of token bows for Jane, the visitors departed.

"Charlotte really is a d-d-detestable p-person," burst out Rachel, as soon as she and Jane were alone in their chamber. "D-Do you know, she collects *p-proposals?* She says she has had f-fifteen offers already, and shows no m-more true f-feeling about them than if they were a box full of shoe-roses!"

"Fifteen proposals of *marriage?*" exclaimed Jane in amazement, and when Rachel nodded, "I do not believe it! Or if so, they must have been from very frippery suitors. I cannot think any sensible man would wish to marry her."

"No, she is a s-selfish, cold-hearted girl. Do you know, she was praising the style of my hair (my gown of course she dismissed as beneath contempt) and when I told her that you had done it, and your own also, she seemed taken aback for a moment, and then said, with *s-such* a curl of the lip — 'Oh, then I suppose she can always be sure of a post as a lady's maid! That is, if my uncle does not propose to dower her?' — giving me a most inquisitive glance!"

"What did you say?"

"L-Luckily at that moment my aunt rose to take leave. I merely g-gave her a *look!*"

Jane said with a sigh, "I wish that I *could* obtain a post as lady's maid. I believe it would be much more amusing than teaching spoiled brats. Most ladies get on very comfortably with their maids — well, they have to, after all, or they would be continually pinched and tweaked and sent down to dinner with their hair in a snarl. I should enjoy dressing my ladies elegantly, and arranging their hair in handsome new fashions — for which you must admit I have a decided talent."

She was engaged in dressing Rachel's hair as she talked, setting grape-like clusters of curls on either side, to give added width to Rachel's narrow features, catching up a swathe at the back in an opera-comb. Rachel had begged for this style, which was much in vogue at the moment, but Jane did not privately think it very becoming to her friend.

"Nobody else will have such a b-bang up fashion," Rachel said contentedly, admiring her bunches of curls in the glass. "It will give me great confidence."

"Rachel! You had better not let Mrs Consett hear you employing such language. You have been talking to the Dixon boys too much."

Rachel laughed. "Perfectly true. Do you know — I could see that Charlotte envies us our friends. I think th-that was why she was so anxious to make sure that we would be at the Assembly."

"Because she wishes to make sure that Matt and Sam and Frank Churchill are there also — oh, *Rachel*! Do you think she hopes to add our friends to her list of declarations?"

The two girls stared at one another in dismay.

"What a d-disgusting notion!" said Rachel. But then she laughed. "S-Still, I think our friends would have more sense."

"Perhaps we had best warn them to make their declarations to her at once, without delay, so as to be done with them," agreed Jane. "Which muslin shall you wear — the tamboured, or the jaconet?"

"The tamboured — the green with a tiny silver thread. Will that do?"

"Your favourite — very elegant!" Jane assured her. "Something tells me that your cousin Charlotte will be far too fine, grossly overdressed, in order to show us poor dowds the proper style for ladies who associate with dukes' daughters."

"N-Now I am afraid you are not d-displaying a proper spirit of charity!"

Lady Selsea and her daughter had remained talking so long that the girls were obliged to scramble through their dressing, and, even so, dinner was late, which put the Colonel, who had a military passion for punctuality, into one of his bad tempers. Also the afternoon's drive had set his lame leg to throbbing painfully.

"Speak louder, girl!" he suddenly bawled at Rachel, having failed to catch one of her soft-voiced remarks, which startled her so greatly that she dropped and broke her glass, which a servant had just filled with lemonade, spilling its contents over her green gauze dress.

"Now look what you have done — bungling, clumsy girl!"

"Oh dear — I am so sorry!" gasped Rachel, and Mrs Campbell calmly said, "You will have to change your gown, Rachel; you cannot possibly go to the Assembly dripping like a mermaid!"

"I — I do not mind it. It is of no consequence," protested Rachel, but all the older ladies cried out at the foolhardiness of such an idea.

"To go out in a wet gown! Quite wild! Besides being very improper — giving rise to all manner of ineligible notions about your upbringing."

"Do as your mother bids you!" thundered the Colonel, in such a voice that two drops of dark blood fell on Rachel's plate. Jane, aghast, sprang up.

"Yes, come, Rachel, do — I will help you change very quickly — we shall be back before you have done drinking tea," she promised, seeing the Colonel's furious scowl and glance at the clock. As they fled from the room he sat angrily tapping his gold watch.

"Bring some ice — quickly!" Jane called to one of the maids, swathing her napkin around Rachel's neck; and she persuaded Rachel to lie back in an armchair with ice packed on her nose and forehead while the fastenings of her gown were undone.

"There: it has stopped. And what a mercy there is no blood on your dress — only lemonade, which will wash out. I am sure I read somewhere that to spill water is lucky — perhaps lemonade is luckier still — perhaps it will bring you fifteen offers of marriage like your cousin Charlotte!"

Jane was gabbling at random in order to soothe Rachel who, she could see, was still painfully shocked and startled by her father's outburst, the first of its kind for some time. Tears stood in her eyes, and her hands shook.

"What shall you put on instead of the green?"

"I don't care. It is all one," muttered Rachel, allowing herself, however, to be divested of her sopping petticoats.

"Well then, how about the pink mull and your corals? They bring out the colour in your cheeks." Privately Jane thought this gown more becoming to Rachel than her favourite green, and she swiftly fetched it and fastened the tiny buttons before any objections could be raised.

"Oh, how unfortunate! Now your hair is tumbled, and I fear there will be no time to re-curl all those clusters — "

"It is of no consequence," Rachel said again, listlessly.

"It certainly is of consequence. Your first ball! But there is no sense putting the Colonel in a passion. I know! I will dress it à La Sauvage — I was studying a picture of that in *La Belle Assemblée* while we were waiting for your grandmother in Harvey's Library yesterday, and I know just how it should be done. Then you will look exactly like a Parisienne."

And, sure enough, in very little time, Jane's clever fingers had built up a wild but impressive turret of brown hair on her friend's head, interspersed with plumes and spangles.

"There! No, do not stop to study yourself — you look very stylish — and it is perfectly safe — guaranteed to survive even a country-dance — Charlotte will be green with envy — your coral fan and gloves — come!"

Clasping her friend's hand, Jane made Rachel positively run down the stairs, so that she arrived in the hall with unwonted colour in her cheeks.

The Colonel, hat, gloves and greatcoat already assumed, stood there tapping his foot impatiently, but during the girls' absence he had been obliged to undergo a fairly thorough trimming from his wife as to the thoughtlessness of upsetting his daughter before her first public ball.

"*Just* when we wanted her to be at her best. It was really inconsiderate of you, James!"

And Mrs Fitzroy had weighed in with a whole shower of sweetly barbed conversational darts. Therefore, when the girls reappeared, the Colonel merely remarked, "That is well. Now let us be off," and hurried his party from the house without passing remark upon his daughter's changed appearance, (which, at another time, he might have strongly criticized,) or, indeed, appearing to take it in at all.

The Assembly Rooms, on the first floor of the Royal Hotel, were already beginning to fill when the Campbell party climbed the stairs, and the joyous tuning scrape of strings could be heard. A military band from the regiment quartered at Radipole Barracks was to play.

The large ballroom, brilliant with lights, had as yet only a sparse company scattered over its bare waxed floor, and the older ladies in their satin gowns lost no time in appropriating seats near to the fire. A number of officers in red coats were strolling about, in and out of the card-room, and new arrivals, chaperons with their carefully dressed and adorned charges, continually surged up the stairs. Much to the comfort of Rachel and Jane the Dixon family soon made an appearance, surrounding the Campbells in a friendly group. They were accompanied by Frank Churchill, who came smiling up to Jane, claiming, it seemed, the right of taking on from where their conversation had broken off that afternoon.

"My aunt was not well enough to undergo the fatigue of such an evening; and my uncle remains to keep her company. But they have given me leave to enjoy myself — " with a smile that was half irony, half straightforward anticipation of the evening's pleasures. "May I congratulate you, Miss Fairfax? You have always such an air of elegance, especially when you wear white."

"Why, thank you," she replied, rather inattentively. "But, Mr Churchill, listen, will you render me a service?" — in a low tone, glancing behind her to make certain that both Rachel and Rachel's father were out of earshot, on the other side of the fireplace, talking to Mrs Dixon.

"Of course! Need you ask? Anything that lies within my power." The real kindness underlying his words could not be mistaken.

"Then — if you please — make much of Rachel this evening! She has received *such* a set-down from her father earlier tonight. And her spirits are so very easily overthrown." In a few swift words Jane gave Frank Churchill the history of what had passed. "The Colonel — wretched man — *never* realises how severely he can undermine her confidence. Pray, Mr Churchill, will you do all that is in your power to ensure that she enjoys herself?"

"Trust me, Miss Fairfax! and I shall urge Matt to do likewise; we shall see that she never lacks for a partner. You are a good friend, Miss Fairfax!"

He bowed, raising her hand to his lips with a sparkling look of complicity. Then he was threading his way through the crowd near the fireplace, to the side of Rachel, who, with the leaping firelight illuminating her rose-coloured gown and piled bright-brown hair, was not at all aware of the interested glances that she was eliciting from strangers as well as friends. Frank spoke a few words to her, Jane saw her give him a pleased, friendly nod, and, the orchestra at that moment striking up, a set began forming, and Frank Churchill led Rachel out on to the floor. Matt Dixon at the same moment approached Jane and asked for the favour of her hand.

"Thank you! I shall be most happy!" she told him with truth. "How is your brother this evening?"

"Well enough, as you see, to be here, but not well enough to dance. He will keep my mother company. He has charged me to inform you that you resemble Finuala, the daughter of Lir; which I am sure I have no need to do, as you must know it already."

"Indeed I do not! Who was Finuala?"

"She was a sea-nymph, daughter of a sea-god; and she was changed to a swan."

Jane thanked him inattentively, as they took their places; the music was making her feet tingle with the wish to be dancing. But, as they were about to begin, they were halted by a disagreeable voice in Jane's ear. It was that of Mr Gillender.

"Hey-dey, Miss? How is this? I thought you and I were engaged to dance together? Here was I, firmly believing that we were bespoke, and now I see you stand up with somebody else! Did I not ask you this afternoon, out by that damned dull lake?"

"Yes, sir, you asked me," replied Jane coolly, "but at the time it was not expected that our party would attend the ball, and if you recall, I did not accept your kind offer."

"Well, upon my soul, that's calm! Now here am I, high and dry for lack of a partner! For Miss Selsea is dancing with Dalrymple — "

"I am sure, sir, the master of ceremonies will soon introduce you to any number of eligible young ladies."

"No such young ladies as I find tolerable!"

Fortunately the demands of the dance now removed Jane and her partner from Mr Gillender's vicinity; but throughout the two dances he kept reappearing at her elbow, from time to time, in the most unwelcome manner, and breaking into her conversation with Matt, who, though in general good-humoured, exclaimed when at last Mr Gillender took himself off into the card-room, "That is a most pestilential fellow! At Cambridge he was thought to be clever, but I could never see it. I always found him a dead bore."

"Oh, so you have known him at Cambridge?"

"A very little." A shade of discomfort seemed at that moment to pass over Matt's face, but it was gone so fast that Jane thought she might have imagined it.

"Do tell me some more about your home in Ireland," she said. "I have such a curiosity to hear about it. The local people sound so very delightful."

And eagerly, as they danced, he continued to do so. Jane presently observed Charlotte, with an expression of strong displeasure on her countenance, not far removed from them in the set. Jane she wholly ignored, but bestowed a gracious smile upon her partner when they passed one another in the set.

"Charlotte is not at all pleased with us," murmured Rachel some time later as they stood getting breath back after the first two dances.

"Well it is not our fault that she arrived too late to lead off the first set! And she can hardly complain about her partner! Is not that Lord Felix Dalrymple?"

"Yes — but do not you think him very puny and disagreeable-looking? He asked me to dance, but I was very happy to be able to tell him that I am engaged throughout the evening."

Indeed Rachel, to her own astonishment, found that she was positively the belle of the ball, her hand being eagerly sought by many who had observed her dancing with Frank Churchill; she danced and danced, her cheeks pink, her eyes shining; while Frank and Matt kept vigilant, though unobtrusive watch to make sure that she was never, at any time, neglected or left without a partner.

Jane herself had quite as much success as she could wish, dancing nearly every dance and receiving a number of compliments, the majority of which she privately thought very silly.

"It was hard luck upon Charlotte," she told Rachel at supper when they sat with the boys, "that your dress is so much prettier than hers, since they are both of the same colour. But hers is too bright."

"You were right in prophesying that it would be overtrimmed! I heard Grandmamma telling her that she should remove all that floss and spangled fringe; it made her like a Punch-and-Judy show, Grandma said. Poor Charlotte!"

It was certainly, for Charlotte, a new and disagreeable experience that her insipid prettiness should, for the length of an evening, be outshone by her plain cousin's unpredictable beauty; and she bore it ill.

"Where in the world did you pick up that notion of doing your hair, Rachel?" she disagreeably demanded, when they were all drinking orgeat in the tea-room. "It resembles nothing so much as a heron's-nest. Oh! I suppose Miss — thing — did it for you?"

"The style is called La Sauvage, and is all the crack in Paris at present," Mrs Fitzroy told her tartly. "It becomes Rachel very well. James! This so-called orgeat is nothing but weak barley-water. Can you not procure us some tea?"

The Colonel grumpily did so, then retired to the card-room, where he had spent most of the evening.

After the tea interval there were two more dances. Frank Churchill, as before, danced with Rachel, and Matt, ignoring a beckoning glance from Charlotte, asked Jane if she would again be his partner.

"With pleasure, sir!" — evading a hopeful officer just approaching.

Fortunately the disgruntled Mr Gillender had departed, as he threatened to do, earlier in the evening "to take himself to a gaming hell" whispered Frank; and Robert Selsea had retired to the card-room to play cassino. After two dances with Jane he had announced his intention of standing up with her again later, but she was relieved at his failure to do so, for she found his conversation, which was entirely about terriers and rat-hunting, singularly dull and, at times, almost incomprehensible.

"Well, girls? Did you enjoy the ball?" inquired Mrs Campbell, rousing herself from heaps of Parliamentary reports to receive a glass of negus from her husband. With a little surprise she eyed Rachel's flushed, animated countenance.

"Oh, yes, Mamma! It was very p-pleasant — was it not, Jane?"

"Rachel had a splendid success!" Jane told Mrs Campbell. "She was the cynosure of all eyes. Was it not so, Colonel Campbell?"

"Why yes — I suppose so — that is, she did not appear to lack for partners — "

But the Colonel, like his mother-in-law, was in a state of acute suffering from tired feet, aching leg, and rheumatic joints; he could not wait to escape to bed. Mrs Fitzroy, in like state, merely said that Charlotte Selsea looked a sight; the girl had no more dress-sense than a Hottentot.

"I shall hear all about it in the morning," promised Mrs Campbell.

In the morning, however, she received by the mail such an

exceedingly gloomy report on the working conditions of mantua-makers that she had no leisure to bestow on her daughter.

But directly after breakfast Charlotte and her brother came round from the White Hart Inn.

"We have arranged a party to Corfe. Come along! These affairs are no fun unless there are plenty of people — numbers are everything. We have your friends the Dixons — and Mr Churchill — and several more. Come along!"

Very reluctantly, Jane and Rachel were obliged to join the excursion. Indeed, during the next week they found themselves continually in the company of Charlotte Selsea and her brother; not from any wish of being so but because, without open discourtesy, there seemed no way to evade these unwelcome incomers. Charlotte and her brother and friend indefatigably arranged picnics, promenades, sightseeing excursions, bathing parties; it seemed plain that the two males followed this programme because that was their chosen way of leading their lives, in continual pursuit of amusement; they must be entertained, even if it bored them. Charlotte, it was equally evident, was after more definite game. On all of their outings, Matt Dixon was her escort; she rode at his side, sat by him on rocks or fallen trees, peered through the telescope he held for her, searched for shells and fossils with him, picked wild-flowers with him. And all the time she continually talked to him in her flat chirping little monotone, telling him tales of doings in high society; amazingly dull, insipid tales they seemed to Jane, if she should chance to overhear a phrase or two, but Matt listened as if entranced.

She has put a spell on him, Jane thought. She has bewitched him.

Rachel seemed utterly stricken at the defection of her dear friend; so much that Jane did not dare discuss the matter with her. It was too painful. She grew pale, and much thinner; her appetite declined; her stammer returned.

"Make haste!" cried Charlotte, coming in one morning before breakfast was done. "There is no time to be lost! We are all going to Abbotsbury and the Chesil Bank. Robert has bespoken a carriage for you at the hotel, and he will drive you; I daresay your companion-lady will not object to sitting bodkin? Or perhaps Miss Fairfax may prefer to remain behind?"

"Going to Abbotsbury? Pray, whom do you mean by 'we all'?" dourly demanded the Colonel. His niece airily replied,

"Oh, Robert and I, and Tom Gillender, and your friends the

Dixons and their mother and Mr Churchill. Matt and Tom and Mr Churchill ride, and Mr Sam Dixon drives his mother."

"I should prefer to ride also," said Rachel with some glint of spirit, but her father told her to put any such notion out of her mind.

"All the way to Abbotsbury? It is five miles at least, very likely six. And the weather most unpromising. And *I* certainly do not find myself well enough to accompany you; my hip today plagues me abominably — "

It was plain that he was within a hair's breadth of forbidding the whole outing and Jane, who had a curiosity to see Abbotsbury and the Chesil Bank, said quickly,

"Perhaps Mrs Campbell may herself like to take part in the excursion? I have heard her express an interest in old monastic foundations."

Mrs Campbell decried any such wish, however. "If Mrs Dixon and Mrs Consett ride with the young people I see no occasion for my presence;" and she returned to her reading.

Jane noticed with interest that Charlotte today wore a new and dashing riding costume, blue velvet, in better taste than her usual dress; also her hair, piled under a feathered shako, was in a style copied from that of Rachel at the Assembly.

"Well, M-Mamma, what d-do you say? Sh-Shall we go?" Rachel asked dispiritedly.

"Oh, by all means, dear child, if you wish it. But do not linger too long. The Grants dine with us, if you recall; it would not do for you to be late for dinner. And you and Jane had better put on warmer gowns; the wind freshens."

"Oh, do not let them stay to dress up, or I daresay they will be hours prinking and pranking!" struck in Robert. "A warm pelisse or a wrap apiece will be all they need. There will be rugs in the carriages, I daresay."

In the event, Rachel drove with her cousins, while Jane and Mrs Consett squeezed in with Mrs Dixon and her younger son. The other gentlemen rode on horseback.

Jane was happy to see Sam Dixon looking rather better, and congratulated him on feeling well enough for the outing, after a week spent indoors. She always felt comfortable with Sam Dixon; he had inherited his mother's easy lack of ceremony and simple unaffected goodness. And the journey was entirely delightful: for a considerable part of it, they were bowling along a ridge road, high above the sea, which gave a magnificent view of Chesil Beach, that remarkable shingle bank, sixteen miles long, extending in an unbroken curve from Abbotsbury to Portland, with a lagoon on its inner side.

"I should not wonder, though, if the weather worsened," said Mrs Dixon, her tone a little less carefree than it had been at the start of the trip. "See how the waves whiten. We must make sure not to remain too long in Abbotsbury. I do not trust those feathery strips of cloud along there to the west."

"Mamma is a famous weather-diviner," Sam said teasingly. "The elders in Baly-Craig always defer to her opinion if there is any dispute. But let us hope that this time her anxieties are unjustified."

Abbotsbury, with its wide main street, raised footpaths, and thatched cottages, was pronounced completely charming, and a luncheon was bespoken at a modest inn; after this refreshment the party strolled about inspecting the swan-lake, the ancient remains of the Abbey, the immense tithe-barn, and the chapel of St Nicholas. The group had dispersed in twos and threes while exploring; Jane remained with Mrs Dixon and her younger son.

While his mother was inspecting some stained glass in the chapel — "What a contrast, is there not," Sam said to Jane, "between Rachel and her cousin. They are not at all alike, are they? There is so much sincerity and candour about Rachel — whereas, although Miss Selsea converses with great ease and chatters very amusingly, I do not find her straightforward. There is a lack of true spontaneity."

"Yes," agreed Jane slowly, "I know what you mean. I suppose it is the result of upbringing. Rachel has spent her life in all kinds of wild places, while her father was on active service, and so had no chance of mixing with clever society people; she has retained a kind of simplicity which I suppose is rare in adults. Whereas her cousin has from an early age lived in the midst of London society."

"Very true! And here we see the results."

Jane liked him the better in that he did not then go on to disparage Charlotte Selsea; instead he praised Rachel, speaking of her in terms of such gentle warmth that Jane, with a queer pang, thought, Sam loves Rachel! He loves her deeply! Oh dear, I wonder if she is aware of this? Poor fellow! He is such a good, kind person!

— Somehow, although she had a great kindness towards Sam, indeed, felt more warmly towards him than almost anybody else she knew, she could not imagine any very prosperous outcome for this love of his. She was certain that Rachel, though fond of him, felt towards him only as a friend.

Yet, she thought, after all, what do I really know about him? Or about Rachel? Why exercise my spirits over two people who should be perfectly capable of conducting their own affairs?

And she paid heed, instead, to Mrs Dixon, who, having inspected the reredos and a plaster tunnel-vault, strolled out of the chapel and said bluntly, "Miss Fairfax, how much longer do these Selseas remain in Weymouth? I own that I *cannot* take to Miss Selsea. She seems a vain, heartless kind of girl, and a designing coquette. How very different from dear Rachel!"

"I do not believe they will stay here very long," said Jane. "They will soon have had enough of Weymouth. They are used to a more entertaining society."

"My son Matt seems hugely taken with her."

"He finds her talk amusing. She knows so many prominent people in London society."

"Knows! Hah! She has heard each of them utter one *bon mot* at a party — or has heard somebody else who has done so! All her gossip comes at second-hand!"

Jane reflected that this was probably true. "Yet she brings it out with such an air of confidence. One cannot but be entertained."

"*I* can!" said Mrs Dixon. "Speak for yourself, Miss Fairfax. Though I notice she never addresses herself to you."

"Oh no, I am far below her notice."

"Well," said Mrs Dixon, her pleasant brow creased with unwonted dislike and disapproval, "I wish she may soon find some likelier prey than my son Matt. — Why not Frank Churchill? He will be heir to a considerable fortune, they say."

"Oh, ma'am, but Mr Churchill is just the sort of gentleman that Miss Selsea has been accustomed to meet — a young London society gentleman, polite, cheerful, agreeable. But Mr Matt Dixon is so much *more* than that. Miss Selsea has probably never come into contact with such a mind in her life!"

"Miss Fairfax, you are a shrewd one!" cried Mrs Dixon, turning on Jane a look of remarkable friendliness and intelligence. "They do think well of him at Cambridge. So you can understand my concern about him — my estimate of his value."

"Indeed I do, ma'am. But I am sure that because — because Mr

Dixon is so far above the lady in real worth of character and — and intelligence — he will not for long be deluded by her apparent charm."

At this moment they were disconcerted by the sudden onset of a shower: large cold drops of rain commencing to fall on them with most unwelcome heaviness and frequency.

"Lord bless me, how very unfortunate! Now, what are we to do? Miss Fairfax, you and Sam had best hurry back to the inn; I know that you, too, are subject to bad colds. And to get a wetting is the very worst thing in the world for my poor boy," cried Mrs Dixon, casting her eyes about for Matt and Miss Selsea, who had last been seen climbing over a stile between two cottages. "Now, where are those others gone? Oh, Mr Churchill — " to Frank, now encountered with an umbrella, gallantly escorting Rachel in the direction of the hostelry — "will you, pray, go in search of my son Matt and Miss Charlotte? We must leave for Weymouth at once, without delay, before the storm worsens; it has come on very much faster than was to have been expected — " casting a harassed and disapproving glance at the heavens, which were indeed very black and threatening.

Frank obligingly gave over his umbrella to Sam.

"I think I know just where the others are to be found: there is a ruin or small chapel on that eminence over there, and they were last seen posting in its direction; Miss Selsea expressed a wish to see it. I will summon them."

The ladies returned with Sam to the inn, which, fortunately, was only a few steps farther along the street. There they found Mrs Consett, leisurely taking a cup of tea, and commissioned with the message that Mr Gillender and Mr Selsea had ridden off (Robert Selsea appropriating Frank Churchill's hired horse for the purpose) in order to attend what they had been informed would be a famous cock-fight at the village of Sherton Abbas inland.

"Well! Upon my word!" exclaimed Mrs Dixon with some indignation. "That's cool! Poor Mr Churchill! How is he supposed to return to Weymouth?"

"Mr Selsea said he might have his turn at driving the ladies."

The two errant young gentlemen had been gone at least twenty minutes, so there was nothing to be done but wait in the parlour for the rest of the party to make their appearance. Rachel was pale and silent. She sat staring at the rain streaming down the windowpanes. Mrs Dixon became increasingly anxious about her son Sam.

"To be obliged to drive back in this downpour! It is above all things unfortunate! I would suggest that you remain here at the inn overnight, my dear boy, but the bedrooms all seem to be wretchedly damp; you would take just as much harm from the beds here, I daresay, as from the storm."

"Oh, beyond doubt! Besides the fact that I have not the least wish to remain overnight in this rustic spot!" said Sam with an affectionate smile for his mother's worries. "In any case, ma'am, you forget that I shall be needed as a driver."

"But where in the world can those others be?" fretted his mother.

It was yet another twenty minutes before the trio made their appearance; Charlotte, it seemed, continually in quest of "a better prospect" had persuaded Matt farther and farther along the ridge beyond the chapel, and Frank had been obliged to walk nearly a mile before he caught up with them. The young lady, sheltered by the umbrella, was cheerful and reasonably dry, whereas both young gentlemen were tolerably wet, and Matt appeared in decidedly low spirits, though Frank Churchill, talkative and gay as usual, took with equanimity the news that his rented horse had been commandeered and that it would be his task to drive some of the ladies back to Weymouth.

As the storm continued unabated and showed no sign of lessening, it was thought best to set off, Sam driving Charlotte and Rachel in the carriage that was supplied with a hood, and Frank in charge of Jane and the two older ladies, all the females and Sam being protected by such additional wraps and umbrellas as the inn was able to provide.

The journey was a silent one, the lashing downpour rendering it impossible for the travellers to see any of the coastal view which had delighted them on the outward trip; while the spirits of all were quenched by the sharp drop in temperature and lamentable change in the weather; and those of Mrs Dixon, in particular, afflicted by much self-blame in ever having agreed to the outing.

Chapter 8

Charlotte came hastening round to see her cousin next morning. The storm had raged all night, but dropped with daybreak, and although great white breakers still rolled in commandingly all round the bay, a bright sun shone on wet pavements and on the beach, piled high with driftwood and weed.

"What, are you all still frowsting indoors?" cried Charlotte exultingly. She seemed in particularly high spirits. "Why, Tom and Robert and I have been out this hour! They are outside. Half the town is on the Esplanade. Will you not join us, with your friends?"

Mrs Campbell, who had heard with great disapproval how, on the previous afternoon, Charlotte's lack of thought for others had subjected the rest of the party to prolonged and hazardous exposure to the weather, greeted Charlotte coldly and expressed the hope that no excursions to far-distant hilltops were under consideration today?

"No, ma'am, no," returned Charlotte, quite indifferent to her aunt's unwelcoming demeanour. "Tom and Robert and I are out enjoying the sight of the surf this fine day, and hoped that my cousin might accompany us; and the Mr Dixons and Mr Churchill if they are here?"

Her face fell when informed that the latter gentlemen were not at present under the Campbells' roof, but, soon recovering her spirits, she exclaimed,

"There! I had made certain they must be here, since they are not abroad. However it's of no consequence! Do, pray, get your bonnet, Rachel. I daresay they will soon join us if we are all seen walking in a party together."

Mrs Campbell offering no objection to this, if Mrs Consett accompanied the girls (Jane's company had not, of course, been requested by Charlotte, but Rachel said, "You'll come, will you not, Jane?" to Charlotte's evident chagrin) the young ladies ran to put on bonnets and pelisses, for the wind was still blustery.

The young ladies with hats on joined the young gentlemen (who had been throwing pebbles to disturb a flock of gulls in dispute over the carcass of a large fish on the beach) and the whole party turned to walk southwards towards the older part of the town, the two cousins ahead with Rachel (Charlotte continually casting her eyes about in search of the missing gentlemen) while Jane found herself in the rear, accompanied by Mr Gillender and Mrs Consett. The latter was no walker, for her elegant nankeen half-boots, a size too small, gave her continual discomfort, and she lagged farther and farther behind. Jane was in no hurry to commence a conversation, for she had long ago formed a very low opinion of Mr Gillender's tastes and mental attainments; but she was perfectly content to enjoy the fresh sea breeze and admire the spectacle of the great white waves casting themselves in majesty upon the sand. Her mind, moreover, was greatly preoccupied by thoughts of the Dixon brothers: a deep anxiety about Sam, and a hope that their absence from the sea-front this morning was not caused by yesterday's experiences. Rachel had related to Jane, with strong indignation, after they arrived home, how Charlotte had, on the return journey, by her continued complaints and lamentations, obliged Sam to give her almost all his own protective coverings, and the umbrella which was the only screen he had from the downpour, "although," said Rachel disgustedly, "she had quite enough wraps of her own already and is in any case as s-strong as a m-mule. I only hope the poor boy has not taken a terrible chill."

"So, Miss Fairfax," began Mr Gillender, after some ten minutes of strolling, "is not this a fine sort of morning? 'Pon honour, who would have reckoned it would turn out so bright last night when Selsea and I were slogging it back from that cock-fight — which, by the by, turned out to be a confounded hum, the most cursedly shabby affair, not worth going five minutes out of one's way for, nor spending sixpence to see; it was a most wretched take-in."

Politeness obliged Jane to offer a few words of sympathy for the young man's disappointment, though in truth she felt how much better it would have been if they had remained with their party, returned home at a reasonable hour, and not deprived Frank Churchill of his horse.

However her reply seemed to delight Mr Gillender, who turned to her with a wide, red-faced grin, and exclaimed, " 'Pon my word, Miss Jane, you and I appear to think alike upon just about everything in the world! Do we not — hey? Have you not observed it? Why, the other day, when you made some devilish clever remark about France, I said to myself, That young lady has took the very words out of my mouth! 'Pon honour, it was so! I never in all my life encountered a gal who had such a knack of knowing what I might be about to say, and then saying it first! It is the most famous thing! Upon my soul, I begin to believe we was made for one another; I do indeed!" And, before she could prevent him, the young gentleman was pouring into Jane's startled ears a fervent proposal of marriage, couched in the most immoderate language: "He was sure, upon his soul he was, that she was the finest creature in Dorset; hang it! for all he knew, in the whole world; for handsome looks, cleverness, ladylike ways, and amiable disposition, her equal was not to be found in the kingdom, no, by G — it wasn't; so he had told Robert, over and over, and so he proposed to tell the Colonel, that grand, good-hearted old fellow, just as soon as they returned from the promenade. Yes! by Joseph, before the day was out, he hoped to have the Colonel's consent to the knot being tied, and then, by Jove! the whole town should know it, soldiers, sailors, and fishermen too for all he cared!"

"Stop a minute, stop a minute, pray, Mr Gillender!" cried Jane, attempting in vain to stem this torrent of eloquence. "There are two words needed to such a bargain and mine has not been given — nor indeed ever will it — "

"Oh, hang it all, Miss Jane! I know it is the fashion for some young ladies to be pishing and pshawing when they receive a declaration. Charlotte Selsea would not have me for she has set her sights on nabbing a title (though I'd have thought the name Gillender good enough for anybody; and all the world knows that Sir Adam took the name of Selsea when he came into the baronetcy; it was plain Jones before, and that is why Lady S keeps him in the closet as much as may be, for he ain't too presentable for public show); but, be that as it may, Miss Jane, I'm a plain blunt fellow, as you can see, wooing ain't my strong point. But I did think that a girl of such downright sense as yours would not descend to such a paltry havering. Consider that part despatched, say I — and let us get to brass tacks. What is to keep us from a speedy entry into the married state? Not a thing, that I know of — "

"Then, sir, you are greatly mistaken," said Jane with energy. "I have no mind to marry at present, and I certainly never entertained the least notion of marrying *you*. You will do me the courtesy of abandoning this subject immediately and never alluding to it again."

"Oh, deuce take it, Miss Jane! How can you snub a fellow so? Come now: I know a gal of your looks and spirit will not be teasing a poor fellow for very long; it ain't in nature for you to be so hard-hearted."

"Indeed it *is*, Mr Gillender! I have not the least wish or intention of marrying you, and I beg that you will put the notion out of your head, at once and entirely. Nor can I conceive why you should ever have imagined that we think alike upon *any* topic: so far as my observation has gone I should say that our tastes were utterly dissimilar."

Having thus administered what she hoped would serve as a crushing and final set-down, Jane walked ahead at a rapid pace to catch up with Rachel and her cousins; but Mr Gillender accompanied her, apparently not a whit discouraged, and cheerfully promising to "speak to the old gentleman before the day was out."

Not choosing to pay him the compliment of rational remonstrance any more, for she began to be convinced that he was simple in his wits, Jane gladly joined the others, who had paused to admire the prowess of a group of fishing vessels that took advantage of a favouring shift of wind to put out from harbour, despite the high seas.

"Lord! Don't they bounce, though!" cried Robert. "I tell you, those sailors are fine fellows to venture out in such cockleshell craft. I say — what a prime lark it would be to hire one of those vessels and enjoy a day on the water! We could sail to Lyme, or to Poole — how about it, ladies? Are you game for such a spree?"

Charlotte cried out upon her brother that it was by far too stormy, they should all be drowned for sure, and very likely become most villainously ill besides.

"Oh, lord! I don't mean today; but one of these days, tomorrow perhaps, or Thursday; the wind will soon drop, to be sure, and one must find something to do in this dead-alive hole. What do you say, Tom?"

Mr Gillender gave his enthusiastic endorsement to the proposal, and Charlotte then recollecting that the Dixon brothers were reputed to be fine sailors, coming as they did from the coast of Cork, famous for its inlets and estuaries, began to be more interested in the project. "But not for several days; not until the weather had entirely settled."

Rachel and Jane cast one another glances of dismay; both had hoped that the Selseas might not prolong their visit beyond a couple more nights. But these words seemed to propose a longer period of residence. Neither Rachel nor Jane, with recent memories of a long sea-voyage from the Indies, had the slightest wish for any unnecessary excursion upon the water. But the rest of the party canvassed the suggestion for many minutes and it ended by Robert's promising to seek out "an old sailor fellow, a capital old tar whom I encountered down by the waterside; he will readily put me in the way of securing a suitable vessel whenever we wish it, within the crack of a whip, I daresay."

At this moment Mrs Consett joined them, full of news; she had encountered an acquaintance from Harvey's Library who told her that poor Mr Dixon the younger was taken shockingly unwell, having contracted a severe chill after yesterday's misadventures. "His poor mother very distressed; but she hopes it will soon pass over."

"We m-must go round to their house at once and inquire about him!" declared Rachel, much agitated. "Oh, p-poor Mrs Dixon! How sorry she must feel that they ever t-took part in yesterday's excursion. Come, Jane — "

Jane was very willing, and Charlotte said that she would accompany her cousin. But the gentlemen had other plans: Robert recollected an engagement to go and inspect an excellent little gig which he had thoughts of buying. "For it is such a bore to be stuck here with nothing but hired affairs, or my mother's old wreck of a carriage, and this is as neat a little rig as one could wish — trunk, sword-case, splashboard, lamps, and the fellow asks only sixty guineas and I daresay I can beat him down to fifty — will you come, Tom?"

Mr Gillender went off with him forthwith, any recollection of his extraordinary proposal to Jane having, apparently, been banished from his head by this new interest. Jane, much relieved, hoped that she would hear no more of the matter.

The ladies turned towards the old town. But Charlotte and Mrs Consett proceeded in a very dawdling manner, stopping at every corner to speak to acquaintances or look into the shop windows that contained articles of wear. Rachel, many yards ahead with Jane, found the opportunity to say to her friend, with strong indignation:

"Jane, d-do you know *why* Charlotte p-persuaded Matt to walk with her such a very long way yesterday? It was b-because, she said, she was 's-screwing him up to the point of m-making an offer!' Is not that abominable?" Her voice shook with outrage; there were tears in her eyes.

Jane, too, felt a grievous pang: part anger, part pure sorrow. That Matt, so good, so brilliant, sincere, candid, full of courage and poetry, should be subjugated, like any common man, by the wiles of such a shoddy little *intrigueuse* was pitiful indeed.

"And — and did he then make the offer — did Charlotte say?" Jane's voice was not quite steady.

"No — thank heavens! Charlotte was very cross — laughably so, if it had not been such an odious matter — Frank Churchill came hallooing after them, she said, just before she had *wound him up to the sticking-point!*"

"But I suppose," said Jane despondently, "there is nothing to prevent his coming back to that point at some future time."

"Charlotte will certainly not wish to be defrauded of her sixteenth offer. She will do her utmost to procure another opportunity. But what a s-strange creature she is, Jane! I said to her, 'Charlotte, what is the p-pleasure, what s-satisfaction can you find in extracting offers from m-men that you have no intention of accepting?' And she answered, 'Oh, lord, my dear creature, what else is there to t-talk to men *about* — unless they are m-making love? Everything else about them is so d-devilish d-dull!' and then she added, 'B-But, as to that, I have a very good m-mind to accept Matt Dixon. After all, he will be Lord K-Kilfinane by and by. Lady Kilfinane sounds well enough!' And, Jane, she *meant* it! Oh, Jane — what sh-shall I d-do if Charlotte marries Matt?"

The unmistakable note of anguish and desolation in Rachel's voice was like a cold hand clutched about Jane's heart. She stopped and looked at her friend. The two tears that stood in Rachel's eyes came out and rolled down her pale cheeks.

"*Oh, Rachel!* Oh, my dear girl!"

"I love him," Rachel said simply. "I think I always have. And I always shall."

"Then," said Jane, with an assumed brisk cheerfulness which she was very far from feeling, "we must place all our hopes on the fact that Matt is far too sensible a creature to be taken-in by Charlotte for long. It can be no more with him than a mere temporary infatuation."

"Yes," said Rachel forlornly, "but if he offers and she accepts him while he is s-still infatuated, then he is lost indeed! For she will never let him go; and Matt is by far too honourable to ask for his release."

Jane's silence acknowledged that this must be so.

The two girls stood for many minutes by the waterside, oblivious to the cries of oysterwomen and the rattle of rowlocks, watching the ferryboat slowly pull towards them, while Jane, mindless of the lively scene before her, admitted in the privacy of her own heart the wretched fact that now, for the first time in their lives, Rachel's interest and her own were in conflict.

For she, too, loved Matt Dixon. The morning's disclosures had made this all too plain to her: first, her astonished, instantaneous rejection of the preposterous Mr Gillender — and then the double pang of anguish with which she had received the news of Matt's interrupted offer to Charlotte and Rachel's misery about it.

So! Jane told herself angrily. You are in a fine fix, and must scold yourself out of it as best you can. For it seems horridly probable that Matt may fall prey to Charlotte's wiles; and — should he have the luck to escape Charlotte — if, by any miraculous chance, he were to turn his attentions in your direction, how could your conscience ever allow you to bring about the total ruin of Rachel's hopes?

There was not the least prospect that some other suitor might come and oust the image of Matt from Rachel's heart; Jane knew this by instinct. Rachel was faithful; where she loved once, she would love for ever. Secret hopes which had been forming in Jane's mind regarding the relations between Rachel and Frank Churchill were now entirely scotched. And, Jane could not help admitting to herself, Rachel and Matt would be very well suited. If only . . .

Just in time, Charlotte and Mrs Consett came hastening up, as the ferryboat nudged its lip against the quayside step; and all four ladies were rowed across the harbour to Trinity Road. There Mrs Dixon received Rachel and Jane very kindly, but her demeanour towards Charlotte was decidedly uncordial; either maternal instinct or Sam's own unguarded revelations had evidently informed her as to Charlotte's selfish behaviour on the return journey yesterday. And she had no cheerful news for the inquirers: the surgeon had called twice, last night and again this morning — a very excellent man, thank heaven, one who had even been honoured by attendance on His Majesty while resident in Weymouth — but he detected a putrid tendency in the disorder; Sam was heavy, restless, and feverish, his pulse low and rapid; at times he was alarmingly active but somewhat disordered in mind; at others he fell into a heavy stupor. No, he most certainly could not be visited, said Mrs Dixon — coldly answering a question of Charlotte's — his brother was sitting with him and must be held excused from coming down; Matt was the only one who, by brotherly attachment and sheer force of personality, could oblige the patient to keep quiet when he rambled and threw himself about.

"Oh, d-dear ma'am, I am so v-very sorry," Rachel said miserably. "If only we had not g-gone on that unlucky excursion. I wish a th-thousand thousand times that we had never set out!"

"Do not be blaming yourself too severely, my dear; I was in equal fault," her hostess assured her sadly. "I rode along too, and enjoyed myself as much as any of you young ones. And we must hope the dear boy will soon throw it off."

"Is there anything that we can bring — anything that we can do for you?" eagerly inquired Jane.

No, the neighbours had all been very kind, exceptionally kind; there was really nothing at present. If there should be, she would be sure to let them know. And pray give her love to dear Colonel and Mrs Campbell.

The latter would be so very sorry to hear about poor Mr Sam, Mrs Consett said, and the party then took their leave, for Mrs Dixon's restless eye, continually roving to the stair, reminded them that she was on tenterhooks to be with her son.

"*Well*!" said Charlotte rather peevishly, when they were all out on the harbour-front once more. "Brotherly affection is all very fine, but I think Matt Dixon might just as well have stepped downstairs to see us! I am sure Robert would have done as much if *I* had been abed."

Nobody disputed this statement.

"It is all very provoking," continued Charlotte, "for now I daresay Matt will, through some exaggerated notions of family duty, feel obliged to keep close to the sickroom — where, as a man, he cannot be of any real use — just when we require his company for our water-party, and — and a hundred other things. It is most vexatious. I have no patience with such selfishness."

And she continued fulminating in this manner as they re-crossed the harbour, despite the remonstrances of Mrs Consett, who observed that such an example of brotherly devotion was truly Christian; nobody could expect Mr Matt Dixon to form one of a party of pleasure while his brother was seriously unwell; and, she furthermore inquired, what *was* this projected water-party, and was Miss Selsea quite sure that Lady Selsea knew and approved of it?

"Oh, stuff!" cried Charlotte, as the ferryboat again reached the northern jetty, "why should Mamma raise any objection? It is but to put out for a few hours in one of the fisher-people's boats — not the least harm in the world. Here are my brother Robert and Mr Gillender, ma'am, who will tell you the same."

For indeed the two young gentlemen were once again to be observed, though whether waiting for the ladies or merely lounging about among the other idlers on the quay, it might be hard to determine.

It seemed that the excellent little gig had turned out a complete disappointment: "No such thing, a most paltry little turn-out, not a sound strip of metal nor plank of wood in the whole construction, rickety as an oysterwife's basket, fit only to be driven by some old parson; and, to make matters worst of all, the miserly curmudgeon would not reduce his price of sixty guineas by a single penny. Not a penny, I assure you! though I told him any fool could see it was ready to fall apart if it were driven above five mile an hour."

The young men, therefore, who had planned a trip to Corfe Castle in the new acquisition, were at a loose end, and glad to rejoin the females. It was proposed that they should all walk to the wishing-well at Upwey. Frank Churchill, who appeared at that moment, having escorted his aunt to the hot bath and back to her residence, was enthusiastic for this project. "He had heard so much about the wishing well and had so many urgent wishes, he could not wait to try its efficacy." Poor Mrs Consett appeared far less happy at the prospect of a two-mile walk, but, luckily for her, Lady Selsea was now to be seen taking the air in a donkey-carriage; she agreed to join the young people and offered to take Mrs Consett up into her equipage, while her children and their friends walked alongside.

Mr Gillender again seized the chance of walking by Jane, who, to deter him from any repetition of his unwelcome offer, immediately began to tell him about poor Sam Dixon's serious condition.

He did not appear to be much moved by the tale, but wagged his head solemnly and said that Sam Dixon was a sad, sickly sort of fellow; the present malady would doubtless carry him off.

"Indeed, I hope not!" said Jane, shocked at such a callous view.

"And, as for the elder brother, I think nothing of him. At Cambridge they said he was brilliant, but I could not see it. You never found him at cock-fighting or any manly kind of sport. True, he lost a great deal at the races — I heard he was shockingly dipped there — "

"What?" cried Jane, who could hardly believe her ears.

"Oh, to be sure, I believe he still owes Bob Selsea some hundreds. And that ain't gentlemanly, you know; a fellow should pay his debts, even if it means borrowing from somebody else — "

Jane, to escape this terribly unwelcome communication, stepped away from Mr Gillender. Rachel was walking with Charlotte and Frank Churchill; she seemed content enough. To keep Mr Gillender at a distance, Jane positioned herself by the two ladies in the donkey-carriage, where she could listen to their desultory conversation or not as she pleased; they paid less heed to her than they might to a floating seagull.

She had much to occupy her mind. Anxieties about Sam Dixon and about Rachel — and now this new one about Matt — there played an almost equal part.

Jane had talked on several occasions with Mrs Dixon and was party to that lady's well-grounded fears about her delicate younger son; this present crisis must be a severe test of his frail constitution. And then, Rachel! For some time it had seemed to Jane happily possible that the friendship between Sam and Rachel, comfortable, teasing, brotherly, sisterly, might grow to something deeper and more enduring. But one instant, listening to the tones in Rachel's voice as she spoke of Matt, had been enough to abolish that hope at a stroke.

Lastly, with a kind of wry despair, Jane considered her own shattered hopes. As a child — and, indeed, into her teens — she had nourished a romantic, impossible vision of Mr Knightley leading her to the altar. She had *known* this to be impossible, with her sober, workaday mind, and yet her inner fantasizing self persisted in spinning stories of how Mr Knightley rescued her from some predicament: found her on Donwell Common with a sprained ankle; defended her from hostile gypsies; snatched her from the path of a runaway horse; and then proceeded to confess his secret but unquenchable passion, in words as well-chosen as they were brief, sincere, and heartfelt . . .

She had often laughed at her own nonsense, but had continued to spin the stories. In the end, as she grew older and wiser, she had almost succeeded in laughing herself out of the habit; but her success, she now wincingly acknowledged, was because recently she had wondered, had suspected, had faint, but hopeful reason to believe that Matt Dixon was interested in her, was not insensible to her looks, her ways, her habits of thought, her attainments. He had talked to her so unguardedly, so pleasantly, in his warm Irish voice, on many evenings, their minds seemed to move together like birds in flight, with ease, with comradeship. They had sung and played together, their taste in music according so well. Matt was such an exceptional creature! Words from poor Mr Gillender's absurd proposal came back to her: "the finest creature in Dorset — for all he knew, in the whole wide world! — " that might certainly be said of Matt Dixon. — The news of his debts was certainly a shock, a blow — but that must have been from youthful, hot-headed excesses during his first year in Cambridge, no doubt; he seemed steady enough now . . . Once having known Matt, who could possibly take an interest in any other man, be he never so well-disposed? Other men's interests were so trivial, their ideas so idle and shallow. — And again Jane's thoughts turned to Mr Gillender: what in the world could have possessed him to declare himself in such a fashion? So early in the day he could hardly be the worse for liquor — what could have incited him to act so? For Lady Selsea and her children made no attempt to conceal their low estimate of Rachel's friend; they behaved to Jane as if she were some kind of upper servant. And hitherto young Mr Gillender had tended to follow their example. What new impulse could have possessed him?

At that moment Jane caught Lady Selsea's eye, and received a frowning glance, a repelling gesture.

"Miss Fairfax, pray do not walk so close; you fidget the donkeys. Rather, go and tell my daughter Miss Selsea, if you please, that she *must* open her parasol or she will come out all over freckles; and Rachel would do well to observe the same precaution — not that

Rachel appears to trouble herself about such things," Lady Selsea added to Mrs Consett, who shook her head in agreement.

Jane, thus hinted away, increased her pace and conveyed the desired mandate to Charlotte, who tossed her head, more at the messenger than the message, but consented to unfold her parasol.

The group ahead, while following the line of the shore, had had its numbers augmented by the addition of two more young men, friends of Robert Selsea; now a general re-shuffle of partners took place; Jane found herself walking with Frank Churchill, an arrangement perfectly agreeable to her, since, though there had never been any especial friendship between them, he was at all times so cheerful and well-mannered that his company must never fail to please, unless one were in desperately miserable spirits. Just now he was extremely welcome.

Jane courteously inquired if he had recently heard from his father, Mr Weston, and if there were any news of Highbury; at once his face lit up.

"Why yes, Miss Fairfax! I have but this morning received tidings which, to me, must be of the most surpassing interest, and since it relates very much to Highbury also, I am sure that you will soon be receiving the same news from your own correspondents there; but I am happy to have the gratification of being first in the field."

Jane looked her eager interest.

"Anything relating to dear Highbury must, you know, Mr Churchill, be of the closest and dearest importance to me; do, pray, tell what has happened?"

"My father is going to be married! As you may know, Miss Fairfax, a year or two back he bought the Randalls estate outside the village, and has been building his house and improving his property; now that his schemes are almost perfected he has lost no time in selecting a chatelaine for the property; and whom do you think he has chosen?"

Jane quickly cast her mind over the various eligible females of Highbury: the Misses Cox — Miss Otway, Miss Caroline Otway, Miss Bickerton — one wild notion did cross her mind, but that was soon dismissed —

"Upon my word, Mr Churchill, your riddle is too difficult for me! I have not the least notion in the world, and can only beseech you not to keep me in suspense."

"It is a Miss Taylor!" he said in triumph. "Are you acquainted with a Miss Taylor?"

"*Miss Taylor?* Gracious heavens! You mean," said Jane, almost doubting her own words, "you mean the Miss Taylor who has for many years been governess and companion to Miss Emma Woodhouse?"

"Yes, that, I am told, is the lady. I have not, of course, had the pleasure of meeting her myself, having, to my own shame let it be said, never set foot in Highbury. But I have it from my father's own pen that Miss Taylor is the peak of perfection — kind, gentle, remarkably well-informed, with a most pleasing sense of humour, the patience of any Griselda, and, best of all, a true attachment to my father, who, I must say, deserves to be the guardian of all these virtues, for he is the kindest, most good-natured man alive. So is not this a fine piece of news?"

"It is indeed," said Jane warmly, "and I am very happy for Mr Weston and sincerely wish him well. If there is any man worthy of such a piece of fortune, it is your father. And I am able to endorse all the good things that he has said about Miss Taylor, for I have known her since I was six. — But I am afraid the news will not be received with such joy in the Woodhouse family; I suspect that old Mr Woodhouse and his daughter Emma will miss the company of their friend most severely."

"Oh, well," said Frank with easy indifference, "it is in the nature of governesses to move on at intervals from family to family, is it not?"

Jane agreed with a slight chill at her heart that this was the case.

"But here," he continued, "they will not be losing the lady to any great distance, after all. She may still be a neighbour and friend. And what a pleasure to lose her so nobly — not to another period of servitude, but to an establishment of her own, a very handsome establishment, and to a strongly attached husband. They must be hard-hearted people if they begrudge her such a future. — Not being acquainted with the Woodhouse family, I cannot, of course, presume to pronounce upon their attitude to this event."

Jane assured him that Mr Woodhouse was a most benevolent old gentleman, and that Miss Woodhouse might be depended on to behave with grace at all times.

"How old is she?"

"My age. She will soon be twenty-one."

"Oh well — then she has no more need for a governess. I tell you, Miss Fairfax," exclaimed Mr Churchill, "this news finally decides me. For some reason, I have never found it easy to obtain my guardians' permission to visit Highbury; one objection or another has always been raised; I hardly know, myself, how it has come about that I have never set foot there, but now the time has come when I must break this embargo. Do you not agree? It is high time that I made my way thither, and a wedding visit would make an excellent pretext for so doing. My guardians could hardly take exception to that, would you think?"

Very warmly, Jane agreed that she could see no reason why the Churchills should forbid such a natural visit. "Why not attend the wedding itself?"

But at that Frank did shake his head doubtfully.

"My aunt, Miss Fairfax, is full of very strong pride, the Churchill pride. I make no attempt to defend it; to me it is a puzzle; I inherit from my good father a republican streak and a lack of proper pride which has often been the despair of my friends. I am as happy talking with a drover as with a duke. — But when my mother, who died at my birth, married Captain Weston, as he was then, the Churchills felt that she had made a hideous misalliance, and cast her off. And the breach formed then has never wholly healed. I fear that when they learn that my father, on his remarriage, is allying himself with a *Miss Taylor* — a governess — their estimate of him will only be reinforced."

Jane could only feel sorry for the young man, brought up in what seemed to her such wrong-headed and unpleasant surroundings.

"Oddly enough," he went on, "I understand that Miss Taylor is a distant connection of Lady Selsea's husband Sir Adam — whose name, you may be aware, had been Jones before his ennoblement." Jane shook her head. "But that, I am afraid, would not endear her any more to my aunt."

Jane had no comment to offer, and they walked for some distance in a comfortable, friendly silence. Their path now lay over a sandy ridge, and the small hamlet of Upwey could be seen not far ahead, in a declivity among a group of trees.

Mr Churchill then, glancing about him, apparently to ensure that he would be unheard, which was the case, for they were removed by several hundred yards from any of their companions, said,

"Miss Fairfax, I am a little troubled in mind about a matter relating to your friend Miss Campbell. May I confide it to you? For I believe your good sense will be able to decide whether any action should be taken, and, if so, what."

"Of course, please do confide in me, Mr Churchill," Jane answered, in some surprise. "Anything that relates to Miss Campbell must be of concern to me — though I am quite at a loss to imagine what the problem may be."

"It is a matter of gossip," said he. "Gossip which is bandied about among such frippery fellows as Gillender and Wisbech and Frome at the Assembly Rooms and coffee houses. Yes, you may well look astonished! But rest assured it is no questionable behaviour on the part of your friend that has called forth such talk, merely a rumour, originating nobody knows where: this has it that Mrs Fitzroy possesses a fabulous collection of jewels which she is bound, by entail, to bequeath to the first of her granddaughters to marry."

"Good heavens!" exclaimed Jane. "What a farrago! Mrs Fitzroy (I need hardly say) has never taken *me* into her confidence about her property, but it has long since been understood in the family that her resources are slender — which was why she was obliged to take up residence with Colonel Campbell in the first place. I would doubt very much if she has more than a few hundred pounds' worth of trinkets; such as she wears are elegant, to be sure, but of no particular value. I wonder who can have started such a tale?"

"Though its origin may be in doubt, there can be none as to its prevalence. It is all over Weymouth, in the clubs and cardhouses. And I am afraid the gentlemen in the clubs are laying odds on the respective chances of the two young ladies, the granddaughters, Miss Campbell and her cousin. It had been thought that Miss Campbell might make a match of it with Mr Dixon. But now Miss Selsea — "

"Good God!" exclaimed Jane. "What a situation!"

But, another group overtaking them at this moment, she was unable to say more, except to ask in a hurried undertone, "Do you think it possible that Miss Selsea has heard this tale? Perhaps from her brother?"

Frank Churchill's expressive nod was all the answer she required.

Chapter 9

The wishing-well at Upwey consisted of a plenteous spring of clear water which gushed, fountain-wise, from an aperture in a fern-fringed rock-face and fell some three or four feet into a basin below, whose sandy floor was liberally besprinkled with offerings, from buttons, ribbon-bows and bent pins to brass rings and half-guinea pieces. The local rector declaimed from time to time in his pulpit against such idolatrous and heathenish practices, but this did nothing to quench the faith of the people round about in the water's efficacy against all known ills, and power to grant wishes for every variety of future happiness. As the spring lay such a pleasant distance from Weymouth, easy walking for an afternoon's promenade, it was a rare summer day that did not see several groups of visitors come on foot to the picturesque spot and make trial of its magical powers.

Today a group of sailors and their female companions had walked out to try the spring's virtues, and there were screams, and laughter, and splashing, and much horse-play; but when this company had tired of the sport and wandered off to the village ale-house, the party of gentry made a more sedate approach.

"Come, now, Miss Selsea," gallantly urged Lord Osbert Wincham, one of Robert's friends who had joined their group, "I understand that it is necessary to drink the water from your cupped hands as it falls from the rock; shall I carry you across? Those tiny boots of yours look far too fine to venture upon the wet, slippery rocks!"

Three flat-topped stepping-stones made a span of the pool but, probably due to the recent rains, they were only just above water-level.

Charlotte gave a little coquettish cry. "Oh! Lord Osbert! I am sure you would drop me! Oh, what shall I do? How can it be approached?"

Frank Churchill, with instant, cheerful address, stepped briskly across the stones, filled his cupped hands with water and, returning, proffered them to Charlotte.

"There, Miss Selsea! You may dip your little finger — or your lips, if you so choose!"

But Charlotte, though she smiled, and thanked, and looked obliged, made such an elaborate business of folding up her parasol and taking a kerchief from her reticule that all the water had drained from Frank's hands before she was ready.

"Oh, dear me! *Now* what is to be done?"

Rachel, with a perfectly blank face, yet contrived to meet Jane's eye as Lord Osbert promptly picked up Miss Selsea and made his way over the rocks, holding the lady so that she might cup a little of the water into her own hand.

"Now you must take a wish, Miss Selsea!"

"O, gracious me! But what must I wish?" She raised her eyes with pretty deference to the gentleman as he set her down safely again upon the bank.

"That must remain a secret or the wish loses its efficacy," pronounced Lord Osbert, who was a tall young man of patrician appearance: that is to say, he had already, at the age of thirty, lost a great deal of hair from the top of his head, and was somewhat deficient in chin. But this deficiency was compensated by a fine nose and a general air of assurance, hardly justified, Jane privately thought, by the gentleman's intellectual endowments.

Charlotte closed her eyes tight, smiling.

Meanwhile Lord Osbert's friend Mr Carlisle had assisted Rachel, by himself chivalrously striding knee-deep through the pool while he supported her progress across the slippery rocks; she drank a little water, laughed, coughed, and with his help returned safely to dry land again.

"Now you, Miss Fairfax!" cried Mr Gillender, who had contrived to place himself at Jane's side. "Allow me to carry you — pray let me be of service!"

"There is not the least need for that, thank you," said Jane, and expeditiously got herself over the stones and back before he could intervene. Sipping the teaspoonful of cold spring water in her palm, she closed her eyes tightly, and thought: *Rachel. My wish is for Rachel.* May I never stand in the way of her happiness.

"Why, Miss Fairfax!" cried Mrs Consett censoriously — the

two ladies in the donkey-carriage had arrived while the wishing ceremony was in process — "look, you have allowed your petticoat to dip in the pool and now it is most shockingly wet!"

Mr Gillender exclaimed with concern: should he run to the inn, procure a cloak, a blanket, what could he do, how could he be of aid?

Jane assured him calmly that it was nothing, the weather was warm and windy, it would dry fast enough on the walk home. She could see that the two older ladies observed with great disapproval this passage between her and the gentleman; she stepped away from him and went to Rachel, who stood at some distance from the group.

"Did you make a good wish?"

Rachel's smile was sufficient answer.

"The best in the world. For a friend."

"Mine too."

"I think mine is already beginning to operate," said Rachel, glancing to where Charlotte was permitting Lord Osbert to dry her hands with his kerchief. "I think, thank heaven, that Matt's star is on the wane already."

"Assisted in its decline by the sum of thirty thousand a year."

"Now, Jane, you are being spiteful."

"No; merely realistic."

Jane reflected that however much Miss Selsea may have been attracted by Matt Dixon's real worth, real charm, she must know that she had little hope of securing him while his brother lay seriously ill; if she believed the absurd rumour about the jewels — or if she merely wished to be the victor in this matrimonial contest, speed was a more important factor than the satisfaction of winning her cousin's beau, and Lord Osbert might offer a safer prospect.

On the way home, Jane again found Frank Churchill at her side. She was pleased: first, because his company kept Mr Gillender at a distance; secondly because she had had time to reflect on the piece of gossip he had given her.

"Mr Churchill: I have been thinking much about what you told me."

"The gems?" he murmured.

"The same. And, while I am almost certain there can be no truth in the story, and it has simply been circulated by some idle mischief-maker, yet I think it would be much better *not* to inform

— my friend — the other lady." He nodded, with a look full of intelligence. "It would do nothing but distress and embarrass her. As matters stand, she has little enough confidence; to be aware of such an odious circumstance as that *wagers* are being laid would cast her utterly down. And to what purpose? If the story were true, she would not be interested in such an inheritance. I have often heard her declare how little sympathy she has for — for the older lady's interest in dress and adornment. Let her keep her peace of mind."

"I am glad that is your opinion," said Mr Churchill. "And I entirely agree. You are a good friend, I think, Miss Fairfax."

"I hope — I try to be," said Jane, thinking of her wish at the pool. "What I *will* do, I think, is to tell Colonel Campbell. He should certainly know. And he may know what proper steps to take."

"Are you sure that he will not believe Miss Campbell should be informed? Or scold her about it? He is not very clear-headed where she is concerned."

"No he is not," agreed Jane, liking Frank the better for his accurate assessment of this relationship. "But he will sometimes listen to me; I hope I can make him see reason."

Jane's intention to ask for an interview with the Colonel that evening was forestalled by his sending for her; she found him in the small apartment which he had pre-empted as his study.

"Miss Fairfax, I have a communication to make to you of which you can possibly guess the import." He seemed half annoyed, half amused. "I hope — I trust — that you will find it neither embarrassing nor distressing."

"Does it refer to Mr Gillender, sir?"

He nodded.

"I hoped," Jane said, "that I had given him sufficient discouragement so that he would not be applying to you. He is not at all a sensible young man. I must apologise for your trouble, sir."

"You will not be bothered by him any more. — But I am sorry about this, Jane," said the Colonel, and he did look, she now observed, both cast-down and vexed. "The reason *why* you were annoyed by his foolish attentions in the first place was, I have discovered, because of a rumour, apparently circulating about this town, that I intend to dower you on equal terms with Rachel; that I have the sum of twelve thousand pounds to bestow on you, also, at your marriage. With all my heart I am sorry it cannot be so, my dear. *No one* is sorrier than I; if I had the money to spare it should freely be given. But — as you know — I have not. And when Mr Gillender heard this news, his change of aspect was laughable to see. He now reckons that he has made a thorough fool of himself, and I should not wonder if he has already left Weymouth, rather than risk seeing you again, or the friends to whom he has probably been boasting of his conquest."

"I see," said Jane.

She could not help feeling somewhat stung and mortified, though she had herself wondered if something of the kind lay behind Mr Gillender's attentions.

"Do not let this disturb you, my dear," added the Colonel kindly. "There are sure to be other suitors, worthier of you, and if one asks who values you as he should, I hope you will have the good sense to accept him."

"Of course, sir. That is to say, if I love him." The Colonel frowned. Jane went on, "And if, and if Rachel is likewise happily settled! I would not be a charge upon you for a day longer than I need; as you know, I have already suggested looking for a situation — "

"No, no; not yet; time enough for that when Rachel has — has established herself," he said quickly.

"But sir — relative to that, there is something you should know — " and Jane put him in possession of the tale about Mrs Fitzroy's legacy.

As she had foreseen, the Colonel was out of all reason vexed and disgusted.

"*Just* like my mother-in-law to have such a tale circulating about her. And not a word of truth in it," he muttered to himself. "I wonder if the other rumour had also stemmed from her?"

"Fortunately Rachel herself knows nothing of the matter; and — and I think should *not* know; it would destroy any confidence she has been gaining here," Jane said with all the force she could command, for she could see that his first impulse was to call the females of his house together and give them a great scold.

"Very well — no, I daresay you are right," he agreed gloomily. "Perhaps we should quit Weymouth — "

"Oh, sir! When it has done Rachel so much good? And — and we could hardly leave the Dixons just now, when poor Mr Sam is so ill — "

"That devilish Charlotte," muttered Colonel Campbell. "All our troubles seem to lie at her door. And I heard from Captain Curtis some discreditable tale of Charlotte and her brother involved in bargaining for smuggled French lace — "

Nothing more likely, Jane thought. But if Charlotte managed to land Lord Osbert, her need for smuggled lace would surely be at an end?

The Colonel was continuing to smoulder.

"What is this scheme I hear from Robert — hiring a boat, sailing to Lyme? It sounds a most ill-considered plan," he pronounced.

Here, Jane could only agree. She assured him that neither she nor Rachel had any interest in such an excursion, nor the least wish to join it; at which the Colonel, lacking the spur of opposition, began to consider that, after all, perhaps there might be no harm in the project, provided some steady-headed older person were on board.

"Mrs Consett tells us that she suffers dreadfully on the water, sir; and Mrs Dixon, naturally, will not leave the bedside of her son; and Lady Selsea is not at all fond of water-parties; but if either yourself or Mrs Campbell — ?"

"Well, we shall see; we shall see."

For another week, no pleasure parties could be under consideration by any friends of the Dixons; Sam continued terribly unwell and none of those to whom he was dear would have wished to take part in such schemes. But at last he was pronounced out of danger, and if some hectic symptoms, which had established themselves on the departure of the fever, imbued his physician with deeper misgivings as to the final outcome, these were not immediately communicated to the mother and brother.

"He is sitting up; he is able to eat a little gruel, Rachel," Mrs Dixon said with tears in her eyes. "Oh, I am the happiest woman in Dorset, I do believe! Of *course* Matt must go with you on a water-party — nothing could do him more good! He has been so wonderful — such a patient nurse to his brother. No woman could have done as much. He certainly deserves a little pleasure and cheerful company, if ever anyone did. But Rachel, my dear girl, I am come down to ask a favour — " Rachel and Jane and Mrs Campbell had called in Trinity Road, and Mrs Dixon had briefly left the sickroom to receive them — "Sam has been thinking of you, has been speaking of you so *continually* during the course of his illness. The name *Rachel, Rachel,* has been for ever on his lips! Would you do him — and me — the great kindness of stepping upstairs for a moment and greeting him? It would mean so much! And the physician assures me there is no risk of infection."

"Of course, ma'am — I shall be only too happy! Dear Sam! I do not believe he can have thought of me more than we have all been thinking of him, wondering how he did, and wishing him well."

She went away with Mrs Dixon, was absent not many minutes, and returned wih her eyes full of tears.

"Oh, Jane! Oh, Mamma!" she burst out, once safely away from the house. "He is so thin and wasted! Hands like claws! And he is so white! Oh, when I think of Charlotte, I could wish her at the bottom of the sea."

Mrs Campbell sighed, but refrained from pointing out that Charlotte's thoughtless and selfish behaviour had, almost certainly, only hastened processes which would have taken place sooner or later even without her intervention.

"My dear, you must take comfort in the fact that your visit was such a pleasure to Sam. Mrs Dixon told me it positively brought colour into his cheeks. I think you should go again, since it does him so much good."

"Oh, I shall! Every day, if his mother allows it!"

Colonel Campbell was not so complaisant about these visits. "What is the use?" he said privily to his wife. "The physician tells Curtis the poor fellow is sinking slowly. It can only be a severe blow to Rachel, and overset her shockingly, when he does go off."

"James! How can you be so callous? So fond as Rachel is of those two boys."

Lady Selsea shook her head over the business when talking with her mother.

"Sitting by a young man's sick-bed! A very queer kind of proceeding! Thank heaven Charlotte was not given to such unladylike behaviour."

But Mrs Fitzroy did not, here, see eye to eye with her elder daughter.

"Your Charlotte, my dear Sophy, had best mind her ways if she wishes to be sure of Wincham. They are a starched, strait-laced lot, those Winchams and Pomfrets; let them get wind of any dealings in *run goods* — or Robert's gaming — and that fellow may sheer off yet, mark my words."

"Oh, nonsense, Mamma, why, he lives in her pocket; he was walking with her all yesterday and asked her to dance three times at the Assembly."

"I hope she did not accept?" With a flash of the older lady's eye.

"Dear me, no! Charlotte knows better than that," replied Lady Selsea calmly.

Colonel Campbell finally gave the water-party his sanction, and even declared his intention of joining it himself "to make certain the young people behaved sensibly and did not get up to any foolish pranks." Whether or not the Colonel's nephew and his friends were grateful for this thought they, at all events, displayed proper obligation, were flattered because the Colonel gave their scheme the favour of his presence, knew that his experience would ensure the success of the excursion, and hardly believed they could have managed without him.

Matt, though still reluctant to leave his brother for so long as a whole day, was firmly ordered off by his mother to refresh his own constitution by sea air and cheerful company.

"I shall do excellently well, with Mrs Campbell, and I do not know how many kind neighbours to sit with me. The dear girls will be so happy to have you on the ship — and here has Mr Robert Selsea been besieging the house daily and asking for you — "

Matt pulled a wry face at the latter information, but went off willingly enough, only bidding his mother send a messenger on horseback to Lyme if she had any anxiety and wished for his return; the hazards of wind and tide made it quite possible that the land journey would be quicker than the sea passage.

Rachel, who had at no time manifested any interest in the water-party, declared, when it came to the day, that she did not wish to go; she had a premonition that one of her nose-bleeds might come on, she felt uneasy, not at all the thing, would prefer to remain quietly at home and sit a while with Sam. No arguments could make her change her mind.

Jane, at this most eagerly declared that she would remain behind and keep Rachel company; she had never been greatly inclined for the trip and her only pleasure in going would have been if Rachel were there; otherwise she had rather not.

"No, dear Jenny, you must go — do, to please me!" said Rachel. "Matt and Frank will be so disappointed if you do not go, and so will Papa! I believe that he has been looking forward to the party and would be sorry to miss it."

So, with great reluctance, Jane allowed herself to be persuaded.

The trip, in fact, fulfilled all her worst expectations, and she could only rejoice for Rachel's sake that the latter had escaped it.

"It was the most miserable day that I have passed in years," she said, laughing and groaning, when safely back at home in the room she shared with Rachel. "Oh, how delicious this lemonade tastes! The sun was abominably hot — there was only one tiny area of shade in the boat, where, of course, Charlotte sat herself down with her parasol, along with Lady Decima Wincham — "

"What is she like, Lady Decima?"

"Very stupid, has not three words to say for herself; needless to say, none of those was addressed to me. No wind blew at all throughout the whole morning, so the boat dawdled beside the same patch of shore, I believe for four hours; and, then, the boat was so very small; at least on the *Thessaly,* coming from the West Indies, we had fair accommodation and a place on deck to sit down; but in this tiny craft there *was* no deck, nothing but coils of rope and great barrels that smelt of fish; Charlotte got a great spot of tar on her skirt and made *such* a commotion; and then, by the time we reached Lyme, it was too late to go ashore, your father insisted we must turn back directly, and of course your cousins were highly displeased at that; so, on the voyage home, everybody was cross, except for Matt and Frank Churchill that is, who behaved beautifully; we all three sang glees and amused ourselves while Charlotte and her friends grumbled and complained."

"And what is this that Papa told me — about Matt having saved your life?" Rachel demanded with eager interest.

Jane laughed and blushed. "Oh, it was nothing! Nothing really! Your father exaggerates. On the way home — the wind had got up by then and the ship was moving quite fast through the waves — Charlotte suddenly gave a loud scream, declaring that water was gushing through a vent-hole and ruining her gown — so she asked me to move quickly and make room for her — I, not realising that the boom was about to swing over — and the ship at that moment giving a great lurch to one side — I suppose I must have slipped — "

"Oh, if I had been there!" cried Rachel. "Though I should have been petrified to see you so nearly swept overboard as Papa says you were — "

"Nonsense! You would doubtless have done just what Matt did, which was to leap forward and grab the folds of my habit — my old blue one, luckily, stitched so strongly by dear Aunt Hetty that it will last till Judgment Day! It was by no stretch of the imagination a romantic rescue. Lady Decima is probably reporting to her mamma the Duchess at this very moment on the shocking lack of lace on my petticoats!"

But Rachel could not see the incident with such levity. "Thank heaven Matt was there!" She gripped Jane's hand tightly.

"Oh, if he had not been, I daresay Frank Churchill would have done me the same service," said Jane, a little uneasily.

After tea that evening both Matt Dixon and Frank Churchill came round to York Buildings to inquire after Rachel's earlier indisposition and whether Jane had suffered any ill-effects from her misadventure. Both young ladies, however, professing themselves quite restored and in good spirits, a walk along the beach was proposed, for the evening that followed such a hot day was remarkably fine, and warm. Colonel and Mrs Campbell were pleased to accompany the girls and their escorts, and the party, pacing slowly back and forth along the Esplanade, was soon joined by several other friends.

After half an hour's strolling Jane found herself, whether by accident or his design she was unable precisely to decide, at some distance from the rest of the party in the company of Matt Dixon, who then, slowing his pace, addressed her in tones of great urgency.

"Miss Fairfax — My dear Miss Fairfax — *Jane!* Is it really true that you suffered no shock, no harm, in today's accident?"

"Upon my honour, Mr Dixon, not the least harm in the world — thanks to your prompt action! For the rest of my life I shall have grateful cause to remember your presence of mind — indeed, but for that, there would have *been* no rest of my life! I am truly sensible of my debt — "

She would have thanked him further, but was deeply alarmed when he interrupted.

"That was nothing — the merest trifle — nothing to what I would wish in future to be able to do for you! Miss Fairfax — Jane — this incident has opened my eyes — I think it cannot have escaped your notice that my feelings for you have lately been increasing to the point where — "

He had gently taken her arm and turned her round so that he might study her countenance in the gathering dusk. But she now interrupted his flow of eager speech by an almost involuntary cry of distress and warning.

"Matt! — Mr Dixon! Oh, pray, *pray* do not say to me what you may later bitterly regret — pray do not — !" He gazed at her in astonishment.

"Why, what can you mean? How could I ever, possibly regret telling you of my warm love and admiration — my respect and devotion? All I ask is — "

"Do not! Do *not*!" she repeated urgently. "Consider those words unsaid! I will forget them — no," she corrected herself, "I cannot, will not, do that, but I will never, never remind you of them — "

"But, Miss Fairfax — my dear Jane — I truly, truly love you! 'Deed and I do!" Under strong emotion the Irish intonation of his voice became more noticeable. I shall remember this moment, Jane thought, for the rest of my days, the way he held me, and the way he spoke.

Involuntarily she closed her eyes for an instant.

"There is nothing in the world I wish more than to make you my — "

"*Listen*, Matt — Mr Dixon! My dear Mr Dixon! Please listen to me. I have valued your friendship very deeply — so deeply that I — that I must take the privilege a sister might to speak to you with absolute honesty. Before you go on to make any proposition to me. — Is it not true that you owe Mr Robert Selsea a large sum of money?"

" — Why, why yes, that is so," Matt answered, after a moment. He sounded shaken and discomposed. "But, but Robert has told me that he is not in any hurry — and what is that to the — "

"No; dear Matt; it *is* to the purpose. I feel so warmly to you —" her voice shook — "that I don't wish you to — to place yourself in a false position — all to no end! Has, by any chance, a rumour reached you that Colonel Campbell purposed to give me a dowry — to bestow a — a sum of money on me at my marriage?"

A long, painful silence followed her question. She drew a deep breath and went on with all the resolution she could muster. "I think I may be right in guessing that it has? From whence such a rumour issued I do not know — though I may guess; but I am able to tell you that it is absolutely groundless. There is no basis to the tale. Kind, fatherly as the Colonel's feelings have always been towards me, he has told me himself that it is out of his power to endow me in that way. When I marry, Mr Dixon, I shall not have a single penny to bring to my husband. The Colonel's fortune must, very properly, go to his own child, and I am glad that it should be so. For I love Rachel like a sister. Now, do you understand me?"

Another long and miserable silence followed. Touching his arm gently, Jane compelled Matt to turn and continue their walk.

"Indeed, dearest Matt, I do feel for you also as a sister," she resumed, after a short while, "and I am very much moved and, and, grateful that you feel these things towards me — that is why I have taken the liberty of speaking to you so. Can you forgive me?"

"Oh, Jane!" She was horribly distressed to discover that he was sobbing. Tears were streaming down his face. Quickly, she drew him down a narrow side street where he paused a moment and leaned his head distractedly against a wall.

"You must think me an utter scoundrel," he muttered. "A low poltroon of a fellow who goes after women simply for their money."

"No, I do not," said Jane, thinking of Charlotte.

"That confounded debt! It has hung over me for two years now. Racing — Newmarket — what a fool I was ever to get involved with such a set. I would never, ever do so again."

"Oh I do hope not, indeed," said Jane warmly.

"But now I am so strapped for cash — if my uncle should discover — then it is goodbye to — "

"Don't despair! *Pray* don't! Surely there must be other ways to raise the money — loans, mortgages — "

"My uncle would be sure to hear of any such measure. He is so stringently against gaming — and the last thing I wish is to distress my mother just now — "

"Is there nothing you could sell? No one you could turn to for advice? Colonel Campbell?"

"Colonel Campbell!" he exclaimed with a groan. And then, recovering himself a little, "Miss Fairfax — Jane — I beg you, do not think too hardly of me! To you I must seem like the most pitiful wretch — but, I assure you — those feelings I spoke of — they are *real*! They come from the deepest level of my heart. Only — I see now — they must be useless — wasted; they can lead nowhere."

"You must not feel that!" she urged him. "True feelings, I believe, are never wasted. They will help you — they will guide you. Oh, trust me, believe me, it must be so — " Her voice was almost choked with tears.

But, with a broken exclamation, he had left her, striding off into the recesses of the old town.

Horribly shaken and discomposed, Jane returned to the Esplanade where, luckily, the dim light enabled her to rejoin Colonel and Mrs Campbell and a group of their friends without her long absence or the perturbation of her countenance being remarked on.

And there, strolling among the others, she was able to review her interview with Matt in such sobriety and sense as she could command; and to feel that, on the whole, and considering the turmoil of her own emotions, she had acquitted herself well.

Which self-congratulation did not prevent her, later that evening, in the room shared with Rachel, from lying awake far into the hours of the morning, both cheeks and pillow soaked with silent, bitter tears.

Chapter 10

Three days later Rachel came to Jane with a troubled look and said,
"Jenny, I must talk with you. I want to ask your advice. Where
can we g-go to be undisturbed?"

"Let us cross the ferry and climb up on to the Mount. Then we
can call in Trinity Road and make inquiries about Sam on our way
home."

A slight cloud appeared to cross Rachel's brow at the mention
of Trinity Road, but she said, "Very well; I will tell Mamma," and in
a few minutes the young ladies were on their way. Both maintained a
silence along the sea-front which was interrupted only by necessary
greetings to friends; and it was not until they had ascended the
steep Nothe headland and were seated on a bench near its summit
that Rachel broke her reserve. Behind them the slit windows of the
fortress peered vigilantly towards France; in front lay the harbour,
full of masts, the great curve of the bay, and the hilly coastline
running eastwards towards Poole.

Rachel said: "Matt has asked me to marry him."

"Oh, Rachel dear! I am so very glad. It is what I had hoped."

Jane was able to bring out her reply with energy because it was
true.

Rachel swung round on the seat and studied her friend sharply,
with close attention.

"*Did* you hope it, Jenny? Did you really do so?"

"With all my heart. You and Matt will be right for one another."

"But what about Charlotte?"

Jane had almost forgotten about Charlotte.

"Oh, that was nothing — a mere butterfly fancy. A year hence
you will both laugh to recall it. It was because she pursued and
teased him so. It will be a salutary lesson — no more."

"But, Jenny, listen: it is not simple, it is complicated. This is the
way it happened. You know I went to see Sam yesterday. And his

mother took me up to his room. He was sitting in the bow window. And, Jenny I — I can see that he will not l-long be with us. His hands are so thin — and his wrists. The light shines through them. He said to m-me — " Rachel's voice quivered — "he said, 'Rachel, I love you dearly. And I once hoped that you would be my wife. But as that cannot happen, it would m-make me very happy if you and Matt were to m-marry. I know Matt loves you very much. And so does my mother. I would s-slip away from this world so peacefully if I knew that you two were going to pass your lives together. Will you please think about this, dear Rachel?'"

"Oh, good God," murmured Jane. Although it was a warm day, she felt a throbbing chill run over her flesh. "So what did you say to him?"

"I said, 'Does Matt know what you are asking?' and he said, 'No. I am not speaking on his instructions. But I know that Matt loves you. I thought I would find out first how you felt. Could you marry him, Rachel?' And I said, 'I don't know, Sam. This is queer. I need to think.' And Mrs Dixon (who was there) said, 'Oh, dear Rachel, do think! Do help my boys if you can!' So I told them both that I would think, and I came away. — Oh, Jenny, what shall I do? I have been thinking about it all night. Why did not Matt himself ask me?"

"He is a humble person — he has a lack of confidence in his own — " But here Jane's voice faded away.

Rachel repeated, "Jenny, what shall I do?"

God help me, thought Jane. She spoke in her strongest voice.

"Do? Why, there can be no question. You marry Matt. He is a sweet, good fellow, and one day he will be a great name. You will marry him — and you will make a very happy marriage of it! His mother loves you — Sam loves you; you are almost part of that family already. I am sure your parents will be overjoyed when you tell them."

"But — but Matt told me he has gaming debts," Rachel said unhappily.

"Well! Your dowry will pay them. And he will avoid gaming from now on."

Will he? Jane wondered. Did he speak the truth when he said, "I would never, ever do so again"? Probably. Young men had to sow a few wild oats. Everybody knew that.

"And — and suppose he flirts with another person — as he did with Charlotte?"

"He did not flirt with Charlotte; she flung herself at him. I think he would always love you best," said Jane firmly. "And, as to the gaming debts, I think — I have a strong feeling that there Matt has learned his lesson. The debts, after all, were contracted several years ago when he was younger, and new to the world. I hope I am right. You will have to wait and see. Matt is not perfect." She paused and drew a breath. "But he is a dear, dear creature, and I am sure you can be very happy together."

"In Baly-Craig?" Rachel said doubtfully. "It is such a long way away. What about — what about my career as a political cartoonist?"

"You will have to wait until your children are grown and then come back to London. By then Matt will be a famous poet and you will have illustrated his poems. Besides drawing a great many mountains and Irish peasants."

"Oh Jane. Are you sure? At one time — not long ago, I thought — I thought that it was you Matt loved. You — you t-take such pleasure t-talking together."

"Of course we do. He will be just like my brother. How could I have borne it if you had married somebody I detested? And," said Jane, looking steadily down the path, "here he comes now. He must have seen us walk past the house. He has come to ask you himself. And I am going to leave you. Mind, now, that you give him a good answer."

She kissed Rachel lightly and started off at speed. Encountering Matt, at the second turn of the path, she told him, "Go and ask her! She is waiting for you," and hurried by, concentrating all her attention on the noble view of cliffs and countryside lying to the north and east of Weymouth town.

When Rachel Campbell and Matt Dixon announced their engagement there was great, if sober rejoicing in both families concerned. Colonel and Mrs Campbell were happy to see their daughter settled with a young man whom they had known and liked for so long; and if, with her twelve thousand, she could have made a more brilliant match in London society, yet, considering her shyness and reserve, and her speech disability, they were glad to know that her future was assured in a family that esteemed her so highly, and would use her so kindly, as the Dixons. Matt's great-uncle, Lord Kilfinane, informed with all speed, returned his approval by post with cautious promises of future assistance and possible augmentation of their income until Matt should succeed to the title and the estates pertaining.

Mrs Dixon had long looked on Rachel almost as a daughter and received her as one with every demonstration of joy; and Sam was filled with silent content.

The single stipulation he made, on hearing of his brother's successful suit, was that the wedding should be soon.

"Otherwise, you know, if I should be taken off suddenly, you would have to wait through a mourning period, and that would be so stupid," he pointed out. "For my sake, dear Matt, dear Rachel, won't you have the knot tied here, now, in Weymouth? Indeed what is there in the world to prevent you?"

And in view of these considerations, as well as Rachel's great aversion to London and horror at the thought of a large fashionable wedding, and Mrs Campbell's dislike of fuss and needless expenditure on fripperies, it was agreed by all the parties concerned that the ceremony should take place as soon and as simply as possible. A date early in October was fixed on, much to the outrage of Mrs Fitzroy who did not see how a proper set of bride-clothes could possibly be assembled in so short a time. "And what about their carriage? And what about their house? And linen? And house-ware and furnishings?"

"But, Mamma, they will be going off to Ireland directly after, to Baly-Craig; it has been decided that they should wait and buy their carriage in Ireland; and the house, you know, is waiting for them there, all complete with furnishings, I daresay."

"Disgraceful! A most paltry business!"

The voices of Lady Selsea and her daughter were not to be heard among the many raised in congratulation. For Charlotte the grapes were sour indeed: Sir Osbert, hearing some word of the French lace transaction, had, as Mrs Fitzroy prophesied, removed himself from the proximity of a young lady who might choose to engage herself in such questionable dealings, and Charlotte was too proud to fall back on his friend Mr Carlisle who had only four thousand a year. Lady Selsea therefore contrived a pressing engagement in Scotland and when Rachel civilly invited her cousin to act as bridesmaid, Charlotte made curt reply that she was unable, for on that date they would be at Lady Clanredesdale's. At the small and unassuming ceremony in St Mary's Church, Jane was Rachel's only attendant.

The single feature of the occasion which transcended the bride's wish for quiet unpretentiousness was an arrangement put in hand by Colonel Campbell's friend Captain Curtis who secretly contrived that the band of the — th Dorset Dragoons should be drawn up outside St Mary's to play the happy couple and their friends back to the Royal Hotel, where the wedding breakfast was to be held.

And this kind thought ended in disaster.

Colonel Campbell with his daughter had ridden to the church in one carriage, Jane, Mrs Campbell and Mrs Fitzroy in a second, the Dixons in a third. On the return journey Rachel, of course, rode with her bridegroom, Jane with Mrs Dixon (Sam had not been well enough to attend the ceremony) and Colonel Campbell was to accompany his wife and mother-in-law. But just after he had handed Mrs Fitzroy into the carriage and stepped in himself, the regimental band broke into such an earsplitting blast on drums, fifes, cornets, and other military instruments that the horse pulling the Colonel's curricle, a young, excitable beast, bolted away up St Mary's Street and on to the sea-front, where the carriage overturned and its occupants were flung into the roadway. The Colonel and his wife escaped with some injuries but Mrs Fitzroy, thrown clear over the balustrade and on to the pebbly beach below, was picked up lifeless.

Naturally such a calamity at once put an end to any thought of celebrations. Poor Rachel had already arrived at the hotel with her husband when informed of the accident; Colonel and Mrs Campbell were carried straight to York Buildings where medical assistance was summoned immediately; and it was discovered that, while Mrs Campbell had escaped with nothing worse than bruises and contusions, the Colonel had a badly broken hip-joint, besides a severe concussion.

So the day that had begun with such joy and promise ended in dismay and total confusion. Rachel insisted that, until her parents were out of danger, she must remain with them, and, Matt and his mother perfectly sympathizing with this filial anxiety, she returned, for the time, to their house, and the Dixons to theirs in Trinity Road, while plans for the journey to Ireland were, for the moment, set aside.

Jane's plans, likewise, received a check.

Before the wedding Rachel had said to her: "Jenny, you *will* come with us to Baly-Craig — will you not? Matt wishes it, I wish it, so much; Papa and Mamma, as you know, are promised to us for a long visit very soon after the wedding; and Mrs Dixon and Sam will come when — when Sam is ready to travel; will you not accompany them? We all want your company so very much. Indeed I do not know how I can manage without you."

But Jane had, with the utmost firmness and tenacity, set her face against all such persuasions, though they were made repeatedly by Rachel and her parents as well as the Dixons. Nothing could sway her. The time had come, she said, when she must make her own way. It had always been agreed that, on reaching the age of twenty-one, or, when Rachel was happily settled in life, she, Jane, must set out upon her allotted career of teaching. And now this moment had arrived. She must delay no further.

The accident had postponed, but only temporarily, this decisive step.

"As soon as your parents are recovered," she told Rachel, "I shall return to London and enrol my name with one of those agencies in Wigmore Street."

"Oh, Jenny!"

"No, Rachel, it must be so. I have waited too long as it is. The day has come."

But the day, as events were to prove, still remained some distance away in the future. The Colonel's injuries took an unexpectedly long time to mend. Strangely enough, while he continued so very unwell, there was nobody so dear, no person so necessary to him as his own daughter. It seemed as if her imminent loss had suddenly awakened him to her value. He complained every time she quitted his chamber and seemed to sense, in some telepathic way, if she ever ventured out of the house to take a walk with her husband. He pined, fretted, and waxed captious and unreasonable unless she were continually by him. Indeed, during this period the relation between father and daughter grew far closer than it had ever been before: Rachel at first performed almost every service for her father; when he was well enough to enjoy it, she read aloud to him untiringly; and the marvel was that, in the occupation of reading to him, her stammer almost completely left her, and returned only at rare intervals thereafter.

Nobody had loved Mrs Fitzroy; nobody felt much grief at her departure; indeed, Rachel, Jane, and the Colonel perceived her absence from the family circle as a positive benefit; she had never attempted to conceal her low opinion of the Colonel or her distrust of Jane and, with advancing years, her temper had only shortened and her prejudices strengthened. Although for Rachel she had at times evinced a kind of waspish, cantankerous preference, this had by no means been reciprocated, and, of the three, it was perhaps Rachel who admitted the greatest relief at her passing. "If only it might have happened sooner; then there need not have been all that dispute about my presentation." "But then we might not have come to Weymouth," argued Jane, "and look how fortunate that proved for you." "Oh, but as soon as I knew that the Dixons were here, I should somehow have contrived to persuade Papa," said Rachel, who, since her marriage, and despite being separated from her husband, had, during the ensuing weeks, acquired a remarkably increased degree of self-confidence; when she did contrive to slip out and spend an hour with Matt, she always returned with pink cheeks and sparkling eyes. Jane, sighing in painful bafflement over her own frustrated and unprofitable emotions, could only wonder if all male attachments were so fleeting and changeable. Matt, with his vehement passion for truth and beauty, his strong notions of right and wrong, had seemed the last person so readily and speedily to transfer his affections from one object to another. — She could not help recalling his tears, his apparent deep distress. Well, there could be no profit in brooding over a state of affairs she had taken pains to bring about; Jane shook off these thoughts when they assailed her, and went to make herself useful to Mrs Campbell, the only member of the family to experience any real sorrow at Mrs Fitzroy's sudden and unexpected demise. Although latterly there had been scant sympathy between the two ladies, the ties of childhood can never be entirely forgotten, and the loss of a parent, however divergent in tastes and habits, must always carry a disquieting impact; furthermore Mrs Campbell remained, for some weeks, too shaken and bruised to resume her normal activities. During this period Jane, by helping with correspondence, making extracts, reading pamphlets aloud, and also by a great deal of sensible affectionate conversation, was able to be of considerable comfort, and to ameliorate the time of confinement.

October, November, and December thus passed away. And on a mournful day in December, the remains of Sam Dixon were laid to rest in the graveyard of St Mary's where the wedding ceremony had taken place. No military band played on this occasion, but the voices of the small congregation were raised in music such as Sam had loved during his lifetime.

Frank Churchill came back to Weymouth for the funeral; his aunt and uncle had, of course, long since returned to London, where they were to remain until February. Mrs Churchill had indeed appeared at the funeral of Mrs Fitzroy (which was considered by many an amazing and distinguished mark of esteem, for Mrs Churchill practically never graced such common occasions with her presence). Jane had studied the great lady with interest as she sat in her carriage but found nothing to admire or wonder at; she was a smallish, very proud-looking personage of uncordial aspect with a sallow complexion, who held herself very upright and looked straight ahead; she was much wrapped up in furs and spoke to no one. Jane sincerely pitied Frank for being under the dominion of such a relative. — But when he returned to Weymouth for Sam's obsequies he spoke of his aunt cheerfully enough.

"She suffers from such continual pain; and I believe she is sincerely fond of me; so I try to bear with her crabbed ways. You and I, Miss Fairfax, have to learn to accept the rough with the smooth; we are both poor orphans and must temper our lamb-like behaviour to the prevailing wind."

Frank had come calling with Matt Dixon the day after Sam's funeral to inquire after the health of the Colonel and, if possible, take the young ladies for an airing on a mild afternoon which seemed more like spring than winter. The Colonel had reluctantly parted with his daughter for an hour and she had availed herself of this sanction to walk with her husband while Frank and Jane strolled together along the deserted shore at a tactful distance behind the married pair.

"So what are your plans now, Miss Fairfax?" Frank presently inquired.

Jane sneezed; the day of the funeral had been wet, and she had become chilled during the graveside proceedings.

"Oh — when they are all gone off to Ireland, I shall seek for a position. And, I suppose, when I have found an eligible one, I shall engage myself."

Her voice showed little enthusiasm for the prospect. She sneezed again. "But first," she added more warmly, "I shall return to Highbury to visit my dear aunt and grandmother. And see all the friends there that I love and esteem so highly. I have not been there for so long! Not since we returned from the Indies. But what of you, Mr Churchill? Have you been to Highbury yet? To visit your father and his new bride?"

He laughed, looking a trifle shame-faced.

"Why — to tell you the truth, Miss Fairfax — and I know not how precisely it has come about — but, believe it or not, one obstacle or another has hitherto prevented my visiting that famed spot! I am really a most conscienceless, discreditable dog! With me it is out of sight, out of mind, I fear! Since I know none of those good people in Highbury, I find it difficult, I think, to take an interest in them. It will be different, I am sure, once I have been there. *You* must show me the way, Miss Fairfax!"

He seemed sincere in his self-denigration, yet Jane could hardly believe that he was quite so shallow or careless as he made out. Had he not, after all, taken the trouble to return to Weymouth for Sam's funeral? And he had seemed sincerely grieved at this death; he had passed several hours yesterday sitting with Mrs Dixon and Matt, condoling, and helping to sort and pack belongings, preparatory to the departure for Baly-Craig. Such was not the behaviour of an insincere or affected man.

"Shall you return to the Campbells' house in Manchester Square?" he next inquired. "When the party have set off for Dublin?"

It had been decided that a sea passage would be less troublesome for the Colonel's mending hip joint than one by land, and the married pair, with Mrs Dixon and Rachel's parents, were now planning to embark from Weymouth, all together, in two weeks' time.

"No, I shall make my way straight to Highbury." Jane sighed, thinking how, when they first travelled down to Weymouth, she had nourished hopes and plans of taking Rachel, on the return journey, to visit her loved friends and relations. "Colonel Campbell, in his kindness, has said that I am to travel post, and has promised me money for the journey."

"And I wish with all my heart that I could escort you," said Frank warmly, "but my aunt, alas, in one of her sudden crotchets, has decided that she must go to Harrogate for the waters, and I am instructed to return tomorrow and bear her company. Poor lady! No amount of experience ever seems to teach her that the air and water of one place will do her no more good than that of another."

"Is she so very ill?"

"Yes," he said soberly. "I am afraid that she is. The rheumatic afflictions are a superficial matter, though they plague her sorely; but her London physician, a very excellent man, has informed my uncle and me that she has a deep-seated malady of the heart which is liable to carry her off without warning at any time; and that, with the best care in the world, she may not be with us for more than a year, or two at the outside. — We therefore indulge her caprices, poor lady — my uncle has more to bear than I do. I, at least, may leave her for short periods — though," he added with a smile, "I do not like to make these too frequent or too prolonged, since I am always certain to find myself in disgrace when I return."

How very lucky I am, Jane thought soberly, that Aunt Hetty and dear Grandmamma are so unfailingly kind and sweet-tempered. I have not had a cross word from either of them, I believe, in the whole of my life. How very different has been my lot from that of Frank Churchill or Rachel! If I am ever inclined to repine at my fate, I should remember that.

She did not feel her good-fortune with such conviction on the afternoon, two weeks later, when, having seen the party aboard in Weymouth harbour and waved her handkerchief so long as the faces were discernible over the rail, she returned to the house in York Buildings, littered with string and scraps of sacking, and all the debris of departure, to pay off the last manservant and await the arrival of her own conveyance.

Bidding goodbye to Rachel had been exceptionally painful. The two girls had embraced each other again and again.

"Oh, Jenny! Oh dear, dear Jenny!" cried Rachel, weeping. "How can I bear to lose you? You *will* come — will you not? — as soon as you possibly can, to visit us at Baly-Craig?"

"Of course she will come, my dear," said the Colonel gruffly. "And will bring a handsome husband along with her, one of these times, I daresay — eh, Jane, my dear? Eh, Matt, my boy?"

Matt was very silent at the parting. He had been silent with Jane, had seldom addressed her except when strictly necessary during the past months — ever since the occasion of his declaration to her. But on the evening before the embarkation he had contrived to waylay her for a moment, as he left York Buildings, and had pressed a little packet into her hands, without a word said.

Later, seizing a rare moment of privacy, she unfolded the paper and found that it was a poem, in Matt's writing:

> *"From this day on*
> *My friend will be the moon*
> *Who many times her light upon us two has thrown.*
>
> *Her stately way*
> *Over the fields of sky*
> *Must pass you too, where'er you chance to stray*
>
> *Since I have lost*
> *The one I love the most*
> *And buy my bread now at such bitter cost*
>
> *O then, dear Artemis*
> *Vouchsafe me only this*
> *Touch my lost friend with your eternal kiss*
>
> *And, as you travel by*
> *Carry my thought across the sky*
> *To Her, in whatsoever bourne she now may lie."*

Jane's first feeling on reading this was indignation. He should not have given it to me, she thought; no, he should not. He is committed to Rachel now and must accept the situation completely. — But then she felt a deep woe, and wondered for the hundredth time if she had done right in encouraging the pair to marry. Would they be happy, off there in Baly-Craig? As for this poem, this paper . . . She snatched a chance, when no one was about, to carry it, torn into tiny pieces, and toss it into the December sea. She had no right to keep it, and it would only bring ill-luck, she felt certain.

"You should kiss Jane goodbye," said Rachel at the parting. "She is your sister now!" But Matt did not do so, nor did he touch her hand.

From Colonel and Mrs Campbell Jane received the affectionate embraces of true parents.

"Write to us every single week," Mrs Campbell said. "I really do not know how we shall contrive without you, Jane. We shall miss you — we shall indeed."

"Remain in Highbury as long as you choose," urged the Colonel. "Stay there to be nursed by your friends and throw off that dismal cold which has so beset you lately. Do not be hurrying yourself, now, into some pitiful position in any niggardly, inferior establishment; you must pick and choose, you know, pick and choose! Wait for the best! Here — " and she found he was hurriedly thrusting into her hand another small packet.

"Oh, sir! You shouldn't! You should not, indeed!" she exclaimed, thinking somewhat wildly of Matt. But *this* one, she later discovered, contained notes amounting to fifty pounds.

"Nonsense! You're a good gel!" the Colonel returned roughly, and strode after the others up the gangway. "Wish I could have done more for you," he called over the rail.

Recalling these farewells later, in the dusty hallway of No 2, York Buildings, with the forlorn, hollow emptiness of the deserted rooms around her, no voice to cheer her solitude, and a small, thick rain falling outside, was it any wonder that Jane should succumb to great despondency of feeling? Or that, thinking herself secure from intrusion, she should sink down upon her trunk, which stood in the hall awaiting collection by the carrier, and abandon herself to a tempest of tears?

She had never felt so lonely in her life.

"Miss Fairfax!" exclaimed a familiar voice. "My dear — my *very* dear Miss Fairfax! Good God! You must not distress yourself like this — alone — when I have a shoulder to offer. Why, you are shivering like an aspen-leaf! You are freezing! Here, let me wrap my greatcoat round you."

Jane, limp and sobbing, offered no resistance. She felt the coat go round her, and a pair of warm, comforting arms.

"Come, lean your head on my shoulder. If you must cry, cry in comfort! What is a friend for? There, let me lend you my handkerchief — yours, I fear, is wholly drenched."

Jane allowed herself the luxury of another burst of tears but, as is often the case, the being given permission to cry ad lib had the effect of drying up the source. She let her head remain in its place for a short while, however, then blew her nose resolutely and, looking up into the solicitous countenance of Frank Churchill, said, "What a poor creature you must think me."

"Indeed I do not! I think — " he checked himself. "Never mind what I think. But what a sad crew of curmudgeons those Campbells and Dixons are, to go off on their ship and leave you so, all alone, to fend for yourself."

"They invited me to go with them. Ever so many times. But I — would not."

"And who's to blame you? I could see how you were situated; *I* could see *that* clearly enough."

Preferring to ignore the implications of this, hoping she misunderstood him, Jane said, "But, Mr Churchill, what are *you* doing here? I thought you had escorted your aunt to Harrogate?"

"And so I should have, but she changed her mind, as she so frequently does. My uncle escorts her to Bath instead. So I snatched the chance to make a detour — I am to meet them there, but came to Weymouth first. How glad I am that I did so! For now I am available to offer myself as companion, attendant, purveyor, friend, whatever you require, until you leave this place. At what time does your carriage come for you?"

"Not until noon."

"Then," said he, "I suggest that we take our way to Harvey's Library. The clouds are lifting; see, the sun begins to shine. I shall buy you a cup of coffee — scandalizing all the gossips of the place, if any remain here — and find you some wonderful novel to amuse you on your journey and distract your sad thoughts. Do you remember how we both laughed over *Mysterious Warnings?* I shall find you another equally mysterious, I promise you!"

Somehow, Jane found herself persuaded into this programme, though she stipulated that she must first wash her face and tidy her hair.

When they had taken coffee together, and he had bought her the novel, besides a bag of sponge-cakes for the journey, at Ryall's, and a beautiful shell with a pearly interior — "So that, sometimes when you look at it, you will remember Weymouth and your friend Frank — " he suggested that they should go and stroll on the Esplanade. Weymouth was almost deserted in this late December season; they had the whole promenade to themselves.

"For I have had a very good, in fact a sovereign idea," Frank said. "And I wish you to give it your earnest and undivided consideration."

Jane, through all his course of small kindlinesses and attentions, had had little to say, despite her gratitude for the comfort; her throat was tired and closed-up from tears; she said nothing now, but followed him passively, walked with him languidly, and leaned obediently beside him on the balustrade when they had followed the curve of the bay to its southernmost end. The waves rolled in roaring, whitecapped, but the sky had cleared to a pale and tender blue.

"Now:" said Frank, "here is my plan. It may very easily have escaped your notice, dear Miss Fairfax, that during these months at Weymouth I have fallen much in love with you, and indeed cherish towards you the very warmest feelings, both of affection and admiration. Circumstanced as I have been, on the edge of your small, happy group, it has been possible for me to observe and understand, perhaps, more clearly than those closer to you, the emotions, the good and beautiful motives that have been prompting you recently on, on several occasions."

Jane opened her mouth to speak but with an uplifted hand he forestalled her.

"Miss Fairfax, I do not ask any questions. I have no wish, none in the world, to be prying or impertinent. I honour you deeply — to me, indeed, you seem like a kind of angel. I almost worship you!"

She tried to speak again, and again he prevented her.

"I *know* that you have no dowry — that Colonel Campbell is unable to help you. I know that! Just as I know," he added irrelevantly, "that you are the most beautiful young lady I have ever seen, and worthy to grace a ducal establishment — even if you have not Mrs Fitzroy's jewels. — Did Miss Campbell get those, on her marriage, by the way?"

"Yes! she did," said Jane laughing, "but they proved to be a very modest collection." He was so odd a mixture of humours that she hardly knew whether to take him seriously.

"Good, I am glad to see you laugh. Too much of this comedy at Weymouth has been played out as high tragedy, and I never like tragedy. I enjoy dancing, dear Miss Fairfax (you are the best dancer I have ever been privileged to lead out) and singing, and piano music, pleasant company, conversation, jokes, and beautiful gardens. Do you not think that we should suit? Do — please — say yes, I beg you! To tell the truth, my heart has been set on you ever since we danced together at that first Assembly when you had done Miss Campbell's hair so cleverly."

"But, Mr Churchill — "

"Now! Do not be raising a whole host of unreasonable objections! Pray take time to think carefully about my offer. You have had, I conjecture, several other offers since you came to Weymouth. But none of them are anything like so eligible as mine! I am very good-tempered, I shall, one day, have command of a handsome fortune, and I love you devotedly. What more could you ask for?"

"I — "

"Yes, there is that," he agreed, without waiting for her to say more. "*You* do not at present love *me*. I am aware of that sad fact. But, dear Miss Fairfax, I am a very well-meaning fellow. And I, on my side, love you most faithfully — do not you think that, given time, you might find it in your kind heart to reciprocate? And — and put out of your heart any other image that might perhaps have taken up lodging there?"

"Perhaps. Perhaps . . . But," said Jane, and now she spoke firmly and resolutely and would not let him stop her, "none of this is to the purpose. We both know, Mr Churchill, that your aunt would never, ever, for one moment, countenance an alliance between you and such a humble, unconnected creature as myself. You know it, and I know it. So how can you, even for one moment, consider it?"

"I am afraid that is quite true," he agreed seriously. "Good, beautiful, gifted as you are, my aunt would see only that you have no great relatives to give you consequence. So — if you are to accept my offer, which I hope with all my heart that you may — we should be obliged to keep our happiness to ourselves."

"A secret engagement, do you mean?" said Jane with distaste.

"There! That is what I love about you!" he exclaimed. "The nail hit on the head every time. No evasions, no circumlocution. Yes, dearest Miss Fairfax, it would mean a secret engagement. I love the idea no better than you, I assure you. I would accept it with joy, nonetheless, since because of it I would feel secure of you. I would not have the agonizing fear of losing you, which has kept me posting back to Weymouth on all possible occasions, always in terror that some other, equally discerning suitor might have anticipated me and snatched the prize from under my nose."

Jane sighed and looked out at the boiling surf. Her expression was very troubled.

"You do not like the idea," he said. "I cannot blame you. But look at it this way, my dear. I — I have good reason to know that at this moment you are lonely and heartsick, that you have lost the family you love (and somebody else besides whom you did not deserve to lose); you have a bleak, uncertain future to face, with no friends and no funds and nowhere of your own to lay your head. Would it not cheer you, in this pass, to know that you *do* have a friend, a secret friend; to know that, instead of the hazardous future, you would, by and by, on the contrary, be sure of a comfortable establishment and a loving companion to share it with you? — And all that is *true*, and *must* come to pass," he ended vehemently. "It is only a matter of waiting with a little patience."

"I *hate* the kind of waiting that depends upon — upon somebody else's misfortune — upon their death," said Jane bluntly.

"You could not do so more than I. And yet we have our own rights too. Do we not? Look," he urged, "let us leave it this way. *I* shall consider myself bound to you — by every tie of honour and devotion. You, on the other hand, may feel free as a bird, so that you need be troubled by no scruples as to — as to the waiting."

"But that would not be fair," she said at once. "If one is bound, the other should be too."

"So you agree!" cried Frank, delighted. "You do agree! You are an angel, and you have the honourable feelings of a queen. And I shall come to Highbury as often as I can, when you are settled there, and, among those good simple people, all those friends whom you love so dearly, and in that rural setting, I shall woo you as warmly as Corydon ever wooed his Phyllida. You shall soon see how constant, how persistent my devotion will be. And for a pledge — " he pulled from his pocket a little box — "as a pledge, dear, dearest Miss Fairfax, will you not accept this?"

The box held a ring, a glint of silver, a tear of opal. "It was my mother's: when young Captain Weston first wooed her, this was all he could afford. Will you keep it for me? Will you wear it round your neck on a ribbon?"

Somehow he had insinuated the box into her hands. "It is very beautiful," she sighed, looking down. "The most beautiful thing."

A mist of tears caused it to shimmer in her vision. One fell into the box.

"I have pressed you too much," said Frank Churchill with remorse. "I have hurried you; I ought not to have thrust myself upon you when you were so wretched and cast down. But I had to take the chance, I could not lose such an opportunity. And I could not bear to leave you so sad and heartsick. Promise me that, at least, you feel a trifle better now; that I have distracted your thoughts just a little?" he ended with his persuasive smile.

She could not help smiling back.

"You know that you have."

"Then I believe that my whole life up to this point has been justified!"

"My coach will soon be arriving," said Jane. "In fact I think I see it there." And she began to hurry towards York Buildings.

Frank Churchill attended her into her conveyance with every care.

"I shall be counting the days until we meet again at Highbury. I shall be counting the hours!"

He held her hand long and warmly.

"Goodbye, Mr Churchill," said Jane, wondering how she could ever have let herself be persuaded into such a wildly untoward course of action, clean contrary to all her sense of right. She feared that, for the sake of present relief, she had rendered herself liable to a future of perpetual agitation and trial.

And yet her heart *was* lighter. He had spoken the truth.

"No, no, not goodbye. Never goodbye!" He had closed the door but left the window open, to exhort her through it. "Till we meet again at Highbury. Let me hear you repeat those words."

"At Highbury, then."

Satisfied, he stepped back; the driver cracked his whip and the horses were at once in motion.

BOOK TWO

After two days' travel, and the intervening night spent at Southampton, Jane reached Highbury in such a state of low spirits and fatigue, and with her cold decidedly worsened, that, after administering hot negus and sandwiches, her fond relatives put her straight to bed, with many lamentations regarding her pallor and thinness.

"Hetty," said Mrs Bates, "the child is as tired as she can be. No talking now."

For once the old lady had her way, and Jane was allowed to sink into the comfort of her own old hammock-shaped mattress in the enfolding luxury of a country silence. But, alas! sleep did not follow so quickly. The future of perpetual agitation and troubled conscience that she had foretold for herself lay in the future no more, but had become the present. Back here in her first home, with the two who loved her most dearly in the world, she found herself hampered by a secret that hung round her neck, along with Frank Churchill's ring, as heavily as any penitential chain. Openness and candor had always been as natural to her as breathing; now they were denied to her.

Next morning Jane insisted that she was well enough to join her aunt and grandmother at breakfast, but they had reason to bewail the smallness of her appetite.

"Only half a slice of bread-and-butter! And our country bread, our country butter is so good, so superior to any that you might procure at Weymouth or London; but we shall soon have you better. We shall indeed! Three whole months at least in Highbury! We never were so long without you before, but three whole months now will make up for that. We shall not know how to make enough of you. All our friends are so rejoiced for us; they will soon be calling themselves — "

The promised friends soon, indeed, began arriving, making their way up the narrow, inconvenient little stairway alongside the barber's shop, and into Mrs Bates's small upstairs front parlour, with its tiny fireplace, window-seat, beaufet, and four prim Windsor chairs. — What will Frank Churchill think when he first sees *this?* was Jane's uncontrollable reaction when plump Mrs Cole and even plumper Mrs Goddard squeezed their way up the stair, with gifts of honey and new-laid eggs, and the whole room seemed crammed with female persons.

"Do you come up too, Mr Knightley!" called Miss Bates out of the casement, seeing him on his horse in the High Street outside. "We have such a pleasant gathering here, Mrs Cole and Mrs Goddard come to congratulate us on having our dear Jane again — "

"Then you will have no room for me," he replied, taking off his hat and bowing. "But pray give Miss Jane Fairfax my kind remembrances and I look forward to seeing her very soon at a time when you have more space withindoors."

Jane caught the tones of his voice and was warmed by the message, but at the same time felt a sorrowful pang. Here was another friend, and a dear and kind friend, to whom her heart could never again be truly open. Nor, even, could her feelings towards him be the same. In the past, she confessed to herself, there had always been that faint bewitching childish hope that some day, some distant future day, he would suddenly reveal that his affections had always been hers — since the time of the riding lessons. But now, even if he did so — and the possibility had certainly grown dimmer in her mind with the accretion of years and common sense — even if he did so, she would be obliged to decline his offers. She was fixed, committed, to another; and another, she could not in her innermost heart deny, of lesser quality than Mr Knightley. Would Mr Knightley ever suggest, ever consent to, a secret engagement? Jane was very certain that he would not. But then, similarly circumstanced, how *would* he behave? Perhaps the comparison was unfair. Mr Knightley was a man of independent fortune, always had been; he was obliged to conciliate nobody. Still, the comparison would recur . . .

"Jane, my dear, your wits are woolgathering," exclaimed her aunt Hetty. "Here is kind Mrs Cole, making you such a generous, obliging offer — "

"Only the other day I was telling Mr Cole that I really am

ashamed to look at our new grand pianoforte in the drawing-room, while I do not know one note from another, and our two little girls, who are but just beginning, perhaps may never make anything of it; you are welcome, my dear, at any hour of the morning or afternoon to come to our house and practise on it to your heart's content; indeed it does seem a shame that you do not have an instrument here — "

"Or, you may come to the school, any afternoon after three, when the girls give over practising," chimed in Mrs Goddard, "though I am obliged to admit that our instrument, due to the continual use it receives, is not of such a quality as one might — "

"I was saying to Mr Cole only yesterday how dreadful it is that poor Jane, who is mistress of music, has not even the pitifullest old spinet in the world to amuse herself with, and he quite agreed — "

Next Mrs Weston arrived, with a gift of some cream cheeses, and Jane looked with renewed interest at this pleasant, fresh-faced lady who had formerly been Emma Woodhouse's governess and was now Frank Churchill's stepmother. And she had not yet met Frank! How strange that was! Jane both dreaded and longed that the conversation might advert to him, to his arrival, or his non-arrival; but it turned, instead, upon Emma Woodhouse and her recent, rather unaccountable friendship with little Harriet Smith.

"I *was* surprised, I must confess, when it first began," Mrs Weston was saying. "Such a difference, you know, in their — in their respective circumstances, and in their mental attainments; but of course for Emma's sake I was very happy; a woman always feels such comfort in the society of one of her own sex. And poor Emma — you know — However Mr Knightley does not agree with me; he feels that the society of such a compliant little creature as Harriet must only increase dear Emma's tendency to lead — "

Jane was listening to this with real interest, but Mrs Cole broke in. "Mr Elton has been calling *very* frequently at Hartfield, has he not? Before Christmas my Lucy — she is niece to Mr Woodhouse's Serle, you know — Lucy said that Mr Elton had been there almost every day! It did seem most particular — but whether — but which young lady he — "

"Oh," struck in Miss Bates, "*I* am not at all quick at those sort of discoveries! What is before me, I see. But I do not conjecture. I am not clever at supposition. Now Jane, here, of course, has never met Mr Elton! — Our new young vicar, you know, Jane dear; he was appointed after the death of our kind Mr Pryor — such a worthy, excellent young man. I am sure any young lady he — At present he is away in Bath, but you will meet him soon enough. So very attentive to your grandmother and me — always insists, you know, on our sitting in the vicarage pew, because of grandmother being a little hard of hearing — "

"Here is Miss Woodhouse, ma'am!" announced Patty up the stairs, and the next moment Emma Woodhouse was among them, looking, Jane had to admit to herself, uncommonly elegant in a fur-trimmed bonnet and pelisse — quite the equal of any of the society ladies at Weymouth. She carried a beautiful plant in a pot.

Mrs Cole reddened, appearing a little conscious, and said that she must really be going; she and Mrs Goddard speedily took themselves away down the stair; but Mrs Weston gave Emma the hearty greeting of old affection, and Emma herself bade Jane welcome back to Highbury with every friendly courtesy and grace. Emma Woodhouse had now, Jane must acknowledge, an appearance that must please any but the severest critic: a pretty height that anybody might think tall, but not too tall; her size perhaps just a fraction plump, but graceful; her complexion bore the exquisite glow and bloom of good health and untroubled temper. Her manner was open, friendly, and conciliating; try as she would, Jane could find no fault with it. She behaved just as she should to the old lady and to Aunt Hetty; asked just the questions she ought about Weymouth, Colonel and Mrs Campbell, Jane's future plans, her present emotions on returning to the place of her birth; acted, in short, so much like a kindly generous friend and neighbour that, when the visit was done, Jane found herself assailed by feelings of guilt and contrition.

"She really is perfectly amiable, simple, and unassuming! I cannot imagine why, all these years, I have been making her into such a monster! She is not to be held responsible for her behaviour at six, just after losing her much-loved mother. And, poor thing, she must be excessively lonely if she finds herself obliged to make friends with such an insipid, dull little creature as I remember that Harriet Smith. Mr Knightley always did want Emma and me to be friends. I will think and act differently towards her, I will indeed, from now on."

But an evening passed at Hartfield two days later reversed these kindly feelings.

"Why does Miss Woodhouse not invite us to dine? Why do we go in *after* dinner?" Jane asked her aunt as they waited for the Hartfield carriage to pick them up.

"Oh! my dear. The Woodhouses very seldom have dinner guests. You know Mr Woodhouse is so — "

"They invite the Westons to dinner. And Mr Knightley. And, I am told, Mr Elton."

"Well: gentlemen are — and Miss Woodhouse knows that we — and ladies, you know, when they are on their own, are — "

In short, thought Jane, ladies on their own must expect lesser consideration. It was an idea that had not, until recently, entered her mind, but must do so more frequently now that she had left the Campbell family and was confronting her own doubtful prospects.

The evening at Hartfield, most regrettably, brought back all Jane's previous antipathetic feelings towards Emma Woodhouse. Former provocations reappeared. Emma's kindly solicitude towards the older ladies could not redeem her other faults. True, tea and coffee were offered repeatedly, and the muffin was handed round twice. But she does that since she knows she owes it to her own consequence, as lady of the house, thought Jane. Not from true open-heartedness.

Mr Knightley was present (had already dined there) and asked for music. The young ladies, both young ladies, played and sang. Emma's conduct, again, appeared impeccable: she praised Jane's performance with taste and discrimination, she asked for more. But it is all hypocrisy, thought Jane. And a kind of wilful self-denigration. She knows, very well, that the standard of her own playing lacks polish; that she could have done far better if she had practised more. She had played some light Scotch and Irish ditties and an overture by Cimarosa. Whereas Jane had played a really difficult set of variations and overture by Pleyel, which was vigorously clapped by her audience, though she suspected that they had not been listening.

Why does Emma not practise more? Jane wondered. She has all the time in the world. What does she *do* with her days? How does she ever get through them? — Here, unexpectedly, like a leaf floating upstream against the current, came a feeling of unbidden pity for Emma. But this vanished with speed when the talk turned to Weymouth. Emma seemed, thought Jane, so very, so *particularly* curious — not to say inquisitorial — about Frank Churchill.

"Was he handsome? Was he agreeable? Had Miss Fairfax known him well? Did he appear a sensible young man, a young man of information? Would he make a pleasant addition to their circle when chance, or his own inclination, at last brought him to Highbury?"

Jane felt there was more than simple neighbourly interest in these deft probings; Emma somehow, by some witchcraft, some prescience of her own, had already, it seemed, fathomed the connection between Jane and Frank; she possessed that kind of instinctive shrewdness, rather than real intellectual power; she would almost certainly be the one to expose their secret and bring it to light.

And when they parted she said laughingly, "You look so beautiful, nowadays, Miss Fairfax, and so elegant, I cannot stop admiring you! Do you remember the days when you wore my old puce-coloured merino pelisse?"

"And your mother left me one hundred pounds," lay unspoken between them; one hundred pounds which still remained intact as an insurance against future exigencies.

Jane could not forgive her.

The gift of a whole fore-quarter of pork from Hartfield next day only deepened the injury. "Now I suppose we shall have to go and thank them yet again," said Jane ungratefully.

"My dear! Indeed we must. A whole quarter. Such bounty! Quite overwhelming. I shall invite the Coles to come and dine off the loin with us — I can do that, you know, on the way back from Hartfield — but first I must run down to ask Patty if we brought the biggest salting-pan with us on our removal from the vicarage — Oh, my dear Jane, will you really go instead? — that is so very obliging of you — "

A knock at the door and the delivery of a note from Mrs Cole changed the direction of Aunt Hetty's thought.

"Why! Good gracious me! Mr Elton is to be married! Only listen to this! Mrs Cole writes to me — Mr Cole having just the moment before informed her, upon receipt of a letter from Mr Elton — he is engaged to a Miss Hawkins of Bath — well! I was never so astonished in my life! A Miss Hawkins — of Bath!"

Here Jane, in imagination, heard Mrs Fitzroy saying, "*Hawkins?* What kind of a name is *that?*"

Aunt Hetty went on: "And there was Mrs Cole remarking, only the other day — but *I* never thought so. Well, you will be happy now, ma'am, will you not?" (To her mother). "The poor old vicarage is to have a mistress again. And a delightful new neighbour for us all. This is excellent news! We must run up to Hartfield directly. Jane, wrap up close in your warmer pelisse, for it may rain later on."

At Hartfield they found Mr Knightley, and Miss Bates was able, but only just, to forestall him with the announcement of Mr Elton's engagement.

"There is the news with which I had hoped to surprise you," said Mr Knightley smiling at Emma — who had received it, Jane thought, with a slightly conscious look; had she hopes of Mr Elton for herself?

"But where could *you* hear the news?" cried Miss Bates, astounded. "Where could you possibly hear it, Mr Knightley?"

"I was with Cole on business an hour and a half ago. He had just read Elton's letter."

How can one hope to keep *anything* hidden in this place? thought Jane.

"A new neighbour for us all, Miss Woodhouse!" repeated Miss Bates joyfully. "My mother is so pleased! Jane, you have never seen Mr Elton — no wonder that you have such a curiosity to see him."

Jane roused herself from a sad reverie, which had taken her back to that last day in Weymouth. Saying goodbye to Rachel, to Matt — his nervous start away from her proffered hand ... Walking up to Hartfield this morning, a mild fresh springlike morning of alternate shine and shower, she had felt almost unreal, as if this familiar Highbury, with its cobbles and narrow passage-ways, its bow-windowed cottages, newer brick houses of more dignity, its church, forge, and stables, were no more than a dream, from which she might at any moment awaken to find herself back on the Esplanade with Rachel, the Campbells — the Selseas, Mr Gillender —

"No: I have never seen Mr Elton," she replied, starting as her aunt addressed her. "Is he — is he a tall man?"

"Who shall answer that question?" cried Emma. "My father would say yes, Mr Knightley no, and Miss Bates and I that he is just the happy medium. When you have been here a little longer, Miss Fairfax, you will understand that Mr Elton is the standard of perfection in Highbury, both in person and mind." She cast a saucy, teasing look at Mr Knightley; plainly, thought Jane, there *was* something relating to Mr Elton.

"If you remember, my dear Jane," said her aunt, "I told you yesterday he was precisely the height of Mr Perry."

"You are silent, Miss Fairfax," said Emma. "But I hope you mean to take an interest in this news? You, who have been hearing and seeing so much of late on these subjects — "

Now, what in the world can she mean by that? thought Jane.

" — who must have been so deep in the business on Miss Campbell's account — we shall not excuse your being indifferent about Mr Elton and Miss Hawkins!"

Emma's eye, clear and sparkling hazel, seemed to pierce Jane's secret like the thrust of a needle into an abscess.

"When I have seen Mr Elton," replied Jane, with all the calm she could muster, "I daresay I *shall* be interested — but I believe it requires that with me. And as it is some months since Miss Campbell married, the impression may be a little worn off."

Fortunately for Jane, her aunt continued to descant upon the subject of Mr Elton's engagement, and her own silence and absence of mind went unremarked until Miss Bates inquired, "Have you heard from Mrs John Knightley lately, Miss Woodhouse? Oh, those dear little children! Jane, do you know I always fancy Mr Dixon like Mr John Knightley."

Jane started violently. "Quite wrong, my dear aunt," she said in haste.

"I mean in person, you know — tall, and with that sort of look — and not very talkative."

"There is no likeness at all, I assure you. Mr Dixon *is* talkative — very talkative, with an Irish cadence to his conversation which — which some people, I believe, find attractive."

"Mr Dixon, you say, is not, strictly speaking, handsome?"

"Handsome? Oh, no — far from it — certainly plain. I told you, Aunt Hetty, that he was plain. Black, shaggy hair, you know, and a long countenance — " Her voice shook a little.

"My dear Jane, you said that Miss Campbell would not allow him to be plain — I remember at one time you wrote me — and that you yourself — "

"Oh, as for me," said Jane quickly, observing Emma's eye still upon her, Emma still taking a deep interest in this interchange, "as for me, my judgment is worth nothing. Where I have regard, I always think a person is well-looking. I gave what I believed the general opinion when I called Mr Dixon plain."

Despite herself, Jane could not avoid her voice lingering on those two words *Mr Dixon*. I shall never see him again in this world, she thought. I may allow myself the luxury of speaking about him, occasionally, if people inquire.

"Well my dear Jane, I believe we must be running away. The weather does not look well and Grandmamma will be uneasy. Jane, you had better go home directly — I would not have you out in a shower. — Oh, Mr Knightley is coming too. Well, that is so very — ! I am sure, if Jane is tired, you will be so kind as to give her your arm as far as — "

Jane found herself being hurried home upon the arm of Mr Knightley.

"If you can sustain this pace, Miss Fairfax, you will just reach your door, I believe, before the rain commences. It was not wise of your aunt to bring you out on such a threatening morning. But I know her love of news! When the days are longer, I hope we shall have you out on horseback again? You look — if I may say so with the blunt kindness of an old friend — somewhat in need of fresh air and building up."

Jane blushed and — such was the friendly solicitude of his tone and the turmoil of her own feelings — felt the ready tears spring to her eyes.

"There!" he said. "I had no intention to offend you. You are still knocked-up from your journey. Go in, go in! In a few days our good air will have restored you."

And he strode off down the street with a quick, kind salutation, as the rain commenced pelting down in good earnest.

Chapter 12

After ten days passed in Highbury, Jane began to receive letters from her friends in Ireland. They were attentive and kind correspondents; seldom did two or three days pass but she had a note from Colonel Campbell, or a slightly longer letter from his wife who, even in Baly-Craig, retained her public interests and her correspondents abroad or in London; while Rachel and Mrs Dixon supplied long, weekly informative and loving epistles, the former ending, sometimes, with a little note: *"Matt asks to be remembered."*

"We are growing very happy," Rachel wrote presently. "I think that in time we shall do very well together. And I become fonder and fonder of Matt's mother; we have invited her to make her home with us always, since Baly-Craig is such a huge barrack of a place, half farm, half castle. I have not been into all the rooms yet, I believe. I draw continually — the hills, the little houses, and the fisher-people! They love Matt, and he loves them. I cannot understand their language. Matt is glad to be back in his own place. A sorrow and lowness, only natural when you consider that he has never been here without Sam, are slowly lifting from him."

And he is forgetting me too, Jane thought. And that is well. I wonder if all men's memories are so short?

But she was to be surprised and comforted by the frequency and affection of Frank Churchill's letters.

"My word, Miss Fairfax, you *do* have a deal of correspondents!" often wonderingly remarked old Mrs Standen, the postmistress, peering over her spectacles in the small steamy office as she handed Jane yet another letter. "Almost every morning there is summat for ye! But there, young folks, they've a deal of time for writing."

And Jane, walking homeward by the longer and more roundabout way, past the George and Dragon Inn, and Mr Cole's livery stables, would have sufficient time to read and absorb Frank's tender words before hiding the folded paper away at the bottom of her reticule.

His letters were amusing too — full of gaiety, friendship, and warmth — he described his activities — hoped he might be able to persuade his aunt and uncle to remove to London — perhaps next month — inquired with genuine solicitude after Jane — was her cold better? — had she been obliged to take to her bed? — was she managing to obtain the necessary air and exercise? — had she time to read? work? play the piano? — was there pleasant company in Highbury? — he had already had charming descriptions of her from his father and stepmother — and he was hers devotedly, hers entirely.

The arrival of such letters, besides the more infrequent, cautious business of replying to them, did indeed help to cheer Jane's days, and the frequency of mail received from Ireland made the concealment of Frank's communications easier to manage. Since there were several letters a week to read aloud from the Dixons or Campbells, an extra one or two from Bath or Yorkshire could pass unregarded among the rest, and Jane's morning walk to the post office before breakfast became the time of day that she valued most, when she was alone, could think, be herself, plan, recollect, and hope.

As the days passed, she became more and more signally aware of how large a part Frank Churchill now played in her life; how important he had become to her; what a difference he, and his projects and promises, made in her otherwise bleak future.

Mr Elton returned from Bath to be fêted, congratulated on his betrothal, and to preen himself a little in the faces of the females of Highbury. — Jane could not like him. She thought he was on the verge of being vulgar — handsome in a pink-faced, obvious way, no doubt, but a smooth, self-satisfied young man, with a genial word, a joke, a smile for everybody; still there was something about him that failed to please. Superficial, thought Jane; I do not believe he has ever thought deeply on any subject as a clergyman ought. And he is vain; he is making a parade of himself and his new engagement; he is showing off in order to attract somebody's notice; I wonder whose? Could it be that of Emma Woodhouse? If so, she has worse taste than I would have credited her with; but then she has so little experience.

To Jane, Mr Elton was civil enough; and she had to admit that he paid very proper and friendly attention to her grandmother and aunt, inviting them always to sit in the vicarage pew, because of Mrs Bates's deafness. But she could not warm to him; compared, for instance, with Frank Churchill, so quick-witted and considerate, he seemed lumpish and over-effusive; and she felt it no loss when he returned, as he very soon did, to Bath, where his marriage to Miss Hawkins would shortly be celebrated.

The day after his departure came more interesting news.

"My aunt and uncle expect elderly guests for two weeks at Enscombe," Frank wrote. "As soon as they have arrived and are settled in I shall post off, spend a night at Oxford, and hope to arrive in Highbury next Tuesday for a whole fortnight! I can be spared for that long! What joy to see you again, and so soon! And in a place of such affectionate interest to us both. Your devoted F.C."

The letter felt like a little nugget of warmth in Jane's muff as she hurried homeward. All day she was in a glow. In the last weeks she had begun to realise how deadly quiet and dull Highbury could be, how she missed the intelligent conversation, the easy communication, interchange of ideas, the daily discussion of books and public topics that she had shared with Rachel and the Campbells, with Frank and the Dixons. In Highbury there was gossip: the old ladies paused in the street to discuss Miss Augusta Hawkins's ten thousand pound dowry and the probable colour of Mr Elton's new carriage; but there was virtually no well-informed, stimulating talk. Frank's talk, she now reflected, had been that; though it could not be compared, perhaps, with Matt Dixon's poetic flights and occasional flashes of genius, yet it was the conversation of a thoroughly sensible, well-educated young man, conversant with public affairs, well-read, well-bred, and, besides that, amusing and witty. What a treasure he now seemed, in retrospect! Perhaps, thought Jane hopefully, Mrs Elton will be a sensible, conversible woman, somebody who may become a real friend, to fill a little of the dreadful gap left by Rachel's loss; now I begin to understand better what poor Aunt Hetty means when she rejoices over the arrival of a new neighbour. In Highbury people were too absorbed in their own affairs to spare much interest for what went on abroad: though, for instance, Jane was known to have visited the West Indies, very few people had invited her opinions or descriptions of the places she had seen, and, of those, even fewer troubled to wait and listen to her answers.

Soon came Mr Weston to proclaim and exult over the news of his son's imminent arrival; and now Jane might feel free to be aware of it and discuss it with her aunt and grandmother.

"Poor Mr Weston had been so disappointed at Christmas when the young man could not come. To be sure, Mr Knightley said he might if he were *truly* resolved, but then, it is not easy to flout the wishes of rich relatives! Mr Knightley was a little hard on the young man. Mr Knightley has his own views about many things — such as the friendship between Miss Woodhouse and that little Miss Smith. Mr Knightley's standards are very high."

Privately Jane agreed with Mr Knightley's views of this particular friendship. She thought that it reflected no credit on Emma Woodhouse. She had observed the two friends together on a number of occasions, and saw how almost slavishly little Miss Smith looked up to, and doated on Miss Woodhouse, agreeing instantly with every word she uttered; and how complaisantly Miss Woodhouse received this uncritical admiration. Mr Knightley shows his usual sense in disapproving of such a relationship, thought Jane; and then, with a slight chill: I wonder what Mr Knightley will think of Frank Churchill, when they meet?

The day came that was appointed for Frank's arrival, and now Jane began to be secretly, anxiously calculating. Then she tried to laugh at herself. It is only Frank Churchill! In Weymouth, often, I hardly noticed whether he was present or absent. — But in Highbury, matters were otherwise. His image had been insensibly changing through the weeks of separation, and she was surprised at the strength of her own wish to see him again. — Prudently, she tried to damp these feelings down. — He will tell his father that he met a Miss Fairfax in Weymouth, whom he believes to be now resident in Highbury; how soon may he call? Perhaps in two days? Perhaps in three? Or might there be a chance of an accidental meeting in the High Street?

But, to her utter amazement, on the very day itself there was heard a knock at the street door, and a moment later Patty the servant came, big-eyed, to announce that an unknown young gentleman, giving his name as Mr Churchill, was asking for Miss Jane.

"Well! What a thing! I wondered — I did wonder!" exclaimed Miss Bates. "Do you recall, Jane — oh, no, I think you were downstairs in the kitchen just then — but, twenty minutes ago, I saw Mr Weston pass by in the street with a strange young man. Oh! said I to your grandmother, I wonder if that can be Mr Weston's son that he is expecting? But no, it cannot be, for Mr Churchill would hardly come on his friends before they thought to see him, and *that* was not to be until this evening — only, if it is *not* Mr Churchill, who else in the world can it be?"

By this time Mr Churchill himself had come smiling up the stair and was waiting to be introduced to the two elder ladies.

"Grandmother, Aunt Hetty," said Jane, blushing, "this is Mr Frank Churchill — of whom you may have heard me speak — "

All the time, while Aunt Hetty was bidding him an effusive welcome, and the old lady offered quieter kindnesses, while he was being pressed to take a slice of sweet cake from the beaufet — or a baked apple, one of Mr Knightley's, a particularly excellent batch — or a glass of spruce-beer, which they had made themselves — Jane kept her eyes carefully away from Frank's countenance. Indeed she dared not look at him. I ought not to be ashamed of my home, she was thinking miserably. I ought not to mind that this place is so different from the house in Manchester Square, from the house in Weymouth. That the room is so tiny, that you can hear the barber talking to his customers down below, that Aunt Hetty is — what she is. I ought not to feel ashamed. If I do so it is a fault in me, not the place.

She looked unhappily out of the window at the narrow cobbled street, where two dogs were fighting over a bone, where an ostler chewed a straw as he dawdled in gossip with a carter, outside the Crown Inn.

She heard Frank say, "Indeed no — I am particularly fond of sweet cake, and this looks particularly excellent. Caraway seed, is it not? Did you make it yourself, Miss Bates? I must beg the receipt from you for my aunt's housekeeper."

With a strong effort, Jane turned at last to meet his eye, and received from him such a friendly sweet smile of reassurance that her spirits, which had been as low as possible, suddenly went soaring up.

He was explaining that he had reached Randalls on the previous evening, having changed his plan in order to travel faster and for longer stages.

"I hate to dawdle," said he, "and there is great pleasure in travelling fast when it is to see friends."

"And you found your father well? And Mrs Weston?"

"They both send their best remembrances. My father has gone to transact some business about hay at Mr Cole's stables. And then he has an errand for my stepmother at Ford's, where I am to meet him shortly. Perhaps you, ma'am, can tell me where Ford's is to be found?"

He was immediately and copiously informed, but seemed to find the directions hard to comprehend. "I turn *left* at the George — or is it right?"

"Perhaps," said Miss Bates, recollecting, "Jane, you might accompany Mr Churchill, then you could ask Mrs Ford, you know, about the gloves that she is ordering for me; the morning is bright, I believe the walk would do you good. Do you find my niece pale, Mr Churchill? You have been used to seeing her in the sea air of Weymouth; do you think she appears paler than she did there? Some people have remarked on it. 'Oh, Miss Bates,' said Mrs Goddard only the other day, 'we do think that Jane grows very pale — does she take enough exercise in the fresh air?' 'Oh, Mrs Goddard,' said I — ''

Frank assured the anxious aunt that her niece was by no means pale. At the moment, indeed, this was true, for Jane's cheeks were suffused with the glow of consciousness; but when the couple were liberated, and in the street, walking as slowly as possible in the direction of Ford's, Frank remarked in a tone of real concern:

"But you *are* pale, you know; paler by far than you were at Weymouth. How comes this about? Are you ill? Does the air of your native place not agree with you?"

"It is nothing," she answered quickly. "I am well — perfectly well."

"And happy?"

"I shall learn to be. *Very* happy in being back here — with my grandmother and dear Aunt Hetty. It is just — the confinement in so small a place — the loss of so many and such dear friends — " She paused and bit her lip.

He ventured to touch her arm, guiding her past a puddle, glancing at her heedfully.

"I know, I can comprehend. But — " in a rallying tone "now *I* am here I hope that may be partially amended. I hope that we can be meeting often?"

"Not *too* often," Jane said in a stifled tone. "Or tongues will start to wag. This is such a place for gossip. And that is the very last thing you can afford."

More acutely than ever, she felt the evil of her position.

"Oh," said Frank cheerfully, "but I have already thought of a ruse to gloss over the fact of our friendship. There are several other young ladies in this village, I find; one of them, in fact, I have already met. I shall cultivate their acquaintance most assiduously, so that it may not be said that I distinguish *one* particularly with my attentions. If I acquire the reputation of a sad flirt, what does that matter? Do you not think this a clever scheme?"

"Very," said Jane, trying to ignore a slightly hollow, sinking sensation. Had her feeling for him changed as much as that? Could this be jealousy? Was she so mean-spirited that she could begrudge even such diversionary tactics? "Which young lady did you meet?" she inquired politely.

"A Miss Woodhouse. My father took me to her house. I imagine you must know her? A *very* self-satisfied young lady — satisfied with her looks, her fortune, and her wit — she will do excellently well as a stalking-horse!" He laughed. "Indeed I could see at once that Papa would be happy for me and Miss Woodhouse to make a match of it."

"And to *that* I am sure your relatives in Yorkshire could have not the least objection," Jane could not help remarking rather coldly; and then wished that she had held her tongue.

Taking her arm again to cross the street Frank said in a low tone, "But you know my own wishes are quite to the contrary. I prefer dark beauty to hazel-eyed comeliness. — Besides, Miss Emma is too plump. And her reputed wit is no such thing. Your friend Rachel had far more real intelligence and understanding."

Comforted, Jane was able to smile at Mr Weston, just emerging from Ford's.

"Ah, there you are, there you are!" cried Frank's father happily. "And with Miss Fairfax, I see! That is right, that is right! Is not my son a fine young sprig, Miss Fairfax? But I am forgetting, you have met before. I am glad to see ye. How is your good aunt, and your grandmother? Well? I am happy to hear it. Now, Frank my boy, we must be running along — we have several other calls to pay, and Mrs Weston will be expecting us — See ye soon, Miss Jane, you and Miss Bates must come out to Randalls one of these evenings, ay, you must come and give us some of your grand music — " and as he took Frank's arm and hurried him off, with hardly time for a hasty "Goodbye" she heard him continue to Frank, "Ay — poor thing — 'tis a kindness to invite her to play, for the Bates ladies, you know, have no instrument — "

Jane, left alone outside Ford's, felt as if air and life had been abruptly sucked out of her. Frank and his father seemed so gay, so secure together. But she — how was she to bear this imposture? How contrive to see Frank again — to converse with him unobserved? Wherever they met, it would be in the presence, under the notice of other people, under cruel constraint. How could they ever manage to communicate at all?

And yet Frank almost seemed to enjoy the prospect of such pretence, such concealment.

What have I done? Jane asked herself again and again. What have I done?

At last she made her way blindly into the shop.

Next morning Jane, glancing from the casement in the front room, had a chance to see Frank Churchill, arm-in-arm with Emma Woodhouse and Mrs Weston, standing on the other side of the the road in front of the Crown Inn. They were apparently discussing the building: the club-room windows stood open, Frank stopped and looked inside, then made some inquiry of his companions. They shook their heads. All seemed to be on the friendliest, the kindliest of terms.

Only pride, and a strong self-discipline, kept Jane from inventing some errand that would take her into the street. — But she could not bear to break into their group. They all seemed delighted with one another.

Not for the first time, Jane now felt most cruelly the lack of a piano. It had always been her habit, at moments of loneliness or low spirits, to sit down and disperse her trouble by a couple of hours' vigorous practice; now that relief was denied her. True, she could go along to the Coles' house; but the little girls were continually in and out, interrupting, so was their talkative mother, there was no chance of privacy... Doggedly, she took out her little desk, which lived under her bed when not in use, placed it on the wash-hand-stand in the bedroom she shared with Aunt Hetty, and continued a half-finished letter to Rachel Dixon.

Next morning Aunt Hetty, glancing out of the window as she did at least every half-hour when at home, exclaimed, "Upon my word, here come Mr and Mrs Weston! But where, I wonder, is the fine young man?"

The Westons had brought a brace of pheasants; Mr Weston and his son, it seemed, had gone out shooting on the previous day in the copses of a neighbouring farmer and had had famous sport; "and somebody was saying, I forget whom," explained Mrs Weston, "that old Mrs Bates was particularly fond of pheasant — "

"Oh! My dear ma'am! My dear sir! What bounty! I always say that for true kindness our neighbours are not to be bettered! But where is your son? Where is the handsome young man?"

The Westons looked a little shame-faced, but laughed it off.

"He has driven to London to have his hair cut; he will be back this evening."

"To *London? Sixteen miles!* To have his hair cut? But what is wrong with Ben Strudwick in the shop below-stairs?"

"Oh, well, Frank, you see, has been brought up to grand tastes. Nothing but the best will serve. I am afraid he is a sad coxcomb," said his father laughing, "but he is young, after all, he must submit to have his leg pulled about it, eh, Miss Jane? When a young gentleman begins to study his appearance we know what to think, do we not?" And he made some playful allusion to Miss Woodhouse which Jane tried not to hear.

Mrs Weston seemed more troubled at this evidence of foppery than her husband. But she said defensively that Frank was really a good boy, a dear, charming boy.

The Bates ladies, when once more alone, could not get over the extravagance.

"Sixteen miles, twice in a day! A chaise from the Crown! *There* is one, you can see, who has never needed to study expenditure!" They were discussing it all afternoon; since a fine rain had set in, Jane was unable to get out of doors. Frank will have had a wet day in London, she thought, and wondered what else he did there, besides getting his hair cut. But, of course, the Churchills must have many friends in London from former periods of residence there. No doubt he was passing his time in pleasant company.

She preferred not to think about it.

Mrs Cole called before twilight to shake her head over the folly and extravagances of young men. "Thank heaven her children were girls!" and to invite the Bates ladies to a gathering on the following Tuesday: "We shall have some music, some fine music; Miss Jane must bring all her best pieces."

"Ay," said Aunt Hetty comfortably when the visitor had left, "the Coles are as friendly and sociable a couple as you could wish to meet. They can afford to be, you know. For his stable, and the hay-and-feed business in London have prospered so well, these last years, that he has been able to throw out a new wing on his house. You will see when we go on Tuesday, Jane."

"I have seen it already, aunt."

"Ay, so you have. How forgetful I grow!" laughing heartily at herself. "And Grandmamma is always happy to go and sit with Mr Woodhouse on such occasions, to keep him company, so that Miss Emma may also attend the party. Mrs Goddard will come to pick up Grandmamma, and they all play backgammon, and Miss Emma always takes care that they are supplied with very agreeable refreshments — wine and cake invariably, and sometimes a little supper — a fricassee of sweetbread, or asparagus, which Grandmamma is very partial to — "

"But why," said Jane, trying and failing to dispel the shade of resentment from her tone, "why should Emma Woodhouse be invited to dinner at the Coles' while you and I may only come in *after* dinner — ?"

Aunt Hetty fidgeted with the fringe of her shawl.

"Oh! well, my dear, the thing is — well, that is, the way that we are circumstanced — unattached ladies, you know, females without gentlemen are an encumbrance at a dinner-party — they must make up their table — "

"But Emma Woodhouse is also an unattached female," said Jane coldly.

"But she, my dear, has thirty thousand at command; she *must* be of the first consequence in Highbury. The Coles know that! Why, they would not have dared even invite her, you know, a year or so ago, before Mr Cole did so well with his hay-and-feed business. And it is quite a condescension on her part to accept — they were not at all sure that she would. — But, of course, she will see so many of her friends there: good Mr and Mrs Weston, and young Mr Churchill — perhaps that is the reason why — and Mr Knightley, and the Ponsonbys, and Mr Cox, and young Mr Cox; the Cox ladies, you know, also come in afterwards, with Miss Smith — and *she* is Emma Woodhouse's *particular* friend; so you have no need, my dear Jane, to feel slighted, not the least in the world — "

Just the same, Jane did feel sore and slighted; she could not help herself.

Next day at church Frank contrived to get near her, after the service, just for a moment, under pretext of inquiring as to the ownership of a dropped prayer-book, and asked in a low tone:

"At what hour is your daily visit to the post office?"

"At half past eight."

His jaw dropped, visibly, but he rallied and said, "Then you may expect to see me there, one of these mornings," before turning to offer the book inquiringly to another lady.

The post office was situated in a turning at the less frequented end of the High Street. On Monday morning Jane looked for Frank there in vain.

But, later that day, such a startling event occurred as must entirely drive Frank's undependable behaviour and the Coles' discriminating hospitality out of Jane's mind: a carter pulled up in front of their house, inquired for Bates, or Fairfax, and proceeded to deliver an enormous, sacking-wrapped package.

"But what *is* it?" cried Aunt Hetty. "What in the world is it? Sure, there must be some mistake!"

But no, the package was carefully addressed to Miss Jane Fairfax, in care of Bates, High Street, Highbury, Surry. And when, with the utmost difficulty, it had been manhandled up the narrow, steep, right-angled stairs and divested of its wrappings in the parlour, it proved to be a handsome upright piano, from Broadwoods, accompanied by a large parcel of music. — There was only *just* room for it, in one corner, by dint of removing one of the Windsor chairs to the bedroom shared by Jane and her aunt, and taking a leaf out of the Pembroke table.

"But from *whom* can it be?" cried Aunt Hetty. "Was there no letter with it? No card? No message, no delivery ticket?"

The carter shook his head.

"Well! That is the greatest mystery in the world! I never was so astonished!" repeated Miss Bates over and over, when the carter had been despatched below-stairs to take a glass of beer in the kitchen with Patty.

"It must, of course, be from Colonel and Mrs Campbell," said Jane calmly, though her heart beat fast.

"So kind! So *very* thoughtful! They know how you must miss your music! But how strange in the Colonel not to have mentioned it in one of his letters! Why did he not write beforehand?"

"Perhaps a letter went astray."

"Ah! true, that might explain it."

The piano, despite being an embarrassment, was of immense

comfort to Jane. She had seen nothing of Frank, beyond the brief glimpse after church; and this token of his thought, of his real consideration for her and her needs, was heartwarming indeed. She practised on the piano for a long time, as long as she thought her relatives and the neighbours could be expected to endure.

On Tuesday morning Frank was at the post office counter, fruitlessly inquiring for a parcel of wools expected by his stepmother. He faced Jane with an expression of laughing guilt on his face.

"Yesterday morning I confess it, I overslept. I am such an idle dog — !"

Jane began a confused, hurried speech of thanks for the piano.

"You should not — indeed you should not have — "

"Indeed I *should*! To find you in want of something which I know to be as necessary to you as breath itself — and I so easily able to supply it — "

The piano, Jane knew, must have cost him at least thirty guineas.

"It is all wrong; it is not right — "

"Shall I see you at the Coles' this evening?" he broke in.

"Yes, Aunt Hetty and I are to come after dinner."

He muttered something derogatory to the Coles' taste in dinner guests.

"Cox and his son! A shambling scrivener and a callow young clerk! — But listen to me now, I have something truly diverting to tell you."

"Oh?"

"It relates to Miss Woodhouse."

"Oh?" said Jane again in a cooler tone.

"Miss Woodhouse, it appears, sets herself up as a matchmaker and diviner of romantic attachments *par excellence*." She would, thought Jane, remembering the wedding game. "It was she, so she herself asserts, who brought Miss Taylor and my father together. Next — so she told my stepmother — she claimed to have detected an embryonic passion between the vicar, Elton, and her own protégée, little Miss Smith. But that, unaccountably, seems to have gone astray; Elton shied off and transferred his affections to a lady in Bath. But now — and I have it from the horse's mouth, from Miss Woodhouse herself, who lost no time in confiding her suspicions to me — she pretends to have discovered a submerged, frustrated romance between — guess who?"

"How can I possibly guess?" said Jane coldly, but with an uncomfortable palpitation of the heart.

"Between yourself and *Mr Dixon*, none other! All this was confided to me — almost a stranger — on our second encounter, when we were walking about the village the other morning with my stepmother. Was it not true, Emma wanted to know, that Mr Dixon greatly preferred your piano playing to that of Miss Campbell? that he perhaps even preferred your person? that he had pleaded for you to accompany the married pair to Ireland?"

"She really asked you such questions?" said Jane, transfixed.

"Yes! Was it not exceedingly singular? That she should make such confidential inquiries — about people she had never seen — to someone like myself whom she had only just met? Oh, she is a strange, free young lady, Miss Emma Woodhouse! It seemed to me singularly indelicate. But very diverting, you must agree!"

"Oh, very," Jane agreed, in a hollow tone.

"And highly convenient for us!" Frank continued cheerfully. "That Miss Woodhouse should, for heaven knows what reasons, harbour such suspicions about you and Dixon must remove from her mind any possibility of observing a connection between you and *me*. The lady is barking up the wrong tree with a vengeance!"

He seemed so entertained by the episode that Jane wondered, in a kind of bemusement, if all those former days at Weymouth had been completely erased from his mind; did the name of Dixon really now mean no more to him than an idle joke? Had she mistaken in him what seemed like a true perception of her feelings for Matt?

Would he prove equally forgetful in other respects? As forgetful as Matt Dixon?

"I must go," she said nervously. "They will be wondering, at home, why I am taking so long."

Again she tried to express her heartfelt thanks for the piano, while deploring the rashness, the extravagance of the gift. But he brushed her thanks aside and waved her a gay farewell, "Till this evening!" striding off in the direction of Randalls, which lay the opposite way to hers.

"I say, though," he turned to call out, laughing, "I wonder what Miss Emma will make of the instrument? She will think that Dixon sent it!"

Chapter 13

The party at the Coles' was a large, cheerful, and fairly informal gathering.

Despite being relegated to the inferior, post-dinner part of the company, Jane had taken great pains over her dress, and even greater pains over her hair. While engaged on this latter task, she could not help sighing for Rachel, and missing her sorely.

"The people in Ireland are queer," Rachel had written in a letter received that day, "but I grow to like them more and more. They are so easy, lively, and entertaining — so very different from Grandmother Fitzroy and her friends! I could listen to them talking forever — they have such a way of expressing themselves. I can see where Matt's poetry comes from. (He is writing again, you will be glad to hear; working very hard.) The Irish even seem to enjoy *my* conversation — they are very kind to me!"

At last, Jane thought, Rachel has found a company that appreciates her. I was right in what I did. Yes, I was right.

Which conviction was no great comfort to her that evening when, with Aunt Hetty, she entered Mrs Cole's new large drawing-room. The ladies who had dined in the house were there already, gathered near the fireplace, the gentlemen not yet entered.

Jane immediately found herself subjected to an inquisition on the subject of the piano, news of which had already flown all over the village; Mrs Weston, Mrs Cole, Mrs Goddard, Mrs Cox, Mrs Otway, Mrs Gilbert, Mrs Ponsonby — all must have their curiosity satisfied as to the make of the instrument, as to tone, touch, and pedal; and had any indication been received regarding the donor? Was it not singular? Had she heard from Colonel Campbell? Or from Mrs Dixon? The piano commanded far greater attention than all Jane's previous history or travels abroad. Very heartily, after ten minutes of this interrogation, did Jane wish that the piano had never arrived in Highbury. Her face felt as false and stiff as a mask. She began to believe that the instrument might be more a penance than a pleasure.

The only person who did *not* approach and make inquiry was Emma Woodhouse. *She* thinks she knows all about it already, thought Jane resentfully, and was not grateful for this consideration. — Emma, beautifully dressed, sat aloof and conversed with her little friend Miss Smith.

After a while some of the gentlemen walked through from the dining-room, flushed and good-humoured with wine and conversation. Frank headed the file, and, after giving them a quick smile, passed clean by Jane and Miss Bates, who were seated near the door, and made his way straight over to Miss Woodhouse. He stood beside Emma and her friend until a seat came vacant, then appropriated it, and remained there, chatting gaily with the two young ladies for what seemed to Jane an interminable time; it might perhaps have been seven or eight minutes.

By degrees, in came more gentlemen, and, following a break and a general movement in the company, Jane saw Mr Churchill glance in her own direction, address some laughing remark to Emma, who also looked towards her, then he stood up and began to thread a path through the crowd, making for her.

At last he stood in front of her, upon his face a broad smile of satisfaction and amusement.

She looked up at him gravely.

"Good evening, Miss Bates!" said he to Aunt Hetty. "I have just been telling Miss Woodhouse how greatly I admire your niece's style of hairdressing. So very original! I see nothing like it here. I conclude that it must be some London or Parisian fashion that she has brought here to dazzle the natives of Surry?"

"Indeed, sir, she does it all herself," said Miss Bates. "Is it not quite wonderful? No hairdresser from London, I think, could — but Jane is so very clever at all that kind of thing! In Weymouth, you know, she was able to study *La Belle Assemblée* and such journals — but, I was forgetting, you were in Weymouth yourself. I grow sadly forgetful! Now, is not this a pleasant party? So many friends — so many good people — "

At this moment Miss Bates was offered a dish of tea by Mrs Cole, and turned away to receive it; Frank took the opportunity of leading Jane a little aside.

"You will be happy to hear that I have a great deal more to tell you in the saga of Miss Woodhouse and her suspicions. I sat by her at dinner and we talked about you a great deal." Am I supposed to be pleased at that? thought Jane. Frank went on, his voice changing to a more serious note, "But first, by what means did you come hither?"

"Mr Knightley kindly sent his carriage for my aunt and myself."

"Oh." Rather disappointed. "My stepmother wished to offer the use of my father's carriage to take you home — it is not right that you should have to walk half a mile in the dark — but, if Knightley already — "

"That was very kind in Mrs Weston," said Jane composedly, "and we are grateful for her thought; but, you see, it is not necessary."

"Knightley seems a good-hearted old fellow. I wonder why he never married? Perhaps some early disappointment . . . But listen, now, while I tell you more. Emma Woodhouse, by this time, is entirely convinced that Dixon is the sender of the piano. She has it all worked out to her own satisfaction. Is not that capital? She assured me of this, most positively, at dinner. She is, truly, an extraordinary lady. I think she must have the most wayward imagination in Surry. I cannot help being entertained by her."

Expertly, he found Jane a seat and placed himself at her side, continuing in a low tone,

"Now that you have had more leisure to try the piano, tell me — does it suit? Was it chosen with sufficient nicety? I had taken as much care as I could, I promise you, to study your tastes, while we were in Weymouth."

"You must be aware," she answered with constraint, "how very precisely it is suited to my tastes."

She felt embarrassed to be seen talking to him, even in this large assembly; felt that every eye must be fixed on them.

"Do you know," he went on, "Miss Woodhouse had somehow heard the history of that episode — did you mention it in a letter to your aunt, perhaps? — the occasion, do you recall it, when you were nearly swept off the boat, thanks to the stupidity of that wretched Charlotte Selsea — and Matt Dixon saved you from falling into the sea? That tale, as you may imagine, added wondrous fuel to her bonfire!"

He chuckled, but Jane was instantly carried back to that ill-starred summer boat-trip: the heat, the glare, the discomfort, the sudden panic as the ship heeled over — Matt Dixon's concerned face bending over hers, his arms around her. It had been later on that same day —

"Aha!" Frank exclaimed. "I see the pianoforte is being wheeled out, that music is now to be the order of the evening. Miss Woodhouse, of course, performs first. Wealth must always take precedence over talent. So be it."

He threw Jane an expressive grimace, then rose and hurried to make himself useful in helping to reposition the piano and sort sheets of music. While Emma played and sang one or two simple ballads he added, uninvited, a tenor part to her singing, and was heartily applauded. His voice had not the quality of Matt's, Jane thought; still it was tuneful enough. After the usual polite acclamations, denials, and excuses, they sang together again, a couple more times; then Emma gracefully gave way, asserting with the prettiest humility that neither in voice nor execution was she fit to sit at the feet of Miss Fairfax who, etc. etc.

And when I think what she has been saying about me! thought Jane.

Frank and Jane now sang together for some considerable time. They sang many of the songs that had been practised by the group in Weymouth; and, carried away by the music and all it meant to her, Jane almost felt herself transported back into that happy period. This, though she was not conscious of it, gave her voice an added texture, a deeper lustre. The applause was tumultuous. They were asked, begged to sing again and yet again, until Jane's voice, from lack of practice, began to grow husky.

Mr Knightley now sharply intervened.

"This must not be!" he said. "Miss Bates, are you mad to let your niece sing herself hoarse in this manner, after she has been plagued by such a bad cold? Go and interfere. They have no mercy on her."

"Oh! Dear! Yes, Mr Knightley, you are very right. Jane, Jane, you must not endanger your throat so — your voice grows thick, indeed, indeed it does! Come, sit by me and let me wrap this kerchief round your neck."

Frank, at once, was all contrition. But Jane heard Mr Knightley say dourly, "That fellow thinks of nothing but showing off his own voice."

Friends now surrounded Jane, applauding and praising; her voice had come on so wonderfully since she was last in Highbury! Frank was soon separated from her by the crowd. — In a few moments the word was for dancing: a joyful buzz swept through the room. Chairs were being moved back, the piano rolled against the wall. Jane, seated by her aunt, had felt, all of a sudden, exceedingly tired; the emotion generated and recalled by the songs had drained her of energy. She was glad to remain still.

But when Mrs Weston, presiding at the piano, began an irresistible waltz, Jane thought what a great pleasure it would be to dance again with Frank. He was such an excellent dancer. She looked about for him.

He was nowhere at hand; then she saw him bow, with a flourish of gallantry, to Emma Woodhouse, and lead her to the top of the set which was forming.

"Ah," said Aunt Hetty comfortably, "there is young Mr Churchill leading out Miss Woodhouse; that is just as it should be; she is the lady of first consequence here. How graciously she smiles on him!"

Plump Mr Cole, her host, invited Jane to dance.

"My word, Miss Fairfax, you certainly showed us the way, with your famous playing and singing. My word, your fingers did rattle over the keys! Indeed it is too bad that you should not be able to stay always in Highbury, else I should not hesitate to invite you to teach our three little girls; Mrs Cole is always saying that she believes our present teacher to be sadly deficient; but what do we know of such matters?"

Yes, that is all I am fit for, thought Jane, listening to Mr Cole's corset creak as he capered beside her. (Caper, from capra, a goat, she thought). The corsets had been one of the penalties of wealth; he had worn them only for the last year, Mrs Cole had told Miss Bates.

Frank and Emma were not far off in the set. Jane caught Frank's eye.

"You look fatigued, Miss Fairfax," he called. "I am afraid I tired you to death with our singing."

There was no time to reply, had she wished to; they were parted again.

Two dances, unfortunately, were all that could be allowed; there was no chance of changing partners again. The party was over.

Jane overheard Frank say to Miss Woodhouse: "Perhaps it is as well! I must have asked Miss Fairfax, and her languid dancing would not have agreed with me after yours."

Mr Knightley, all kindness and care, handed Jane and Miss Bates into his carriage. He himself proposed to walk home, so as not to inconvenience them, but Miss Bates cried out at such an idea.

"Here is plenty of room for three! All the way to Donwell — a whole mile! In the dark! With his own carriage at hand! What a notion. He must not think of it. He must accompany them."

"Very well," he said. "But I will not incommode you with conversation. I believe that Miss Fairfax is dangerously tired."

Jane found a kind of forlorn comfort in his large silent presence between her and Aunt Hetty who, for once, perhaps under the influence of Mr Knightley, had nothing to say on the short drive home.

Parties are hateful occasions, thought Jane. I shall never wish to attend another.

Next morning, however, brought an early call from Frank and Mrs Weston "to inquire after Miss Fairfax's throat. Had it recovered from last night's over-exertion? Frank had been so sorry — so bitterly ashamed afterwards that he had not noticed sooner — "

Miss Bates was able to assure them that Jane was quite herself again this morning, only a little languid. "Indeed, so am I — such late hours, I assure you, are not at all what we are accustomed to. But, now, here is a thing — the rivet has come out of my mother's spectacles — and we are all at sixes and sevens — for a bushel of apples came over from dear Mr Knightley — so kind as he is always — I had meant to take over the spectacles, before, to John Saunders, but, what with one thing and another — "

"Let me see the spectacles," said Frank. "Oh, I think I may be able to fasten that rivet, if you will allow me, ma'am? Indeed, I like a job of that kind excessively! All you need is to supply me with a little, sharp, pointed knife. I feel certain I shall be able to repair it." And, to his stepmother, "Were you not planning to visit Ford's, ma'am? Why do you not leave me here, at my silversmith's work, and come back with my father presently — I know he, too, wishes to hear the tone of Miss Fairfax's new acquisition."

"Very well," said Mrs Weston good-naturedly. "And I believe I see Miss Woodhouse out there in the street; I must inquire how her father enjoyed the evening with Mrs Goddard — "

"Miss Woodhouse there? So she is!" cried Aunt Hetty. "Then I will just run out with you and invite her to come up and hear the new piano as well — she will be delighted with its tone I am sure, such a judge as she is — "

Miss Bates and Mrs Weston both left the little parlour.

Old Mrs Bates, deprived of her spectacles and therefore of her drawn-thread-work, sat slumbering gently in the armchair by the little hearth. Voices could be heard from the street outside — Good morning! Such a delightful evening! Such exquisite music! — amid the clatter of hoofs as Mr Perry rode by, his horse slipping on the cobbles. But for the pair inside, the external world seemed far distant; they were enclosed together in a small brief capsule of silence. At last Frank said softly,

"I wished so very much to dance with you."

Jane found voice enough to reply "Indeed?" remembering his last remark to Emma Woodhouse. The cool dry note in her tone must have caught his ear; he went on with great warmth: "But I have since had a famous notion! I shall ask my father and stepmother to hold a little party at Randalls — a party expressly for dancing, you know, just the people who formed the set last night — five or six couple. I am sure there might be space in the drawing-room at Randalls. And then — and then we can dance together as we did at Weymouth. That night was such a joy to me — "

"Had you not better apply yourself to your task?" said Jane coldly. "I can hear voices at the street door."

He had approached her, in evident hope of taking her hand; she turned away from him abruptly, stepped to the piano, and began rearranging the pile of music on it.

They could hear Miss Bates below: "Pray take care, Mrs Weston, there is a step at the turning. Pray take care, Miss Woodhouse, ours is rather a dark staircase — Miss Smith, pray take care. Miss Woodhouse, I am quite concerned, I am sure you hit your foot. Miss Smith, the step at the turning!"

Next minute the room was filled again with people. Miss Woodhouse, Miss Smith must be greeted, and seated, and offered baked apples and cake.

"What!" said Mrs Weston to her stepson, finding him still at work on the glasses, "have you not done yet? *You* would not earn a very good living as a silversmith!"

Frank explained that he had been helping Miss Fairfax wedge one of the piano legs with paper. He bade a very civil good-morning to Miss Woodhouse — *more* than civil; he was soon sitting beside her and choosing the best baked apple for her.

"Do, pray, Miss Fairfax, give us the pleasure of hearing your new piano!" exclaimed Mrs Weston kindly. "It is such a handsome instrument, I am sure it has a splendid tone. And your playing last night was such a treat — so far superior to what we are accustomed to." She is protesting too much, thought Jane unhappily. Does she do it to cover up the fact that her stepson is paying marked attentions to Miss Woodhouse? But then, why should that trouble her? No doubt she feels it would be a most desirable match.

Oh, when shall I ever be free from these horrible feelings of discomfort, guilt, jealousy, suspicion?

Jane sat at the keyboard and played; she hardly knew what. Everybody was very civil in praising her execution and the tone of the instrument.

"Whomever Colonel Campbell might employ in the business," Frank said loudly to Emma, "he has not chosen ill. I heard a great deal of Colonel Campbell's taste in Weymouth; and the softness of the upper notes I am sure is exactly what he and *all that party* would particularly prize. I dare say, Miss Fairfax, that Colonel Campbell either gave his friend very minute directions; or else wrote to Broadwood himself. Do you not think so?"

His tone was laughing, teasing. Jane did not reply, so he went on,

"How *much* your friends in Ireland must be enjoying your pleasure on this occasion, Miss Fairfax. — There! It is done. I have the pleasure, madam" (to Mrs Bates) "of restoring your spectacles, healed for the present."

After handing the old lady her glasses, Frank walked to the piano and selected a waltz from the sheet music. He put it before Jane.

"Such a delightful tune! You did not enjoy it as I did, last night, Miss Fairfax; you appeared tired. I believe you were glad we danced no longer. But I would have given worlds — all the worlds one ever has to give — for another half-hour. I beg you, play it now!"

She played.

After a few minutes Frank said, still in his teasing tone: "If I mistake not, that was danced at Weymouth?"

Blushing with irritation, very conscious of Emma close at hand listening to every word, Jane switched to another melody, and heard Frank addressing Emma behind her:

"All this music was sent with the instrument, you know, Miss Woodhouse. Very thoughtful of Colonel Campbell, was it not? I honour that part of the attention particularly. Nothing hastily done, nothing incomplete. *True* affection only could have prompted it."

How *can* he? thought Jane.

And, with even greater indignation, she caught Emma's reply, in a laughing, conscious tone: "Hush! You speak too plain. She must understand you."

"I hope she does," said Frank nonchalantly. "She is playing 'Robin Adair' at the moment — *his* favourite."

Furious, Jane played louder, and the pair behind her moved farther away.

Miss Bates now observing Mr Knightley in the street outside threw open the casement and called out of it, inviting him to come up. "Here are Miss Woodhouse and Mr Frank Churchill. Was not their dancing delightful last night! Did you ever see anything to equal it?"

"Oh, very delightful indeed!" he answered drily. "I can say nothing less, for I suppose Miss Woodhouse and Mr Churchill are hearing everything that passes. And," (raising his voice still more) "I do not see why Miss Fairfax should not be mentioned too. I think Miss Fairfax dances very well; and Mrs Weston is the very best country-dance player, without exception, in England — "

"Oh, Mr Knightley — something of greater consequence — " And Miss Bates began to thank him effusively for the apples. "Ah — he is off! He never can bear to be thanked — "

Mr Knightley does not like Frank Churchill, Jane thought. I wonder if he sees through his play-acting?

"We must be running along," said Mrs Weston. "Look at the time! Come, Emma, come, Miss Smith; we have discommoded Mrs Bates and Miss Bates quite long enough. Frank and I will accompany you as far as Hartfield."

The party removed themselves; and Jane had time for only one quick burning look of reproach at Frank before he was gone.

A couple of days passed before Jane saw Frank Churchill again. He did not present himself during her morning visits to the post office; but she heard that he was repeatedly seen walking with Mrs Weston and Miss Woodhouse; and that the party from Randalls had spent an evening at Hartfield.

He is capricious, thought Jane.

Then she blamed herself. I have frightened him away with my coldness and irritability. It is my own fault.

But still, her heart was sore.

Jane's next view of Frank was in very different circumstances.

Miss Bates and her mother were not, of course, rich enough to be capable of such acts of charity to the poor of the village as were the prerogative of the wealthy Miss Woodhouse; but still the two ladies, in their quiet way, did perform many small kindnesses; through the offices of Mrs Cole, or other well-disposed persons, they obtained yarn and flannel from which to make up garments for the indigent; and many an old cottage-woman or turned-off field worker had cause to bless them in the cold winter days for a warm red petticoat or pair of sturdily knitted stockings. Sickness and poverty would always command their friendly efforts; Mrs Bates had a bookful of receipts for tried and tested remedies which, in the old days, had been available from the vicarage for any that needed them; and she still kept in her pantry various bottles of embrocation, Camphire Julep, and Black Plaister. Jane one day had been entrusted with such a remedy — a bottle of liniment for rheumatic gout — and was glad of the opportunity for a solitary walk to a cottage situated at some distance from the village, down Vicarage Lane, but a quarter of a mile beyond the vicarage itself. Arrived at her destination she delivered the bottle, was cordially thanked by the recipient, old John Abdy, and rewarded with copious anecdotes about her grandfather, the former vicar, to whom Abdy had been clerk for twenty-seven years. Lingering, listening, averse to take her leave before the old man's flow of narrative had dwindled to its natural conclusion, Jane became aware of voices outside. There came a tap on the door, and somebody called, "May I come in?"

Next moment the door opened and Miss Woodhouse made her appearance, with Mrs Weston behind her, bearing a jug of soup. Over the shoulder of the latter, Jane perceived the face of Frank Churchill, which lit up at sight of her.

Emma was being extremely gracious.

"Some of your grandmother's famous lotion, Miss Fairfax. How very kind! I have heard wonders as to its healing properties."

Emma, it seemed, had come to give the old man the benefit of her assistance in writing a letter about parish relief. She had brought paper and ink, and sat down directly in a businesslike manner to her task.

Jane bade the new arrivals a civil good-day and was taking her leave when, to her surprise, Frank announced that he would accompany her. "My father will be waiting for me at the Crown; we are to ride to Kingston together. The beauty of the day encouraged me to accompany my stepmother on her errand, and we fell in with Miss Woodhouse. But the two of them will be excellent company for one another on the return journey; indeed, they may well prefer my absence." And he made some joke about ladies' confidences which Jane, in a slight state of confusion, failed to catch.

"Was this prudent?" she demanded of him nervously, when they were at some distance from the cottage, in the seclusion of a little hollow where the lane ascended a hill between high banks.

For answer he threw his hat in the air, then kissed her gloved hand before she could prevent him.

"I so very seldom catch a glimpse of you without a host of witnesses — all those dear, good dull souls, listening like munching cattle to our every syllable, and not understanding one word in twenty! I am sure that Highbury is populated by folk of sterling virtue, but you must allow that they are not quick-minded. That tedious party at the Coles'! You lost nothing by missing the dinner, I assure you; the dancing was the only tolerable part of the affair; and that was wrecked for me by the frustration of not dancing with *you!* But it passes comprehension how the people here can value you so low. *Oh, yes, Miss Fairfax!* they say; a nice pretty young lady who can play the pianoforte! You, who speak so many languages, who have travelled abroad, visited the West Indies, who in a few months read more books than most of them peruse in the whole course of their stupid lives — !"

Jane laughed, and forgave him his parting remark to Emma at the Coles'. "I must confess that I find them dull, too; but they are perfectly well-meaning; they do not mean to slight me by failing to ask for my impressions of the West Indies. Simply, they have so little interest in what occurs outside the confines of the village."

"It makes me wild with indignation," said he, "to think of you immured here, in this intellectual desert, month after month. Highbury is all very fine for a visit — "

"The term of my stay is at my own command," Jane pointed out. "I can always apply for a teaching post — "

"Do not speak of that," he exclaimed hurriedly. "I cannot *bear* the notion."

"But it must be so — "

"Look!" he interrupted. They had reached the top of the short rise; where the lane turned a corner the hedgerow was fortified by a very fine old oak-tree which had spread its massive bulk among the hazel and blackthorn. In the oak's knobbed and fissured trunk was a deep cavity, not immediately visible from the lane, for it was low down behind a protruding bole. "Look," said Frank, thrusting his arm in up to the elbow, "it is quite dry; some squirrel's forgotten larder. The perfect letter-box for us! I have been exercising my mind as to how, while I stay with my father, I can communicate with you privately. Here we have the solution!"

"Oh, but — "

"But me no buts! You will often be calling to inquire how that poor old gentleman goes on down there; and across the meadows this tree is only ten minutes' run from my father's house; I can see his chimneys from here. Every day I shall be able to leave a message here, to remind you of my existence!"

Jane could not gainsay the comfort of this arrangement. And his promise was amply fulfilled by many affectionate notes, many tiny gifts.

One morning Frank arrived at Miss Bates's abode in person, and in high spirits.

"Do come, Miss Bates. And you, too, of course, Miss Fairfax. We need your sage and expert advice."

"Advice? What in the world can *my* advice be good for?" fluttered Aunt Hetty. "But still — if you say so Mr Churchill — so kind — so very much obliged for the repair of those spectacles — come, Jane — do not omit to button your pelisse for the wind is in the east — "

They were to go, Frank told Jane as they crossed the street, no farther than the Crown Inn, where Mr and Mrs Weston were already gathered with Emma Woodhouse, debating the possibilities of using the club meeting chamber as a ballroom. It had been decided that the drawing-room at Randalls was not large enough for such a purpose.

Half an hour was most agreeably spent in the large, dusty chamber discussing the essential questions of lights and music, tables and chairs, tea and supper: could the card-room be used as a supper-room or was it too small? Would the older members of the party *expect* to play cards? Might a second room at the end of a passage be suitable for supper or was it too far distant?

"This wallpaper is dreadfully dirty!" said Mrs Weston distastefully. "And the paint so yellow and forlorn!"

"My dear, who will notice that by candle-light?" exclaimed her husband, exchanging smiles with Frank, and Emma said to Jane,

"The room itself is such a spacious, pleasant size; it would accommodate nine or ten couple very comfortably. I own, I do think this is a charming plan, do you not, Miss Fairfax? Are you not fond of dancing? I am sure you are! Do you not miss it? Here in Highbury we have so few opportunities."

She spoke with such apparent spontaneity that Jane warmed and felt, for a moment, purely kindly towards her; but these feelings were impaired when, not long after, she heard Frank engaging Miss Woodhouse for the first two dances.

Why does he have to do that? thought Jane resentfully. Is Emma Woodhouse *always* to be of the first consequence?

A date for the ball was canvassed. "Nothing can possibly be achieved in less than a week, you know," Mrs Weston was protesting to her husband. "Frank, can you not obtain permission from your aunt and uncle to remain with us for a third week?"

Frank thought that he might; hoped that he would be successful. — Three more days went by in animated planning. Jane saw Frank several times. Music and dances were discussed.

Emma Woodhouse even came to call on Jane, to ask, in the most friendly, unaffected way, if Jane would teach her (or her maid) that particularly elegant fashion of dressing her hair which had been so remarked at the Coles' evening party. "Your hair is so beautiful, Miss Fairfax. I am sure it must curl naturally. Whereas mine is nothing but a trouble — has to be curled every night — "

Jane, disarmed, provided the necessary instructions, and exclaimed involuntarily, in the charity of the moment: "Oh, Miss Woodhouse, I hope nothing may happen to prevent this ball! What a disappointment it would be. I do look forward to it, I own, with *very* great pleasure."

But her heart, accustomed to disappointment, misgave her; and with reason, as matters proved: two days later an express letter from Mr Churchill ordered his nephew's instant return. Mrs Churchill was very unwell — too ill to trifle — Frank must set off for Enscombe without delay.

He called early at the Bateses', to announce this melancholy news. Aunt Hetty was out of the house, gone to morning service, as she did on certain days; old Mrs Bates not yet up. Frank and Jane had ten minutes alone together.

She was in a flutter of low spirits. "We have done dreadfully amiss! I would never, *never* have consented to such a scheme if I had considered what it would entail. Such a course of concealment — of hypocrisy! We are acting clean contrary to our sense of right. It can never lead to good. Do, pray, Mr Churchill, take back your ring — " she was pulling it from its ribbon as she spoke — "do, pray, consider yourself free from this engagement. It is not right. I know it is not right. And what can we ever hope from it, what is the use of it?"

But he would not be persuaded. "What, and leave you free to engage yourself to Knightley? or to young Cox? Never! I cannot endure to lose you! Being obliged to leave you here and return to Yorkshire is hard enough, but the thought that I would have no more right to hear from you, no expectation of seeing you again as my dearest and best hope on this earth — no, believe me, that would not be bearable. You forget what a forlorn and lonely life I have of it, up there at Enscombe."

He actually fell on his knees, clasping her hand, and looking so sincerely miserable that in the end she allowed herself to be persuaded, and tucked the ring back inside her fichu, just before Aunt Hetty walked up the stair.

Chapter 14

The toll exerted upon Jane's constitution by Frank Churchill's visit to Highbury had been so severe that, for several days after his departure, she was obliged to take to her bed and lie there with a shawl over her eyes, flinching from the smallest gleam of light, and crying out, when she could not help it, from the atrocious pain of her headache. Nothing Mr Perry prescribed had any success in alleviating the agony. But by degrees it abated and she was able to creep about the house, wan, listless, and lacking appetite. — To her very great relief, by the time she was capable, once again, of meeting neighbours, the topic of Frank Churchill had ceased to be of paramount interest, superseded by the return of Mr Elton with his new bride.

Mrs Elton was first to be seen in church, and then Miss Bates thought it proper to call.

"After all your grandmamma, my dear, was once mistress of that same vicarage. One must not be behindhand in this sort of thing, especially to a new-married lady."

Jane, though not eager, was persuaded to accompany her aunt. "It will do you good, my dear, to see new faces — ah, I am forgetting, you have met Mr Elton, but not often. It will give a new turn to your thoughts."

Jane remembered her former hope that Mr Elton's wife might prove a pleasant companion, a substitute for Rachel. Dispiritedly, she walked with Miss Bates along Vicarage Lane.

Mrs Elton proved to be a short, thin, vivacious lady, not in her first youth. — She might be seven- or eight-and-twenty. Her hair was dark, not very plentiful, most elegantly dressed, her complexion somewhat sallow, her teeth very fine, a little prominent; she displayed them a great deal in laughing and talking. Her gown, too, Aunt Hetty thought remarkably elegant; Jane found it somewhat overtrimmed. — She was very ready to admire Jane and be friends.

"Oh! Miss Jane! Your fame has gone before you!" (laughing affectedly). "While in Bath I have been for ever hearing about you and your talents."

"In Bath?" said Jane, perplexed. "I do not believe that I have any acquaintance in Bath?" Her thoughts flew wildly to Frank, visiting the town with his aunt in January; but she felt very certain that Mrs Churchill would not move in the same circles as Miss Hawkins.

"Oh, but, Miss Fairfax, you do! A very old friend! And although I do not know the lady herself, I am acquainted, most intimately, with a lady who frequently visits her; a particular friend of mine, a Mrs Partridge; and from her I have been hearing such stories about the talents of Miss Jane Fairfax and her superior performance on the pianoforte, and all her other accomplishments. I assure you, it has been the greatest satisfaction, comfort, and delight to me to know there was the prospect of such an interesting acquaintance in the new society I am got into. You and I, Miss Fairfax, must, I think, establish a musical club here in Highbury; we must have many sweet little concerts here. Do not you think that a good plan?"

Jane was not very favourably impressed by Mrs Elton. She replied with caution: "I may not remain in Highbury very long — "

"Oh! my dear!" cried out her aunt. "You said — you are promised to us for at least three months. Now, did you not?"

"But pray tell me, Mrs Elton, for I am consumed with curiosity," said Jane, hoping to evade this issue, "who is your connection in Bath who knows me so very well?"

The lady in question turned out to be Mrs Pryor, widow of the former incumbent, now living in reduced circumstances in Westgate Buildings. "She is always busy, I believe," said Mrs Elton, "she makes a quantity of little thread-papers, pin-cushions and card-cases, which my friend Mrs Partridge is able to dispose of for her."

Jane's heart bled for her kind former teacher, reduced to such a pass. Oh, if only I could do something for her, she thought; thank heaven my aunt and grandmother have such thoughtful, attentive neighbours here.

And then, with a cold chill: Might I ever be reduced to such a level?

"But, pray, Miss Fairfax, tell me," went on Mrs Elton, "are you a great friend of Miss Emma Woodhouse? Seriously now, I wish to know. Everybody here informs me that Miss Emma is the first lady of the village, but — I own — I cannot warm to her! There is a something so very arrogant, so very disdainful about her — and what is she, after all? Hartfield is no bigger than my brother-in-law Mr Suckling's place at Maple Grove! I find her airs, her pretensions hard to bear, I must acknowledge."

"Oh, but my dear ma'am!" cried Aunt Hetty in distress, "Miss Woodhouse is so very gracious — so condescending — so kind to all of us — why, I could not enumerate the times that my mother has been up to take tea with old Mr Woodhouse — or a little supper — which is always so nice — and to play back-gammon — and then, if they kill a pig, Miss Woodhouse never omits to send us a leg — "

"*Mr* Woodhouse, I grant you — a dear old gentleman — quite old-fashioned in his courtesies — which I dearly love — my sister Selina often tells me I am absolutely old-fashioned in my own ways — but the daughter, with her cold stiff airs and manners — I must confess she is *not* to my taste! They say she is affianced to that rich young man, Mrs Weston's son-in-law?"

"We have not heard that? Is it indeed so?" exclaimed Aunt Hetty with the liveliest interest.

"No? Perhaps I may mistake. But, my dear Jane — (I know we are going to be great friends, you see, so I address you familiarly) — do you know what Miss Emma Woodhouse had the amazing impertinence — the effrontery — to assert? That my husband — that Mr Elton had been paying marked attentions to that little nobody, that Miss Smith, her friend, and that he was in duty bound to offer for her. Needless to say, it was no such thing, as he very soon made her understand! All this, of course — " laughing — "was before it had fallen to Mr E's lot to encounter little me at the Pump Room — "

"Is that so, indeed?" said Miss Bates. "Now you come to mention it, I do remember it was hinted at one time — Mrs Cole dropped a word to me about little Miss Smith — but I fear I am not quick at such things — "

That accounts, thought Jane, for the looks of decided ill-will that I have seen Mr Elton casting towards Emma Woodhouse. I wondered why he seemed to dislike her so. She expected him to marry her protégée. Perhaps the gentleman himself had higher expectations? Perhaps *he* hoped to marry Miss Woodhouse herself? Mercy on me! I am becoming as parochial and gossip-minded as the worst old lady in the village.

"Miss Smith!" continued Mrs Elton with fine scorn. "Why — nobody even knows who her parents were!"

Mr Elton came in, glossy with self-satisfaction and the married state.

"I have been telling Miss Jane, Mr E," cried his wife, "that she and I must join forces and start a musical club. A soirée every Thursday night! Do you not think that a famous plan?"

Jane demurred again that she did not know how long it would be within her power to remain in Highbury. — She had a strong notion that Frank Churchill would detest Mrs Elton.

"I have a letter today from my friends in Ireland — Colonel and Mrs Campbell — this very day — suggesting that I join them, for they are now to remain until midsummer. They are so very pressing — "

"Oh, but my dear," wailed Aunt Hetty in agitation. "You told me, you did tell me, that you were going to refuse their kind offer?"

"I am certain that your Irish friends can spare you to us for a while longer, dear Jane. No, no! I cannot afford to lose the best musical talent in Highbury until my musical programme is well established. We shall not permit you to leave us yet!" declared Mrs Elton with an arch smile.

Without at all liking her situation, Jane found herself being manoeuvred into promises of far greater intimacy with the Eltons than she either wished or intended. I am finely served, she thought with some irony, for my dissatisfaction with my lot and feeling the lack of a friend. Now I am supplied with one, and what a friend! Emma Woodhouse would be infinitely superior. And, because the Eltons appeared to be arrayed in enmity against Emma, Jane began to feel more kindly towards her.

"Mrs Elton seems such a clever, kind-hearted lady," said Aunt Hetty, with simple satisfaction on the walk home. "It will be a fine thing for you, my dear, to be going over to the vicarage for musical evenings and exploring parties, getting away from us old people for a while; you must not be closeted with grandmamma and me all the time, you know, or you will fall into the dismals. And then, Mrs Elton has such great connections! She has promised me that she will look about her, by and by, and find a situation for you. Not that we wish you to leave us — never that! But a situation that was not too far distant from Highbury — with some elegant, respectable family — we could not, in conscience, decline. I am sure Colonel Campbell would agree with me there."

Oh, Frank! thought Jane. What am I to do?

Willy-nilly, she saw herself being whisked off to some Maple Grove, to the residence of some Mrs Suckling.

Two days later, however, came an exultant letter from Frank himself. "I have persuaded my aunt and uncle that a remove to London will do them both good. We shall soon be in Manchester Street, perhaps in April; certainly in May. What a joy to know that then I shall be only sixteen miles distant from you — that scarcely more than an hour's ride will bring me the chance of seeing you, of being near you. I think of you continually — dream of you every night — am consumed with longing for that time."

Jane could not help feeling happier. His letters were so loving, so warm, so spontaneous. They always raised her spirits. She had missed, she must acknowedge to herself, the daily flow of notes, verses, and absurd tiny gifts which he had contrived to deposit in the hollow oak-tree, while he was staying with Mr Weston. And yet, she thought, what real benefit will it bring me to have him close at hand? It entails a continual charade, a lie told to every person I know — which is so odious. I have no gift for pretending, acting a part, disguising my feelings to the people I love best. It is strange that Frank does not seem to object to that part of the affair — in honest fact, I believe he almost enjoys it!

Her thoughts were running on these lines as she sat on a stile three-quarters of a mile outside the village, after re-reading Frank's letter — for it was a fine warm afternoon of late March — when, unexpectedly close, she heard voices, and saw Emma and Harriet Smith approaching along a footpath.

"Ah, good-day, Miss Fairfax!" cried Emma cordially. "Is it not charming weather? We, as you see, have been gathering catkins for our drawing programme. — Do you receive good news from your friends in Ireland?" for Jane, blushing, had hastily stuffed the sheets of Frank's letter into her muff. She thought she saw Emma's eyes on the paper. Annoyed, Jane blushed even deeper at the recollection of Frank and Emma's light-hearted teasing on the subject of Matt Dixon. How *could* they? How could Frank talk of Matt Dixon in such a manner, in such a context, when he at least knew how much the name really meant to her?

She answered Emma composedly that her friends in Ireland were well, and that they had repeatedly invited her to join them — which, after all, was the truth; but that at present she would not leave her aunt and grandmother.

"Ah, very dutiful — very right," said Emma. "Is it not, Harriet?"

"Oh *yes*! Miss Woodhouse!"

Jane thought Harriet a tedious little creature. Her conversation seemed to consist entirely of "Oh, yes, Miss Woodhouse! Oh, no, Miss Woodhouse!" How could Emma put up with it, day after day? Not, in truth, that she has much alternative, thought Jane. Then she wondered briefly how Harriet had taken the defection of Mr Elton. Had she been in love with Elton? Had she been greatly grieved? She seemed cheerful enough now.

"I am having a little dinner party next week," said Emma. "For Mr and Mrs Elton. We must pay proper attention to our new-married pair, must we not? I have persuaded Papa that it is our duty and he has — reluctantly — agreed, provided there be no more than eight persons. Mr and Mrs Weston of course will come, and Mr Knightley — Harriet is unable, for she has a previous engagement — " (here Harriet did look a little conscious) " — will you graciously make up our table, Miss Fairfax? Mr Knightley, I know, always enjoys talking to you."

Jane could not help a small glow at these words, though she suspected they were spoken mainly in mockery. — She thanked and accepted.

On the day of the dinner party, which was a wet one, heavy with sleety April showers, Mr and Mrs Elton offered to pick up Jane in their carriage. — She had far rather the offer had come from Mr Knightley; she was not very happy to arrive at Hartfield under the aegis, as it were, of the Eltons. — Coming to Hartfield was always a little strange, a little painful for Jane, because, although the house did not seem to welcome her now, so much of her childhood was connected with it; she could never enter the grounds, or the rooms, without recalling those long, fulfilled, peaceful days of childhood, those tranquil hours at the piano, with Mrs Woodhouse silently listening in the next room; and the strange unhappy week spent with the newly-bereaved Emma. Does *she* ever think of those days? Jane wondered.

To her surprise and pleasure she had discovered, earlier in the day, that Mr John Knightley was also to be one of the guests. She had met him in the village with his two little boys. It seemed that he had come down from London to escort these, the eldest of his children, who were to pay a visit to their grandfather and aunt. — To do Emma justice, she does seem to be an affectionate aunt, thought Jane. — But how will Mr Woodhouse endure such an enlargement of his group, if he cannot tolerate more than eight people round the dinner table? And how will Mr John Knightley enjoy being plunged into the middle of a social gathering? Of old, Jane knew him for a somewhat taciturn, unsociable individual.

Fortunately for Mr Woodhouse's peace of mind, Mr Weston had been unexpectedly summoned to town, and was not able to present himself at dinner-time. The numbers around the table were no more than they should be.

Mr John Knightley, who had always, in his quiet, reserved way, been fond of Jane, talked to her before dinner, while his brother and Mrs Weston engaged the Eltons.

"I hope you did not venture far, Miss Fairfax, this morning, or I am sure you must have been wet?"

"I went only to the post office," said Jane, "and reached home before the rain was much. It is my daily errand. A walk before breakfast does me good."

"Not a walk in the rain, I imagine," he said drily. "When you have lived to my age you will begin to think that letters are never worth going through the rain for."

"I cannot expect," said Jane, "that simply growing older should make me indifferent about letters."

"Letters are no matter of indifference; they are generally a very positive curse."

"I can easily believe that letters are very little to *you*!" cried Jane. "You have everybody dearest to you always at hand! I, probably, never shall again; and therefore, till I have outlived all my affections, a post office, I think, must always have power to draw me out, even in worse weather than today."

Mr Woodhouse, approaching, remarked, "I am very sorry to hear, Miss Fairfax, of your being out this morning in the rain. Young ladies should take care of themselves. Young ladies are delicate plants. — My dear, did you change your stockings?"

"Yes, sir, I did indeed; and I am very much obliged by your kind solicitude."

Mrs Elton, catching part of this conversation, now opened fire upon Jane.

"My dear Jane, what is this I hear? — Going to the post office in the rain? This must not be! You sad girl, how could you do such a thing? — Mrs Weston, did you ever hear the like? You and I must positively assert our authority! We will not allow her to do such a thing again! There must be some arrangement made, there must indeed. The man who fetches our letters every morning (one of our men, I forget his name) shall bring yours to you."

"You are extremely kind," said Jane, alarmed, "but I cannot give up my early walk."

"My dear Jane, say no more about it — consider that point as settled."

"Excuse me," said Jane earnestly. "I cannot by any means consent to such an arrangement — "

Unintentionally, she caught Emma's eye. A deep intelligence seemed to flash between them.

She has guessed something, thought Jane. She knows something. But knows *what?*

Hastily, almost at random, she began speaking again — about the post office — its efficiency in despatching letters to their correct destinations — the great variety of hand-writings — their general indecipherability; the talk turned next to similarities of hand-writing within a family — Emma's writing and that of her sister Isabella were cited as examples.

Emma herself suddenly struck in, rather wide of the point at issue.

"Mr Frank Churchill writes one of the best gentleman's hands I ever saw."

Good God! thought Jane, transfixed. Then she did see his letter! She recognised his writing on the paper in my hand, last week in the meadow!

The rest of the discussion was no more than a confused murmur in Jane's mind; she was deeply relieved when dinner was announced, not long after, and she heard Mrs Elton say, with her artificial laugh:

"Must I go first? I really am ashamed of always leading the way!"

Emma gave Jane a smiling, sidelong conscious glance as she took the other girl's arm and led her to the dining-room; any observer might have considered the appearance of goodwill as highly becoming to the beauty and grace of each.

After dinner Mrs Elton, ignoring her hostess in a manner which Jane could not help finding ill-bred and highly inappropriate to the occasion, led Jane aside and after first giving her another scold on the folly of her walks to the post office, brought the conversation round to her future career.

"Here is April come," she said. "I get quite anxious about you. Have you really heard of nothing?"

"I do not wish to make any inquiry yet."

"Oh, my dear child, your inexperience really amuses me! Indeed, indeed, we must begin inquiring directly."

"When I am quite determined as to the time — which I am not at present," said Jane firmly, "there are places in town — offices for the sale, not quite of human flesh, but of human intellect — "

"Oh, my dear, you quite shock me; — but, you know, it will not satisfy your friends to have you taking up with any inferior, commonplace situation — "

"I am quite serious," said Jane positively, "in wishing *nothing* to be done till the summer."

"And I am quite serious too, I assure you," replied Mrs Elton gaily, "in resolving to be always on the watch, that nothing really unexceptionable may pass by — "

Vexed, harassed almost beyond endurance, Jane hardly knew how to make a polite response. Fortunately, soon afterwards, Mr Weston made his appearance among them. He was cheerful and exultant after a satisfactory day in London, and because of a letter from Frank which he had found at home and handed to his wife.

"Read it, read it: he is coming, you see; good news, I think! In town next week, you see. They will stay a good while when they do come, and Frank will be half his time with us!"

Turning to Mrs Elton, who was close at hand, Mr Weston said, "I hope, ma'am, I shall soon have the pleasure of introducing my son to you."

Chapter 15

Soon the Churchills were known to be in London. Jane, returning with Aunt Hetty from a call on Mrs Cole, was thunderstruck, one morning, to see Frank in the street, on horseback. Though why should I be so startled? she reprimanded herself. Nothing is more natural, after all. — He had just ridden down for a couple of hours, he told them; had been at Randalls with his stepmother; in ten minutes or so, might he impose himself on them for a short visit? He was so eager to hear again that delightful upper register of Miss Fairfax's new piano. And had she yet — with a conspiratorial smile at Jane — heard anything about it from Colonel Campbell?

He came — after considerably more than a ten-minute interval — listened to the piano, pronounced it even mellower in tone than he had recalled, and informed them with great satisfaction that the ball at the Crown Inn was once again under practical consideration.

Though happy to hear this news, Jane was not a little piqued to find that, after the encounter in the street, and before coming to call on them, he had been visiting at Hartfield. — He seemed unusually flushed and excited. Was that because he had been talking to Emma? There was no opportunity for a private word between them. All must be open, public, such as might be heard by any person. There seemed no end to the evils of their situation. Jane longed to ask him what was the matter, but found no possibility of doing so.

This was the only sight of Frank she was to be granted for ten days. He was often hoping, intending to come, but as often prevented. That his aunt was really ill was very certain. And it soon appeared that London was not the place for her. She could not endure its noise. Her nerves were under continual irritation and suffering; and by the ten days' end a letter from Frank to his father communicated a change of plan. They were going to remove immediately to Richmond. Mrs Churchill had been recommended to the medical skill of an eminent practitioner there, and had otherwise a fancy for the place. A ready-furnished house was engaged for May and June.

Mr Weston was overjoyed. "Now we shall *really* have Frank in our neighbourhood! What are nine miles to an active young man — an hour's ride! He will be able to visit us almost every day — Richmond is the very distance for easy intercourse. *Now* we can name a day for our ball — a May ball! What could be better? Even dear Mr Woodhouse can have no alarms on the score of draughts or damp."

The day for the ball was fixed; but Jane, after so many alterations of plan, found herself almost indifferent to its arrival. What pleasure can it hold for me? she asked herself. And she prepared herself quietly and mechanically for the evening's gaiety, piling up her hair in the Parisian style that she had once achieved for Rachel, interweaving it with spangles and beads.

"Oh, my dear! Your hair!" cried her aunt. "I am sure everyone will be — Well! It is so very — ! And here is kind Mr Knightley's carriage, ready to take Grandmamma to Hartfield. Mind, now, ma'am, you take your shawl — for the evenings are not warm — your large new shawl that Mrs Dixon sent you — our friends are so kind! — such a beautiful blue. Colonel Campbell rather preferred an olive, I remember, Jane said, but I am sure blue better becomes — there were three, Jane said, under consideration, but in the end the blue was chosen. Now, ma'am, I shall just run round from the ball so as to bring you home, for I know Mr Woodhouse does not like to sit up too late; you may expect me at half-past nine — our best regards of course to dear Mr Woodhouse — well, Jane, are you ready? Here now is Mr Elton's carriage for us — dear me, so many carriages stopping at our door, people will think — and it is only just across the road, after all, no more than a hop, skip and jump — but, true, it rains just a little — or almost rains — what Patty would call a mizzle — "

Frank was at the door of the Crown to receive them, with smiles and umbrellas. His eyes told Jane how much he admired her looks. — She began to feel happier. And the large old spacious rooms looked very well, thronged with cheerful people who all knew one another, the darkened paint and stained paper softened and made mellow in a blaze of candlelight.

The Eltons had arrived already and been introduced to Frank; Jane heard Mrs Elton's comments on him:

"A very fine young man indeed, Mr Weston! I am happy to say that I am extremely pleased with him — so truly the gentleman, without the least conceit or puppyism. You must know I have a vast dislike of puppies — quite a horror of them. They were *never* tolerated at my brother-in-law's house, at Maple Grove. — Ah, Jane dear! Did the carriage collect you as it ought? You wear white — very right. I like to see a young girl — and your hair, always so clever. How do you like my gown? Do you approve this trimming? I rely on your taste. — How has Wright done my hair? What do you think of this fashion? *Nobody* can think of dress less than I do *as a rule*, — but, since this ball is given in compliment to me — I see very few pearls in the room except mine — even Miss Woodhouse does not — What do you think of this lace? Is it not charming? — So: Frank Churchill is a capital dancer! We shall see if our styles suit. A very fine young man, certainly, is Frank Churchill; I like him very well."

Frank, happening to catch Jane's eye at this moment, gave her a wink, a slow deliberate wink on the side of his face away from Mrs Elton; Jane gasped, choked into her fan, and quickly looked away. But her spirits rose.

They sank again, quickly, when the ball opened; Mr Weston with Mrs Elton led the way, Frank followed with Emma Woodhouse, having claimed the promise made by her to him when they inspected the room. Jane, dejected, must settle for dancing with Mr Elton, whose style did not suit her at all, though he evidently thought well of it himself, for he bowed and flourished and was in a continual course of smiles.

Mr Knightley, Jane observed, was not dancing; he stood among the older men and looked rather gloomy; Jane thought, not for the first time, how handsome and distinguished he appeared among the bulky country squires and thickset shoulders. Why did he come to the ball, if not to dance? she wondered. She had far rather he had been her partner than Elton. The evils of her patronage by the Eltons were incalculable. She wished there were some way — any way — in which she might distance herself from them.

Even more so did she wish it just before the supper interval when she saw Mr Elton give poor Harriet Smith a sharp and surely undeserved snub. Invited by Mrs Weston to dance with Miss Smith, the only young lady at that moment sitting down, he replied in a loud carrying tone: "Miss Smith — oh! I had not observed. But I am an old married man, Mrs Weston — my dancing days are over."

As he had been dancing with Jane herself not half an hour before, she could imagine with what surprise and mortification Miss Smith heard these words — especially since Mr Elton and his wife were now exchanging meaning smiles.

Next moment Mr Knightley stepped forward and invited Harriet to dance.

Jane, standing next them in the set, partnered this time by Frank, saw that Harriet's eyes were swimming with tears, and that she was directing towards Mr Knightley a gaze almost of worship. Poor little thing, she looked as if she had been reprieved from the scaffold. This should, at any rate, cure her of any partiality for Mr Elton, thought Jane. What an odious piece of behaviour! — She was pleased to observe the villain in question retreat to the card-room looking decidedly foolish.

Supper was announced, and now Jane must feel more comfortable, for Frank escorted her to the supper-room, along with Aunt Hetty, newly returned from seeing old Mrs Bates home after her evening with Mr Woodhouse. "I ran away, as I said I should, to help grandmamma to bed, and got back, and nobody missed me. Dear Jane, how shall we ever recollect half the dishes for grandmamma? Soup too! Bless me! I should not be helped so soon, but it smells most excellent — "

"Will you dance with me again?" Frank asked Jane after supper.

"Would not that look too particular?"

"Oh, no, I am sure not."

"Should you not dance with Miss Woodhouse?" she said rather coldly.

"No, why? See, she is walking on to the floor with Knightley. And looks very happy to do so."

"Oh well — in that case — "

"Come, Miss Woodhouse, Miss Otway, Miss Fairfax," cried Mrs Weston, "What are you all doing? Come, Emma, set your companions an example. You are all lazy! Everybody is asleep!"

Another set formed, and the ball proceeded.

Jane went home from it thinking better even than before of Mr Knightley (if that were possible) and worse of the Eltons, which was not at all difficult.

On the day succeeding the ball, a dramatic event occurred at Highbury, involving Mr Frank Churchill and Miss Harriet Smith.

Jane Fairfax did not witness it, but was, in the course of time, told about it by a large number of persons who had not been at the scene either, but knew all about it from one source or another.

Frank, expected back at Richmond by the middle of the day, was due to leave early in the morning. — He did, however, contrive a short call at the Bateses', on pretext of returning Aunt Hetty's scissors which he had borrowed during the ball to trim a candle-wick. Miss Bates being out at church he had achieved five minutes' private conversation with Jane in which they both agreed that Elton had behaved odiously to poor Harriet, and that his wife was unremittingly vulgar.

"Emma was in such a rage about it — she was saying to me that Elton had behaved disgracefully."

"Whereas Mr Knightley behaved beautifully," said Jane, wishful to get away from the subject of Emma, who seemed to recur a great deal in Frank's conversation at present.

"Knightley is a very decent fellow. I am sorry that he has taken such a strong dislike to me. I cannot think why!" said Frank cheerfully.

Then he insisted on talking about Switzerland.

"Since we can make no immediate plans," he declared, "let us prepare far-distant ones. I shall take you one day to Geneva — the Castle of Chillon — oh, how you will love those lakes and mountains. How their background will set off your beauty!"

"Oh, how unpractical you are!" sighed Jane. But nonetheless she was a little soothed by his promises, and by the fact that he had contrived to come and see her.

It was not until later in the day that, from Mrs Goddard, they heard of his subsequent adventure. Having taken a shortcut on foot and arranged to meet his chaise a mile beyond Highbury, he had heard female cries of distress as he walked forward, and found Harriet Smith and Miss Bickerton, a fellow-pupil at Mrs Goddard's, being harried by a band of gypsies in a deep, narrow lane. Miss Bickerton had managed to escape the troop by climbing up the bank and running across a field, Miss Smith, trembling and terrified, had given the gypsies a shilling and was being assailed by demands for more.

The troop, mostly children, were at once frightened off by young Mr Churchill, who then escorted the petrified, palpitating Miss

Smith to the nearest house (Hartfield, as it happened) where she immediately fainted.

Such an adventure as this — a fine young man and a lovely young woman thrown together in such romantic circumstances — could hardly fail of suggesting certain ideas to the ready minds and readier tongues of Highbury. Within half a day gossip had Mr Churchill and Miss Smith marked down as a most peculiarly interesting couple; and Jane, who, whatever and among all her jealous anxieties, could not impute to Frank the smallest interest in foolish little Harriet, could breathe easy for a while.

One of the worst evils of their situation, she had decided, was the growth of misunderstandings and misapprehensions which, based perhaps in the first place on small, inadvertent errors, had no chance of being talked away in the natural course of communication, but grew and festered.

She was assured by Frank that he had no real interest in Emma Woodhouse, and yet, when she saw his manner to her, and, even more, the way in which Emma received these attentions, it was hard for Jane to remain tranquil and unperturbed. — Emma would have him in a moment if he offered, I am sure of it, she thought. Oh! how trapped I feel here, how I wish that I could get away and occupy my mind with something sensible, instead of these morbid fancies. — I wonder if Emma feels trapped here too?

During the week following the ball at the Crown a fair was held in Highbury; this was an annual event, instituted centuries ago as a horse- and hiring-fair; there were still nowadays to be found a few booths selling cloth, leather articles, tools, produce, and cheeses, but the greater part of the proceedings were now given over to sports, merriment, fortune-telling, maypole- and morris-dancing, and the sale of knick-knacks. Jane, as a child, had always longed to visit the fair, but it was not patronised by the gentry. "There are too many rough, rude doings," had said Aunt Hetty, "it is not an affair for gently-bred little folk. Mrs Woodhouse never takes Isabella or Emma, you may be sure!" and so small Jane had sighed out her longing from a distance, listening through an open bedroom window to the joyful sounds of kettledrum, pipes, and fiddle in the big meadow behind the George and Dragon.

Only half seriously she had once suggested to Frank that this would be an occasion when formality might be waived, if he wished to escort her and Harriet Smith (who, likewise, had been heard one day voicing a plaintive wish to see the jollifications, and being most decidedly set down by Emma, who told her that it was a noisy, tawdry affair, in no way befitting the notice of persons of quality).

Frank, however, had shown a reluctance to accede to Jane's suggestions; greatly though he would enjoy accompanying his dear Jane and little Miss Smith to the village junketings, he doubted if his aunt would countenance another visit to Highbury quite so soon after the ball; the matter was therefore left indefinite; and, by the day of the fair, Jane still had not heard from him. Boldly, therefore, she resolved to ignore convention, to see and enjoy the festivity for herself; and she communicated her intention to Harriet Smith, who was overjoyed to be her companion. Accordingly the two young ladies, having paid their sixpence at the gate, began with caution to explore the aisles between the canvas booths.

"Oh, Miss Fairfax, is not this entertaining? *Do* look at the little pigs in that pen — and the sheep-shearing, oh, how fast they do it! — Gracious me! What enormous cheeses! Only see those muslins, how very cheap, I wonder if I should buy a length? Or a kerchief, or a posy? But then one would have to carry them. And here are mops and pails, but I do not wish to purchase a mop . . . Oh, Miss Fairfax, a fortune-teller! Only a penny! Should we have our fortunes told?"

But Jane, with a slight shiver, dragged the over-enthusiastic Miss Smith away from the fortune-teller's booth, with its tinsel moon and stars; she felt far too uncertain of her own future to wish to put it to the question.

"Let us watch the maypole-dancing," she proposed instead.

"Oh yes! Let us!" agreed Harriet with perfect docility.

The maypole-dancing was pure delight, with its white garlanded pole and light-footedly expert boys and girls, each holding the end of a different-coloured ribbon, twining these into webs and patterns, sometimes closely enfolding the pole, sometimes spread out into an airy curtain. The music made one long to be in there dancing also . . .

"If only Frank were here to enjoy this with me," thought Jane, at that moment honestly longing for him; and the next instant she saw Frank himself, on the opposite side of the circular space round the maypole, in the company of Emma Woodhouse. At the same time he saw Jane — looked amused and delighted and self-congratulatory; then he, along with Emma, was eagerly threading his way through the crowd towards Miss Smith and herself. His explanations for arriving thus unexpectedly, and with the wrong lady, were entirely reasonable:

"Was not this famous? At the very last, his aunt had relented, so rode at top speed to Highbury; learned that Miss Fairfax and Miss Smith had gone to the fair on their own — doughty young ladies! — Had started off, accordingly, in search of them, and by the post office had encountered Miss Woodhouse who, pleased by the music in the distance, had finally allowed him to persuade her . . . "

All this was run through very gaily, and the smile he gave Jane was entirely confident, full of affection. But had he not — Jane asked herself — been giving just such another smile to Miss Woodhouse a moment before?

"Now, ladies, what would you wish to see next?" said he. "The Learned Pig? The blacksmith's shop? The fish stall? Miss Fairfax, would not your aunt enjoy a fine fresh fish for her supper? I am entirely at your service."

"Oh — good gracious!" cried out Harriet. "Look, Miss Woodhouse — there is Mr Martin with his sisters — " pointing to a ruddy-faced young farmer accompanying a pair of plain, sensible-looking girls. "Oh, should I not go and bid them good-day?"

"No, no, certainly not," said Emma, "they have not seen you, there is not the least occasion to go out of your way to distinguish them. Mr Churchill, I thank you for your escort; and I must aver that the fair is just as I expected: a noisy, vulgar romp, worth a five-minutes' visit, no more. I shall now be equally obliged for your company back to Hartfield; and, Harriet, I think you had best return with me; spending more than a brief time at such an event as this will do you no credit; let us hope that no one of consequence in Highbury has noticed you here."

"Very well, Miss Woodhouse," murmured Harriet, quite quenched; and Jane, deprived of her companion, had no option but to quit the scene with the others.

She was silent on the return walk and when Frank asked if, having escorted Miss Woodhouse home, he might call on her aunt and grandmother, she replied to him coolly that they would not be at home; they were bidden to the vicarage later that day.

"Sooner you than I!" said Emma. "Then, Mr Churchill, you are kindly welcome to come in and entertain my father, who is always happy to see you."

May, with its primroses and hawthorn blossom, was warming into June when the Eltons gave a party.

Mrs Elton, arriving in Highbury, had been greatly shocked at the inferior standards of the social evenings there, at the want of ice, the smallness of the rooms, the pitiful quantity and quality of rout-cakes, and the unblushing use of dog-eared packs of cards that had plainly been dealt and shuffled many times before. — She now proposed to make a return for all the hospitality she had received by one very superior and prestigious party.

"Will it be necessary for us to invite the Woodhouses?" she said to her husband. He, after due consideration, replied,

"I fear we must, my love; old Mr W is, after all, the chief churchwarden; but let us wait to invite them until a week after all the other invitations have been sent out; that will show proud Miss Emma at what value we hold her!"

This small piece of spite had an effect which he had not foreseen: apprised in advance of this gala by Mr Knightley and other friends who had received invitations, Emma was able to be ready with a previous engagement of her own: she was so very sorry but that was the evening on which her sister, Mrs Isabella Knightley, was to be with them to collect the little boys, John and Henry . . . So, honour was satisfied on both sides.

Frank happened to be spending that evening with his father and stepmother and was graciously included in their invitation; he was, of course, happy for a chance to be anywhere in company with Jane, especially in a large concourse of people where, it was to be hoped, his attentions to her might not be remarked.

As it fell out, the younger and more frivolous members of the party were assembled at a large table, playing Speculation, while the older and more sober guests were on the other side of the room, engaged in whist. Frank Churchill contrived to get himself seated by Jane, who had never played Speculation before, and he amused himself by teaching her the fine points of the game and, in general, looking after her hand. Mr Knightley, among the whist players, began to notice, across the room, what he interpreted as signs of unusual intelligence between the pair — certainly looks of great, almost proprietorial admiration, of far more than mere liking, on the gentleman's side, and a kind of consciousness, of some deeper understanding, on the part of the lady.

Knightley was troubled; he had always, since her childhood, had a considerable regard for Jane Fairfax, and he could not endure the notion that she might have become involved in any kind of clandestine relation — especially with young Mr Churchill, to whom, from the start, for reasons only known to himself, he had taken a strong dislike. — He studied them with greater attention, and, moving their way when the cards were at an end and the company standing in a loose group near the fire, waiting for carriages, heard Frank say in a low tone:

"Do you know what I count as my most treasured possession?"

The talk in the group had been about what should be saved first in a conflagration, supposing one had only a moment in which to choose.

Jane shook her head, deliberately moving away from him, searching with her eyes for her aunt.

"A small handful of letters," Frank said. "A packet no bigger than would fit into the palm of a glove — that should be *my* first object — "

But Jane had left him and was saying to Miss Bates, "Aunt Hetty, should we not go home? It grows late and Grandmamma will be anxious — "

"May I not escort you home?" began Frank, but she shook her head vehemently, and was out of the door before he could attract the attention of his father and stepmother.

This looks very bad, thought Knightley to himself; this has all the air of downright collusion. Just what I would have thought of Frank Churchill — an idle, trifling sort of fellow! But how can Jane Fairfax, a girl of superior discretion and understanding — how can *she* have become so enmeshed?

A week later another series of events brought him yet stronger suspicions.

The Westons and their son had been out walking, and had persuaded Miss Bates and her niece to accompany them. It was a fine June evening and, not far from Hartfield, they encountered Mr Knightley escorting Harriet and Emma homewards from a stroll down Donwell Lane. At Hartfield gates Emma, who knew it was exactly the sort of visiting that would please her father best, urged them all to go in and drink tea with him.

As they were turning in at Hartfield gates, Mr Perry passed on his horse.

"Did Perry, then, never set up his carriage?" asked Frank idly.

"Carriage?" said Mrs Weston. "I did not know that he had any such plan."

"Nay, I had it from you! You wrote me of it three months ago."

"Me? Impossible! I never heard of such a plan."

"Never? Really, never? Then I must have dreamed it. I am a great dreamer," Frank said laughing. "I dream of all my friends at Highbury when I am away, and when I have gone through them, then I dream of Mr Perry."

"Why, to own the truth," cried Miss Bates, "there *was* such an idea last spring, for Mrs Perry herself mentioned it to my mother — but it was quite a secret, and only thought of about three days — Mrs Perry thought she had prevailed on him to buy a carriage. Jane, don't you remember grandmamma's telling us of it — where is Jane? Oh, just behind. Extraordinary that Mr Churchill should have such a dream!"

Mr Knightley saw, or thought he saw, in Frank Churchill's face, confusion suppressed, or laughed away; he had involuntarily turned towards Jane, but she was behind, busy with her shawl. Mr Knightley suspected in Frank Churchill the determination of catching her eye — he seemed watching her intently — in vain, however, Jane passed between them into the hall and looked at neither.

"Miss Woodhouse," said Frank Churchill later, when they were all seated at the large round table, having drunk tea, "Miss Woodhouse, did your nephews take away their alphabets? We had great amusement with those letters one morning. I want to puzzle you again."

Emma, pleased with the thought, produced the box, and the table was quickly scattered over with the letters that she had written on small squares of board for the two little boys.

Frank was now, Knightley observed with strong disapprobation, directing a great deal of attention — what could only be categorized as *flirtatious* attention — towards Emma, as if to throw a veil over his real thoughts or intentions; after he and Emma had mutually amused one another for a good many minutes by forming words for the other to solve, he, with a rather too casual air, pushed a word in front of Miss Fairfax, who applied herself to it. Frank was next to Emma, Jane opposite them, and Mr Knightley was so placed as to see them all. The word was discovered and, with a faint smile, re-jumbled and pushed away. Harriet Smith, eager after every fresh word, directly took it up. She was sitting next to Mr Knightley and turned to him for help. The word was *blunder*; and as Harriet exultingly proclaimed it, there was a blush on Jane's cheek which gave it a meaning not otherwise ostensible. Mr Knightley connected it with the dream, but how it all connected was beyond his comprehension. How the delicacy, the discretion, of his favourite could have been so laid asleep! He feared there must be some decided involvement. Disingenuousness and double dealing seemed to meet him at every turn.

Continuing to watch, he saw a short word prepared for Emma and given to her with a look sly and demure. She found it highly entertaining, though it was something which she judged it proper to appear to censure, for she said, "Nonsense! For shame!"

He heard Frank Churchill next say, with a glance towards Jane, "I will give it to her — shall I?" and as clearly heard Emma opposing it with eager, laughing warmth — "No, no, you must not, you shall not, indeed."

It was done, however, and Mr Knightley, darting his eye towards it, saw the word to be *Dixon*. Jane Fairfax was evidently displeased: looking up, seeing herself watched, she blushed more deeply than Knightley had ever perceived her and saying only, "I did not know that proper names were allowed," pushed the letters angrily away and turned to her aunt.

"Ay, very true!" cried the latter. "It is time for us to be going, indeed."

Frank Churchill anxiously pushed towards Jane another collection of letters, but these were ignored.

Jane, wrapped in her shawl, bidding goodnight to Mr Knightley, felt in his parting salutation a gravity, a coldness, a displeasure which, from him, she had never expected to receive; on the walk home with Aunt Hetty, listening to her aunt's chat, she answered never a word, but walked in silence, sunk in despondency, impotence, and a bitter feeling of injustice.

While Knightley, for his part, strode furiously back to Donwell, feeling that the arrival of Frank Churchill at Highbury had corrupted his two favourite people in it: Emma Woodhouse and Jane Fairfax had both, in different ways, been injured by the young man's company and had become sly and spiteful on the one hand, deceitful and secretive on the other. — He wished to heaven that the contemptible young puppy had never left Yorkshire.

Chapter 16

It was now the middle of June, and the weather very fine; Frank was repeatedly at Highbury, and Jane had the greatest difficulty in persuading him that it would be wrong — disastrous — the greatest piece of folly imaginable — for him to walk alone with her through the copses, heaths, and hayfields, or along the lanes bespangled with wild-rose and honeysuckle.

"It is such a waste!" cried he. "Am I *never* to see you alone? Notes and tokens are fine, but it is your dear presence that I so desperately need and want! In this charming weather, in this delightful country? It is too hard, it is too unfair! Here have I made all these efforts to come to Highbury — persuaded my aunt and uncle to remove from Yorkshire, from London — and now all I get is a glimpse of you at some atrocious card party at the Eltons'!"

For Jane, miserably jealous and angry with Emma over the unkind joke in the letter-game, had resolved never to set foot in Hartfield again. With a rankling sense of injury she began to feel that Emma, wealthy, happy, cheerful, and free, was far better suited to Frank Churchill than she herself; they enjoyed the same kind of jokes, they were not fettered by the considerations of conduct, of propriety, of rectitude that prevented Jane from taking advantage of brief, stolen meetings with her lover; in short, she feared, now that Frank had had time to become thoroughly acquainted with Miss Woodhouse, that he had begun to regret his illicit connection, and to wish to be rid of it. And small wonder! Jane thought sometimes, remorsefully. For when he did succeed in a short private meeting it was only, more often than not, to receive cold words, reproaches, almost hostility. And this was the more unfair, she acknowledged to herself, because, in her present constricted existence, Frank was almost the only source of cheer and comfort. — She received, these days, fewer letters from Ireland, and must admit sadly that distance and the passage of time were playing their inevitable part in cooling and diminishing those once vital relationships. Colonel and Mrs Campbell wrote of a possible return to London in August; but this return had been deferred so often that another postponement seemed highly possible. — Whereas Frank's attentions and solicitude never diminished; in between his assiduous calls at Hartfield, his walks and talks and ostensible courtship of Miss Woodhouse, he still found time for an immense number of little notes and tiny trinkets tucked into the crevice of the oak tree; the notes sometimes no more than a line, or a verse:

> " 'One moment may with bliss repay
> Unnumbered hours of pain
> Such was the throb and mutual sob
> Of the knight embracing Jane . . . '

Would that *I* had been that knight! But this may serve to show that I am ever thinking of thee, ever thine — F. C."

Since Jane, remonstrating with Frank over the gift of the piano, had begged him never, never to compromise her in such a way again — as the cramped accommodation at her grandmother's entirely precluded the possibility of concealing any new article — he exercised the utmost ingenuity in finding her objects of such minute size that they might be hidden in the finger of a glove or the fold of a handkerchief: a diminutive Chinese ivory dog "to watch over you" said Frank; a Venetian glass bead of glowing colours "which will one day be restored to its twenty-nine brothers; meanwhile accept it as an earnest of what is to come"; a pea-sized silk purse containing Maundy money, silver pieces of which the biggest was no larger than her finger-nail. She had to admit that his gifts were enchanting, and showed the most imaginative affection. Which made her own behaviour all the more unreasonable. But she could not help herself.

Meanwhile she found the life of Highbury more and more insufferably confined, stifling, and petty. How had Emma endured it for so many years? The course of conversation was always the same. Daily Jane was obliged to listen to conjectures from Mrs Cole, Mrs Goddard, Mrs Cox, Mrs Otway, regarding the probable alliance of Mr Churchill and Miss Woodhouse: "Such a good match! Such a charming young couple! So well suited!" — or sometimes, as an alternative, that of Mr Churchill and Miss Smith: "So very romantic as that would be! But, you know, his grand family would never permit it, for she is nobody!" Another source of speculation was a reported friendship between Mr Knightley and Miss Smith: "He has been taking a great deal of notice of her lately! And that, you know, he never did before." This suggestion, coming out of the blue, caught Jane unguarded and gave her a wholly unforeseen wrench of anguish: "No!" she thought. "It cannot be true! He would never waste himself on that little ninny!" She was not, it seemed, quite prepared yet to forego her dreams of Mr Knightley.

To such discourse, Jane's only alternative was the Eltons' ill-judged malice against Emma, and Mrs Elton's officious and wholly exasperating attempts to hustle Jane into some undesired teaching post. — The fact that her own conscience told her she should no longer be a charge upon Colonel Campbell's purse made these ministrations no easier to bear.

And if she mentioned the subject to Frank, he simply brushed it aside; his attitude to this matter was another source of almost unbearable irritation. "Teach? You? What nonsense! The idea is not to be thought of!"

"But it *has* been thought of," said Jane stiffly and angrily. "The whole of my education has been directed to that end. It has been thought of, and it must be thought of."

"Well, I, for one, refuse to think of it," said Frank, and he tickled her wrist with a buttercup — they were walking over Highbury Common with Miss Bates, the Westons, and the Eltons.

"Mr Churchill!" cried Mrs Elton ahead of them, turning round, "shall you be in Highbury next Friday? I purpose that day for our exploration to Box Hill — I am relying on you to make one of the party! It is to be a *fête-champêtre*, you know — we shall carry shepherds' crooks and play on pipes, and the ladies will wear wreaths of wild-roses round their hats. It was to have been this week, but one of our carriage-horses fell lame — so vexatious!"

Frank promised to be one of the party to Box Hill, though he disclaimed any ability to play upon pipes, and as none of the other guests invited possessed the requisite skill, that part of the programme had regretfully to be abandoned.

Jane felt small expectation of pleasure from the affair, having learned that Emma was to be one of those present: Frank's manner to Emma in public was now that of the acknowledged suitor, and hers one of gracious encouragement and acceptance; each, to Jane, was about as agreeable as salt upon a wound.

But before the Box Hill excursion lay another social hurdle which Jane would also gladly have avoided, though she saw no means of doing so. This was an invitation to all his friends in the village from Mr Knightley to walk out to Donwell Abbey, partake of a nuncheon, and pick as many of his strawberries as they wished.

"So very kind!" cried Aunt Hetty. "And indeed the Donwell strawberries are the best in the country. Not that I may partake of them myself — you know how sadly unwell they make me — but if you and I, Jane, pick hard for an hour or so, we shall be able to carry home enough to make at least half a dozen pots of preserve for Grandmamma — and you know strawberry is her very favourite!"

So there was no avoiding the day at Donwell. Mr Knightley's manner to Jane, ever since the evening of the letter-game at Hartfield, had been so distant, so grave, so unbending, that she felt herself utterly cut off from his favour and former cordial friendship. No more mention had been made of horseback riding excursions. So a day spent at his house must be penitential, not pleasurable, for she saw no means in the world of regaining his esteem.

The day, indeed, proved exactly what she had expected. Donwell Abbey was a beautiful old place, rambling and cool, low and sheltered; its ample gardens, extending down to an encircling stream, were justly famous; there was a lime avenue, and a handsome view to the river where lay the Abbey Mill Farm, nestling under a tree-clad escarpment.

And the weather was almost unbearably hot.

"That, you know, is where the Martins live," said Aunt Hetty, pointing to the farm, after they had picked as many berries as they could, and were strolling, to grow cool, in the shade. "I recall, at *one* time, there was talk of Harriet Smith marrying Mr Robert Martin — Mrs Goddard said he had offered for her indeed — Miss Smith was very friendly with the Martin sisters — but I daresay Miss Woodhouse will have dissuaded her from the match. She could do better for herself, no doubt! Mrs Cole has been saying — Mr Frank Churchill — or, I have sometimes thought, Mr Knightley — he did dance with her, you recall, at the Crown, and that seemed so very — and there he is, indeed, walking with her now — "

Oh, this insufferable place! thought Jane. Never, ever free from somebody's observation! A neighbourhood of voluntary spies! Every act, every word is noticed, is heard!

She looked quickly, unhappily towards Mr Knightley, pacing

along the lime walk with Harriet on his arm. — He had not spoken to her, Jane, all day, except briefly to bid her good-morning. — Well, Harriet certainly could not do better than Mr Knightley, though surely he will find her conversation utterly lacking in substance? Still, they seemed *now* to be finding topics of conversation, to be talking together very comfortably.

With remorse, Jane took Aunt Hetty's arm and drew her to a seat under a spreading beech-tree. There Mrs Elton pounced upon them.

"Aha, my dear Jane! Now you *must* listen to this! A Mrs Smallridge, own cousin to Mrs Bragge, a friend of my sister Selina, a lady well known at Maple Grove — delightful people! Charming situation! — and she is in need of just such a clever young lady as yourself — very best circles of society — not at all far from Bristol — you would be given the very first consideration (even although you are not able to play the harp) — treated as a person of consequence; indeed you *shall*, you *must* take this opportunity! I will brook no denial. I will not indeed! Pray, now, my dear, dear Jane, now do, do authorize me to write off by return of post — only heard from Selina this very morning — *must* close with such an offer immediately — "

Jane, repeatedly thanking, declining, shaking her head, felt in despair as if she were trying to fight off a cloud of stinging gnats. It was torture. Glancing past Mrs Elton, she saw Emma pass by with Mrs Weston and caught Emma's eye; almost, she felt she saw there a glance of friendship, of commiseration.

When a remove was made to the house, Jane was immensely relieved; they were all invited in to a shadowed, cool dining-room, where cold meat, fruit, and cake were laid out, and then they might carry their food to eat it where they chose.

Emma's father, old Mr Woodhouse, had been indoors all morning by a fire; he would not go out, for he found the hot sun deleterious, but had been well entertained with books of engravings, cameos, shells, corals, and drawers full of coins and medals. Jane was happy to go and sit with him for a while — she had always been fond of Mr Woodhouse — and listen to his simple admiration of these simple things.

In the distance she heard the voice of Mr Weston, reassuring his wife:

"Nonsense! my dear, the black mare is as steady a mount as could be wished. No, depend upon it, Frank's lateness will have been caused by some crotchet, some sudden whim of Mrs Churchill; be sure, that is all it will be. The boy will arrive soon enough, mark my words."

Frank's lateness, which would once have distressed Jane, now seemed, if anything, a relief, the removal of one cause of stress. And the look on the face of Mr Knightley, she observed, appeared to denote that he, for one, would be perfectly happy if young Mr Churchill failed to arrive entirely.

After the meal they were all to go out of doors again, and now Mrs Elton recaptured Jane and was even more unflagging in her unwelcome applications.

"Excuse me," Jane said at last, driven beyond endurance, "I see Miss Woodhouse over there — I have something I wish to say to her — " knowing well that Mrs Elton, who daily slandered Miss Woodhouse to the top of her powers, would never choose to follow her into *that* company.

Miss Woodhouse was strolling towards a side entrance that led into the house; Jane followed, and caught her withindoors.

"Miss Woodhouse! Will you be so kind, when I am missed, as to say that I am gone home? My aunt is not aware how late it is; but I am sure my grandmother will want us; I am determined to go directly. When they come in, will you have the goodness to say that I am gone? I know Mr and Mrs Elton will drive my aunt home."

Emma's sympathy, her kindly interest, were caught directly.

"Certainly, if you wish it? But you are not going to walk to Highbury *alone*?"

"Yes, what should hurt me? I walk fast, I shall be at home in twenty minutes."

"But it is too far — let my father's servant accompany you — let me order the carriage — "

"Thank you — thank you — no. I had rather walk. And for *me* to be afraid of walking alone — I, who may so soon have to guard others!"

And, when Emma still tried to dissuade her: "Miss Woodhouse, we all know at times what it is to be wearied in spirits. Mine, I confess are exhausted. The greatest kindness you can show me will be to let me have my way."

"I do understand you, perfectly," said Emma, and saw her out of the front door with all the zeal of a friend.

"Oh, Miss Woodhouse!" exclaimed Jane, from a full heart, "the *comfort* of being sometimes alone!"

She saw on the other girl's face a sudden flash of startled comprehension, which showed that if Emma had not always given much thought to Jane's situation, she at least did so now.

Alone in Donwell Lane, enjoying the wonderful solace of the silence around her, Jane was saddened by the reflection that, had circumstances turned out otherwise, she and Emma Woodhouse might indeed have become such good friends as, at that moment, they almost seemed.

Once well away from the Abbey, Jane pulled out a letter from her reticule and re-read it, as she slowly paced along. It was from Rachel: a letter overflowing with joy to announce that she and Matt Dixon were now the delighted parents of a son. "If it had been a daughter, dearest Jenny, we should have named her after you; but as he is a son we have christened him little Sam, and only hope that he may grow up as dear, good, beloved and clever as his uncle. My father and mother are overjoyed at being grandparents, and have agreed to remain with us here at least until October. — Matt sends his best love to you, Jenny dear, and so do I; when, *when* will you come to make the acquaintance of this newest Dixon?"

Joyful news, there could be no question; justification of all her actions; and yet, with it, somehow, Jane felt that a door had closed; her relation with Rachel could never again be quite what it had been; Rachel and Matt were now cemented together into a proper married pair. And Jane's connection with Matt? That was gone, entirely — forgotten — blotted out. He was lost to her for ever.

Having reached which point in her reflection, she heard the sound of hoofs, and, rounding a bend in the lane, saw Frank Churchill before her, mounted on the black mare. He looked hot, and decidedly out of spirits.

His greeting of Jane lacked the usual unfeigned delight.

"But what are you doing *here*? — I do not understand? — Is not this rather singular? Besides, I had hoped to see you at the house, at Donwell — what will people think?"

"Oh, think — think!" cried Jane, out of all patience. "What do I care what people think? No," she corrected herself. "I do care. But — Mrs Elton was not to be borne — and Mr Knightley is so angry with me — I am sure he has discovered our secret — and it was so hot — and that odious woman has found yet another situation which she *insists* I must accept — "

"Will you not return with me now to Donwell?" said he, only partly attending.

"Are you mad? Not on any account! What would people think *then*? No — no — you go on to Donwell — talk to Miss Woodhouse — have a pleasant day — "

"How could I do so? I suppose," he said, but not at all graciously, "I suppose I must accompany you back to Highbury. It is not at all right that you should walk this lane alone — neither safe nor proper. Remember what happened to Miss Smith!"

"And you think it would be proper for me to be seen walking along the lane in *your* company?" cried Jane furiously. "Is it not enough that my friends — people whose esteem I really value — already look on me coldly, and — and — " a strangled sob choked her utterance. After a moment she said more calmly, "Please leave me, Mr Churchill. I am in no need of your escort and do not wish it."

"Thank you," said he in an accent of deep mortification, remounted his mare, and rode on towards Donwell.

Gulping back her tears, Jane completed the walk to Highbury.

The picnic to Box Hill, on the following day, could hardly, under such auspices, have been expected to be successful; and it was not. In the first place, the party was too ill-assorted. Emma and the Eltons were hardly on speaking terms, Mrs Weston, a kind, good-humoured lady and a peace-keeper, remained at home, for she was within ten days of her confinement. Mr Knightley displayed gloomy disapproval towards Frank Churchill, who seemed unaware of it, and towards Jane, who was all too conscious of it. Mr Weston, good-natured and a little foolish, was wholly unaware of these undercurrents. Harriet Smith seemed nervous, Frank dull and depressed, Emma rather bored. Only Miss Bates was her cheerful self. And the weather was as hot as ever.

Over the cold collation, which they ate sitting upon the grass, Frank perked up and began to flirt outrageously with Emma. She responded in kind. It was very plain, Jane thought, that Frank's silly gallantries were simply intended to hurt and annoy herself; but what could be Emma's motive? In the normal way she was too well-bred to act as she was acting now. Once or twice, intercepting a saucy, teasing look which seemed directed at Mr Knightley, Jane wondered if Emma's wish was to pique that gentleman; if so, she was certainly successful, for his aspect became more and more lowering as the day proceeded.

— All in all, it was a horrible excursion. And the culminating point of discomfort and shame was reached after Frank announced:

"Ladies and gentlemen, I am ordered by Miss Woodhouse — who, wherever she is, presides — to say that she demands from each of you, either one thing very clever; or two things moderately clever; or three things very dull indeed; and she engages to laugh heartily at them all."

"Oh, very well!" exclaimed Miss Bates, who had been happily unconscious of all the nuances under the conversation hitherto, "Three things very dull indeed! That will just do for me, you know. I shall be sure to say three dull things as soon as ever I open my mouth — shan't I?" — looking round with the most good-humoured dependence on everybody's assent.

"Ah, but ma'am!" cried Emma. "There may be a difficulty. Pardon me, but you will be limited as to number — only three *at once*."

Miss Bates did not immediately catch Emma's meaning, but Jane, blushing scarlet, sprang up and walked a short distance away from the group. Then, mastering herself, she came back and sat down.

Frank tried to catch her eye, but she would not look at anybody.

Mrs Elton was now speaking in a high, affronted voice.

"Miss Woodhouse must excuse *me*. *I* am not one of those who have witty things at everybody's service. I have a great deal of vivacity *in my own way*, but really I must be allowed when to speak and when to hold my tongue. Pass us, if you please, Mr Churchill; pass Mr E, Jane, and myself."

"Shall we walk, Augusta?" said her husband.

"With all my heart! Come Jane, take my other arm."

Jane shook her head, however, and the husband and wife walked off.

"Happy couple!" said Frank. "How well they suit! Marrying, as they did, upon an acquaintance formed in a public place! It is only by seeing women in their own homes that you can form any just judgment. Short of that, it is all guess and luck — and will generally be *ill*-luck. How many a man has committed himself on a short acquaintance and rued it all the rest of his life!"

He was looking straight at Jane, who icily replied, "A hasty, imprudent attachment *may* arise; but there is generally time to recover from it afterwards. It can be only weak, irresolute characters who will suffer an unfortunate acquaintance to be an inconvenience — an oppression — for ever." He made no reply. "Now, ma'am," said Jane to her aunt, "Shall we join Mrs Elton?"

Miss Bates quietly agreed; as they walked away from the group, Jane heard Frank's voice behind her raised in what sounded like decidedly forced and false merriment.

The sight of the servants looking out for them to give notice of the carriages was a joyful one; though the ride back with the angry Eltons was a hardship to be endured, as much as possible, in silence.

"I was mistaken in that young man — *quite* mistaken! A puppy! An insufferable puppy! What he can see in Emma Woodhouse! Though she herself is no better! Who could tolerate her unpardonable rudeness to your aunt, my dear Jane? Quite unpardonable. But no more than might be expected — "

Jane, too, thought Emma had been unpardonable. But Miss Bates herself said tolerantly, "Oh, well you know, I do run on. I am a talker, I know I am a talker. And Miss Woodhouse — and her father — so kind as they are, always — so many attentions as we are always receiving from them — indeed, Miss Woodhouse must often find me very tiresome. I should try to hold my tongue more often than I do, I should indeed."

"Now!" cried Mrs Elton, when Jane and her aunt were dropped at their own door, "I wish you all to come round to the vicarage this evening." Oh, no, thought Jane. "I will not take no for an answer, mark my words!" went on Mrs Elton. "Such a tiresome day as this has been, such sad, tiresome company. But a quiet, pleasant evening, among true friends — now do, Miss Bates, do, my dear Jane, say that you will come! Otherwise, you know, Mr E and I must be thrown upon one another's company, and we are both out of spirits. Is not that so, Mr E? Help me to persuade them — and you must bring your mother too, bring dear old Mrs Bates — will not that be charming, Mr E?"

"Yes," said he grumpily, in a tone wholly lacking conviction.

Jane, with sinking heart, saw there was to be no escape.

Chapter 17

On the day following the excursion to Box Hill, Jane woke with a sick sensation of sorrow and loss, and the usual symptoms that accompanied one of her acute headaches — a constriction as of an iron band clamped across her forehead, nausea, an inability to eat or swallow, and impaired vision that made it painful to look towards light. She would have been glad to remain all day in bed, yet there were many things she must do.

The first was a letter to Frank. — She penned a brief note to him, breaking off their engagement — she felt it to be a source of repentance and misery to both. She asked for the return of her letters. She sent back his ring. — Next she wrote to Mrs Smallridge, the great friend of Mrs Elton's sister's friend Mrs Bragge, accepting her offer of a post as governess to the four little Smallridges. Thirdly, she wrote to Colonel and Mrs Campbell, informing them of her decision. Fourthly, a note to Rachel Dixon, congratulating her upon her happiness . . .

Having reached this last beginning, however, she was obliged to stop. Tears blinding her vision, she laid her head down upon the pillow; but the pain in her temples was too severe; standing up again, she began to pace about the shaded room.

Aunt Hetty put her head round the door. Heads had been poking round it all morning: Mrs Elton, Mrs Cole, Mrs Goddard and Mrs Cox, to inquire how she did and to congratulate her upon her fine new post. This time, it seemed, it was Miss Woodhouse.

"Miss Woodhouse!" gasped Jane, who was barely able to articulate. "What in the world does *she* want with us?" Has she not done us enough mischief? was what she felt inclined to say. "I cannot see her. I can see *nobody*."

Frank, she knew, was back in Richmond; he had left yesterday evening, directly after the return from the picnic, by chaise, because his horse had a cold; Mr Elton had learned this from the ostler at the Crown.

"Well," said Aunt Hetty, hesitating in the doorway, "I will tell Miss Woodhouse that you are laid down upon the bed."

"Tell her what you choose," said Jane, and recommenced her desperate pacing to and fro. Through the door she heard Emma's voice: "Ah, madam, you will be very sorry to lose her; and will not Colonel and Mrs Campbell be sorry to find she has engaged herself before their return?" The voice *did* sound sincerely sympathetic; can she be wishing to atone for her hateful behaviour? thought Jane. But it is too late, by far too late.

"Ay, and what are we to do with the pianoforte, you will be thinking! Our dear Colonel Campbell will have to decide about that, Jane says. It will be for him to say."

Shortly afterwards, Emma was heard to take her leave; and Jane's headache becoming even more agonizing, she was forced to lie down with a cold compress upon her brow and Aunt Hetty's smelling salts at hand; neither of which remedies afforded her any relief whatsoever.

The following day brought news from Richmond of a startling nature. An express arrived at Randalls to announce the death of Mrs Churchill. Mr Weston's loquacity being almost as unbridled as that of Miss Bates, this information was not slow in spreading all over the village. Mrs Cole brought word of it to the Bateses. — A sudden seizure, of a completely different nature from anything foreboded by her general state, had carried the unfortunate lady off after a short struggle. Frank Churchill's redoubtable aunt was no more.

For Jane this news seemed bizarre, almost unreal. Her headache, even after two days, was still very severe; she suffered from nervous fever, and Mr Perry, who had been called in, strongly doubted the possibility of her being able to keep her engagement with Mrs Smallridge at the time originally proposed. Mr Perry, indeed, suggested that Jane had undertaken more than she was equal to. "But what, then, *can* I do?" said Jane piteously. "I must work, I must earn my living."

It seemed strange to reflect that the news of Mrs Churchill's death, had it arrived last week, would have opened to her such a very different prospect. For it was well understood that the lady's husband, of a good-humoured, pliant disposition, was completely different from his wife; that there would be no difficulty, not the least in the world, about reconciling Mr Churchill to Frank's marrying any young lady he chose; the chief obstacle to matrimony was suddenly removed. If it had only happened last week! She had lost Frank Churchill; she had lost a delightful, sweet-natured, intelligent young man who had seemed, at the commencement, to love her most sincerely.

"But matters are far better as they have fallen out," resolved Jane, trying to find a cool spot on her pillow. "We should never have suited; that fact was becoming abundantly plain. He will be better off with Emma Woodhouse — and I heartily wish them joy of each other." So she told herself, trying to suppress the agonizing doubts, the sharp misgivings that persisted in telling her she had thrown away something of inestimable value.

Emma Woodhouse, meanwhile, appeared to be sincerely contrite, either for her vulgar and illtimed flirtation with Mr Churchill, or her heartless rudeness to Miss Bates; or both; kind messages continued to flow in from her daily. Could she not take Miss Fairfax for a ride in her carriage? Would Miss Fairfax not come up to Hartfield for a day and sit in the garden? Would Miss Fairfax accept some arrowroot — some calves-feet jelly — some fine old Constantia wine? All offers were refused, all gifts were returned immediately, despite Miss Bates's pleas and protests. Jane felt that, just then, she could not endure to receive *anything* from Emma Woodhouse, in whatever spirit it was sent. — Developing a hunger for fresh air and solitude, Jane left her bed, went out of doors, and walked about the meadows outside Highbury, careless of who might see her.

Meantime — and this formed the most acute point in Jane's scale of suffering — she had heard nothing from Frank. No acknowledgment of her note — nor of a second note, repeating the burden of the first — no return of her letters to him. *Nothing*. She hated him, she never wished to hear his voice again — but why did he not reply? She had resolved never to think about him, but this total severance was a kind of torture; she had never expected that it would be so bad. Had he forgotten her trivial existence, in the press of family business? Were the uncle and nephew removed to Yorkshire? What had *become* of him?

For ten days Jane subsisted on such scraps of gossip as percolated from Randalls, and these were now necessarily few. Mrs Weston, now very near her lying-in, did not venture from the house, and her solicitous husband remained close by her. But it was presently rumoured that Frank and his uncle had removed to friends at Windsor; next, that they would in due course return to Enscombe.

Then, on the tenth day, Jane, weary and depressed, having taken one of her now habitual solitary rambles in the pastures between Highbury and Donwell, was returning homewards, when she heard the sound of hoofs in the lane and, over the top of the hedgerow, saw the countenance of Frank Churchill. — At the same instant he caught sight of her, and pulled up his horse.

"Jane — Jane!" he called urgently. *"Jane!"*

She would have turned and fled, but there was nowhere she could flee to; the field was a large one, and she was halfway across it.

Next moment Frank, having consigned his horse's reins to a very untrustworthy-looking elder-bush, was forcing his way through the hedge. It was thick; he had quite a struggle. Then he was racing across the grass to Jane — caught hold of her hand — and, despite considerable resistance, pulled her into his arms.

"My darling girl! Now I can truly call you mine — in the face of all Highbury!" He laughed, looking about; not a soul, not a roof, was visible.

"Now I can kiss you if I wish and no human being on earth can raise any objection."

"But wait — wait — " she was fending him off — "I wrote to you. I wrote *twice*. Did you not receive my letters? I said — "

"I know what you said. The engagement was a source of repentance and misery to us both; you dissolved it. Do you think those words have not been etched in fire on my heart?"

"Then why — *why* — did you never reply?"

"I did, I did! Wait till I tell you. Oh, I am such a stupid, careless dog! When we are married, you will have to manage all our business affairs. Your dreadful letter reached me on the very morning of my poor aunt's death. I answered it immediately; but, from the confusion of the time, and all the tasks that were falling to me just then, my answer, instead of being sent off with all the business letters of that day, somehow became locked up in my writing-desk. I had written to refuse your rupture, to tell you that all secrecy could now be at an end, that my uncle consented to our engagement, that all would now be well with us; I had written in deep contrition and shame to apologise for my disgraceful — my outrageous behaviour — born

245

of frustration and impatience — I had written to declare my deep, undying love and beg you to reconsider. Here is that letter. I have it with me now. Would you wish to read it?"

"I think, perhaps, I do not need to," she said, smiling a little, looking up into his face.

"I do not deserve you, Jane. Indeed I don't. I am well aware of that! But — to hear that you had engaged yourself to this terrible Mrs Smallridge! To know that within two weeks you were to leave Highbury — to remove yourself entirely out of my reach — oh, that was purgatory indeed!"

"So your uncle knows about us?" she asked wonderingly, almost unbelievingly.

"He knows — he entirely approves — he only waits to make your acquaintance. Poor man! I think — when he grows accustomed to his new state of loneliness and liberty — he may be a changed creature, and will be very glad of such angelic company as yours. If you can consider making your home with him at Enscombe — "

"Oh," said Jane, laughing and colouring, "that is far too distant a prospect as yet to be considered."

She looked up at Frank.

He was not Matt Dixon. He was not Mr Knightley. (With an internal smile at herself she acknowledged that she must now renounce that childish daydream once and for all.) But he was a dear, kind fellow, he was himself, and he loved her. And she loved him too; yes, she did, in spite of all. Together they would do well enough.

Slowly, hand-in-hand, they walked across to the field gate and Frank, in the lane, reclaimed his horse.

"Have you told your father and stepmother yet?" she asked.

"No, I am on my way there now. My first errand was to you. I would have claimed you in the presence of your family (and no doubt also that of Mrs Cole, Mrs Goddard, Mrs Cox, and Mrs Elton) but I am very glad that it has fallen out this way. I would be happy to keep our love a private thing between us two for just a little longer. If you do not object?"

"You really enjoy keeping it a secret," she said smiling. "You are a born conspirator, I believe. And what about Miss Woodhouse? When is she to know? Will it not be a severe shock to her?"

"No," said Frank seriously, "there, I believe you wrong Miss

Woodhouse. I believe that *she* has been party to our secret for a very long time — almost since my first visit to Highbury. — Once I almost told her. Yes, yes, I know she flirted with me scandalously, but I am quite sure, and always have been, that with her it was only a game — otherwise I would never have dared carry it to the lengths I did. Miss Woodhouse has never been in love with me. Where her heart is, I cannot pretend to say. Maybe she will never marry?"

Jane thought fleetingly of Knightley, but said nothing, and Frank went on, "Next time we meet, it will be as acknowledged *promessi sposi*. Will not that be conventional and dull? Let us part here, now, like Romeo and Juliet, on this corner, hoping that we are unobserved. Goodbye, my dearest, dearest heart. I am the happiest man in Highbury this day, I believe!"

"Why not in all Surry?" Jane called after him mockingly as he rode off, and he turned, kissing his hand, to catch the startled eye of Mr Elton, coming out of the churchyard gate.

Chapter 18

A few days later, Emma came again to call at the Bates's. Miss Bates, as it happened, was out, but Mrs Elton was there. Jane was sorry for this circumstance; she knew the dislike the two ladies bore for each other, and would have much preferred to see Miss Woodhouse on her own.

Considerable placating of Mrs Elton had been necessary. In producing explanations of why she had first accepted the position offered by Mrs Smallridge, and then suddenly declined it, Jane had been obliged to acquaint Mrs Elton with some of the true facts of the case. Far from being offended, the lady was then all interest and eagerness, especially as she believed that she was the only one in Highbury entrusted with the secret.

"Do you not think, Miss Woodhouse," she now gaily exclaimed, "that our saucy little friend here is charmingly recovered? Do you not think her cure does Perry the highest credit?" And, under her breath to Jane, "We do not say a word of any assistance that Perry might have; not a word of a certain young physician from Windsor! Oh, no! Perry shall have all the credit."

Mrs Elton's opinion of Frank Churchill as a puppy seemed to have been rapidly modified.

Mr Elton soon came in search of his wife; he seemed hot and out of spirits. "Hunting for Knightley all over town! Not even a message! Forgot our appointment entirely! I found his servant William Larkins who said his master seemed strangely out of humour these days, he could hardly ever get speech of him. Very extraordinary!"

Emma declared that she must be going. She, Jane thought, seemed unwontedly lively; in a fine glow of humour. Meeting Jane's eye she smiled with such significance that Jane accompanied her down the stair. Emma had, Jane knew, been told her own news privately by the Westons; she was relieved that it seemed to have been so cordially received.

Indeed, on the stairway, Emma said, clasping Jane's hand, "I am very, *very* happy for you. In fact, had you not been surrounded by other friends, I might have been tempted to ask questions, to speak more openly than would have been strictly correct. I feel that I should certainly have been impertinent."

"Oh," cried Jane, blushing, "I am sure there would have been no danger of that! Indeed I have not time for half that I wish to say! I long to make apologies, excuses, to urge something for myself. I have been so unfriendly, so rebuffing. If your compassion does not stand my friend — "

"You are too scrupulous!" cried Emma warmly, squeezing her hand. "Everybody is so perfectly satisfied, delighted, even — "

"You are very kind, but I know what my manners were to you. So cold and artificial! I had always a part to act. It was a life of deceit. I *know* that I disgusted you. Frank — Mr Churchill — once told me something that you had said to him regarding my reserve — that it was a most repulsive quality — "

"Pray, say no more! I feel that all the apologies should be on *my* side. When I think of that picnic — Let us forgive one another at once. We must do whatever is to be done quickest, and I think our feelings will lose no time there."

Here now, thought Jane, is the *real* Emma, and why have I been so blind as never to see her before?

"Oh!" she cried out, "why were we not friends from the very beginning?"

"And the next news," said Emma with a smile of comprehension, "the next news, I suppose, will be that we are to lose you — just as I begin to know you."

And how much do I know *you*? wondered Jane as she watched Emma cross the street and walk rapidly towards Mr Knightley, who stood outside the Crown. Why are you in such abounding spirits? Is it entirely because of my news? Or is there something more?

Mrs Weston's friends were soon made happy by the news of a daughter, safely born to her; and shortly after that a most startling, an almost unbelievable rumour began to percolate through the village.

This was no less than the engagement of Emma Woodhouse to Mr Knightley; kept secret from every soul, apparently, until Mrs Weston's recovery made her the properest party to help reconcile old Mr Woodhouse to the arrangement. — It had been agreed that, for the time being, Mr Knightley should leave Donwell Abbey and live at Hartfield; in no other possible way could Mr Woodhouse, never at any time a friend to matrimony, have been reconciled to the marriage.

Mrs Elton, when the tidings reached the vicarage, was incredulous, then disgusted. "Poor Knightley — *poor* fellow! Sad business for him. How *could* he be so taken in? There would be an end of all pleasant intercourse with him. Shocking plan, living together. It would never do. She knew a family near Maple Grove who tried it, and had been obliged to separate before the end of the first quarter."

Mr Elton hoped the young lady's pride would now be contented; no doubt she had always meant to catch Knightley if she could.

Jane, receiving the news, felt a surprizing, a shaming pang. There, she thought ruefully, is another little bit of my heart broken. How many times can a woman's heart be broken in the course of a lifetime? I had believed that I was wholly recovered from my childish worship — for such it almost was — of Mr Knightley; but this seems to show that I mistook myself. I find that becoming entirely adult is a far slower process than one supposes . . . Knightley is a better man than Frank; I cannot deny it; and Emma Woodhouse is remarkably lucky to have him; and he will be good for her, he will soon teach her that it is not necessary for happiness to be the first in consequence; though I believe she has been learning that for some time now. It is queer: I have noticed a change in her ever since the day at Donwell and that dreadful picnic at Box Hill. Perhaps her own behaviour then taught her a lesson, when she had leisure to think it over. Knightley will be good for her; and I shall be good for Frank. But Frank will be good for me too; I am sure he will be kind, and unfailingly cheerful, and cherish me and show me things to laugh about. — And he did know my friends at Weymouth, Rachel and Matt and Sam.

A note soon came from Randalls: Frank would be there next day. Could Miss Fairfax be spared for the afternoon?

Jane had already been for a carriage-ride with Mrs Weston, her future mother-in-law: a long, comfortable heart-to-heart, during which Jane had wept a little, and unburdened herself, and received assurances that what she and Frank had done was not so very bad, could readily be forgiven, and they all loved her as a daughter already, could not be happier at Frank's choice. Indeed she soon felt that in Mrs Weston, kind, domestic, and fond of female company — and who had, after all, known her from the age of six — she might well discover more of a mother than Mrs Campbell, friendly but always absorbed in the *Analytical Journal*, had ever been.

At Randalls, there was Frank: loving, laughing, half ashamed of the long imposture, half ready to boast about it. His welcome to Jane was irresistible. Emma and her father had come as well, to visit the baby, and Emma said teasingly to Frank,

"I do suspect that in the midst of your perplexities you had very great amusement in tricking us all! I am sure it was a consolation to you?"

"Oh, no, no, no! How can you suspect me of such a thing? I was the most miserable wretch."

"No; I am sure it was a source of high entertainment to you. Perhaps I am the readier to suspect because, to tell you the truth, I think it might have been some amusement to myself. I think there is a little likeness between us; if not in ourselves, in our destiny, which bids fair to connect us with two characters so superior to our own."

"True, true," he answered warmly.

"Do you remember the wedding game that we used to play?" Emma said to Jane when the two girls, apart from the others, were walking in Mrs Weston's herb garden.

"I always hated it," said Jane involuntarily.

"How queer! Why?"

"I don't quite know. Perhaps because I was afraid that *I* would never get married. I was so plain. And I hated talking about clothes, because I never had any new ones of my own."

"And now you are so elegant!" Emma laughed. "Do you know, I used to envy you so! I almost hated you, because my mother used to listen to you playing the piano; she never listened to me. And she left you that hundred pounds. For years I bore you a grudge over that. And people were always saying we should be friends, because we were the same age; that seemed, somehow, to make us into rivals. And you were so much better than I was at everything — lessons, and music and races — "

"How horrible! I suppose," said Jane, thinking, "in a small neighbourhood such as this, people like us, who have some similarities, are almost forced into rivalry by their acquaintances continually comparing them — "

"And then, later, when you kept going away and coming back — *then* I envied you even more. Because you had seen the world and I had not! London — the West Indies — Weymouth; can you believe it, I have never left Highbury in my whole existence! I think that is why I like to make up stories about people. It is something I *can* do, it gives me a feeling of power, of being able to alter their lives."

"Rather dangerous?" said Jane doubtfully.

"Very much so! Now, I believe you are right. It led me into idle, mischievous ways — matchmaking, trying to dissuade poor little Harriet from wishing to marry Robert Martin."

"*Did* she wish to, then? And you dissuaded her?"

"Yes I did; to my black shame be it said. And worse than that! But all came right; she is to marry him after all, now." A shade of trouble, and then a blush, crossed Emma's face; Jane wondered if Knightley (whom she had not seen since the engagement was announced) had any hand in the business, and was confirmed in her guess when Emma said, "Mr Knightley put it right. Mr Knightley always puts me right when I go wrong. I think that he and I have always loved one another, though we did not discover it until so very recently. When we are married, he says that I had better begin to write novels — that will satisfy the inventive part of my frivolous nature."

"Oh!" cried Jane on a simple note of pure sorrow, "What a great deal of time we have wasted!" With an aching sense of loss she remembered those acorn tea-cups that she had kept for so long, in hopes that some day Emma would come and share a small festivity with her. Half mocking herself, and Emma too, she added, "And Mr Knightley always wanted us to be friends!"

"Yes, and if we had been we should have changed each other's lives."

"To an incalculable extent," agreed Jane, thinking of Rachel Dixon. "Now we shall never have the chance; it is too late."

And Emma said with equal sadness: "Yes, that is true. But at least we have stopped being enemies."

MANSFIELD REVISITED

Joan Aiken

What happened after Fanny Price's marriage to Edmund Bertram? Here, by the author of ELIZA'S DAUGHTER, is a witty and entertaining sequel to Jane Austen's classic novel, concentrating on the story of Fanny's lively young sister, Susan, who replaces Fanny as Lady Bertram's companion. Soon there are new surprises and new scandals at Mansfield Park . . .

'A lovely read – and you don't have to have read MANSFIELD PARK to enjoy it'   *Woman's Own*

'Worth reading if only for the excellent Lady Bertram, as funny as ever'   *Punch*

'Jane Austen fans will love the book, exclaiming with pleasure at the cleverness and cunning'   *Literary Review*

'Her sense of time and place is impeccable. Others may try but nobody comes close to Aiken in writing Jane Austen sequels'
Publishers Weekly

£5.99   0 575 40024 2

INDIGO

JANE AUSTEN
Elizabeth Jenkins

'Everything a biography should be: beautifully written, full of atmosphere, lively in humour and wisely critical'   Hugh Walpole

An acknowledged triumph of literary insight, Elizabeth Jenkins's life
of Jane Austen has been for many years a favourite portrait of this
remarkable woman. At the same time it is an absorbing evocation of
social life among the country gentry of Georgian England. This is
the world of Jane's small circle of friends and her large and affectionate family – the world she depicted so brilliantly in her novels.

By drawing on the writer's sparkling correspondence with her
sister, on family reminiscences and on the novels themselves, Elizabeth Jenkins builds up a sensitive picture of Jane Austen's emotional
and creative life. In doing so she shows how her great gifts developed
from the early novels to the remarkable achievements of her
maturity: PRIDE AND PREJUDICE, MANSFIELD PARK, EMMA and
PERSUASION.

'Invaluable'   Lord David Cecil

'Filled me with unstinted delight . . . A book I shall never lend to
anybody – I should so dread its loss'   Molly Keane, *Sunday Times*

£7.99   0 575 40057 9

*IND*I*GO*

Out of the blue...

INDIGO
the best in modern writing

FICTION

Nick Hornby *High Fidelity*	£5.99	0 575 40018 8
Kurt Vonnegut *The Sirens of Titan*	£5.99	0 575 40023 4
Joan Aiken *Mansfield Revisited*	£5.99	0 575 40024 2
Daniel Keyes *Flowers for Algernon*	£5.99	0 575 40020 x
Joe R. Lansdale *Mucho Mojo*	£5.99	0 575 40001 3
Stephen Amidon *The Primitive*	£5.99	0 575 40017 x
Julian Rathbone *Intimacy*	£5.99	0 575 40019 6
Janet Burroway *Cutting Stone*	£6.99	0 575 40021 8

NON-FICTION

Gary Paulsen *Winterdance*	£5.99	0 575 40008 0
Robert K. Massie *Nicholas and Alexandra*	£7.99	0 575 40006 4
Hank Wangford *Lost Cowboys*	£6.99	0 575 40003 x
Biruté M. F. Galdikas *Reflections of Eden*	£7.99	0 575 40002 1
Stuart Nicholson *Billie Holiday*	£7.99	0 575 40016 1
Giles Whittell *Extreme Continental*	£6.99	0 575 40007 2

INDIGO books are available from all good bookshops or from:

Cassell C.S.
Book Service By Post
PO Box 29, Douglas I-O-M
IM99 1BQ
telephone: 01624 675137, fax: 01624 670923

While every effort is made to keep prices steady, it is sometimes necessary to increase prices at short notice. Cassell plc reserves the right to show on covers and charge new retail prices which may differ from those advertised in the text or elsewhere.